Daniel Thompson

The rangers 1777

The Tory's daughter: A tale. Tenth Edition

Daniel Thompson

The rangers 1777
The Tory's daughter: A tale. Tenth Edition

ISBN/EAN: 9783337174705

Printed in Europe, USA, Canada, Australia, Japan

Cover: Foto ©Andreas Hilbeck / pixelio.de

More available books at **www.hansebooks.com**

THE RANGERS

OR

THE TORY'S DAUGHTER

A TALE

ILLUSTRATIVE OF THE

REVOLUTIONARY HISTORY OF VERMONT

AND THE

NORTHERN CAMPAIGN OF 1777

BY THE AUTHOR OF "THE GREEN MOUNTAIN BOYS"

TWO VOLUMES IN ONE

TENTH EDITION

BOSTON 1895
LEE AND SHEPARD PUBLISHERS
10 MILK STREET NEXT "THE OLD SOUTH MEETING HOUSE"

VOLUME I.

On commencing his former work, illustrative of the revolutionary history of Vermont, — THE GREEN MOUNTAIN BOYS, — it was the design of the author to have embraced the battle of Bennington, and other events of historic interest which occurred in the older and more southerly parts of the state; but finding, as he proceeded, that the unity and interest of his effort would be endangered by embracing so much ground, a part of the original design was relinquished, or rather its execution was deferred for a new and separate work, wherein better justice could be done to the rich and unappropriated materials of which his researches had put him in possession. That work, after an interval of ten years, and the writing and publishing of several intermediate ones, is now presented to the public, and with the single remark, that if it is made to possess less interest, as a mere tale, than its predecessor, the excuse must be found in the author's greater anxiety to give a true historic version of the interesting and important events he has undertaken to illustrate.

THE RANGERS;

OR,

THE TORY'S DAUGHTER

CHAPTER I.

" Sing on ! sing on ! my mountain home,
The paths where erst I used to roam,
The thundering torrent lost in foam,
The snow-hill side all bathed in light, —
All, all are bursting on my sight ! "

TOWARDS night, on the twelfth of March, 1775, a richly-equipped double sleigh, filled with a goodly company of well-dressed persons of the different sexes, was seen descending from the eastern side of the Green Mountains, along what may now be considered the principal thoroughfare leading from the upper navigable portions of the Hudson to those of the Connecticut River. The progress of the travellers was not only slow, but extremely toilsome, as was plainly evinced by the appearance of the reeking and jaded horses, as they labored and floundered along the sloppy and slumping snow paths of the winter road, which was obviously now fast resolving itself into the element of which it was composed. Up to the previous evening, the dreary reign of winter had continued wholly uninterrupted by the advent of his more gentle successor in the changing rounds of the seasons ; and the snowy waste which enveloped the earth would, that morning, have apparently withstood the rains and suns of

1

months before yielding entirely to their influences. But du.ing the night there had occurred one of those great and sudden transitions from cold to heat, which can only be ex|erienced in northern climes, and which can be accounted for only on the supposition, that the earth, at stated intervals, rapidly gives out large quantities of its internal heats, or that the air becomes suddenl⸗ rarefied by some essential change or modification in the state ol the electric fluid. The morning had been c.:udless; and the rising sun, with rays no longer dimly struggling through the dense, obstructing medium of the dark months gone by, but, with the restored beams of his natural brightness, fell upon the smoking earth with the genial warmth of summer. A new atmosphere, indeed, seemed to have been suddenly created, so warm and bland was the whole air; while, occasionally, a breeze came over the face of the traveller, which seemed like the breath of a heated oven. As the day advanced, the sky gradually became overcast — a strong south wind sprung up, before whose warm puffs the drifted snow-banks seemed literally to be cut down, like grass before the scythe of the mower; and, at length, from the thickening mass of cloud above, the rain began to descend in torrents to the mutely recipient earth. All this, for a while, however, produced no very visible effects on the general face of nature; for the melting snow was many hours in becoming saturated with its own and water from above. Nor had our travellers, for the greater part of the day, been much incommoded by the rain, or the thaw, that was in silent, but rapid progress around and beneath them; as their vehicle was a covered one, and as the hard-trodden paths of the road were the last to be affected. But, during the last hour, a great change in the face of the landscape had become apparent; and the evidence of what had been going on unseen, through the day, was now growing every moment more and more palpable. The snow along the bottom of every valley was marked by a long, dark streak, indicating the presence of the fast-collecting waters beneath. The stifled sounds of rushing streams were heard issuing from the hidden beds of every natural rill; while the larger brooks were beginning to burst through their wintry coverings, and throw up and push on before them the rending ice and snow that obstructed their courses to the rivers below, to which they were hurrying with increasing speed, and with seemingly growing impatience at every obstacle they met in their way The road had also become so soft, that the horses sunk nearly to the 'lank at almost every step, and the plunging sleigh drove heavily along the plashy path. The whole mass of the now saturated and dissolving snow, indeed, though lying, that morning, more than three feet deep on a level, seemed to quiver and move, as if on the point of flowing away in a body to the nearest channels.

The company we have introduced consisted of four gentlemen and two ladies, all belonging, very evidently, to the most wealthy, and, up to that time, the most honored and influential class of society. But though all seemed to be of the same caste, yet their natural characters, as any physiognomist, at a glance, would have discovered, were, for so small a party, unusually diversified. Of the two men occupying the front seat, both under the age of thirty, the one sitting on the right and acting as driver was tall, showily dressed, and of a haughty, aristocratic air; while his sharp features, which set out in the shape of a half-moon, the convex outline being preserved by a retreating forehead, an aquiline nose, and a chin sloping inward, combined to give him a cold, repulsive countenance, fraught with expressions denoting selfishness and insincerity. The other occupant of the same seat was, on the contrary, a young man of an unassuming demeanor, shapely features, and a mild, pleasing countenance. The remaining two gentlemen of the party were much older, but scarcely less dissimilar in their appearance than the two just described. One of them was a gaunt, harsh-featured man, of the middle age, with an air of corresponding arrogance and assumption. The other, who was still more elderly, was a thick-set and rather portly personage, of that quiet, reserved, and somewhat haughty demeanor, which usually belongs to men of much self-esteem, and of an unyielding, opinionated disposition. The ladies were both young, and in the full bloom of maidenly beauty. But their native characters, like those of their male companions, seemed to be very strongly contrasted. The one seated on the left was fair, extremely fair, indeed; and her golden locks, clustering in rich profusion around her snowy neck and temples, gave peculiar effect to the picture-like beauty of her face. But her beauty consisted of pretty features, and her countenance spoke rather of the affections than of the mind, being of that tender, pleading cast, which is better calculated to call forth sympathy than command respect, and which showed her to be one of those confiding, dependent persons, whose destinies are in the hands of those whom they consider their friends, rather than in their own keeping. The other maiden, with an equally fine form and no less beautiful features, was still of an entirely different appearance. She, indeed, was, to the one first described what the rose, with its hardy stem, is to the lily leaning on the surrounding herbage for its support; and though less delicately fair in mere complexion, she was yet more commandingly beautiful; for there was an expression in the bright, discriminating glances of her deep hazel eyes, and in the commingling smile that played over the whole of her serene and benignant countenance, that told of intellects that could act independently, as well as of a heart that glowed with the kindly affections.

"Father," said the last described female, addressing the eldest gentleman, for the purpose, apparently, of giving a new turn to the conversation, which had now, for some time, been lagging, — "father, I think you promised us, on starting from Bennington this morning, not only a fair day, but a safe arrival at Westminster Court-House, by sunset, did you not?"

"Why, yes, perhaps I did," replied the person addressed; "for I know I calculated that we should get through by daylight."

"Well, my weatherwise father, to say nothing about this storm, instead of the promised sunshine, does the progress, made and now making, augur very brightly for the other part of the result?"

"I fear me not, Sabrey," answered the old gentleman, "though, with the road as good as when we started, we should have easily accomplished it. But who would have dreamed of a thaw so sudden and powerful as this? Why, the very road before us looks like a running river! Indeed, I think we shall do well to reach Westminster at all to-night. What say you, Mr. Peters, — will the horses hold out to do it?" he added, addressing the young man of the repulsive look, who had charge of the team, as before mentioned.

"They *must* do it, at all events, Squire Haviland," replied Peters. "Sheriff Patterson, here," he continued, glancing at the hard-featured man before described, "has particular reasons for being on the ground to-night. I must also be there, and likewise friend Jones, if we can persuade him to forego his intended stop at Brattleborough; for, being of a military turn, we will give him the command of the forces, if he will go on immediately with us."

"Thank you, Mr. Peters," replied Jones, smiling. "I do not covet the honor of a command, though I should be ready to go on and assist, if I really believed that military forces would be needed."

"Military forces needed for what?" asked Haviland, in some surprise.

"Why, have you not heard, Squire Haviland," said the sheriff, "that threats have been thrown out, that our coming court would not be suffered to sit?"

"Yes, something of the kind, perhaps," replied Haviland, contemptuously; "but I looked upon them only as the silly vaporings of a few disaffected creatures, who, having heard of the rebellious movements in the Bay State, have thrown out these idle threats with the hope of intimidating our authorities, and so prevent the holding of a court, which they fear might bring too many of them to justice."

"So I viewed the case for a while," rejoined Patterson; "but a few days ago, I received secret information, on which I could rely, that these disorganizing rascals were actually combining, in considerable numbers, with the intention of attempting to drive us from the Court-House."

"Impossible! impossible! Patterson," said the squire; "they will never be so audacious as to attempt to assail the king's court."

"They are making a movement for that purpose, nevertheless," returned the former; "for, in addition to the information I have named, I received a letter from Judge Chandler, just as I was leaving my house in Brattleborough, yesterday morning, in which the judge stated, that about forty men, from Rockingham, came to him in a body, at his house in Chester, and warned him against holding the court; and had the boldness to tell him, that blood would be shed, if it was attempted, especially if the sheriff appeared with an armed *posse*."

"Indeed! why, I am astonished at their insolence!" exclaimed the squire. "But what did the judge tell them?"

"Why the judge, you know, has an oily way of getting along with ugly customers," replied the sheriff, with a significant wink; "so he thanked them all kindly for calling on him, and gravely told them he agreed with them, that no court should be holden at this time. But, as there was one case of murder to be tried, he supposed the court must come together to dispose of that; after which they would immediately adjourn. And promising them that he would give the sheriff directions not to appear with any armed assistants, he dismissed them, and sat down and wrote me an account of the affair, winding off with giving me the directions he had promised, but adding in a postscript, that I was such a contrary fellow, that he doubted whether I should obey his directions; and he should not be surprised to see me there with a hundred men, each with a gun or pistol under his great-coat! Ha ha! The judge is a sly one."

"One word about that case of murder, to which you have alluded, Mr. Patterson," interposed Jones, after the jeering laugh
with which the sheriff's account was received by Haviland and
Peters, had subsided. "I have heard several mysterious hints
thrown out by our opponents about it, which seemed to imply
that the prosecution of the prisoner was got up for private purposes; and I think I have heard the name of Secretary Brush
coupled with the affair. Now, who is the alleged murderer?
and where and when was the crime committed?"

"The fellow passes by the name of Herriot, though it is suspected that this is not his true name," responded the sheriff.
"The crime was committed at Albany, several years ago, when
he killed, or mortally wounded, an intimate friend of Mr. Brush."

"Under what circumstances?"

"Why, from what I have gathered, I should think the story
might be something like this: that, some time previous to the
murder, this Herriot had come to Albany, got into company
above his true place, dashed away a while in high life, gam-
bled deeply, and, losing all his own money, and running up a
large debt to this, and other friends of Brush, gave them his obligations and absconded. But coming there again, for some purpose, a year or two after, with a large sum of money, it was
thought, which had been left or given him by a rich Spaniard,
whose life he had saved, or something of the kind, those whom
he owed beset him to pay them, or play again. But he refused
to play, pretending to have become pious, and also held back
about paying up his old debts. Their debts, however, they determined to have, and went to him for that purpose; when an affray
arose, and one of them was killed by Herriot, who escaped, and
fled, it seems, to this section of the country, where he kept himself secluded in some hut in the mountains, occasionally appear
ing abroad to preach religion and rebellion to the people, by
which means he was discovered, arrested, and imprisoned in
Westminster jail, where he awaits his trial at the coming term
of the court. And I presume he will be convicted and hung,
unless he makes friends with Brush to intercede for a pardon,
which he probably might do, if the fellow would disgorge enough
of his hidden treasures to pay his debts, and cease disaffecting
the people, which is treason and a hanging matter of itself, for
which he, and fifty others in this quarter, ought, in justice, to
be dealt with without benefit of the clergy. — What say you,
Squire Haviland?"

"I agree with you fully," replied the squire. "But to return to Judge Chandler's communication: what steps have you taken, if any, in order to sustain the court in the threatened emergency?"

"Why, just the steps that Chandler knew I should take—sent off one messenger to Brush, there on the ground at Westminster; another to Rogers, of Kent; and yet another to a trusty friend in Guilford, requesting each to be on, with a small band of resolute fellows; while I whipped over to Newfane myself, fixed matters there, and came round to Bennington to enlist David Redding, and a friend or two more; as I did, after I arrived, last night, though I was compelled to leave them my sleigh and horses to bring them over, which accounts for my begging a passage with you. So, you see, that if this beggarly rabble offer to make any disturbance, I shall be prepared to teach them the cost of attempting to put down the king's court."

"Things are getting to a strange pass among these deluded people, that is certain. I cannot, however, yet believe them so infatuated as to take this step. But if they should, decided measures should be taken — such, indeed, as shall silence this alarming spirit at once and forever."

"I hope," observed Miss Haviland, who had been a silent but attentive listener to the dialogue, "I hope no violence is really intended, either on the part of the authorities or their opponents. But what do these people complain of? There must be some cause, by which they, at least, *think* themselves justified in the movement, surely. Do they consider themselves aggrieved by any past decisions of the court?"

"O, there are grumblers enough, doubtless, in that respect," answered the sheriff. "And among other things, they complain that their property is taken and sold to pay their honest debts, when money is so scarce, they say, that they cannot pay their creditors in currency — just as if the court could make money for the idle knaves! But that is mere pretence. They have other motives, and those, too, of a more dangerous character to the public peace."

"And what may those motives be, if it be proper for me to inquire, sir?" resumed the fair questioner.

"Why, in the first place," replied the sheriff, "they have an old and inveterate grudge against New York, whose jurisdiction they are much predisposed to resist. But to this they might have continued to demur and submit, as they have done this side of the mountain, had New York adopted the resolves of the Continental Congress of last December, and come into the

American Association, as it is called, which has no less for its object, in reality, than the entire overthrow of all royal authority in this country. But as our colony has nobly refused to do this, they are now intent on committing a double treason — that of making war on New York and the king too."

"Well, I should have little suspected," remarked Haviland, "that the people of this section, who have shown themselves commendably conservative, for the most part, had any intention of yielding to the mob-laws of Ethan Allen, Warner, and others, who place the laws of New York at defiance on the other side of the mountains; and much less that they would heed the resolves of that self-constituted body of knaves, ignoramuses, and rebels, calling themselves the Continental Congress."

"Are you not too severe on that body of men, father?" said Miss Haviland, lifting her expressive eye reprovingly to the face of the speaker. "I have recently read over a list of the members of the Congress; when I noticed among them the names of men, who, but a short time since, stood very high, both for learning and worth, as I have often heard you say yourself. Now, what has changed the characters of these men so suddenly?"

"Why is it, Sabrey," said the old gentleman, with an air of petulance, and without deigning any direct answer to the troublesome question, — "why is it that you cannot take the opinion of your friends, who know so much more than you do about these matters, instead of raising, as I have noticed you have lately seemed inclined to do, questions which seem to imply doubts of the correctness of the measures of our gracious sovereign and his wise ministers?"

"Why, father," replied the other, with an ingenuous, but somewhat abashed look, "if I have raised such questions, in relation to the quarrel between the colonies and the mother country, I have gone on the ground that the party which has the most right on its side would, of course, have the best reasons for its measures; and as I have not always been able to perceive good reasons for all the king's measures, I had supposed you would be proud to give them."

The old gentleman, though evidently disturbed and angry at this reply, did not seem inclined to push the debate any further with his daughter. The other gentlemen, also, looked rather glum; and for many moments not a word was spoken; when the other young lady, who had not yet spoken, after glancing round on the gentlemen in seeming expectation that those better reasons would be given, at length ventured to remark, —

"Well, for my part, it is enough for me that my friends all belong to the loyal party; and whatever might be said, I know I should always feel that they were in the right, and their opposers in the wrong."

"And in that, Jane, I think you are wise," responded Jones, with an approving smile. "The complaints of these disaffected people are based on mistaken notions. They are too ill informed, I fear, to appreciate the justice and necessity of the measures of our ministers, or to understand very clearly what they are quar-relling about."

"Ah, that is it," warmly responded Haviland. "That is what I have always said of them. They don't understand their own rights, or what is for their own good, and should be treated ac-cordingly. And I think some of our leading men miss it in trying to reason with them. Reason with them! Ridiculous! As if the common people could understand an argument!"

"You are perfectly right, squire," responded Peters, with eager promptness. "My own experience among the lower classes fully confirms your opinion. My business, for several years past, has brought me often in contact with them, in a certain quarter; and I have found them not only ignorant of what properly belongs to their own rights and privileges, but jealous and obstinate to a degree that is excessively annoying."

"Friend Peters probably alludes to his experience in the great republic of Guilford," said Jones, archly.

"There and elsewhere," rejoined the former; "though I have seen quite enough of republicanism there, for my purpose. One year, the party outvoting their opponents, and coming into power, upsets every thing done by their predecessors. The next year the upsetters themselves get upset; and all the measures they had established are reversed for others no better; and so they go on from year to year, forever quarrelling and forever changing."

"And yet, Peters," resumed Jones, banteringly, "I doubt whether you have been much the loser by their quarrels."

"How so, Mr. Jones?" asked Haviland, who noticed that Peters had answered only by a significant smile.

"Why, you know, Squire Haviland," replied Jones, "that I have been on to attend several of the last sessions of your court, as the agent of Secretary Fanning,* to see to his landed interests in

---

* Edward Fanning, secretary to Governor Tryon, New York, before the revolution, obtained, by an act of favoritism from his master, a gran. of the township of Stratton, which, in 1780, Fanning having been appoint-ed a colonel of a regiment of tories, was confiscated, and re-granted. by

this quarter. Well, friend Peters, here, who has gone consider ably into land speculations east of the mountains, you know, had brought, it seems, several suits for the possession of lands, mostly in this same Guilford ; and among the rest, one for a right of land in possession of a sturdy young log-roller, whom they called Harry Woodburn, who appeared in court in his striped woollen frock, and insisted on defending his own case, as he proceeded to do with a great deal of confidence. But when he came to produce his deed for the land he contended was his own, it was found, to his utter astonishment, to bear a later date than the one pro- duced by Peters. This seemed to settle the case against him. But he appeared to have no notion of giving up so ; and, by favor of court, the further hearing of the case was deferred a day or two, to enable him to procure the town records, which, he con- tended, would show the priority of his deed. So he posted back to Guilford for the purpose ; but, on arriving there, found, to his dismay, that the records were nowhere to be found. One of the belligerent parties of that town, it seems, had broken into the clerk's office, stolen the records, and buried them somewhere in the ground. The fellow, therefore, had to return, and submit to a judgment against him. Still, however, he clung to his case, and obtained a review of it, in expectation that the records would be found before the next court. But the poor fellow seemed doomed to disappointment. At the next court, no records were forth- coming ; and though he defended his case with great zeal, he was thrown in his suit again ; when he concluded, I suppose, to yield to his fate without further ado."

" Not by any means," said Peters, in a tone of raillery. " He has petitioned for a new trial ; and the question is to come on at this court."

" Indeed ! " exclaimed Jones, laughing. " Well, I must con- fess I have never seen so much dogged determination exhibited in so hopeless a case. And I really could not help admiring the fellow's spirit and uncultured force of mind, as much misapplied as, of course, I suppose it to have been. Your lawyer, Stevens, really appeared, once or twice, to be quite annoyed at his home thrusts ; while lawyer Knights, or Rough-hewn Sam, as they call him, who, either from a sly wish to see his friend Stevens both- ered, or from a real wish to help Harry, volunteered to whisper a

the legislature of Vermont, to William Williams and others. Kent, af- terwards Londonderry, which had been granted to James Rogers, who has been introduced, and who became a tory officer, was also, in like manner, confiscated and re-granted.

few suggestions in his ear occasionally, sat by, and laughed out of his eyes, till they ran over with tears, to see a court lawyer so hard pushed by a country bumpkin."

"Pooh! you make too much of the fellow," said Peters, with assumed contempt. "Why, he is a mere obstinate boor, whose self-will and vanity led him to set up and persevere in a defence in which he knows there is neither law nor justice."

"And yet, Mr. Peters," observed Miss Haviland, inquiringly, ' the young man must have known that he was making great expense for himself, in obtaining delays and new trials, in the hope that the lost records would be found. If he was not very confident those records would have established his right, why should he have done this? "

"O, that was a mere pretence about the records altering the case, doubtless," replied Peters, with the air of one wishing to hear no more on the subject.

"It may have been so," rejoined the former, doubtfully; "but I should have hardly inferred it from Mr. Jones's description of the man and his conduct."

"Nor I," interposed the other lady, playfully, but with considerable spirit. "Mr. Jones has really excited my curiosity by his account of this young plough-jogger. I should like to get a sight of him—shouldn't you, Sabrey?"

But the latter, though evidently musing on the subject, and mentally discussing some unpleasant doubts and inferences which it seemed to present to her active mind, yet evaded the question, and turned the conversation, by directing the attention of her companion and the rest of the company to a distant object in the wild landscape, which here opened to their view. This was the tall, rugged mountain, which, rising from the eastern shore of the Connecticut, was here, through an opening in the trees, seen looming and lifting its snowy crest to the clouds, and greeting the gladdened eyes of the way-worn travellers with the silent but welcome announcement that they were now within a few miles of the great river, and in the still more immediate vicinity of their intended halting-place — the thriving little village which was then just starting into life, under the auspices of the man from whom its name was derived — the enterprising Colonel Brattle, of Massachusetts.

Having now the advantage of a road, which, as it received the many concentrating paths of a thicker settlement, here began to be comparatively firm, the travellers passed rapidly over the descending grounds, and, in a short time, entered the village. As

they were dashing along towards the village inn, at a full trot,
a man, with a vehicle drawn by one horse, approaching in an
intersecting road from the south, struck into the same street a
short distance before them.   His whole equipment was very
obviously of the most simple character, — a rough board box,
resting on four upright wooden pins inserted into a couple of
saplings, which were bent up in front for runners — the whole
making what, in New England phrase, is termed a *jumper*, constituted his sleigh.   And this vehicle was drawn by a long switch-
tailed young pony, whose unsteady gait, as he briskly ambled
along the street, pricking up his ears and veering about at every
new object by the way-side, showed him to be but imperfectly
broken.   The owner of this rude contrivance for locomotion was
evidently some young farmer from the neighboring country.
But although his dress and mode of travelling seemed thus to
characterize him, yet there was that in his personal appearance,
as plain as was his homespun garb, which was calculated to command at once both attention and respect.   And as he now rose
and stood firmly planted in his sleigh, occasionally looking back
to watch the motions of the team behind him, with his long, toga-
like woollen frock drawn snugly over his finely-sloping shoulders
and well-expanded bust, and closely girt about at the waist by a
neatly-knotted Indian belt, while the flowing folds below streamed
gracefully aside in the wind, he displayed one of those compact,
shapely figures, which the old Grecian sculptors so delighted to
delineate.   And in addition to these advantages of figure, he
possessed an extremely fine set of features, which were shown
off effectively by the profusion of short, jetty locks, that curled
naturally around his white temples and his bold, high forehead.

  " Miss McRea — Jane," said Jones, turning round to the amiable girl, and tapping her on the shoulder, with the confiding
smile and tender playfulness of the accepted lover, as he was, —
" Jane, you said, I think, that you should like to get a sight of
that spunky opponent of Mr. Peters, whom we were talking of a
little while since — did you not ? "

  " O, yes, yes, to be sure I did," replied the other briskly ; " but
why that question, just at this time ? "

  " Because, if I do not greatly mistake, that man who is pushing on before us, in yon crazy-looking establishment, is the self-
same young fellow.   Is it not so, Peters ? "

  " I have not noticed him particularly, nor do I care whether it
is he or not," answered Peters, with an affected indifference, with
which his uneasy and frowning glances, as he kept his eye keenly
fixed on the person in question, but illy comported.

" Well that is the fellow — that is Harry Woodburn, you may rely on it, ladies," rejoined Jones, gayly, as he faced about in his seat.

Both young ladies now threw intent and curious glances forward on the man thus pointed out to them, till they caught, as they did the next moment, a full and fair view of his personal appearance ; when they turned and looked at each other with expressions of surprise, which plainly indicated that the object of their thoughts was quite a different person from what they had been led to expect.

" His dress, to be sure, *is* rather coarse," observed Miss Haviland to her companion, in a low tone ; " but he is no boor ; nor can every one boast of —— " Here she threw a furtive glance at Peters, when she appeared to read something in his countenance which caused her to suspend the involuntary comparison which was evidently passing in her mind, and to keep her eye fixed on his motions.

The arrogant personage last named, wholly unconscious of this scrutiny, now began to incite his horses afresh, frequently applying the lash with unwonted severity, and then suddenly curbing them in, till the spirited animals became so frantic that they could scarcely be restrained from dashing off at a run. The young farmer, in the mean while, finding himself closely pressed by those behind him, without any apparent disposition on thei. part to turn out and pass by him, now veered partly out of the road, to give the others, with the same change in their course to the opposite side, an opportunity, if they chose, of going by, as might easily have been done with safety to all concerned.

" Mr. Peters !" suddenly exclaimed Miss Haviland, in a tone of energetic remonstrance, at the same time catching at his arm, as if to restrain him from some intended movement, which her watchful eye had detected.

This appeal, however, which was rather acted than spoken, was unheeded, or came too late ; for, at that instant, the chafing and maddened horses dashed furiously forward, directly over the exposed corner of the young man's vehicle, which, under the iron-bound feet of the fiercely-treading animals, and the heavy sleigh runners that followed, came down with a crash to the ground, leaving him barely time to clear himself from the wreck, by leaping forward into the snow. Startled by the noise behind him, the frightened pony made a sudden but vain effort to spring forward with the still connected remains of the jumper, which were, at the instant, confined down by the passing runners of the large sleigh ; when

2   B

snorting and wild with desperation, he reared himself upright on his hinder legs, and fell over backwards, striking, with nearly the whole weight of his body, upon his doubled neck, which all saw at a glance was broken by the fall.

With eyes flashing with indignation, young Woodburn bounded forward to the head of the aggressing team, boldly seized the nearest horse by his nostrils and bridle curb, and, in spite of his desperate rearing and plunging, under the rapidly applied whip of the enraged driver, soon succeeded, by daring and powerful efforts, in bringing him and his mate to a stand.

" Let go there, fellow, on your peril ! " shouted Peters, chok-ing with rage at his defeat in attempting to ride over and escape his bold antagonist.

" Not till I know what all this means, sir ! " retorted Woodburn, with unflinching spirit.

" Detain us if you dare, you young ruffian ! " exclaimed the sheriff, protruding his harsh visage from one side of the sleigh. " Begone ! or I will arrest you in the king's name, sir ! "

" You will show your warrant for it first, Mr. Sheriff," replied the former, turning to Patterson with cool disdain. " I have nothing to do with you, sir ; but I hold this horse till the outrage I have just received is atoned for, or at least explained."

" My good friend," interposed Jones, in a respectful manner, " you must not suppose we have designedly caused your disaster. Our horses, which are high-mettled, as you see, took a sudden start, and the mischief was done before they could be turned or checked."

" Now, let go that horse, will you, scoundrel ? " again ex-claimed Peters, still chafing with anger, but evidently disturbed and uneasy under the cold, searching looks of the other.

" Hear me first, John Peters ! " replied Woodburn, with the same determined manner as before. " I care not for your abusive epithets, and have only to say of them, that they are worthy of the source from which they proceed. But you have knowingly and wickedly defrauded me of my farm ; unless I obtain redress, as I little expect, from a court which seems so easily to see merits in a rich man's claim. Yes, you have defrauded me, sir, out of my hard-earned farm ; and there," he continued, pointing to his gasping horse, — " there lies nearly half of all my remaining property — dead and gone ! ay, and by your act, which, from signs I had previously noticed, and from the tones of that young lady's exclamation at the instant, (and God bless her for a heart which could be kind in such company,) I shall always believe *was wilfully committed. And if I can make good my suspicions and a court of law will not give me justice, I will have it elsewhere! There, sir, go," he added, relinquishing his hold on the horse, and stepping aside, — " go! but remember I claim a future reckoning at your hands!"

The sleigh now passed on to the yard of the inn, where the company alighted, and soon disappeared within its doors, leaving the young man standing alone in the road, gazing after them with that moody and disquieted kind of countenance which usually settles on the face on the subsidence of a strong gust of passion. " Poor pony!" he at length muttered, sadly, as, rousing himself, he now turned towards his petted beast, that lay dead in his rude harness, — " poor pony! But there is no help for you now, nor for me either, I fear, as illy as I can afford to lose you. But it is not so much the loss, as the manner — the manner!" he repeated, bitterly, as he proceeded to undo the fastenings of the tackle, with the view of removing the carcass and the broken sleigh from the road.

While he was thus engaged, a number of men, most of them his townsmen, who being, like himself, on their way to court, had stopped at the inn, or store, near by, where the noise of the fray had aroused them, now came hastening to the spot.

" What is all this, Harry?" exclaimed the foremost, as he came up and threw a glance of surprise and concern on the ruins before him.

" You can see for yourselves," was his moody reply, as others now arrived, and, with inquiring looks, gathered around him.

" Yes, yes; but how was it done?"

" John Peters, who just drove up to the tavern, yonder, with a load of court gentry, run over me — that's all," he answered, with an air that showed his feelings to be still too much irritated to be communicative.

But the company, among whom he seemed to be a favorite were not to be repulsed by a humor for which they appeared to understand how to make allowance, but continued to press him with inquiries and soothing words, till their manifestations of sympathy and offers of assistance had gradually won him into a more cheerful mood; when, throwing off his reserve, he thanked them kindly, and frankly related what he knew of the affair, the particulars of which obviously produced a deep sensation among the listeners. All present, after hearing the recital of the facts, and on coupling them with the well-known disposition of Peters, and his previous injuries to Woodburn, at once declared their belief that the aggression was intentional, and warmly espoused the cause of their outraged friend and townsman. A sort of council of war was then holden; the affair was discussed and set down as another item in the catalogue of injuries and oppressions of which the court party had been guilty. Individuals were despatched into all the nearest houses, and elsewhere, for the purpose of discovering what evidence might be obtained towards sustaining a prosecution. It was soon ascertained, however, that no one had seen the fracas, except the parties in interest,—all Peters's company being so accounted,—and that, consequently, no hope remained of any legal redress. On this, some proposed measures of club-law retaliation, some recommended reprisals on the same principle, and others to force Peters, as soon as he should appear in the street, to make restitution for the loss he had occasioned. And so great was the excitement, that had the latter then made his appearance,—which, it seemed, he was careful not to do,—it is difficult to say what might have been his reception. But contrary to the expectations of all, Woodburn, who had been thoughtfully pacing up and down the road, a little aloof from the rest, during he discussion, now came forward, and, in a firm and manly manner, opposed all the propositions which had been made in his behalf.

"No," said he, in conclusion, "such measures will not bear thinking of. I threatened him myself with something of the kind you have proposed. But a little reflection has convinced me I was wrong; for should I take this method of obtaining redress, nowever richly he might deserve it at my hands, I should but be doing just what I condemn in him, and thus place myself on a level with him in his despicable conduct. No, we will let him alone, and give him all the rope he will take; and if he don't hang for his misdeeds, he will doubtless, by his conduct, aid in hastening on the time, which, from signs not to be mistaken, cannot, I think, be far distant, when a general outbreak will place him, and all like him, who have been riding over us here rough-shod for years, in a spot where he and they will need us much of our pity as they now have of our hatred and fear."

"Ay, ay," responded several, with significant nods and looks; that time will come, and sooner than they dream of."

"And then," said one, "it will not be with us as it was with me last fall; when, just as the winter was coming on, and milk was half our dependence for the children, our only cow was knocked off by a winking sheriff, for eleven and threepence, to this same Peters."

"Nor as it was with me," said another poorly-clad man of the crowd, "when for a debt, which, before it was sued, was only the price of a bushel of wheat I bought to keep wife and little ones from starving, my pair of two-year-olds and seven sheep were all seized and sold under the hammer, for just enough to pay the debt and costs, to Squire Gale, the clerk of the court, who is another of those conniving big bugs, who are seen going round with the sheriff, at such times, with their pockets full of money to buy up the poor man's property for a song, though never a dollar will they lend him to redeem it with"

"No, my friends," said a tall, stout, broad-chested man, with a clear, frank, and fearless countenance, who, having arrived at the spot as Woodburn began to speak, had been standing outside of the crowd, silently listening to the remarks of the different speakers, —"no, my friends; when the time just predicted arrives, it will no longer be as it has been with *any* of us. We shall *then*, I trust, all be allowed to exercise the right which, according to my notions, we have from God—that of choosing our own rulers, who, then, would be men from among ourselves, knowing something about the wants and wishes of the people, and willing to provide for their distresses in times like these. I have little to say about individual men, or their acts of oppression; for such men and such acts we may expect to see, so long as this accursed system of foreign rule is suffered to remain. We had better, therefore, not waste much of our ammunition on this or that tool of royalty, but save it for higher purposes. And, for this reason, I highly approve of the course that my young neighbor, Woodburn, has just taken, in *his* case; although, from what I have heard I suspect it was an outrageous one."

'Thank you, thank you, Colonel Carpenter," said Woodburn, coming forward and cordially offering the other his hand; "the approbation of a man like you more than reconciles me to the course which, I confess, cost me a hard struggle to adopt."

"Ay, you were right, Harry," rejoined the former, "though a hard matter to bear; and though I am willing this, and all such outrages, should go in to swell the cup of our grievances, that it may the sooner overflow, yet you were right; and it was spoken, too. like a man. But let me suggest, whether you, and all present, had not better now disperse. The powers that be will soon have their eyes upon us, and I would rather not excite their jealousy, at this time, on account of certain measures we have in contemplation, which I will explain to you hereafter."

"Your advice is good," returned Woodburn, "and I will see

2 *

that it is followed, as soon as I can find some one to dispose of the body of my luckless pony; for then I propose to throw the harness into some sleigh, and join such of the company here as are on foot on their way to court."

" Put your harness aboard my double sleigh standing in the tavern yard yonder, Harry.   And I am sorry I have too much of a load to ask you to ride yourself.   But where shall I leave the harness ? "

"At Greenleaf's store, at the river, if you will ; for I conclude you are bound to Westminster, as well as the rest of us."

" I am, and shall soon be along after you, as I wish to go through to-night, if possible, being suspicious of a flood, that may prevent me from getting there with a team, by to-morrow.   Neither the rain nor thaw is over yet, if I can read prognostics.   How strong and hot this south wind blows !   And just cast your eye over on to West River mountain, yonder — how rapidly those long, ragged masses of fog are creeping up its sides towards the summit !   That sign is never failing."

Woodburn's brief arrangements were soon completed ; when he and his newly-encountered foot companions, each provided with a pair of rackets, or snow-shoes, — articles with which foot-travellers, when the snow was deep, often, in those times, went furnished, — took up their line of march down the road leading to the Connecticut, leaving Peters and his company, as well as all others who had teams, refresing themselves or their horses at the village inn.

But, before we close this chapter, in order that the reader not versed in the antiquarian lore of those times may more clearly understand some of the allusions of the preceding pages, and also that he may not question the probability that such a company as we have introduced should be thus brought together, and be thus on their way to a court so far into the interior of a new settlement, it may not be amiss here to observe, that the sale and purchase of lands in Vermont at this period constituted one of the principal matters of speculation among men of property, not only those residing here, but those residing in the neighboring colonies, and especially in that of New York ; and that the frequent controversies, arising out of disputed titles, made up the chief business of the court, which, on the erection of a new county by the legislature of New York, embracing all the south-eastern part of the *Grants*, and known by the name of Cumberland, had here, several years before, been established.   And it was business of this kind, and the personal, in addition to the political, interest they had in sustaining a court, the judges of which were themselves said to be engaged in these speculations, and therefore expected to favor, as far as might be decent, their brother speculators, that led to the journey of the present company of loyalists, consisting as before seen, of Haviland, a large landholder of Bennington; Peters, an unconscientious speculator in the same kind of property, belonging to a noted family of tories of that name, residing in Pownal, and an adjoining town in New York; and Jones, the agent of Fanning, from the vicinity of Fort Edward; the fated Miss McRea, of sad historical memory, from the same place, having been induced to come on with her lover, at the previous solicitation of her friend, Miss Haviland, to join her, her father, and Peters, to whom she was affianced in their proposed excursion over the mountains to court.

CHAPTER II.

' Now forced aloft, bright bounding through the air
   Moves the bleak ice, and sheds a dazzling glare ,
   The torn foundations on the surface ride,
   And wrecks of winter load the downward tide.''

AFTER travelling a short distance in the road, Woodburn and his companions halted, put on their snow-shoes, and, turning out to the left into the woods, commenced, with the long, loping step peculiar to the racket-shod woodsman, their march over the surface of the untrodden snow. The road just named, which formed the usual route from the village they had quitted to their place of destination, led first directly to the Connecticut, in an easterly direction, and then, turning to the north, passed up the river near its western banks, thus describing in its course a right angle, at the point of which, resting on the river, stood the store of Stephen Greenleaf, the first, and, for a while, the only merchant in Vermont; whose buildings, with those perhaps of one or two dependants, constituted the then unpromising nucleus around which has since grown up the wealthy and populous village of East Brattleborough. Such being the course of the travelled route, it will readily be seen, that the main object of our foot company, in leaving it, was the saving of distance, to be effected by striking across this angle to some eligible point on the northern road. And they accordingly pitched their course so as to enter the road near its intersection with the Wantastiquet, or West River, — one of the larger tributaries of the Connecticut, — which here comes rolling down from the eastern side of the Green Mountains, and pours its rock-lashed and rapid waters into the comparatively quiet bosom of the ingulfing stream below.

After a walk of about half an hour, through alternating fields and forest, they arrived, as they had calculated, at the banks of the tributary above named, where it was crossed on the ice by the winter road, which, owing to the failure of the rude bridge near the mouth of the stream, and the difficulty of descending the bank in its immediate vicinity, had been broken out through the adjoining meadow and over the river at this point, which was consequently a considerable distance above the ordinary place of crossing

On reaching this spot, it was found that the flood, which, on the high grounds, where we have last been taking the reader, was but little observable, had made, and was evidently still making, a most rapid progress.   The rising waters had already forced them-selves through the small but constantly widening outlets of their strong, imprisoning barriers, and were beginning to hurry along, in two dark, turbid streams, over the surface of the ice, beneath the opposite banks, where it was still too strongly confined to the roots and frozen earth to permit of its rising; while the uplifting mass, in the middle of the river, had nearly attained the level of the surrounding meadows.   And, although the main body still remained unbroken, yet the deep, dull reports that rose in quick succession to the ear from the cracking mass in every direction around, and the sharp, hissing, gurgling sounds of the water, which was gushing violently upwards through the fast multiplying fissures, together with the visible, tremor-like agitation that per-vaded the whole, plainly evinced that it could not long withstand the tremendous pressure of the laboring column of waters be-neath.

The travellers, who were not to be turned back by a foot or two of water in their path over the ice, so long as the foundation remained firm, drew up a long spruce pole from a neighboring fence, and, shooting it forward through the first stream of water, passed over upon it to the uncovered ice; and then, drawing their spar-bridge to the water next the other bank, went through the same process, till they had all reached the opposite shore un-wet and in safety.

Here they again paused to note the appearance of the disturbed elements; for, in addition to the threatening aspect which the river was here fast assuming, a slight trembling of the ground began occasionally to be perceptible; while unusual sounds seemed to come mingling from a distance, with the roaring of the wind and the noise of rushing waters, as if earth, air, and water were all joining their disturbed forces for some general commotion.

"The water and ice are strangely agitated, it appears to me," observed Woodburn to his companions, as they stood looking or the scene before them.   "See how like a pot the water boils up through that crevice yonder!   Then hear that swift, lumbering rush of the stream beneath!   The whole river, indeed, seems fairly to groan, like some huge animal confined down by an in-supportable burden, from which it is laboring to free itself.   I have noticed such appearances, I think, when the ice was on the point of breaking up; but that can hardly be the case here, at present can it?"

" On the point of breaking up, now ? " said one of the company in reply. " No, indeed ! Why, the ice is more than three feet thick, and as sound and solid as a rock. Should it rain from this time till to-morrow noon, it won't start."

" Well, now, I don't know about that," remarked an observant old settler, who had been silently regarding the different portents to which we have alluded. " I don't know about the ice staying here twenty hours, or even one. This has been no common thaw, hat we have had for the last six or eight hours, let me tell you."

"And still," observed Woodburn, " I should not think the water high enough as yet to cause a breaking up, should you ? "

" With a slow rise, and in a still time, perhaps not, Harry. But when the water is rising rapidly, as now, and especially if there is a strong wind, like this, to increase the motion, as it does either by outward pressure, or by forcing the air through the chinks in under the ice, I have always noticed that the stream acts on the ice at a much less height, and much more powerfully, than when the rise is slow and the weather calm."

" Then you look upon the appearances I named as indications that such an event is soon to take place here, do you ? "

" I do, Harry, much sooner than you are expecting; for the signs you name are not the only ones which tell that story, as I will soon convince you all, if you will be still and listen a moment."

This remark caused the company to pause and place them-selves in a listening attitude.

" There," resumed the speaker, pointing up to the bold, shaggy steeps of the mountain, which we have before alluded to, and which, from the opposite side of the Connecticut, and within a few furlongs from the spot where they now stood, rose, half con cealed in its " misty shroud," like some huge battlement, to the heavens — " there ! do you hear that dull roar, with occasionally a crashing sound, away up there among those clouds of fog near the top peaks of the mountain ? "

"Ay, ay, quite distinctly."

" Well, that is an echo, which, strangely enough, we can hear when we can't the original sound, and which is made by the striking up there of the roar of the river above us ; that of course must be open, having already broken up and got the ice in mo-tion somewhere. But hark again ! Now, don't you hear that rumbling noise ? Can't you, now, both hear and feel those quick, irregular, deep, jarring sounds ? "

" Yes, plainly — very plainly, now — you are right. Sure enough, the ice in the river above us is on the move !" re-sponded all, with excited looks.

" To be sure it is; and from the noise it makes, it must be com·
ing down upon us with the speed of a race-horse ! Let us all to
the hills, boys, where we can get a fair view of the spectacle."

The company, accordingly, now all ran to gain the top of a
neighboring swell, which commanded a view of West River for a
long distance up the stream, as well as one of a considerable
reach of the more distant Connecticut, both of which views were
obstructed, at the spot they had just left, by a point of woods and
turn in the river in the former instance, and by intervening hills
in the latter.

Among the many wild and imposing exhibitions of nature, peculiar to the mountainous regions of our northern clime, there is
no one, perhaps, of more fearful magnificence, than that which
is sometimes presented in the breaking up of one of our large
rivers by a winter flood ; when the ice, in its full strength, enor-
mous thickness, and rock-like solidity, is rent asunder, with loud,
crashing explosions, and hurled up into ragged mountains, and
borne onward before the raging torrent with inconceivable force
and frightful velocity, spreading devastation along the banks in
its course, and sweeping away the strongest fabrics of human
power which stand opposed to its progress, like the feeble weeds
that disappear from the path of a tornado.

Such a spectacle, as they reached their proposed stand, now
burst on the view of the astonished travellers. As far as the eye
could reach upwards along the windings of the stream, the whole
channel was filled with the mighty mass of ice, driving down
towards them with fearful rapidity, and tumbling, crashing, grind-
ing, and forcing its way, as it came, with collisions that shook the
surrounding forest, and with the din and tumult of an army of
chariots rushing together in battle. Here, tall trees on the bank
were beaten down and overwhelmed, or, wrenched off at the roots
and thrown upwards, were whirled along on the top of the rushing volume, like feathers on the tossing wave. There, the charging mass was seen swelling up into mountain-like elevations, to
roll onward a while, and, then gradually sinking away, be succeeded by another in another form ; while, with resistless front,
the whole immense moving body drove steadily on, ploughing
and rending its way into the unbroken sheet of ice before it,
which burst, divided, and was borne down beneath the boiling
flood, or hurled upwards into the air, with a noise sometimes
resembling the sounds of exploding muskets, and sometimes the
crash of falling towers.

But the noise of another and similar commotion n an opposite direction, now attracted their attention.   They turned, and their eyes were greeted with a scene, which, though less startling from its distance, yet even surpassed, in picturesque grandeur, the one they had just been witnessing.   Through the whole visible reach of the Connecticut, a long, white, glittering column of ice, with its ridgy and bristling top towering high above the adjacent banks, was sweeping by and onward, like the serried lines of an army advancing to the charge ; while the broad valley around, even back to the summits of the far-off hills, was resounding with the deafening din that rose from the extended line of the booming avalanche, with the deep rumblings of an earthquake mingled with the tumultuous roar of an approaching tempest.

The attention of the company, however, was now drawn from this magnificent display of the power of the elements, by an object of more immediate interest to their feelings.   This was an open double sleigh, approaching, on the opposite side of the river, towards the place at which they had just crossed over, in the manner we have described.   The mountain mass of ice that was still forcing its way down the river before them, with increasing impetus, was now within three hundred yards of the pass, to which those in the sleigh were hastening, with the evident design of crossing.   And though the latter, owing to a point of woods that intervened at a bend in the stream a short distance above, could not see the coming ice, yet they seemed aware of its dangerous proximity ; for, as they now drove down to the edge of the water, they paused, and a large man, who appeared to have control of the team, rose to his feet, and with words that could not be distinguished in the roaring of the wind and the noise from the scene above, made an appealing gesture, which was readily understood by our foot travellers as an inquiry whether the team would have time to cross before the ice reached the spot.

"It is Colonel Carpenter and his company," said Woodburn. "He will have no time to spare, but enough, I think, if he instantly improves it, to get safely over.   He has smart horses, and is anxious to be on this side of the river.   Let him come."

Accordingly, they returned him encouraging gestures, which being seen and understood by him, he instantly whipped up his horses, and, forcing them on the ice, soon effected his passage in safety, and drove rapidly down the road, leading along the northern bank of the stream to Connecticut, the object of his speed being obviously to keep forward of the icy flood, which by his progress might otherwise be soon obstructed.

"There," resumed Woodburn, breaking the silence with which

he and his companions had been witnessing the rather hazardous passage of their friends, — "there, the colonel is well over;
but his is the last sleigh to cross this year, unless it be drawn
by winged horses."

"Well, winged, or not winged, there is another, it seems, about
to make the attempt," said one of the company, pointing across
the river, where a covered double sleigh, with showy equipage
was dashing at full speed down the road towards the stream.

"It is a hostile craft!" "Peters and his gang!" "We owe
them no favors!" "Let the enemy take care of themselves!"
were the exclamations which burst from the recently-incensed
group, as all eyes were now turned to the spot.

"O, no! no!" exclaimed Woodburn, with looks of the most
lively concern. "Be they foes or friends, they must not be suffered to enter upon that river. Why, the breaking ice has already
nearly reached the bend, and unless it stops there, that path
across the stream, within five minutes, will be as traceless as
the ocean! Run down to the bank, and hail them!" he continued, turning to those around him. "I fear they would not listen
to me. Will no one go to warn them against an attempt which
must prove their destruction?" he added, reproachfully glancing
around him.

"Shall we interfere unasked?" said one, who was smarting
under a sense of former injuries; "ay, and interfere, too, to save
such a man as Peters, that he may go on robbing us of our
farms?"

"And save such a man as Sheriff Patterson, also, that he may
hang the innocent and pious Herriot?" said another, bitterly.

"And save them all, that they may keep up the court which will
soon hang or rob the whole of us?" added a third, in the same
spirit.

"O, wrong — wickedly wrong! and, if no one will go, I must,"
cried Woodburn, turning hastily from the spot, and making his
way down the hill towards the river with all the speed he was
master of.

A few seconds sufficed to bring him to the edge of the stream,
when, in a voice that rose above the roar of the wind and waters
around, he called on Peters, who was already urging his reluctant
and snorting horses down the opposite bank into the water, warned
him of the situation of the ice, and begged him, as he valued the
lives of his friends, to desist from his perilous attempt.

"Do you think to frighten me?" shouted Peters, who, per
ceiving the speaker to be his despised opponent, became suspi

3

cious, as the latter had feared, that the warning was but a *ruse* to prevent him from going on that night, — "do you think to frighten me back, liar, when a heavy team has just passed safely over before my eyes?"

And, in defiance of the timely caution he had received, and the warning sounds, of which his senses might have apprised him, had he paused a moment to listen, he furiously applied the whip, and plunged madly through the water towards the middle ice. But as rapidly as he drove, the team had not passed over more than one third of the distance across, before he and all with him became fully aware of the fearful peril they had so recklessly incurred ; for, at this critical moment, with awful brunt, the mountain wave of icy ruins came rolling round the screening point into full view, and not fifty yards above them. A cry of alarm at once burst from every occupant of the menaced vehicle and Peters, no less frightened than the rest, suddenly checked the horses, with the half-formed design of turning and attempting to regain the shore he had just left. But on glancing round, he beheld, to his dismay, the ice burst upward from its winter moorings along the shore, leaving between them and the bank a dark chasm of whirling waters, over which it were madness to think of repassing. At that instant, with a deep and startling report, the broad sheet of ice confining the agitated river burst asunder, parted, and was afloat in a hundred pieces around them. Another piercing cry of terror and distress issued from the devoted sleigh and Miss Haviland, with an involuntary impulse at the fearful shock, leaped out on to the large cake of ice on which the sleigh and horses were resting. She seemed instantly to perceive her error ; but before she could regain the sleigh, or even be caught by the extended hands of her friends, the frightened horses made a sudden and desperate lunge forward, and, with a speed that could neither be checked nor controlled, dashed onward over the dissevering mass, leaping from piece to piece of their sinking support, and each in turn falling in, to be drawn out by his mate, till they reached the shore, and rushed furiously up the bank, beyond the sweep of the dreadful torrent from which they had so miraculously escaped.

"O God of heaven, have mercy on my daughter ! " exclaimed Haviland, in a piteous burst of anguish, as he sprang out of the sleigh among the company, who, with horror-stricken looks, stood on the bank mutely gazing on the fast receding form of the luckless maiden, thus left behind, to be borne away, in all human probability, to speedy destruction.

For a moment no one stirred or spoke, all standing amazed, and seemingly paralyzed at the thought of her awful situation. having no hope of her rescue, and expecting every instant to see her crushed, or ingulfed among the ice that was wildly heaving and tumbling on every side around her. But fortunately for her, the broad, solid block, on which she had alighted, and on which she continued still to retain her stand, was, by the submerged and rising masses beneath, gradually and evenly forced upwards to the top of the column, with which it was moving swiftly down the current. And there she stood, like a marble statue on its pedestal, sculptured for some image of woe, her bonnet thrown back from her blanched features, and her loosened hair streaming wildly in the wind ; while one hand was extended doubtfully towards the shore, and the other lifted imploringly to heaven, as if in supplication for that aid from above, which she now scarcely hoped to receive from her friends below.

" O Sabrey, Sabrey ! must you indeed perish ? " at length burst convulsively from Miss McRea, in the most touching accents of distress.

" Is there no help ? Can no one save her ? " added the agonized father.

" Yes, save her — save her ! " exclaimed Peters, now eagerly addressing the men he affected so to despise. "Can't some of you get on to the ice there, and bring her off ? Five guineas to the man who will do it ; yes, ten ! Quick ! run, run, or you'll be too late," he added, turning, from one to another, without offering to start himself.

Throwing a look of silent scorn on his contemptible foe, Woodburn, having been anxiously casting about him in thought for some means of rescuing the ill-fated girl from her impending doom, now, with the air of one acting only on his own responsibility, hastily called on his companions to follow him, and led the way, with rapid strides, down along the banks of the stream, as near the main channel as the water and ice, already bursting over the banks into the road, would permit. But although he could easily keep abreast of the fair object of his anxiety, of whom he occasionally obtained such glimpses through the brushwood here lining the banks as to show him that she still retained her footing on the same block of ice, which still continued to be borne on with the surrounding mass, yet he could perceive no way of reaching her — no earthly means by which she could be snatched from the terrible doom that seemed so certainly to await her ; for along the whole extent of the moving ice, and even many rods in advance

of it, the water, dammed up, and forced from the choked chan
nel, was gushing over the banks, and sweeping down by their
sides in a stream that nothing could withstand.   And, to add to
the almost utter hopelessness with which he was compelled to view
her situation, he now soon began to be admonished that she was
immediately threatened by a danger from which she had thus far
been so providentially preserved — that of being crushed or
swallowed up at once in the broken ice. He could perceive, from
the increasing commotion of the ice around her, that her hitherto
level and unbroken support was growing every moment more
insecure and uncertain.   And as it rose and fell, or was pitched
forward and thrown up aslant, in the changing volume, he could
plainly hear her piteous shrieks, and see her flying from side to
side of the plunging body, to avoid being hurled into the frightful
chasms which were continually yawning to receive her.

"Lost! lost!" he uttered with a sigh ; "no earthly aid can now
avail her.   But stay! stay!" he continued, as his eye fell on the
two or three remaining beams or string-pieces of the old bridge
still extended across the river a short distance below.   "If she
reaches that place alive, and I can but gain the spot in time, I
may yet save her.   O Heaven, help me to the speed and the
means of rescuing her from this dreadful death!"

And calling loudly to his companions, whom he had already
outstripped, to come on, he now set forward, with all possible
speed, for the place which afforded the last chance for the poor
girl's rescue.   The banks of the river, at the point which it was
now his object to gain, were so much more elevated than those
above, that he had little fear of finding the path leading on to the
bridge obstructed by the water.   And it had glanced through his
mind, as he descried this forgotten spot, and saw the remains of
the bridge still standing, that the maiden might here be assisted
to escape on to the bank, or be drawn up by a cord, or some other
implement, to the top of the bridge, which, being high above the
ordinary level of the water, would not probably be swept away by
the ice, at least not till that part of it on which she was situated
should have passed under it.   There was an occupied log-house
standing but a short distance from the place, and the owner, as
Woodburn drew near, was, luckily, just making his appearance at
the door.

"A rope, a rope! be ready with a rope," shouted Woodburn,
pointing to the scene of trouble, as soon as he could make himself understood by the wondering settler.

The man, after a hurried glance from the speaker to the indi cated scene, and thence to the bridge below, during wh.ch he seemed to comprehend the nature of the emergency, instantly disappeared within the door. In another moment Woodburn came up, and burst into the house, where he found the settler and his wife eagerly running out the rope of their bedstead, which had been hastily stripped of the bed and clothing, and the fastenings cut, for the purpose. The instant the rope was disengaged, was seized by the young man, who, bidding the other to follow, rushed out of the house, and bounded forward to the bridge, which they both reached just as the unbroken ice was here beginning to quake and move from the impulse of the vast body above, which, now scarcely fifty paces distant, was driving down, with deafening crash, towards them.

"Thank Heaven, she yet lives, and is nearing us!" exclaimed Woodburn, as he ran out on to the partially covered beams of the bridge, where he could obtain a clear view of the channel above. She is there, hedged in, though as yet riding securely in the midst of that hideous jam, but, if not drawn up here, will be the next moment lost among the spreading mass, as it is disgorged into the Connecticut here below."

"Shall we throw down an end of the rope for her to catch?" said the settler, hastening to Woodburn's side.

"I dare not risk her strength to hold on to it; I must go down myself," said Woodburn, hurriedly knotting the two ends of the cord round his body. "Now stand by me, my friend. Brace yourself back firmly on this string-piece; let me down, and the instant I have secured her in my arms, draw us both up together."

"I can let you down; but to draw you both up ——" replied the other, hesitating at the thought of the hazardous attempt.

"You must try it," eagerly interrupted the intrepid young man. "My friends will be here in a moment to aid you. There she comes! be ready! Now!"

Accordingly, sliding over the edge of the bridge, Woodburn was gradually let down by the strong and steady hands of the settler, till he was swinging in the air, on a level with that part of the approaching mass on which stood the half-senseless object of his perilous adventure. The foremost of the broken ice was now sweeping swiftly by, just beneath his feet. Another moment, and she will be there! She evidently sees the preparation for her deliverance; a faint cry of joy escapes her lips, and her hands are extended towards the proffered aid. And now, riding high on the billowy column, she is borne on nearer and nearer towards those who wait, in breathless silence, for her

approach. And now she comes — she is here ! She is caught in
the eager grasp of the brave youth ; and, the next instant, by
the giant effort of the strong man above them, they are together
drawn up within a few feet of the bending and tottering bridge.
But with all his desperate exertions, he can raise them no higher,
and there they hang suspended over the dark abyss of whirling
waters that had opened in the disrupturing mass beneath, at the
instant, as if to receive them ; while a mountain billow of ice,
that must overwhelm them with certain destruction, is rolling
down, with angry roar, within a few rods of the spot. A groan
of despair burst from the exhausted man at the rope ; and his
grasp was about to give way.

"Hold on there, an instant ! one instant longer ! " cried a loud
voice on the right, where a tall, muscular form was seen bounding forward to the spot.

"Quick, Colonel Carpenter ! quick ! O, for God's sake, quick !"
exclaimed the settler, throwing an anguished and beseeching
glance over his shoulder towards the other.

The next instant, the powerful frame of the new-comer was
bending over the grasped rope ; and, in another, both preservers
and preserved were on the bridge, from which they had barely
time to escape, before it was swept away, with a loud crash, and
borne off on the top of the mighty torrent. They were met on
the bank by the companions of Woodburn, and the friends of the
rescued maiden, who came promiscuously running to the spot;
when loud and long were the gushing acclamations of joy and
gratitude that rang wildly up to heaven at the unexpected deliverance.

CHAPTER III.

*"The king can make a belted knight,
Confer proud names, and a' that;
But pith of sense and pride of worth
Are brighter ranks than a' that."*

THE village of Westminster yields, perhaps, in t ie tranquil and picturesque beauty of its location, to few others in New England. In addition to the advantage of a situation along the banks of that magnificent river, of which our earliest epic poet, Barlow, in his liquid numbers, has sung,

*"No watery glades through richer valleys shine,
Nor drinks the sea a lovelier wave than thine,"*

it stands upon an elevated plain, that could scarcely have been made more level had it been smoothed and evened, by the instruments of art, to fit it for the arena of some vast amphitheatre, which the place, with the aid of a little fancy, may be very easily thought to resemble ; for, from the principal street, which is nearly a mile in extent, broad and beautiful fields sweep away in every direction, till they meet, in the distance, that crescent-like chain of hills, by which, with the river, the place is enclosed.

It was probably this natural beauty of the place, together with its proximity to the old fort at Walpole, at which a military establishment was once maintained by the government of New Hampshire for the protection of its frontier, that led to the early settlement and rapid growth of this charming spot, which, having been entered by the pioneers as far back as 1741, continued so to increase and prosper, though on the edge of a wilderness unbroken, for many years, for hundreds of miles on the north, that, at the opening of the American revolution, it was the most pop.i·lous and best built village in Vermont.

This place, at the period chosen for the beginning of our tale, had been, for several years, the seat of justice for all the southern part of this disputed territory, under the assumed jurisdiction of New York, in which a majority of the inhabitants seemed to have tacitly acquiesced. And the most prominent of its public buildings, as might be expected, was the Court House, embracing the jail under the same roof. This was a spacious square ed fice conspicuous.y located, and of very respectable architecture for the times. The village, also, contained a meeting-house, school house, and the usual proportion of stores and taverns. The whole place, indeed, had now nearly passed into the second stage of existence, in American villages, when the pioneer log-houses have given place to the more airy and elegant framed buildings; and, compared with other towns, which, in this new settlement, were then just emerging from the wilderness, it wore quite an ancient appearance.

Among the most commodious and handsome of the many respectable dwellings which had here been erected, was that of Crean Brush, Esquire, colonial deputy secretary of New York, and also an active member of the legislature of that colony for this part of her claimed territory. This house, at the sessions of the courts, especially, was the fashionable place of resort for what was termed the court party gentry, and other distinguished persons from abroad. To the interior of this well-furnished and affectedly aristocratic establishment, we will now repair, in order to resume the thread of our narrative.

In an upper chamber of the house, at a late hour of the same evening on which occurred the exciting scenes described in the preceding pages, sat the two young ladies, to whom the reader has already been introduced, silently indulging in their different reveries before an open fire. They had safely arrived in town, about an hour before, with all their company, except Jones, who had been left at Brattleborough; and having been consigned to the family of this mansion, with whom they had formed a previous acquaintance at Albany, where Brush, the greater part of the year, resided, and where both of the young ladies were educated, they had taken some refreshment, and retired to the apartment prepared for their reception. The demeanor of these fair companions, always widely different, was particularly so at the present moment. Miss Haviland, with her chin gracefully resting on one folded hand, and her calm and beautiful, but now deeply-clouded brow, shaded by the white, taper fingers of the other, was abstractedly gazing into the glowing coals on the hearth before her, while the gentle, but less reflective McRea, with a countenance disturbed only by the passing emotions of sympathy that occasionally flitted over it, as she glanced at the downcast face of her friend, sat quietly preparing for bed, by removing her ornaments, and adjusting those long, golden tresses, with which, in after times, her memory was destined to become associated in the minds of tearful thousands, while reading the melancholy history of her tragic fate.

"Come, Sabrey," at length said the latter, soothingly, "come, cheer up. I cannot bear to see you so dejected. I would not brood over that frightful scene any longer, but, feeling grateful and happy at my escape, would dismiss it as soon as possible from my mind."

"I am, Jane," responded the other, partially rousing herself from her reverie; "I am both grateful and happy at my providential escape. But you are mistaken in supposing it is that scene which disquiets me to-night."

"Indeed!" replied the former, with a look of mingled surprise and curiosity. "Why, I have been attributing your dejection and absence of mind, this evening, to that cause alone. What else can have occurred to disturb your thoughts to-night, let me ask?"

"Jane, in confidence, I will tell you," replied Miss Haviland, looking the other in the face, and speaking in a low, serious tone. "It is the discovery which I have made, or at least think I have, this day, made, respecting the true character of one who should command, in the relation I stand with him, my entire esteem."

"Mr. Peters? Though of course it is he to whom you allude. But what new trait have you discovered in him, to-day, that leads you to distrust his character?"

"What I wish I had not; what I still hope I may be deceived in; but what, nevertheless, forces itself upon my mind, in spite of all my endeavors to resist it. You recollect Mr. Jones's account of the lawsuit, in which Mr. Peters succeeded in obtaining the farm of this Mr. Woodburn, whose gallant conduct we have all this afternoon witnessed?"

"Yes, certainly."

"Well, did you think that story, when rightly viewed, was very creditable to Mr. Peters?"

"I am not sure I understood the case sufficiently to judge; did you?"

'Well enough, Jane, with the significant winks that passed between Peters and the sheriff, to convince me that an unjust advantage had been taken. But perhaps I could have been brought to believe myself mistaken in this conclusion, had I seen nothing else to confirm it, and lower him still more in my esteem."

"What else *did* you see?

"An exhibition of malice, Jane, which astonished as much as

it pained me. That pretended accident, in running over Woodburn, was designed — ay, coolly designed."

" Why, Sabrey Haviland ! how can you talk, how can you believe, so about one whose betrothing ring is now on your fin-ger ? "

" It is indeed painful to do so ; but truth compels me."

" Might you not have been mistaken ? "

" No ; I saw the whole movement. I had been watching him some time, and I noticed how he prepared those fiery horses of his for a sudden spring, and saw the look of malicious exultation accompanying the final act. And even now, I shudder to think what guilt he might have incurred ! Even as it resulted, only in the destruction of property, how can I help being shocked at the dis-covery of a secret disposition which could have prompted such a deed ? O, how different has been the conduct of him who has thus been made the victim of his misusage ! "

" Different ! Why, what has he done ? I was not aware ——"

" True, I am reminded that I have not told you. That loqua-cious landlady, where we stopped to dine, told me, as we were coming away, that there had been a great excitement among the people in the street, about the outrage ; and that Peters would certainly have been mobbed, if Woodburn had not interfered and prevented it."

" Indeed ! I should have hardly expected so much magnanimity in one of his class. It was truly a noble return for the injuries he had received from Peters."

' Ay, and by this last act of saving my life, he has still more nobly revenged himself upon Peters, and upon us all."

" Assisted to save you, I conclude you mean ; for I heard Pe-ters tell your father, that 't was the settler who lived in the house near by, and Colonel Carpenter, who finally rescued you."

" Did he tell my father that story, without mentioning Wood-burn ? " asked Miss Haviland, with a look of mingled surprise and displeasure.

" Yes, as he came back to meet us with the news, while we were getting round with the sleigh to the spot."

" Well, my father shall know the truth of the case ; and Mr. Woodburn, though he did not boast of his services, nor even stay to give me an opportunity to thank him for what he had done, shall also know that we are not insensible to his gallant conduct ; for, whatever they may say, Jane, I am indebted to him for my life. As dreadful as was my situation among that crashing mass of ice, with which I was borne onward down the stream, I saw all that was done. He led the way from the first, contrived the plan, and with the assistance of the hesitating settler, carried it into execution, with a promptitude that alone could have saved me. It is true, that we both must have perished but for the timely arrival of Colonel Carpenter; but that detracts nothing from the merits of Mr. Woodburn, who, as we hung suspended over that frightful abyss, I knew and felt, was throwing his life to the winds to save mine. O, why could it not have been, as I have often said to myself during our cheerless ride this evening, — why could it not have been Peters, to perform all that I have this day seen in that poor, despised, and persecuted young man?"

" Why, Mr. Peters certainly appeared much alarmed, and anxious that something should be done to save you," replied Miss McRea, after a thoughtful pause, produced by the words and fervid manner of her companion.

'Then why did he leave it to another to save me?" responded the former, severely.

" That I do not know, certainly," replied the other; " but he at once bestirred himself, and I heard him offer five guineas, and I think he doubled the price the next moment, to any one who would go on to the ice and bring you off."

" Five guineas!" exclaimed Miss Haviland, starting to her feet, with a countenance eloquent with scorn and contempt   five guineas, and at a pinch, ten! What a singular fountain must that be, from which such a thought, at such a time, could have flowed! Had it been one of those favorite horses, it would have sounded well enough, perhaps, though I think he would have offered more. It is well, however, that I now know the price at which I am estimated," she added, bitterly.

" It *does* sound rather strangely, now you have named it," responded Miss McRea, abashed at the unexpected construction put on what she had communicated, and mortified and half vexed, that every attempt she had made to remove her friend's difficulties only made the matter worse: " it sounds oddly, to be sure, but I presume he did not mean any thing."

" O, no, I dare say; nor did he do any thing, as I can learn, through the whole affair, except attempt to deprive Woodburn of the credit he had gained. Jane," she continued, with softened tone, " what would you have thought, had you been in my situation, and your lover had acted such a part?"

" I should have thought — I don't know what I should have thought," replied the other, with a feeling which showed how quickly the appeal had taken effect. " But I should have had no

occasion to have a y thought about it; for I *know* he would hav:
been the one to save me, or die with me. O, I wish Mr. Jones
had come on with us, for had *he* been there, so good and so brave
as he is, I am sure even you need not have become so deeply
indebted to this low young fellow."

"Low, Jane, low?" said the former, reprovingly. "Was it low
to overlook so easily the injury and affront he had received from
Peters, and then return good for evil? And was it low to rescue
me from the raging flood, by exertions and risk of life, which
would have done credit to the first hero in the land?"

"O, no, not that; I did not mean that; for his conduct has been
generous and noble indeed; and from the first, when I heard Mr.
Jones's account of him, I was disposed to think highly of the
man, for one in his situation of life. I only meant that he did
not belong to our party, but was one of the lower classes of
society."

"It is true he may not belong to our party, Jane; but how
much should that weigh in the argument? Perhaps at this very
·our, two thirds of the American people would count it as weight
· the other part of the balance. And even I, trained as I have
)een by and among the highest toned loyalists, wish I could help
doubting that our party is the only one that has right and reason
on its side. And as to the claim of belonging to what is called
ne first society, I can only say that I wish many, who are allowed
that claim among us, were as worthy of the place as I think
Woodburn is. I have always loved Justice for her beautiful self
and hated her opposite; and I never could see how those who are
guided by her and the kindred virtues, could be accounted low,
or how, or why, those who lack these qualities could claim to be
called high. Is it any wonder then, Jane, that I should fee
troubled and distressed at discoveries which, in my mind, reverse
the situation that my friends assign to the two individuals of
whom we have been speaking?"

"O, you are too much of a philosopher for me in all that," replied Jane. "Come, be a woman now, Sabrey, and I will dis-
cuss the matter with you, claiming, perhaps, a little, a very little,
of the right of the confessor. I can easily understand how painful it would be to have doubts of the character of one's lover, and
I can also understand," she continued, looking a little archly,
"how one, who did not love a suitor very hard, could feel grateful
—yes, very grateful—to a good-looking young man who had
behaved gallantly. And I have a good mind to half suspect—"

"Hark!" interrupted the other, hurriedly, while a slight tinge became visible on her cheek — "hark! did you hear the striking of the house clock below? It is telling the hour of midnight. Let us dismiss these embarrassing thoughts, and retire to our repose. Your prospects, Jane," she continued, rising and speaking in a sad and gently expostulatory tone — " your prospects are bright with love and happiness ; and it will be ungenerous and cruel in you to say aught which will deepen the shade that I fear is coming over mine."

"O, I will not, Sabrey," warmly returned the kind-hearted Jane. " I did not intend it. Forgive me, do ; and we will dismiss the subject for something which will give us pleasanter dreams, and then, as you say, go to rest and enjoy them."

Leaving these fair friends to their slumbers, disquieted or sweetened by the various visions which the incidents of the day had been calculated to excite in the bosom of each, we will now repair to a lower apartment of the house, to note the doings of a select band of court dignitaries there assembled, for a purpose concerning which a spectator, at the first glance, might, from the appearances, be at a loss to decide whether it was one of revelry or secret consultation, so much did it partake of the character of both.

Around a long table, well furnished with wine and glasses, sat a select company of gentlemen, whose dress and deportment denoted them to be persons of the first consequence. And such, indeed, may be said to have been the fact, till the present time, for the party embraced the judges and officers of the court, and such of the most stanch and influential of their supporters as could be convened for a special consultation, which, it was considered, the portents of the times demanded. Here was the aristocratic and haughty Brush, the host, and leading spirit of the party, with his florid face, cracking his jokes and ridiculing " the boorish settlers," in which he was sure to find a ready response in the boisterous laugh of Peters and other young supporters of the court and loyal party. Here, too, sat the fiery and profane Gale, the clerk of the court, with his thin, angular features, and forbidding brow, occasionally exploding with his short, bitter, barking laugh, as, with many an oath, he dealt out anticipated vengeance on all those who should dare cross the path of the established authorities. And here also was Chandler, the chief judge of the court, with his plausible manners, affectedly sincere look, and deferential smile, as he exchanged the whisper and meaning glance with his colleague, Judge Sabin, a stern, reserved, and bigoted loyalist, or as he nodded approbation to the

4

remarks, wnatever they might be, of those around him. These
with Stearns, a tory lawyer of some note, Rogers, a tory landholder, Haviland, and a few others, all leading and trusty supporters of the court party, constituted the company, or rather the
cabinet council, here convened, all of whom, as appeared by the
entire freedom of their remarks, were fully in each other's confidence.

There was one perso in the room, however, who had no
thought or feeling in com non with the rest of those present, but
who did not appear to be deemed by them of sufficient consequence to be interrogated in relation to his opinions, or of sufficient capacity to comprehend what was said in his presence, at
least not to any degree which might render it unsafe that he
should hear the discussion so unreservedly going forward. This
person, who was acting in the capacity of waiter to the company,
being under a temporary engagement to the master of the house,
to serve him in such work as might be wanted about the house
and stables, was a youth, of perhaps eighteen, of quite an ordinary, and even singular appearance. His figure was low and
slight, and he was made to appear the more diminutive, perhaps,
by his dress, which consisted of short trousers, a long, coarse
jacket, and a flat woollen cap, drawn down to the eyebrows. His
hair, hanging, in lank locks, to his shoulders, was light and sandy,
and his face was deeply freckled ; while a pair of long, falling
eyelashes contributed to add still further to the peculiarity of his
looks, and to give his countenance, with those who did not note
the keen, bright orbs that occasionally peeped from their usually
impenetrable coverts, a sleepy and listless appearance. He now
sat on the top of a high wood-box, placed near one corner of the
chimney, with his legs dangling over one end of the box, and his
head drooping sluggishly towards the fire, apparently as unconscious of what was said and done in the room, as the little black
dog that lay sleeping on the floor beneath his feet.

" Here, Bart," exclaimed Brush, as the company, having
dropped the discussion of all weighty matters, were now briskly
circulating the bottle, and beginning to give way to noisy merriment — " here, Bart, you sleepy devil, come and snuff these can-
dles. Our chap here," he continued, winking archly to those
around him — " our chap Bart, or Barty Burt, to give the whole of
his euphonious name, gentlemen, may be considered an excellent
specimen of the rebel party, who talk so wisely about self-government, sitting under one's own vine and fig-tree, and all that
sort of thing; for, in the first place, he has a great deal of wis-

dom, handy to be got at, it all lying in his face. And then he is so much for self-government that no one can govern him in anything. Then again, as to the idea of sitting under a fig-tree, I think it is one that Bart would most naturally entertain; for had he a tree to sit under, be it fig or bass-wood, and enough to eat, he would sit there till he was gray, before he would think of moving."

"Not badly drawn, that similitude," said Stearns, after the burst of laughter, by which these remarks were greeted, had a little subsided; "but methinks I see a flaw therein, friend Brush: you said our young republican's wisdom, alias ideas, all lay in his face; and then, in the matter of the fig-tree, you go on to intimate he *has one* distinct idea in his head, thereby lessening the force and exactness of the comparison, as I think you will allow."

"I crave pardon, gentlemen," cried the secretary; "I should have qualified; for, really, I have several times seriously sus-pected Bart to have ideas, or, at least, one whole idea of his own; and if you think that is too much to allow the individuals of the party generally, with whom I have compared him, why, then I must knock under, that's all."

"You are down! you are down, then, Brush!" shouted sev-eral, with another uproarious burst of laughter.

Bart, the chief butt of this ridicule, in the mean while, was mov-ing quietly about the room in performance of his bidden tasks, without appearing to notice a word that was uttered; and but for a certain rapid twinkling that might have been seen in his eyes, which, as he deliberately returned to his seat in the corner, were opened to an unusual extent, one would have supposed him utterly insensible to all the taunts and jeering laughter of which he had thus publicly been made the victim.

"Ah! Patterson, here you are then, at last," exclaimed Gale, as the former, with a disturbed and angry countenance, now came pushing his way into the midst of the company. "We have done nothing but drink and joke since you went out, scarcely; at all events, we have concluded on nothing, except to wait and learn the result of your discoveries: so now for your report."

"Ay, ay, Mr. Sheriff," responded Brush. "But stay, take breath, and a glass of this glorious old Madeira, first. There! now tell us how the land lies abroad to-night."

"It lies but little to my liking," growled the sheriff, with an oath 'The rascally dogs have altogether stolen the march of us. They have been swarming into town all the evening, as thick as bees, while not more than a dozen of our flint-and-steel men have yet got on the ground. It beats Beelzebub !——"

"Our witnesses," quickly interposed Judge Chandler, bowing with a significant smile and cautionary wink, while he threw a sidelong glance towards Bart, whom the wary eye of the judge had detected in slightly changing his position, so as to bring his ear more directly towards the speakers—"our witnesses and quarrelling suitors in court you mean, of course ?"

"Why, yes—yes, your honor—if you think that necessary," replied Patterson, following the direction of the other's glance, and then looking inquiringly at Brush, as if to ask whether there was any danger to be apprehended from talking before the servant.

"Pooh — nonsense !" said Brush, readily understanding the mute appeal. "Nonsense! You could not make him comprehend what we are talking about in six weeks, if you should do your prettiest. Why, the fellow has not two ideas above a jackass ! — so talk out."

"Well, then," resumed the sheriff, in a lower tone, "I have satisfied myself that the rebels are plotting like so many Satans, and are in earnest about carrying their threat into execution. Now, the question is, what shall be done — yield the point and submit to be turned out of the Court House to-morrow, as if we were a pack of unruly boys, or what ? "

"Yield !" fiercely exclaimed Gale —"not till my pistol bullets have drank the heart's blood of the d——d rascals, first."

"Ay, Gale," responded Brush, "that would be well enough, but for one small difficulty, which is, that these demi-savages understand quite as much of that kind of play as we do ; and so long as they outnumber us so greatly, the fun of doing what you would propose might be less than talking about it. Let us have Chandler's opinion. What course is it best to take, judge ? "

"Temporize !" replied the latter, in a low, emphatic tone, and with a look of peculiar significance —"temporize till ——"

"Till we can help ourselves," said Patterson, taking up the sentence where the other left it, or rather finishing in words what had been expressed by looks.

"That's just my notion," remarked Stearns. "Let them see and be assured that we are for peace, and want nothing but what is right ; all of which may be said truly And in this manner, if the thing is well managed, their suspicions can be allayed; and we can get possession of the Court House as soon as our friends get on, which will be by to-morrow noon — will it not, Patterson ? "

" Yes, unless this cussed flood has carried away all the roads, as well as bridges," gruffly replied the sheriff. " Yes, and if these mobbing knaves can be kept quiet then, we shall be in a situation to ask no favors."

"And grant none," said Sabin, with cool bitterness.

" You don't learn," asked Chandler, with feigned indifference — " you don't learn that the people have brought any offensive implements with them, do you, Patterson? It might be done covertly, you know. Has this been seen to, by proper measures, — such as examining the straw in the bottoms of their sleighs, and the like ? "

" Yes, thoroughly," returned the former; " they have brought no arms with them, at any rate. We are undoubtedly indebted to your honor's skilful management with them at Chester for that."

"Ay, ay," interposed Stearns, " nobody but the judge could have executed that piece of diplomacy with the fellows. And no one but he can carry out the business successfully now. His honor must be the one to undertake it."

" Certainly." " The very man." " He must do it." " They would listen to none of us." " The thing is settled, and he must go " unanimously responded the company.

" I really feel flattered, gentlemen," replied Chandler, bowing and waving his hand towards the company — " highly flattered by your opinion of my capacity to negotiate in this delicate affair. But you will understand, in case I accede to your wishes, gentlemen," he continued, with a look of peculiar meaning — " you will understand that I am to be considered, on all hands, as utterly opposed to coercive measures — to all — I am understood, I suppose, gentlemen ? "

" Yes, yes, judge," returned the others, with knowing winks and laughter, " we will all understand that you are opposed to the whole move."

Having thus arranged business for the morrow to their satisfaction, these astute personages, who, like their party generally in America, at that period, seemed to have acted on an entirely false estimate of the intelligence and spirit of the common people, now rose and retired to their respective lodgings, inwardly chuckling at their sagacity, in being able to concoct what they believed would prove a successful scheme of overreaching and putting down their opponents, and, at the same time, of establishing their own tottering authority on a basis which might bid defiance to all future attempts to overturn it.

4 *

CHAPTER IV.

As soon as the company, described in the preceding chapter, had all retired from the room, Brush, bidding Bart to rake up the fire and go to bed, proceeded to lock all the outer doors of the house, muttering to himself as he did so, " It can't be as Chandler fears, I think, about this fellow's going out to blab to-night ; but as this will put an end to the possibillity of his doing it, I may as well make all fast, and then there will be no chance for blame for suffering him to remain in the room."

So saying, and putting the different keys in his pocket, he at once disappeared, on his way to his own apartment. When the sound of his retiring footsteps had ceased to be heard, Bart, who had lingered in the room, suddenly changed his sleepy, abject appearance for a prompt, decisive look and an erect attitude.

"Two ideas above a jackass! — two ideas above a jackass, eh ? " he said, and slowly repeated, as with flashing eyes he nodded significantly in the direction his master had taken. " You may yet find out, Squire Brush, that my ears aint sich a disput sight longer than yourn, arter all."

With this he blew out the last remaining light, and groped his way to his own humble sleeping-room, in the low attic story of the back kitchen. Here, however, he manifested no disposition to go to bed, but sitting down upon the side of his miserable pallet, he remained motionless and silent for fifteen or twenty minutes, when he began to soliloquize: " Jackass! — sleepy devil ! — not wit enough to see what they are at in six weeks, eh ? Barty Burt, you are one of small fishes, it is true ; but, for all that, you needn't be walloped about at this rate, and bamboozled, and swallowed entirely up by the big ones of this court-and-king party. You know enough to take care of yourself ; yes, and at the same time, you can be doing something towards paying these gentry for the beautiful compliments you have had from them to-night. and at other times. The fact is, Bart, you are a rebel now — honestly one of them — you feel it in you, and you may as well let it out. So here goes for their meeting, if it is to be found, if I am hanged for it."

Having, in this whimsical manner, made a sort of manifesto of his principles and intentions, as if to give them, with himself, a more fixed and definite character, he now rose buttoned up his jacket, carefully raised the window of his room, let himself down to the roof of a shed beneath it, and from that descended to the ground, with the easy and rapid motions of a squirrel engaged in nut-gathering. Here he cast a furtive glance around him, and paused some moments, in apparent hesitation, respecting the course to be taken to find those of whom he was in quest. Soon, however, appearing to come to a determination, he struck out into the main street, and, with a quick step, proceeded on, perhaps a furlong, when he suddenly stopped short, and exclaimed, "Hold up, Bart. What did that sly judge say about searching in folks' sleighs, for — what was that word now? — But never mind, it meant guns. And what did the sheriff say about a dozen flint-and-steel men having come? Put that and that together now, Bart, and see if it don't mean that the only guns brought into town to-night are packed away in the straw, in the bottom of the sleighs of the court party understrappers? Let's go and mouse round their stopping-place a little, Bart. Perhaps you'll get more news to carry to the rebels," he added, turning round and making towards the tavern at which those in the interests of the loyalists were known generally to put up.

On reaching the tavern, and finding all there still and dark, he proceeded directly to the barn shed, and commenced a search, which was soon rewarded by finding, in the different sleighs about the place, twelve muskets, carefully concealed in hay or blankets. With a low chuckle of delight at his discovery, Bart took as many as he could conveniently carry at one load, and, going with them into the barn, thrust them one by one into the hay mow, under the girts and beams, so as effectually to conceal them. He then returned for others, and continued his employment till the whole were thus disposed of; when he left the place, and resumed his walk to the northerly end of the village. After pursuing his way through the street, and some distance down the road beyond the village, he paused against a low, long log-house, standing endwise to the road. This house was occupied by a middle-aged, single man, known by the name of Tom Dunning, though often called Ditter Dunning, and sometimes Der Ditter, on account of his frequent use of these terms as prefixes to his words and sentences, arising from a natural impediment of speech. He was a hunter by profession, and passed most of his time in the woods, or round the Connecticut in catching salmon, which, at that period, were found in the river in considerable numbers, as far up as Bellows Falls. Though he mingled but little in society, yet he was known to be well informed respecting all the public movements of the times; and it was also believed that he had enrolled himself among the far-famed band of Green Mountain Boys, and often joined them in their operations against the Yorkers, on the other side of the mountains. Very little however, was known about the man, except that he was a shrewd, resolute fellow, extremely eccentric, and perfectly impenetrable to all but the few in whom he confided.

Bart, from some remark he had overheard in the street, in the early part of the evening, had been led to conclude that the company he now sought were assembled at this house. And though he was personally unacquainted with the owner, and knew nothing of his principles, yet he was resolved to enter and trust to luck to make his introduction, if the company were present, and, if not, to rely on his own wit to discover whether it were safe to unfold his errand.

As he was approaching the house, Dunning hastily emerged from the door, and, advancing with a quick step, confronted him in the path with an air which seemed to imply an expectation that his business would be at once announced. Bart, who was not to be discomposed by any thing of this kind, manifested no hurry to name his errand, and seemed to prefer that the other should be the first to break the silence.

" Ditter — seems to me I have seen you somewhere? " at length said Dunning, inquiringly.

" Very likely. I have often been there," replied Bart, with the utmost gravity.

" Ditter — devil you have! And what did you — der — ditter — find there, my foxy young friend? "

" Nothing that I was looking for."

" Der — what was that? "

" The meeting."

" Der — what meeting? "

" The one I'd like to go to, may be."

" You are a bright pup; but — der — don't spit this way; it might be der — ditter — dangerous business to me; for you must have been eating razors to-night."

" No, I haven't; don't love 'em. But you haven't yet told me where the meeting is? "

" Ditter — look here, my little chap," said Dunning, getting impatient and vexed that he could not decide whether the other was a knave, simpleton, or neither — "ditter — look here ; — der — don't your folks want you ?" Hadn't you better run along now ?"

" Reckon I shall, when you tell me where to go and not run against snags."

" Ditter well, der go back the way you come, about ditter as far again as half way ; der then, ditter turn to the ditter right, then to the ditter left, then der — ditter — ditter — ditter — go along ! you'll get there before I can tell you."

" In no sort of hurry ; will wait till you get your mouth off ; may be it will shoot near the mark arter all."

" Ditter, dog, my cat, if I — der — don't begin to believe you are considerable of a critter : and I've half a mind to risk you a piece ; so come into the house, and, der — let me take a squint at your phiz in the light."

Taking no exceptions to the character of the invitation, Bart now followed the other into the house, and, sitting down on a bench by the fire, began very unconcernedly to whistle, on a low key, the tune of Yankee Doodle, which was then just begin-ning to be considered a patriotic air. Dunning, in the mean time, taking a seat in the opposite corner, commenced his proposed scrutiny, which he continued, with one eye partly closed, and with a certain dubious expression of countenance, for some mo-ments, when he observed,

" You are a ditter queer chicken, that's a fact. But I der find now that I know you, as the ditter divil did his pigs, by sight ; I know also the sort of folks you have been living amorgst lately ; and der knowing all that, it's reasonable that I should be a snuffing a little for the ditter smell of brimstone. So now, 'f you are a court party tory, and come here for mischief, you've got into a place that will ditter prove too hot for you ; but if, as I rather think, you are, or der want to be, something better, and can let us into the shape and fix of matters and things over there at ditter head-quarters, you may be the chap we would like to see. Out speak out therefore, like a man, and no more of your ditter squizzling."

After a few more evasive remarks, in which he succeeded in drawing out the other more fully, and causing him the more com-pletely to commit himself, Bart threw aside all bantering and proceeded to relate all his discoveries relative to the contemplated movement of the court party.

' Ditter devils and dumplings !" exclaimed the hunter, as, with eyes sparkling with excitement, he sprang to his feet, as the other finished his recital. " This must be made known directly

Come — der follow me, and I'll take you to the company you
ditter said you wished to see."

So saying, he immediately led the way through a dark entry to
a room in the rear of the house, which the two now entered;
when Bart found himself in a company of nearly twenty grave
and stern-looking men, deliberating in a regularly organized
meeting.

"Ditter here, Captain Wright," eagerly commenced Dunning,
as he entered, addressing the chairman, a prompt, fine-looking
man, and the leading whig of the village ; "here is one," he
continued, pointing to Bart, " one who brings ditter news that——'

" Esquire Knowlton, of Townsend, has the floor now," said
the chairman, interrupting the speaker, and directing his attention
to a middle-aged man of a gentlemanly, intelligent appearance,
who was standing on one side of the room, having suspended the
remarks he was making at the entrance of Dunning and his companion.

' As I was remarking, Mr. Chairman," now resumed the gentleman who had been thus interrupted in his speech, " the tory
party, acting under various disguises, have been, for several
months past, secretly using every means within their reach to
strengthen their unrighteous rule in this already sadly oppressed
section of the country. They aim to bring the people into a state
of bondage and slavery. When no cash is stirring, with which
debts can be paid, they purposely multiply suits, seize property,
which they well know can never be redeemed, and take it into
their hands, that they may make the people dependent on them,
and subservient to their party purposes. And just so far as they
find themselves strengthened by these and other disguised movements, so far they betray their intention to curtail all freedom of
opinion, and to overawe us by open acts of oppression. Here,
one man has been thrown into prison on the charge of high treason ; when all they proved against him was the remark, that if
the king had signed the Quebec bill, he had broken his corona-
tion oath. There, another, a poor harmless recluse, as I have
ever supposed him, is dragged from his hut in the mountains
and imprisoned to await his trial for an alleged murder, committed long ago, and in another jurisdiction ; when his only
crime, with his prosecutors, probably, is his bold denunciations of
their tyranny, unless, as some suspect, even a baser motive actu-
ates them. They even proclaim, that *all* who dare question the
king's right to tax us without our consent, are guilty of high treason and worthy of death ! For myself, I seek not the suspension

of this court at this time, on account of the questionable jurisdiction of New York merely, but because the court, itself bitterly tory in all its branches, is sustained by a colony which refuses to adopt the resolves of the Continental Congress, and thereby continues to force upon us the royal authority, which our brethren of the other colonies have almost every where put down, and which in our case, Heaven knows, is not the least deserving the fate it has met elsewhere. And the question, then, now comes home to us, Shall we tolerate it any longer? The hearts of the people, though their tongues may often be awed into silence — the hearts of the people are ready to respond their indignant *no!* And I, for one, am ready to join in the cry, and stepping into the first rank of the opposers of arbitrary power, breast the storm in discharging my duty to my country."

"Amen!" was the deep and general response of the company.

"Mr. Dunning will now be heard," said the chairman, motioning to the former to come forward.

"Ditter well, Captain — der — ditter Mr. Moderator, I mean. I, being on the watch against ditter interlopers, you know, have just picked up an odd coon, here, who ditter seems to have ears in one place and tongue in another : and his story is a ditter loud one. But let him tell it in his own way. So now, Barty Burt," he continued, going up to the other, who stood by the fire, kicking the fore-stick with his usual air of indifference; "come forward, and tell the meeting all you have der seen and heard, in the ditter camp of the Philistines."

Bart, then, mostly in the way of answers to a series of rapid questions, put by the chairman, who seemed to know him, and understand the best way of drawing him out, — Bart then related his discoveries to his astonished and indignant auditors, giving such imitations of the manner of each of the company, whose words he was repeating, as not only showed their meaning in its full force, but at once convinced all present of the truth of his story.

No sooner had Bart closed, than a half dozen of the company sprang to their feet, in their eagerness to express their indignation and abhorrence of the bloody plot, which their opponents under the garb of peace and fair promises, had, it was now evident, been hatching against them.

"Order, gentlemen!" cried the chairman: "I don't wonder you all want to denounce the detestable and cowardly conduct of the tyrants. But one only can be heard at a time, and Mr.

French, I rather think, was fairly up first, and he will therefore proceed."

While all others, on hearing this remark of the chairman,
resumed their seats, the person thus named, as privileged to
speak first, remained standing. He was a young man, of about
twenty-two, of a ready, animated appearance, while every look
and motion of his ardent countenance and restless muscles proclaimed him to be of the most sanguine temperament and enthu-
siastic feelings. An almost unnatural excitement was sparkling
in his kindling eyes, and a sort of wild, fitful, sad, and prophetic
air characterized his whole appearance as he began.

"It has come at last, then! I knew it was coming. I have
felt it for months; waking and sleeping, I have felt it. In my
dreams I have seen blood in the skies, and heard sounds of battle
in the air and earth. Dreams of themselves, I know, are generally without sign or significance; but when the spirit of a dream
remains on the mind through the waking hours, as it has on
mine, I know it has a meaning. Something has been hurrying
me to be ready for the great event. I could not help coming
here to-night. I cannot help being here to-morrow. The event
and the time are at hand! I see it now — resistance, and battle,
and blood! Let it come! the victims are ready; and their blood,
poured out on the wood on the altar of liberty, will bring down
fire from heaven to consume the oppressors!"

There was a short silence among the company, who seemed to
pause, in surprise and awe at the strange words and manner of
the young man, which evidently made an impression on his hearers at the time, and which were afterwards remembered, and
often repeated, at the fireside, in recounting his untimely fate."

"Mr. Fletcher," at length observed the chairman, breaking
the silence — "Mr. Fletcher, of Newfane, is next entitled to
speak, I believe."

"I rose, Mr. Chairman," said the latter, a fine specimen of the
hardy, resolute, and intelligent yeoman of the times — "I rose but
to ask whether the news just received can be relied on : "can it
be, that Judge Chandler, after his pledge to us at Chester, would
be guilty of conduct reflecting so deeply on his character as a
man?"

"I am not wholly unprepared to believe the story mysel',"
replied the chairman; "our young friend here may have his peculiarities; but I consider him a thousand times more honest and
honorable, than some of those whose sly hints and treacherous
conduct he has so well described."

"Ditter, look here, Mr. Moderator," interposed Dunning. "I was once, ditter travelling, in the Bay State, with a friend, when we came across a meeting-house with eight sides, and my friend asked me what order of architecture I called it. Ditter well, I was fairly treed, and couldn't tell. But I should be able to tell now. I should ditter call it the Chandler order."

A desultory but animated debate now arose. Various methods of accomplishing what appeared to be the settled determination of all — that of preventing the sitting of the court — were suggested. Some proposed to dismantle or tear down the Court House; others were for arming the people, seizing the building, and bidding open defiance to their opponents. At this stage of the deliberations, Colonel Carpenter, whose character had secured him great influence, rose, and requested to be heard.

"From the gathering signs of the times," said he, "we have good reason to believe that the smouldering fires of liberty will soon burst forth into open revolution throughout these oppressed and insulted colonies. Our movements here may lead to the opening scene of the great drama; and we must give our foes no advantages by our imprudence. If we are the first to appear in arms, it may weaken our cause, while it strengthens theirs. Let *them* be the first to do this — let us place *them* in the wrong, and then, if they have recourse to violence and bloodshed, *we* will act; and no fear but the people will find means to arm themselves. Let us, therefore, go into the Court House to-morrow, in a body, but without a single offensive implement, and resist peacefully, but firmly; and then, if they dare make a martyr, his blood will do more for our cause than would now a regiment of rifles."

Although this prudent and far-sighted proposal was for a while opposed, by the more ardent and unthinking part of the company, yet it was at length adopted by the whole; and having made arrangements to carry it into effect, the meeting broke up, and all retired to their respective lodgings.

CHAPTER V.

" Thou ever strong upon the strongest side

ALTHOUGH many were the anxious consultations, and deep plot-tings, among the belligerent parties within doors, during the fore part of the memorable 13th of March, yet it was not till the after-noon of that day had considerably advanced, that any indications of the events which followed became observable in the streets of Westminster. About this time, one of the doors of Crean Brush's guest-filled mansion suddenly flew open, and the crouched and cringing form of our humble friend Barty Burt, hotly pursued by his recent employer with uplifted cane, was seen coming down the steps of the entrance, in flying leaps, to the ground.

"There, you infernal booby! please consider this caning and kicking as a farewell to my house and employ forever!" ex-claimed the enraged master, standing in the door-way, and look-ing down with ineffable scorn upon the prostrate person of the ejected Bart, as he lay sprawled out upon the spot where he landed, without manifesting any disposition to rise.

"I should like to know what I've done criminal, squire?" responded the latter, looking back over his shoulder at the other, with a doleful grimace.

"What have you done?" sharply retorted Brush. "Why, you impertinent puppy, you have done every thing wrong, and nothing right, ever since you got your lubberly carcass out of bed, at the fine time of eight o'clock this morning! and now, to crown all, in clearing off the table, you must go, with your load of meats and half-filled gravy dishes, through the parlor, where you had no business to go, and there, like a blundering jackass, as you are, you must fall down and ruin the best carpet in the house! I've had quite enough of you, sir: so up with you there and clear out, you vagabond!"

"Well, I 'spose I know what you want," muttered Bart, by way of reply to this tirade — " you want to accuse, and drive me away, so you won't have to pay me the two crowns you owe me for work, and other things."

"I don't owe you half that sum, you lying lout," returned Brush, fiercely. "But to get rid of such a pest, and prevent your going round town with that lie in your mouth, I'll give you all you ask; and there they are!" he continued, pulling out and disdainfully tossing the coins down at the other's feet. "Your dirty rags, if you have any in the house, shall be thrown out to you; and then, if you aint off, I'll set the dogs on ye."

With this, and an expressive slam of the door behind him, the secretary returned into the house; and in a few moments, the sash of a garret window was thrown up, and a pair of shoes, a pair of old summer pantaloons, a spare coarse shirt, and pair of stockings, were successively flung down into the yard, near where the owner was still lying, by the hand of a grinning and blushing servant maid, while her dainty-fingered master stood by, directing the operation.

"Well, Bart," now soon began to mutter this singular being, in his usual manner of addressing himself as a second person, when alone — "well, Bart, your plan of getting driv away has worked to a shaving. You've got your pay, too, jest in the way you cal-culated would fetch it; yes, all your honest pay, and one crown more; but you charged that, you know, when you told him two crowns, as damage for the kick and cane lick you got. So that's settled. And as to the other accounts against him, and the rest of 'em there, you'll be in a way to square all, fore long, guess; for you will be your own rebel, now, Bart, you know."

While thus communing with himself, he had slowly, and with many winces of affected pain, gathered up his limbs, risen on to his feet, pocketed his two crowns, and collected and tied up his clothes. And he was now, with a grieved look, as if sorrowing for the loss of his home, looking back to the house, where several curious, half-laughing, half-pitying countenances were seen peer-'ng through the windows to witness his departure. He then looked hesitatingly abroad, one way and then the other, with the sad and despairing air of one who feels there is no place in the wide world where he can find a friendly shelter. After this, with a wince and groan at every step, he slowly hobbled off up the street, losing his lameness, and converting his groans into snickers of low, exulting laughter, as soon as he was out of eye-shot of the company he had left behind him.

"Kinder 'pears to me, Bart," he at length said, resuming his soliloquy, as he glanced keenly at the tavern, which was the scene of his last night's exploit, and which he was now passing— "'pears to me, there's a good many heads rather close together

in spots, round that tory nest over yonder. They act as if they
were in a sort of stew about something. I wonder if they lost
their guns last night, or anything, that puts them in such a
pucker," he continued with a chuckle. "But suppose, Bart, as
going this way is only a sham, suppose we now haul up here,
and edge over there among 'em a little, to learn what they are
up to, before you go to join the company at the Court House."

On reaching the yard of the tavern, Bart found that the company, numbering perhaps twenty in all, had broken from the
separate groups in which they had been conversing, and had
now gathered round one man, who, having just come out of the
tavern, appeared to be communicating to the crowd something
that obviously produced considerable sensation. This person
was a man of the ordinary size, of fair complexion, light eyes,
and an unsettled and vacillating countenance, rendered the more
strikingly so, perhaps, by the quick, eager, and restless motions
and manner by which his whole appearance was characterized.
Bart soon contrived to work his way into this circle, till he gained
a position from which he could hear what was said.

"You may rely on what I have told you," said the speaker, as
Bart came within hearing; "for I have just had it from the
sheriff and lawyer Stearns. The rebels have been in possession
of the Court House about an hour, posted sentinels at all the
doors, and openly declare, that the judges and officers shall never
enter to hold another court. Nobody dreamed of their daring
on such a bold step, or we should have been before them in
taking possession of the house, even with the force we had on
the ground. But, thinking it best to go strong-handed, the judges
concluded they would not go in to open the court till enough
of friends should arrive to put down all opposition at a blow.
The rebels think now, doubtless, that they have got an advantage
which they will be able to maintain. But they will find themselves a little mistaken, I fancy; for Patterson says he has now
got them in just the spot he wanted. This act both he and
Stearns decide to be overt treason, which will justify him in
taking the course he intends, unless they yield and scatter, on
the first summons. But as they won't do that, and our forces will
shortly be here, you can all guess what we shall now soon see
follow," he added, with a significant wink.

"Then why not be getting out our guns at once?" asked
one of the company.

"No," resumed the speaker; "the plan is to leave that till
be last thing before we march upon them, lest the rebels

should take alarm and go and arm themselves, and we thus thwart our own intention of taking them by surprise. You, however, can be kinder carelessly looking up clubs for such as may have no arms, and a few axes and crowbars for breaking into the Court House, if that should be necessary. But, as I said, let the guns remain hid in the sleighs till you have orders to take them out. For it is not exactly settled yet whether we shall march upon them as soon as our reënforcements arrive, and besiege them in the house, or coax them out, and so get possession ourselves. But, at any rate, you will have work on hand soon; and if we don't see fun before to-morrow morning, my name aint David Redding. But come, let's all adjourn to the bar-room, and take a drop to warm us up a little."

Leaving Redding to his despicable task of endeavoring, in compliance with the directions of those whose base tool he was, to inflame the company he had collected, and work up their feelings to such a pitch of enmity and recklessness as should prepare them to imbrue their hands in the blood of their neighbors and countrymen, we will now proceed to note the conduct of more important personages in the events of the day.

While the scene above described was transpiring, Patterson, Gale, Stearns, and one or two other tory leaders, who had been consulting at this tavern, and making their arrangements for active movements, left the house, and, with hasty steps, took their way to the mansion of the haughty secretary, which, by his special invitation, at this crisis, was made the permanent quarters of the judges and principal officers of the court, as well as of his numerous guests.

" Upon the whole, perhaps you are right, Stearns," said Patterson, as they were about to enter the house. " We will start off Chandler to the Court House to make one of his smooth speeches, and play Sir Plausible with the rebel rascals, as agreed on last night, and though he should have done it before, yet he may, even now, succeed in flattering them to quit the house long enough for us to get possession; if not, we will take the other course."

In a few moments after these worthies had disappeared within the house, the door was again opened, and Chief Justice Chandler, the man to whose singularly compounded character, made up of timidity, selfishness, vanity, thirst of power, kindness, and duplicity, or rather the conduct that flowed from it, may be mainly attributed the bloody tragedy that ensued, now made his appearance in the street. He wore a powdered wig, according

5 *

to the fashion of the times among men of his official station, and his whole toilet had evidently been made with much attention. Carelessly flirting a light cane in his hand, and assuming an air of easy unconcern, he leisurely took his way along the street, towards the Court House, bowing low, and blandly smiling to every one he met, and often even crossing to the opposite side of the street to exchange salutations with the passer-by, to each of whom, whatever his party or station, he was sure to say something complimentary, and aimed with no little sagacity to reach the peculiar feelings and interests of the person addressed.

"This is Mr. French, I believe," he said, turning out of his course to speak to the young man introduced in the last chapter, who, with the same restless, anxious look he then wore, was unobservantly hurrying by the other, on his way to the Cour House.

"Yes, yes, sir," replied French, slightly checking his speed, and looking back, with a half-surprised, half-vacant expression.

"Ay, I was sure I knew you," rejoined the judge. "How are the times with you, Mr. French? You will pardon my freedom, sir, but the great interest I take in the success of our enterprising and intelligent young men like yourself —— But no matter now. I see you are in haste. I will not detain you, sir. A very good day to you, Mr. French."

"Well, upon my word, now, here is my friend Colonel Carpenter!" he again exclaimed, as, turning from the person he had just saluted with such poor success, his quick and wary eye caught sight of the gentleman thus addressed coming up behind him. "Most happy to fall in with you, colonel," he continued, grasping and warmly shaking the hand of the other. "How are your family, sir? Shall I confess it, colonel? I have really sometimes greatly envied you."

"Why so, sir?" asked Carpenter, with a little coolness.

"Envied you your well-deserved appellation — that of *Friend of the People*, as they call you," replied the judge.

"The people need a friend at this crisis, I think, sir," responded the unbought yeoman, with cold dignity.

"If there is one title that I should covet above all others," resumed the judge, without appearing to notice the drift of the other's remark, "it would be the one I have named. What can be a more truly honorable distinction? I have often regretted being so trammelled by my station on the bench, as to prevent me from acting as I would otherwise like to do. But a judge, you know, colonel, in party times, must not act openly on any particular side."

"He had better do that, however, than act *secretly* on *all* sides," returned the other, with biting significance.

"O, doubtless, doubtless, sir," rejoined the judge, with a forced laugh, but with the air of one perfectly unsuspicious of any intended personalities. "Yes, indeed. But, ah!" he continued, slightly motioning towards the Court House, against which they had now arrived. "What have we here? A public meeting?"

"Quite possible. At all events I think of going in myself," said Carpenter, quietly turning from the other into the Court House yard, but soon pausing a little, though without looking round, to hear the remarks which the other seemed intent on making.

"Indeed! Why, I had not heard of it, else I should have been pleased to have dropped in. I came out, be sure, only for a little exercise, but —— "

Here he paused, in expectation that the other would speak; but finding himself disappointed, and left alone in the street, he resumed his walk, while his now unguarded countenance very plainly showed the disquiet he felt at the rebuffs he had received in his attempts to conciliate Colonel Carpenter, and obtain from him an invitation to go into the meeting, which, in reality, it was his only object in coming out to attend.

While digesting his mortification, and occupied in conjecturing how he could have become an object of suspicion among the opponents of the court party, as every thing now seemed to indicate, his attention was again arrested by the sounds of approaching footsteps; and, looking up, his eyes encountered the sarcastic countenance of Tom Dunning, who, coming from an opposite direction, was also on his way to join the company at the Court House.

"Ah, Mr. Dunning!" exclaimed the judge, starting from his reverie and downcast attitude, while his face instantly brightened into smiles summoned for the occasion; "right glad to meet you, sir. I have been thinking I must engage some such expert and lucky sportsman, as they say you are, to catch and send me up a fresh salmon, occasionally. I suppose your never-failing spear will be put in requisition again, when the spring opens; will it not?"

"Der — yes, your worship, unless I turn my attention to the catching — ditter — eels, or other slippery varments," returned the hunter, with a sly, significant twinkling of his eyes, as he brushed by the rebuked cajoler, and pushed on without waiting for a reply.

The judge did not pursue his walk much farther; but now, soon facing about, began, with a quickened step and a look of increasing uneasiness, to retrace his way to his quarters.

While these little incidents were occurring in the streets, about one hundred sturdy and determined men had collected within the walls of the Court House. As the construction of this building was somewhat peculiar, for one designed for such purposes, it may be necessary, for a clear understanding of the descriptions which follow, to say a few words respecting its interior arrangements. The court-room was in the upper story, which was all occupied as such, except the east and south corners, that had been partitioned off for sleeping apartments. In the lower story, there was a wide passage running through the middle of the building, with doors at both ends; while the stairs leading up into the court room faced the principal entrance, on the north-east side of the house. After passing by the stairs, there was a small passage leading from the large one, at right angles, and running back between prison-rooms, whose doors opened into it. The part of this lower story, on the opposite side of the main passage, consisted also of two rooms, with doors opening into it, and an entry, or short passage, leading out into the street. One of these rooms was used as a common, or bar-room, and the other as a sort of parlor, being both occupied by the jailer and his family.

Although there had been, for many weeks, a growing disposition among the party here assembled to prevent the session of a court avowedly acting under royal authority, and spurning all the recommendations of Congress, yet there had been no settled intention among them to resort to any other than the peaceful measures of petition and remonstrance, which they believed would be sufficient to effect the desired result. It had been decided, therefore, that the court should be permitted to come together; when such representations and arguments were to be laid before them, as could not fail, it was supposed, to convince any reasonable men of the wisdom of listening to the voice of the people. But when, on the preceding evening, it was discovered, in the way before related, and from other sources, that the people had been duped by the duplicity of Chandler, and that it was the secret purpose of the court, in defiance of all pledges to the contrary, to hold a full session, under the protection of an armed force, the hitherto modest and quiet spirit of patriotism was at once aroused among this resolute little band of revolutionists, and they came to the bold determination, as we have before seen, of seizing the Court House in advance of their opponents, and holding it till their remonstrances should be heard and heeded.

This object, so far as respected the possession of the building, being now obtained, the company proceeded to organize and make arrangements for maintaining their advantage through the night. Their possession, however, was not destined to remain long undisputed. In a short time after they had begun to act, their new recruit, Barty Burt, who could not forego his desire of remaining among the tories (where we left him acting the un-suspected spy on their movements) till they should look for their guns, that he might have the pleasure of witnessing their discom-fiture on discovering their loss, now arrived with news, that the latter, as soon as they made the discovery that their arms had been abstracted, were thrown into the greatest commotion; and that under the direction of Patterson and Gale, both foaming with rage, they had hastily collected all the offensive implements they could find, with the avowed determination of making an immedi ate assault on their opponents at the Court House. But notwith-standing this startling intelligence, no one manifested the least disposition of quitting his post. And although there was not a weapon of defence, beyond a cane, in the whole company, yet they seemed none the less inclined to maintain their position in consequence of the threatening aspect which the affair was be-ginning to assume; but resolving, by acclamation, to keep pos-session of the house till compelled by force of arms to relinquish it, they placed a few strong and resolute men as guards at every door, and quietly awaited the result. And they were not kept long in suspense. In a short time, Patterson and his posse, armed with several old muskets, swords, pistols, and clubs, made their appearance, and, with many hostile manifestations, came rushing up within a few yards of the door. Commanding a halt, the sheriff then, in a loud and arrogant tone, summoned the company within to come forth and disperse. No voice, however, was heard to respond to the summons. Gale, the clerk, then proceeded, upon the intimation of the former, to read the king's proclamation to the outward walls of the house, or the supposed listeners within, with great form and solemnity.

"Ditter—dickins!" exclaimed Tom Dunning, after listening a moment to the reading of the riot act, or proclamation, as it was usually called, as, with several others, he stood just within the entrance. "Now I wonder if they expect to rout a body of Green Mountain Boys with that sort of — ditter — ammunition ?"

"There!" fiercely cried Patterson, as the reader concluded his task. "There, you d——d rascals, now disperse, or, by Heaven, I will blow a lane through ye!"

"Only — ditter — hear that!" again remaked the hunter, contemptuously, at the menace and profanity of the haughty officer. "Natural enough, though, mayhap, for a bag of wind to blow, if it does any thing. He is rather smart at — der — swearing, too, I think. But even at that, I guess he would have to haul in his horns a little, if old Ethan Allen was here, as I wish he was, to let off a few blasts of his — ditter — damnations at him."

Captain Wright, after a brief consultation with the other leaders, now coming down from the court-room, opened the door, (Dunning and another strong-armed man having hold of it to guard against a rush,) and addressed the besiegers.

"Why is all this, gentlemen?" he said, in a respectful, but firm manner. "Are you come here for war? We are here for no such purpose, ourselves. We came with none other than peaceful intentions. And so long as we can say that, and say, also, above all, that we have come together with the approbation of the chief judge of your court, who has promised us a fair hearing of our grievances; and so long as, in direct violation of that judge's pledge to us, you appear here in arms, to intimidate us, let me assure you, we shall not disperse under your threats. We, however, will permit you to come in, if you will lay aside your arms; or we will hold a parley with you as you are."

"D——n your parley!" exclaimed Gale, furiously. "D——n the parley with such d——d rascals as you are! I will hold no parley with such d——d rascals, but by this!" he added, drawing a pistol, and brandishing it towards his opponents.

"Ay! ay!" cried Redding, who, next to the sheriff and clerk, appeared to be the most violent and officious among the assailants: "talk about being here without arms, and for peace, do ye? when you have stolen a dozen of our guns, and have now got them in there among you. Pretty fellows, to talk about parley? We will give you a parley that will send you all to hell before morning!"

Wright here began a denial of the charge made by the last speaker; when he was interrupted by Dunning, who, jogging him said, in an undertone, —

"Let 'em — der — believe it. They are such — ditter — cowards, that the idea of a dozen guns among us will make 'em more mannerly than all the preaching you could — ditter — do in a month."

Concluding to profit by this suggestion of the sagacious hunter Wright now retired within doors, followed by the hisses, curses and all manner of abusive epithets, of the assailants.

The besiegers, now finding that the king's proclamation, on whose potency for quelling the risings of the rebellious colonists, the tory authorities, at the commencement of the revolution seemed to have greatly counted, did not annihilate their opponents, and, not seeing fit to attempt to carry their threats into execution at present, they soon drew off a short distance, and apparently held a consultation. While they were thus occupied, a small deputation was sent out to them from the Court House, with another offer to hold a conference. But their proposals being received with fresh insults and abuse, they returned to the house, while Patterson and his forces, evidently fearing to venture an attack, with their present strength, on the other party, whom they suspected to be armed with the lost guns, now moved off to head-quarters, to report progress, and wait for the expected reënforcement, to hasten whose arrival, expresses had been despatched several hours before.

A short time after the disappearance of Patterson's band, Judge Chandler unexpectedly came up to the Court House, wholly unattended, and being readily admitted, he at once ascended into the court-room, and entered the somewhat surprised, but unmoved assembly, bowing low to individuals on the right and left, as he passed on to an unoffered seat, with the gratified air of one, who, after many detentions, has the satisfaction of getting at length into the company of his friends.

After a rather embarrassing pause, the judge rose, and made a short speech, which left his hearers but little the wiser respecting his real wishes and intentions, though he had much to say about his solicitude for the welfare of the people, and his anxiety that they should do nothing to injure their cause. After he was seated, Wright, Carpenter, and Knowlton, each in turn, addressed him, stating, in general terms, the views and wishes of their party, and reminding him of his pledge, that no arms should be brought by the officers of the court, the recent violation of which they hoped he would be able to explain..

Upon this, the former rejoined, declaring with great assurance, and not a little to the surprise of many in the room, that the arms complained of had been brought without his knowledge and against his express wishes ; and he concluded by assuring his friends, as he said he was proud to believe he might safely call them, that he would go and immediately secure the arms in question ; so that the company might now retire, in full confidence that their petitions would obtain a fair hearing, when the court came together the next morning. The speaker then resumed his seat, and glanced persuasively around him for some tokens of assent or approbation. But the men, whom he had thus undertaken to wheedle, had been taught by experience to heed the caution so well recommended by the tuneful Burns, —

"Beware the tongue that's smoothly hung," —

and a chilling silence was the only response that greeted him.

"You hear his honor's remarks," observed the chairman, at length breaking the ominous silence. "Have you any propositions to make before the judge retires."

Another long interval of deep silence ensued ; when Tom Dunning's tall, sinewy form, and sharp, bronzed features, screwed up with an expression of sly mischief, was seen rising from a back seat in the room.

"Seeing no one else," he said, "seems — ditter — disposed to accept your invitation, Mr. Moderator, I don't — ditter — know but I will make a small proposition on the occasion. Now, as I take it, we are to remain here to-night ; and as we have now learned that the judge and the people here are the — ditter — best of friends, I would just move, Mr. Moderator, that his honor be — der — ditter — invited to take up lodgings with us in the Court House to-night , so that, if the enemy comes," he added, imitating the manner of the judge, as described by Bart, " he can assist us to — ditter — ' temporize — temporize — till '—— "

Here the hunter bobbed down into his seat, while explosive bursts of laughter rose from several parts of the room, and a low, half-smothered titter ran through the whole assembly, at this sly, but cutting allusion to the part last night taken by the double-dealing judge, who now sat before them, looking, for the moment, like a suddenly detected criminal. He, however, while the chairman was calling to order, recovered his command of countenance, and, by the time the tumult had subsided into the less noisy expressions of mirth, he was smiling as gayly as the rest, and affecting to consider the remarks of the stammering humorist as merely a pleasant joke.

"There is no cheating our friend Dunning out of his joke. !

perceive," he said, rising and taking up his hat; "and, indeed, I don't know that I can blame a hardy woodsman for laughing at the idea of one of our in-door and tender professional men, like myself, sleeping on floors and benches. I am afraid we deserve it for our effeminacy. Yes, yes, a good joke, truly! and a good laughter-moving joke is an excellent thing to go to bed upon, they say," he added, as with a merry, gleeful look, he bowed himself out of the assembly.

No further comments were offered by any of the company upon the communications of this official double-dealer, after his departure; for all seemed to think that the single shot of Dunning had rendered all further comments on his speech, and his motives in coming there to make it, entirely superfluous. And they therefore proceeded, as if nothing but an ordinary interruption had occurred, to the business on which they were engaged when the judge came in — that of passing some fresh resolves expressive of their determination to hold the Court House in defiance of the threats of their opponents, and of their now settled purpose of no longer submitting, on any conditions, to the continuance of a court which had proved itself so corrupt and treacherous. After this, and making arrangements for the posting and relieving of guards at the doors for the night, a part of the company left the house to seek lodgings elsewhere, as the usual hour of rest had now arrived.

When the nonplused and disconcerted Chandler left the Court House, he rapidly took his way back to his quarters, from which he had been started out by Patterson and Gale, to see if he might not be able to accomplish by fair words what they had failed to effect by foul. Although he had put the best possible face upon the mortifying occurrence he had just been compelled to meet, and had made, as he believed, a handsome exit from the company, yet he felt keenly conscious that he had not only utterly failed in the object of his visit, but that much of his late base conduct was known. He perceived this in the allusions of Dunning, the pith of which he had affected not to understand. He had seen it, he had felt it, in the significant and knowing glances that had been exchanged on every side around him, and especially in the bitter derisive laugh that had assailed his tingling ears. He had also been taught a new lesson in the interview! He had seen, in the firm manner and determined looks of those he had been confronting — he had seen that which told him of a spirit at work among the people, that the loyal party, with all their boasted strength, might not long be able to quell. He

6

began now, with the instinctive sagacity of the true office-seeker, to perceive the possibility, perhaps probability, that the power of dispensing office and patronage was about to change hands, and he inwardly trembled for his own safety. He found himself, in short, in one of those straits, to which men of his character are not unfrequently reduced — that of being wholly at a loss to decide which side was most likely to become the strongest. Could he have foreseen and decided this, his mind would have been comparatively at ease ; for he could have then trimmed his sails, so as to steer clear of the political breakers which he knew were somewhere ahead. Some course, however, he must decide upon ; and after lamenting his inability to pierce the future, so far as to know which party was destined to prevail, and thus secure the important advantages that might be derived from shaping his present course accordingly, he at length resolved to keep aloof, at present, from both parties, believing he had so adroitly managed thus far, that whichever side might triumph, he could put in a specious claim of having acted with it, in reality, from the first.

And having now made up his mind to this course, he avoided meeting the tory leaders again ; and, seeking out a safe messenger, and sending him to tell them, that " he had left the company at the Court House as he found it," and that " a forgotten business engagement had compelled him to be absent from their councils for a few hours," he took his way to a distant part of the village, where he called on an acquaintance of neutral politics. And here becoming much engaged in conversation, and feigning to have forgotten the hour of the night, he was at last prevailed on to accept, as he did with great seeming reluctance, the invitation of his host to tarry till morning.

After Patterson and his minions retreated from the Court House, they returned to the tory tavern, and there remained several hours, alternately cursing their opponents for rebellious obstinacy in not yielding to their commands and menaces, and their expected friends for their tardiness in reaching the place. And affairs remaining in this situation till a late hour in the evening, they were on the point of giving up all thoughts of renewing the attack that night, when the long and anxiously looked for reenforcement, consisting of thirty or forty armed men, came hurrying on to the ground. The sinking spirits and waning courage of the blustering sheriff and his confederates now instantly revived ; and, exulting that they now had the power to glut their vengeance, they resolved on making an immediate assault. And after mortifying their courage with liberal potations of brandy, the whole party, now swelled, not only by the freshly arrived forces, but by Brush, Peters, Stearns, and many others, who had declined joining in the first sally, to nearly one hundred men, eagerly set forward to the scene of action.

The other party, in the mean time, though still maintaining a watchful guard at the doors of the Court House, had yet been so long exempted from an attack of their foes, that they were now in but little expectation of being any further molested till the next morning. And some were lying stretched upon the benches in the court-room, asleep; some, with their great-coats under their heads, were reposing on the floors of the different passages of the house; while others were sitting round the fires, engaged in smoking and conversation.

Among those taking their turns as sentries, at this juncture, were Woodburn and Bart, who, with each a stout cane or cudgel in his hand, were now stationed at the principal entrance.

"They are coming!" cried Bart, who, having gone out into the street to ascertain what might be the noise which they had heard at a distance, now came running up, with an excited air to his companion; "they are upon us again, with twice as many men as before, and plenty of guns!"

"In with the news!" said Woodburn, as the appearance of the hostile party wheeling up towards the Court House the next instant confirmed the other's statement — "in with the news, and tell them to man the doors, or in two minutes we shall be routed."

Instantly springing into the door, which he unfortunately left open, Bart made the announcement to French, who was restlessly moving about in the passage, and who repeated the same in a voice which started all, both above and below to their feet.

"They are coming for our blood!" he added, in a tone of strange, wild glee. "Ay, there they come! I see them levelling their guns in the yard! Now for the victims! Let us die like —— "

The report of two or three muskets, and the whistling of bullets through the passage just over his head, cut short the speaker. A moment of breathless silence ensued; when the harsh, ruffian voice of Patterson was heard from without, —

"Damn ye, why don't you fire?"

A general discharge of the fire-arms of the assailants, flashing fiercely on the surrounding darkness, and sending their deadly missiles through the passage, windows, and sides of the house, in every direction, instantly followed the ferocious order. And, in the expiring light, the fated French was seen to leap into the air; and then, spinning giddily round and round an instant, fall, with a low, short screech, prostrate on the floor; while mingled groans, rising from a half dozen others along the passage, told also the fearful effect of the murderous volley.

With the discharge of their arms, the assailing force, guided by their torch-bearers, made a rush for the Court House. As they approached the door, Woodburn, who had kept his post, unhurt, on one side of the steps, sprang forward to dispute their passage, and, after knocking up the swords and bayonets that were aimed at his breast, laid about him so lustily with his cudgel, that the whole party were, for some moments, kept at bay. At length, however, Peters, who was near the rear of the hostile column, perceiving it was his hated opponent who was disputing the pass so resolutely, stealthily crept round those in front, and coming up partly behind his intended victim, with a protruded sabre, aimed a deadly lunge at his body, exultingly exclaiming with the supposed fatal thrust, —

"There! d——d rebel, take that!"

"And you that!" cried the other, who, having, from a lucky turn in his body at the instant, received only a flesh-wound on the inner side of his arm, now, with an upward sweep of his cudgel, knocked the sword of the detestable assassin twenty feet into the air — "and you that! ay, and that!" he added, as, with a quickly repeated blow over the head, he sent his foe reeling to the earth.

But the weapon of the intrepid young man being now caught, and his body fiercely grappled by four or five of his exasperated foes, he was soon disarmed, and, in spite of his desperate struggles, borne into the court-house with the crowd, who now rushed furiously along the passages, wounding with their swords, and beating down with their guns and clubs, without distinction or mercy, all whom they met in their way.

"Guard the doors instantly!" shouted Patterson, who perceived that numbers of the vanquished party were retreating through the different doors; "don't let another of the d——d rascals escape! And, hallo there, jailer! bring on the keys of the prison-rooms; we will cage the whole lot, dead or alive, and let 'em be enjoying a few of the fruits of their rebellion now, and the blessed anticipations of being hung for high treason hereafter."

The obsequious jailer soon appeared with the required keys and the doors of both prison-rooms were speedily unlocked and thrown open by the directions of the sheriff.

"Now, tumble them in, boys!" resumed the sheriff, with look and tone of savage exultation.

Eager to obey, the supple tools of arbitrary power now commenced driving all those of their prisoners who had not been too much disabled by their wounds to stand, together into the prison-rooms. They then seized hold of the wounded, who lay weltering in their blood in different parts of the floor of the long passage, and began dragging them along by their limbs to the same destination.

"Monster!" exclaimed Woodburn, looking back from the felon's cell which he was about to enter, and addressing Redding, who stood mimicking, with fiendish glee, the groans and contortions of French, as he lay gasping and writhing in mortal agony on the spot where he fell, just beyond the short passage dividing the prison-rooms — "monster," he repeated, "would you insult the dying?"

"Yes, d—n you!" savagely interposed Gale, stepping forward; "he has got just what he deserved; and I wish there were forty more of you in the same predicament. Drag him along in there with the rest of 'em, Redding!"

"Ay, ay," responded Patterson, "in with him! And I can tell the rest of them, they had better be saving their pity for themselves, for they will all be in hell before to-morrow night!"

It is needless to say that this brutal order was promptly obeyed. And when the dying and insensible victim, pierced through head and body, and all the wounded, had been drawn in and thrown promiscuously together, on the cold, damp floors of the prison-rooms, the keys were turned upon them; and their remorseless butchers, making not the least provision for the sufferers, by way of medical aid or otherwise, returned, after posting a strong guard at the doors, to the tavern or the house of Brush, to celebrate their victory in a drunken carousal.

6 *

CHAPTER VI

' The brand is on their brows,
A dark and guilty spot ;
'Tis ne'er to be erased,
'Tis ne'er to be forgot."

WHATEVER may be the result of the present public movement
for the abolition of capital punishment, and however far future
experiments may go towards establishing the expediency and
safety of such a change in criminal jurisprudence, the history of
every nation and people will show, we believe, the remarkable
fact, that ever since Cain stood before his Maker with his hands
reeking with the blood of his murdered brother, and his heart so
deeply smitten with the consciousness of having justly forfeited
his own life by taking the life of another, that he could not divest
himself of the belief that all men would seek to slay him, no one
principle has been found to be more deeply implanted in the
human breast than the desire to see the wilful shedding of blood
atoned for by the blood of the perpetrator. So strong, so active,
and so impelling, indeed, seems this principle, that no sooner goes
forth the dread tale of homicide, than all community rise up,
as one man, instinctively impressed with the duty of hunting down
the guilty and bringing them to justice ; while the guilty them
selves seem no less instinctively impressed with the abiding con
sciousness that the doom, which heaven and earth has decreed to
their crimes, must inevitably overtake them.

Deep and fearful was the excitement, in the hitherto quiet and
peaceful village of Westminster, as from mouth to mouth, and
house to house, spread the startling intelligence, that a meeting
of unarmed citizens, assembled at the Court House, had been
assailed, and numbers shot down in cold blood by the minions of
British authority. The whole town was soon in commotion. No
loud noise or clamor of voices, it is true, was heard proclaiming
the deed on the midnight air ; but the rapid footfalls of men hurrying along the streets, the hastily exchanged inquiry, the eager,
suppressed tones of those conversing in small groups at the corners
and by-places around the village, the hasty opening and shutting of
doors, and the dancing of lights in every direction, gave ominous
indication of the feeling that had every where been awakened,

and the secret movement which was everywhere afoot among the people.

A small band, who had gathered in the yard of what was called the People's Tavern, were listening, with many a demonstration of horror and indignation, to the account of one who had escaped from the Court House after the tories had got possession.

"Where are our leaders, Morris?" asked one of the listeners, as the speaker, a fluent, energetic young man, closed his recital of the atrocities he had witnessed. "Did they escape, or are they among the wounded and prisoners?"

"Wright and Carpenter had gone off before we were attacked," was the reply, "the rest, not among the wounded I have named escaped in the confusion, I think, except Dr. Jones, of Rockingham, who was driven into the felon's hole with other prisoners; and it may be well that he was, perhaps, as those bloodthirsty brutes would have suffered no surgeon to be sent for to attend those who are not past help."

"And Tom Dunning, whose rifle we shall need, — what became of him?"

"He got out in the same manner I did. We stood in a dark corner, at the head of the stairs, taking note of the proceedings below; when that crafty little chap, that joined us from Brush's, came wriggling like an eel out from between the legs of the crowding tories, in the passage; and, working himself up stairs unnoticed, in the same way, beckoned us to follow him, as we did, into the court-room, where, at his suggestion, we stripped off the sheets of a bed, in one of those corner sleeping cuddies, made a rope, and by it let ourselves down through a window to the ground in the rear of the house; when we separated, Dunning going home, as he said, to arm himself. But here he comes," added the speaker, peering out towards the street, from which several forms were dimly seen approaching — "here he comes, and those just behind him I should judge to be Carpenter and Fletcher, by their gait."

"Well, Dunning," asked one of the company, as the hunter came striding up to the spot, "what is your response to all this?"

"Der — sixty bullets, and a — ditter — pound of powder!" was the stern and significant reply of the other, as with one hand he struck his rattling bullet-pouch and huge powder-horn, and with the other brought down the breech of his rifle with a heavy blow upon the ground.

"That's the man for me!" exclaimed Fletcher, now coming up with Carpenter.

"Ay, Dunning is right!" said Carpenter, with emphasis. If we hold our peace now, the very stones will cry out for vengeance. But talking is only a small part of what must be done. We must act. And first of all, this tale of murder and outrage must instantly be thrown upon the four winds of heaven, and carried into every town in this part of the settlement. Who will volunteer to ride express with the news? — news which, if I know anything of the spirit of the great mass of our people, will be taken as a call to arms, and responded to accordingly."

Several eager voices announced their readiness to start off at once on the proposed mission.

"Follow me to the stables, then," resumed the stanch patriot, hastily leading the way to the barn, and throwing open a stable door. "There!" he continued, pointing to a pair of large, active-looking brutes, feeding together in one stall — "there are my two horses — take them. Let one of their riders go north, the other south; and spare no horse-flesh of mine in an emergency like this · but ride and rally, till you have sent the bloody tale to every house and hut this side the mountains. And you, Morris and Dunning, accompany me to Captain Wright's. More messengers must be despatched west and east, into the borders of New Hampshire, and much other business done before morning.'

A far different scene, in the mean while, was in progress among the inmates of the loyal mansion, which we have before described, and which was destined to give shelter that night to the last conclave of royal office-holders ever known in the Green Mountains. Although the leaders of the court party had returned from the sanguinary scene they had enacted, in high exultation at the decisive victory they supposed they had achieved over their despised opponents, yet neither their own vain boastings, nor the deeply-quaffed wines of their host, could long keep up their spirits. Conscience soon began to be busy among them; and their hearts waxed faint and fearful at the thought of what they had done. They instinctively drew close together, conversed in subdued tones, or sat uneasily listening to the sounds that occasionally reached them from without. And whatever they might have said to keep up their own and each other's courage, it soon became apparent that secret misgivings, fears, and forebodings of a coming retribution had taken possession of their guilt-smitten bosoms.

And there was another person in that house, to whom the tragical events of the night brought deep disquietude; but it was a disquietude of quite a different character from that which was experienced by the troubled wretches we have named : that person was the *Tory's Daughter*—the pure, guileless, and noble-minded Sabrey Haviland.

Having been apprised of the intention of Patterson and his confederates to make an assault upon their opponents as soon as the expected reinforcements arrived, her anxieties on the subject had prevented her from retiring to rest, as her less concerned companion did, at the usual hour. And when the startling report of fire-arms broke upon the stillness of the night, she was not, like many others in the village, at loss to know the cause ; and her fears led her to divine but too well the fatal result. And after an interval of painful suspense, which was terminated by the return of the tory leaders to the house, she stole softly out of her chamber to the head of the stairs, and there listened with mingled emotions of horror and disgust to the boastful recital of their sanguinary deeds, as given by the heartless Gale and others, to her father and Judge Sabin, who had remained in the house, but who, she perceived with sorrow, were warm approvers of all that had been done. But, as revolting to her gentle nature as was the general description of the event, the particulars the exulting narrators soon proceeded to give were much more so. And when she heard them relate the affray between Woodburn and Peters, and heard the latter, while making light of his own hurts, boast that he had first given the other a thrust with his sword through the body, which must finish him before morning ; she could listen no longer, but, hastily retiring to her room, she walked the apartment for nearly an hour in the deepest agitation and distress.

Among the many excellent traits of Miss Haviland's character, a lively sense of right and wrong, together with a deep and abiding love of truth and justice, unquestionably predominated. So strong and controlling, indeed, was this principle in her bosom, that it exhibited itself in all her conversation, and seemed to be the governing motive of all her actions. And when she had once discovered the truth and the right, at which she appeared to arrive with intuitive quickness, no wheedling or sophistry could blind her to their force ; and no inducements could be offered sufficient to cause her to waver in their support. And yet this peculiar trait, as deeply seated as it was, and as firmly as it was ever exercised, was so beautifully tempered by the benevolence of her heart, the equanimity of her mind, and the engaging sweetness of her demeanor, that it never seemed to impart the least tinge c' arrogance to her character, or harshness to her manners. On the contrary, she was all gentleness and devotion, and ever ready to comply with the wishes of others, when a compliance did not contravene, in her opinion, any of the principles of even-handed justice; and, in case she felt bound to refuse to yield to their requests, her refusal was made and maintained with such mild firmness, that none could be offended, none feel inclined to charge her with obstinacy or perverseness. She was at this time the mistress of her father's household, her exemplary and intellectual mother having several years before deceased, and her elder and only sister, the year previous, married one of the leading loyalists of Guilford. And it had been mainly through the influence of this sister and her husband, that she had been induced, the preceding fall, to take the step which was destined to cause her years of sorrow and perplexity — that of engaging herself in marriage to Peters. She had found few or no opportunities of studying this man's character, having known him only as a parlor acquaintance, of easy manners and considerable intelligence. And although she saw nothing particularly objectionable in him, and although she knew that, in point of wealth and family distinction, he was considered what is termed a desirable match, yet she had entered into the engagement with many misgivings, and in compliance rather with the wishes of her friends above named, seconded by the urgent request of her father, than in accordance with the dictates of her own judgment and inclination. But whatever her doubts at that time, or during the months immediately following, they had not been sufficient to disturb the usual even tenor of her feelings, till she left home on her present excursion, during which, as already intimated, she had seen the character of her affianced in a new light — a light which showed him to be possessed of traits as abhorrent to her feelings, as, to her mind, they were base and reprehensible in themselves. And now, to crown all, he had, by an act of deliberate, private malice, even according to his own account, inflicted a mortal wound on the victim of his former injuries — the man who, but the day before, had snatched her, whom the other professed to hold as the highest object of his earthly solicitude, from a watery grave. It was these painful reflections that were now agitating her bosom ; for the more she pondered upon the conduct of Peters, the more did her heart reject and despise him ; and in proportion as her feelings rose up against him were her sympathies drawn towards his victim, Woodburn, whose noble act had created so strong a claim upon her gratitude, and whose character and appearance had alike awakened her interest and admiration.

"Is it indeed thus," she at length uttered, as if summing up the thoughts that had been passing through her mind, "that he who saved my life, at the risk of his own, must die by the hand of one who should have been the first to thank and reward him? Ay, and die, too, without receiving from me, or mine, one word of acknowledgement, even, of the service he so nobly rendered? perhaps the thought of our ingratitude is now embittering his dying moments! Can I, should I suffer this so to remain?"

Here she relapsed into silence, and, slowly resuming her walk round the room, seemed for a while immersed in anxious thought; when she suddenly paused, and, after a moment of apparent irresolution, stepped to the wall, and gave two or three pulls at the wire connected with the servants' bell in the kitchen. In a few minutes the summons was answered by the appearance of the chamber-maid.

"Will you go down to the gentlemen's sitting-room," said Miss Haviland, "ask out my father, and tell him I would see him a moment in my own room?"

The girl disappeared, and, in a short time, Esquire Haviland, with a slightly disturbed and anxious air, entered the room, and said, —

"What's the matter, Sabrey? Are you sick to-night, that you are yet up and send for me?"

"O, no," replied the other; "nothing of that kind led me to send for you, but my wish to make a request which I was unwilling to delay."

The squire cast a somewhat surprised and inquiring look at his daughter, but remained silent, while the latter resumed: —

"You recollect that this morning, after apprising you of the extent of our obligations to Mr. Woodburn, about which you seem to have been so misinformed, I suggested that a personal acknowledgment, with offers of some more substantial token of our gratitude, should be immediately made to him. Has this been done?"

"No," replied he, with a gathering frown: "having understood the fellow was assorting with the rebels in their treasonable plots, I did not feel myself bound to seek him in such company. Is that all you wish of me?"

"It is not, sir," she answered seriously, and with the air of one determined not to be repulsed. "I have accidentally become apprised that Mr. Woodburn, in the affray of to-night, has been dangerously wounded, and, in this condition, thrust into prison. And, as we have now an opportunity of testifying our sense of

his services, it is my earnest request that you procure his release
from prison, for which your influence here, I know, is sufficient;
that he may be brought out to-night and properly attended."

"Insane girl!" muttered the father, angrily, "what can have
put that absurd project into your head? Had you been abed
hours ago, as you ought, instead of being up and prying into
the doings of our authorities, with which a woman has no concern, I should have been spared this exhibition of folly. Why,
the wretched fellow is but receiving the just deserts of his
crimes. He is in prison for high treason; and had I the will,
which I have not, I could not procure his release."

"I cannot believe these opposers of the court will be held to
answer for such a crime. Indeed, it has occurred to me that the
authorities themselves may be called to account for firing upon
these unarmed men; and therefore I still hope you will use your
exertions for Woodburn's release," urged the fair pleader.

"You are to be the judge what is treason, then, hey? And
you are ready to side with these daring and desperate fellows,
and condemn our authorities, are you? What assurance! You
will hardly persuade me to favor your mad projects, I think,"
harshly retorted the bigoted old gentleman.

"You can, at least, go to the prison and return him the ac-
knowledgments which our character and credit require of us,"
still persisted the former.

"Well, I shall do no such thing," replied the other, with
angry impatience; "for I consider the fellow's conduct to-night
has wholly absolved me from my obligations to him, if I was
ever under any," he added, rising to depart.

"I do not view it so, father," returned the unmoved girl, in a
mild, expostulating tone, "and I am sorry for your decision;
for, if those whose place it more properly is to do this, refuse to
perform it, I know not why I should not myself undertake the
duty."

"You!"

"Yes, father.'

"What, to-night?"

"Certainly; another day may be too late."

"Madness and folly! Why, who is to attend you, silly girl?"

"If no gentleman is to be found with courtesy enough to
attend me, I shall not hesitate to go alone, sir."

"We will see if you do!" exclaimed the old gentleman, looking
back from the entrance at the other, with an expression of scorn-
ful defiance — "we will see if you do, madam!" he repeated

closing the door after him, and turning the key on his daughter, whom he thus left a prisoner in her own room.

As Miss Haviland listened to the springing bolt and her father's departing steps, a slight flush overspread her face at the thought of the indignity thus put upon her, and she rose, and, after putting her hand to the door to assure herself that she was not mistaken, proceeded, with a calm, determined air, to a table on one side of the room, on which stood the materials for writing; and here, taking pen and paper, she seated herself, and addressed a brief note to Woodburn, delicately expressing her sense of obligation to him, and concluding with the hope that she might soon have it in her power to do something towards alleviating his present situation. Having signed, sealed, and superscribed the billet, she rose and stood some time hesitating and irresolute.

By what means could this note, now it was written, be made to reach its destination? Should she again summon the chamber-maid, she presumed her father had so managed that the call would not be answered; besides, she felt a repugnance to the thought of resorting to such means. What other method could then be devised?

While thus casting about her for some expedient for effecting her purpose, she thought she heard some one placing a ladder against the side of the house, beneath a window, opening from the rear end of the passage adjoining her room; and, after listening a moment, she distinctly heard the person cautiously ascending. Not being of a timid cast, she quickly removed the thick, heavy curtains of the window in her room next and very near the one under which the unknown intruder was mounting the ladder, and, throwing up the sash, peered out; when, to her surprise, she beheld, and at once recognized, the queer-looking figure of Barty Burt, standing on the top round of the ladder, scratching his head, and giving other tokens of embarrassment at being thus unexpectedly caught in this situation.

"Master Bart," said Miss Haviland, who had become somewhat acquainted with the other, while supplying her room with fuel, previous to his ejection from the house, to which she was knowing, "your appearance, at this time, to say the least of it, causes me much surprise."

"I returns the compliment, miss," replied Bart; "so that makes us even, and no questions on ither side, don't it?"

"Perhaps not, sir," returned the former, with seriousness: 'at all events, you should be able to give a good reason for your

7

appearance here, under such circumstances : please explain your object."

"And if I don't, you will sing out for the squire, you said ? Well, I can get down, and off, before he can get here, I reckon," responded Bart, in a tone of roguish defiance.

"I did not say I would call Esquire Brush; but, unless you explain ——"

"Yes, yes, jest as lieves as not, and will, if you'll keep shut till I can run up garret and back."

"Your purpose there, sir ? "

"An honest one — only to get my gun up there, which the squire didn't have put out for me, when he dismissed me with his high-heeled shoes, to-day, and which I darsent name then, fear he'd have that thrown down, like my 'tother duds, and break it — only that — and if you'll say nothing, and let me whip in, and up to get it, I'll lay it up against you, as a great oblige, to be paid for, by a good turn to you some time, miss."

"If that is all, go — and I may wish to speak with you when you come back."

So saying, she gently let down the sash, and, withdrawing a little from her window, stood awaiting the result; when she soon heard the other, with the light and stealthy movements of a cat, enter the house, and ascend into the garret, through a small side-door, opening from the passage we have named. Scarcely a minute had elapsed before she again heard his footsteps stealing back by her door to the window, through which he had so noise-lessly entered; when, once more raising the sash of her own, she found him already standing on the top of the ladder where she last saw him, he having effected his ingress and egress with such celerity, that but for the light fusil he now held in his hand, she would have believed herself mistaken in supposing he had entered at all.

"Well, miss, I am waiting for your say so," he said, in a low tone, peering warily around him.

"Have you been to the Court House to-night ? " hesitatingly asked the other.

"Well, now," replied Bart, hesitating in his turn, "without more token for knowing what you're up to, I'll say, may be so and may be no so."

"You need not fear me, Bart," replied Sabrey, conjecturing the cause of his hesitation; "I am no enemy of those who have suffered there to-night. But do you know Mr. Wood-burn ?

" Harry, who got you out of that river scrape ? Yes, ived
n his town last summer."

" He is among the wounded and prisoners in jail, it is said ? "

" Dreadful true, miss."

" Could you get this small letter to him to-night ? " she timidly
asked.

" Yes, through the grate; glad to do it, glad of it, twice
over," replied Bart, reaching out and grasping the proffered
billet.

" Why, why do you say that ? " asked Sabrey, with an air of
mingled doubt and curiosity.

" Cause, in the first place, you'll now keep my secret of being
here ; and nextly, glad to find there's one among the court folks
that feels decent about this bloody business. But I must be off.
Yes, I'll get it to him," said Bart, beginning to descend.

" S ay, Barty. Is there any hope that Mr. Woodburn will survive his wounds ? "

" Survive ? Live, do you mean ? O, yes; though the lunge
which that —— But no matter. It was well meant for the heart,
and the fellow wan't at all to blame that it didn't reach it, instead
of the inner part of the arm."

" Indeed ! " exclaimed Miss Haviland, in a tone of joyful surprise ; which the next instant, however, gave way to one of
embarrassment. " Why, I heard — have written, indeed, under
the belief that — and perhaps —— Barty, I think, on the whole,
I will not send that billet now."

As Bart heard these last words of the fair speaker, so inconsistent with all which both her words and manner had just expressed, he looked up with a stare of surprise to her face, now
sufficiently revealed, by the glancing light standing near her in the
room, to betray its varying expressions. But, as he ran his keen
gray eyes over her hesitating and slightly confused countenance,
he soon seemed to read the secret cause of her sudden change
of purpose, arising from that curious and beautiful trait in
woman's heart, which, by some gush of awakened sympathy,
often unfolds all the lurking secrets of the breast, but which,
when the cause of that sympathy is removed, closes up the
avenue, and conceals them from view, in the cold reserve of
shrinking delicacy — the colder and more impenetrable in proportion as the disclosure has been complete.

" O, yes, I will carry it," said Bart, pretending to misunderstand the other, while he pocketed ᵊ billet and began to glide
down the ladder.

" Nc," commenced Miss Haviland ; " no, Bart, I saic ———"

" Yes, yes, I will have it there in a jiffy," interrupted Bart, hastening his descent, and the next instant dodging away in the dark beneath the foot of the ladder.

" Well, let it go," said the foiled and somewhat mortified maiden to herself, after the disappearance of her strange visitor. " If what I expressed, when I thought him dying, was right and proper, it cannot be very wrong now."

As soon as she had thus reconciled herself to the unexpected turn which this matter had taken, Miss Haviland now began to reflect more on Bart's motives in coming, at such an hour of the night, for his gun ; when it, for the first time, occurred to her mind, that he had been induced to take this step in consequence of some particular call for arms having reference to the events of the evening. Fearing she might have done wrong in suffering him to take away the gun, if it was to be used for hostile purposes, and anxious to know whether her conjectures relative to a rising of the people were well founded, she proceeded to an end window of her room, which overlooked a range of buildings known to her to be mostly occupied by the opposers of royal authority ; and removing the curtains and raising the sash, she leaned out and listened for any unusual sounds which might reach her from without. And it was not long before she became well convinced that her apprehensions were not groundless. Some extraordinary movement was evidently going on in the village. The low hum of suppressed voices, mingled with various sounds of busy prepa ration, came up, on the dense night air, from almost every direction around her. Here, was heard the small hammer, the grating file, with the occasional clicking of the firelock, undergoing repairs by the use of the instruments just named. There, could be distinguished the pecking of flints, the rattling of ramrods, and the regularly repeated rapping of bullet-moulds to disengage the freshly-cast balls. In other places could be perceived the hasty movements of men about the stables, evidently engaged in leading out and saddling horses, and making other preparations for mounting ; and then followed the sounds of the quick, short gallop of their steeds, starting off, on express, in various directions, under the sharply applied lashes of excited riders, and distinctly revealing their different routes out of the village, by the streams of fire that flew from their rapidly striking hoofs on the gravelly and frozen ground. All, indeed, seemed to be in silent commotion through the town. Bart's object in coming for his gun, at such an hour of the night, was now sufficiently explained ; for tne quick and discerning mind of Miss Haviland at once told her that the country was indeed rising in arms to avenge the atrocities just committed by the party among whom were all her relatives and friends; and she shuddered at the thought of to-morrow, feeling, as she did, a secret and boding consciousness that their downfall, brought about by their arrogance and crimes, was now at hand.

7 *   F

CHAPTER VII

"A shout as of waters — a long-uttered cry:
Hark! hark! how it leaps from the earth to the sky
From the sky to the earth, from the earth to the sea
It is grandly reëchoed, We are free, we are free!"

Every thing, the next morning, seemed as quiet and peaceful in the village, as if nothing unusual had occurred there. The commotion of the preceding night appeared to have wholly subsided. With such secrecy and caution, indeed, had the revolutionists managed, that no knowledge of their movements had yet reached the ears of any of their opponents. And so guarded was their conduct, through the whole morning, that the court party leaders, although their spies had early been out, prowling round the whole village, were yet kept in entire ignorance of all that had transpired among the former during the night. Being consequently deceived by the false appearance which every thing within the reach of their observation had been made to wear, and feeling thus relieved of their last night's guilty fears of a popular outbreak, these cruel and dastardly minions of royalty now counted on their triumph as complete , and, soon giving way to noisy exultation, they began openly to boast of the sanguinary measure by which their supposed victory had been achieved. And, about nine o'clock in the forenoon, the judges and officers of court, with a select number of their most devoted adherents, all in high spirits, and wholly unsuspicious of the storm that was silently gathering around them, formed a procession at the house of Brush, and, attended by a strong armed escort, marched ostentatiously through the street to the Court House, and entered the court-room to commence the session.

After the judges had been ushered to their seats, and while they were waiting for the crowd to enter and settle in their places, Chandler, who had kept aloof till the procession had begun to form, was seen to run his wary and watchful eye several times over the assembly, to ascertain whether there were any discoverable indications there pointing to any different state of things from the one so confidently assumed by his confederates, when he soon appeared to have noted some circumstance which caused him suddenly to exchange the bland smile he had been wearing for a look of thoughtfulness and concern.

"Do you notice anything unusual in the crowd this morning, Judge Sabin?" he said to his colleague, in an anxious whisper as he closed his scrutiny.

"No, your honor," replied the other, "unless it be the cheering sight of encountering none but friendly faces, instead of the hostile ones, which a man would have been led to expect to meet here, after so much clamor about popular disaffection.

"Ay," responded the former, with a dubious shake of the head — "ay, but that is the very circumstance that puzzles me. Had a portion of the assembly been made up of our opponents, quietly mingling with the rest, as I had rather hoped, I should have construed it into a token of submission; or, had a committee been here to present a petition, or a remonstrance or two, I should have been prepared for that, and could have managed, by a little encouragement, and a good deal of delay, to give every troublesome thing the go-by, till the storm had blown over. But this entire absence of the disaffected looks a little suspicious, don't it?"

"Why, no," answered the stiff and stolid Sabin; "I can see nothing suspicious about it. Indeed, it goes to show me that the rebellion is crushed; for, as I presume, the honest but well-meaning part of the rebels are ashamed, and their leaders afraid to show their faces here to-day, after last night's lesson."

"I hope it may be as you suppose; but I have my doubts in the matter," returned Chandler, with another dissenting shake of the head, as he turned away to renew his observations on the company before him.

On resuming his scrutiny, the uneasy judge soon perceived that the assembly, during his conversation with his colleague, had received an accession of several individuals, whom he recognized as belonging to the party whose absence had awakened his suspicions. But the presence of these persons, after he had carefully noted their appearance, instead of tending to allay only went to confirm, his apprehensions; for, as he closely scanned the bearing and countenance of each, and marked the assured and determined look and covert smile which spoke of anticipated triumph, attended with an occasional expectant glance through the windows, he there read, with the instinctive sagacity sometimes seen in men of his cast of character, enough to convince him, with what he had previously observed, that a movement of a dangerous magnitude was somewhere in progress, and soon to be developed against the court party. And he instantly resolved to lose no time before trimming his sails and preparing to meet the coming storm.   And the next moment, to the surprise of his colleague and the officers of the court, he was on his feet, requesting silence that he might address the assembly. He then proceeded to remark on the unfortunate occurrences of the previous night, with a show of much feeling and regret, and concluded by expressing his disapprobation of the course taken in the affair by the sheriff and his abettors, in a manner that would have given the highest offence to all implicated, had they not believed that the speech was secretly designed only as a game on their opponents, whom he might think it expedient to quiet and delude a little longer.   They, therefore, winked know- ingly to each other, and remained silent; while the speaker sat down with the mental exclamation, —

"There, let it come now!   That speech will do to be quoted. I can refer them to it as the public expression of my views before I knew what was coming."

Having thus placed himself in a position, as he believed, where he could easily turn himself to meet any contingency, — where, in case the apprehended overthrow of the court party took place, he could easily and safely leap the next hour to a favorable, if not a high stand among the new dispensers of place and power, or where, should the present authorities be able to sustain them- selves, he could as easily explain away his objectionable doings, and retain his standing among them.   Having done this, he then turned his attention to the official duties of his place, and ordered the crier to give the usual notice, that the court was now open for business.   This being formally done, the court docket was called over, and the causes there entered variously disposed of for the time being, by the judges, till they came to that of Wood- burn versus Peters; which was a petition for a new trial for the recovery of the petitioner's alleged farm, that had been decided, at the preceding term, to be the property of Peters, on the ground and in the manner mentioned in a former chapter.

"Who answers for this Woodburn?" said Sabin, with a con- temptuous air.   Significant glances were exchanged among the tory lawyers and officers about the bar at the question, and a malicious smile stole over the features of Peters, who had found a seat among them.

"I move the court," said Stearns, the attorney of Peters, "for a judgment in favor of my client for his costs, and also for a writ of possession of his land, of which he has been so unjustly kept out by this vexatious proceeding.   And, as the petitioner has not entered his appearance according to rule, whereby he tacitly

admits that his cause cannot be sustained, I will not permit myself to doubt that the court will so order, even at this early hour —
they certainly have the power to do so."

" They have also the power to postpone the hearing, even to the
last day of the term, before rendering judgment," bluntly interposed Knights, a large, plain-looking practitioner at the bar, who
had taken no active part either for or against the court party.
" We all know how this young man is debarred from appearing
here to-day ; and it seems to me manifestly unjust that any power
which deprives a man of the opportunity of appearing at court,
should render judgment against him in consequence of his non-
appearance. I would, therefore, suggest a delay in this cause.
Perhaps, within a short time, he will employ counsel, or be liberated."

"And perhaps be hung for treason," said Stearns, in a sneer-
ing under-tone.

" Do you answer for him or not, Mr. Knights?" demanded
Sabin, impatiently.

" No, your honor ; he has not authorized me. I only made a
suggestion," answered the former.

" Then judgment must go for buters," rejoined Sabin, with
ill suppressed warmth. " Traitors and rebels must look somewhere else for favor, beside this court, while I hold a seat here."

" Nobody has yet been convicted of treason, I believe,"
promptly responded Knights, while an expression of indignant
scorn flashed over his manly and intelligent countenance ; " and
till such is the case, I take it the rights of all have an equal claim
on the court. I should be pleased to hear the opinion of the chief
justice in this matter."

"Although I may have my doubts on this subject, Mr. Knights,"
graciously replied Chandler, " you could hardly expect me to be
guilty of so great a discourtesy to my colleague here, as to interfere, after the intimation he has just given."

" Make the entry, Mr. Clerk," said Sabin, hastily ; "judgment
for costs, and a writ of possession. I am not troubled with any
doubts in the matter, and will take the responsibility of the decision."

Scarcely was the cause thus decided before Peters glided up
to the clerk, and whispered in his ear ; when the latter, nodding
assentingly, opened his desk, and taking out two nicely-folded
papers, handed them slyly to the other, who, receiving them in
the same manner, immediately left the court-room and proceeded
down stairs. As the exulting suitor passed through the crowd

gathered round the main entrance, he beckoned to a shon, hick-
set, harsh-featured fellow, who immediately followed him around
a corner of the building.

"Well, Fitch," said Peters, pausing as soon as they were out
of the reach of observation, "have you done up your business in
town, so as to be ready for a start for Guilford?"

"Yes; don't know but I have. But you can't have got your
decision, papers made out, and all, so soon as this?" replied the
other.

"All complete!" returned Peters, triumphantly.

"Why, the court has not been in session an hour!"

"True, but I had spoken to Judge Sabin to have my case taken
up this morning; and, as nobody was authorized to answer for
Woodburn, the case was disposed of in a hurry. And the clerk,
with whom I had also arranged matters, had made out the papers
before going into court, and got them all signed off and ready, in
anticipation; and here they are, ready for your hands, Mr. Constable."

"Ay, I see; but what is the necessity of serving them so immediately?"

"Why, there's no knowing what may happen, Fitch. If the
rebels, in revenge for last night's peppering, should send over the
mountain for old Ethan Allen and his gang to come here to stir
up and lead on the disaffected, all legal proceedings might be
stopped. I know most of our folks think, this morning, that the
enemy are fairly under foot. But Chandler, who is as keen as a
fox for smelling out trouble, acts to me as if he was frightened;
and I think he must have scented mischief brewing, somewhere."

"Some say he is a very timorsome man."

"Yes; but watchful and sagacious, and therefore an index
not to be disregarded."

"May be so. But what are your orders about these papers?"

"With this, the writ of possession, go, in the first place, and
turn the old woman, his mother, neck and heels, from the house;
and then get some stiff fellow in for a tenant, rent free the first
year, if you can do no better, provided he will defend the premises against Woodburn, if he escapes unhung. And with this
paper, an execution for costs, as you will see, seize the fellow's
cow and oxen, and all else you can find, and sell them as soon
as the law will let you.

"Why, you won't leave enough of the fellow for a grease spot."

"Blast him; I don't intend to. But now is the time to do it, before he can get out of jail and back there to give fight and trouble us. So you fix all these matters about right for me, Fitch und I'll do the handsome thing by you when I come over, after the roads get settled, in the spring."

"Never fear me, as long as I know what a friend's wishes are," replied the constable, with a significant wink, as he stuffed the documents into his hat, and bustled off on the detestable mission of his more detestable employer.

While Peters and his official minion was thus engaged, Tom Dunning was seen coming, with hasty strides, along the road, from the direction of his cabin, which was situated without the village, about a half mile north of the Court House, from which it would have been visible but for the pine thicket by which it was partially enclosed. As the hunter was entering the village, he met Morris, hastening up the street, from the opposite part of the town.

"Well met," said Morris; "for I was bound to your quarters with a message, which —— "

"Which I am ditter ready to receive, and give you one, which I started to carry to your folks, in return. So, first for yours."

"Mine is, that we are now drawn up, two hundred strong, in the first woods south of the village, and are ready to march."

"And mine, that we are der ditto; besides being a hundred better than you, all chafing, like ditter tied-up dogs, to be let on."

"I will back, then, to my post with the news; and in less than a half hour, tell them, they shall hear our signal of entering the village, as agreed, which we will expect you to answer, and then rush on, as fast as you please, to effect a junction, as we wheel into the court-yard. But stay: have the prisoners been apprized that their deliverance is at hand?"

"Yes; I ran up at the time the court ditter went in, and, in the bustle, got a chance to tell them through the grate."

"All right; but how are the wounded doing?"

"Ditter well, except French, who is fast going"

"Indeed! Poor fellow! But his blood will now soon be avenged," said Morris, as the two now separated and hastened back to their respective posts.

After Peters had despatched the constable on his work of legal plunder and revenge, he returned to the court-room for the purpose of pressing to a hearing some other cases which he had pending against political opponents, and which he hoped, through

the favor of a biased and corrupt court, to carry as casily as the one
wherein he had just so wickedly triumphed. But he was not permit‐
ted to reap any more of his despicable advantages; for he found that
another, actuated by motives no less unworthy than his own, had
already gained the attention of the court to a case of which he
had been the prime mover and complainant. This was Secretary
Brush ; and the trial he had been urging on, through Stearns, the
acting state's attorney, was that of the alleged murderer, to
whose somewhat mysterious, as well as suspicious, arrest and im‐
prisonment allusion has already been made.

"As you say the witnesses are in court, Mr. Stearns," observed
Chandler, after a moment's consultation with his colleague, "as
all the witnesses are here, we have concluded to take up the
criminal case in question. You may therefore direct the sheriff
to bring the prisoner into court without delay."

The sheriff, accordingly, left the court-room, and, in a short
time, reappeared with the prisoner, followed by two armed men,
who closely guarded and conducted him forward to the crimi‐
nal's box.

The prisoner was a man of the apparent age of sixty, of rather
slight proportions of body, but with a large head, and coarse fea‐
tures, that seemed to be kept almost constantly in play by a lively,
flashing countenance, in which meekness and fire, kindness and
austerity, were curiously blended. As he seated himself, he
turned round and faced the court with a fearless and even scorn‐
ful air, but promptly rose, at the bidding of the chief judge, to
listen to the information, which the clerk proceeded to read
against him at length, closing by addressing to the respondent the
usual question as to his guilt or innocence of the charge.

"I once," calmly responded the prisoner — "I once knocked up
a pistol, pointed at my breast by a robber. It went off and killed
one of his fellows, and —— "

"Say, guilty or not guilty ? " sternly interrupted the clerk.

"Not guilty, then," answered the other, determined, while
going through these preliminary forms, that his accusers, the
court, and audience, should hear what, under other circumstances,
he would have reserved for the more appropriate time of making
his defence, or left to his counsel. "Ay, not guilty ; and that
gentleman," he rapidly continued, pointing to Brush, "that gentle‐
man, who has offered to free me if I would submit to be robbed,
well knows the truth of what I say. The witnesses, wl om he has
suborned, also know it, if they know any thing about that luck‐
'ess affray."

" Liar ! " shouted Brush, springing up, in high excitement, as soon as he could recover from the surprise and confusion into which this bold and unexpected charge had thrown him.

" The man's insane — evidently insane, your honors ! " cried Stearns, who, in his anxiety to shield his friend Brush, thought not of the effect of such a remark.

" I thank the attorney for the government for that admission, may it please the court," said Knights, rising, with a sarcastic glance at Stearns. " I may wish to make use of it."

" Are you counsel for the prisoner, sir ? " sharply demanded the other.

" I am, sir," coolly replied Knights ; " and you may find, before we get through the trial, that what the prisoner has said, as much out of place as it was, is not the only truth to be developed. But before the case proceeds any further, I offer a plea to the jurisdiction of this court, and at once submit, whether a man can be tried here for an offence alleged to have been committed in another county, without a special order from the governor for that purpose."

" That order is obtained and on file, sir. So that learned bubble is burst, as will all the rest you can raise in favor of the miserable wretch you have stooped to defend," said Stevens, exultingly. " Mr. Clerk, pass up that order to the court."

" Are you satisfied now, Mr. Knights ? " asked Sabin, with undignified feeling, after glancing at the order which had been laid before the judges. " Mr. Stearns, proceed with the cause."

But that court, on whom the subservient attorney and his corrupt and arrogant friend depended to convict an innocent man of an infamous crime, that a private and nefarious object might thereby be enforced — that court were now destined to be arrested in their career of judicial oppression before they had time to add another stain to their already blackened characters : for, at this moment, a deep and piercing groan, issuing from one of the prison-rooms beneath, resounded through the building so fearfully distinct, as to cause every individual of the assembly to start, and even to bring the judges and officers of the court to a dead pause in their proceedings. A moment of death-like silence ensued ; when another and a sharper groan of anguish, bursting evidently from the same lips, and swelling up to the highest compass of the human voice, and ending in a prolonged screech of mortal agony, rang through the apartment, sending a thrill of horror to the very hearts of the appalled multitude !

' Who ? What ? For God's sake, what is that ? " exclaimed

8

a dozen eager and trembling voices at once, as nearly the whole assembly started to their feet, and stood with amazed and per plexed countenances, inquiringly gazing at each other.

" Don't your consciences tell you that ? " exclaimed the pris-oner, Herriot, in a loud, fearless voice, running his stern, indignant eye over the court, its officers, and leading partisans around the bar. " Don't your consciences tell you what it was ? Then I will ! It was the death-screech of the poor murdered French, whose tortured spirit, now beyond the reach of your power, went out with that fearful cry which has just assailed your guilty ears ! "

" Mr. Sheriff ! Mr. Sheriff ! " sputtered Sabin, boiling with wrath, and pointing menacingly to the prisoner.

" Silence, there, blabbing miscreant ! " thundered Patterson.

" Ah ! No wonder ye want silence, when that name is men tioned," returned Herriot, unflinchingly.

Struck dumb with astonishment at the unexpected audacity of the prisoner in thus throwing out, in open court, such bold and cutting intimations of their guilty conduct, the judges and officers seemed perfectly at a loss how to act, or give vent to their mad-dened feelings, for some moments. Soon, however, the most prompt and reckless among them found the use of their tongues.

" Shoot him down, Patterson ! " exclaimed Brush, with an oath.

" Treason ! I charge him with treason, and demand that he be ironed and gagged on the spot ! " shouted Gale, bringing down his clinched fist heavily on the desk before him !

" Yes, high treason ; let us re-arrest him, and see if we can hang him on that, should he escape on the other charge," chimed in Stearns.

" I have my doubts," began Chandler, who was growing every moment more wavering and uneasy.

" No doubts about it," interrupted Sabin, almost choking with rage. " I'll not sit here and see the king's authority insulted, and his court treated with such contempt and treasonable defiance ; and I order him instantly in irons — chains — yes, chains, Mr. Sheriff ! "

" You can chain the body, but shall not fetter the tongue," responded Herriot, in no way dismayed by the threats of his enraged persecutors, or their preparations to confine and torture his person ; " for I *will* speak, and you shall *hear*, ye tyrants ! Listen then, ye red-handed assassins ! The blood of your mur-dered victim has cried up to God for vengeance. The cry has been heard! the unseen hand has already traced your doom on the wall! and this day, ay, within this hour," he continued, glancing through the window to a dark mass of men, who might now be partially discerned drawn up behind the point of woods at the north — "ay, within this very hour, that doom shall be fulfilled! Hark!" he added, in startling tones, after a momentary pause —" hark! do ye hear those signal guns, echoing from post to post, round your beleaguered Babylon? Do you hear those shouts? The avengers of blood are even now at your doors. Hear, and tremble!"

As the speaker closed his bold denunciations, he descended from the bench which he had mounted for the purpose, and, advancing to the sheriff and his assistants, now standing mute and doubtful with their hastily procured fetters in their hands, he paused, and stood confronting them with an ironical smile, and with folded arms, in token of his readiness now to submit himself to their hands. But a wonderful change had suddenly come over the whole band of these tory dignitaries. The dark and angry scowls of meditated revenge, and the more fiery expressions of undisguised wrath, which were bent on the dauntless old man during the first part of his denunciations, had, by the time he made his closing announcement, all given way to looks of surprise and apprehension. No one offered to lay hands on him; for, as the truth of what he said was every moment more strongly confirmed by the increasing tumult without, no one had any thoughts to spare for any but himself. And soon the whole assembly broke from their places, and, in spite of the loud calls of the officers for silence and order, began to cry out in eager inquiries, and run about the room in the utmost confusion and alarm. At this juncture, David Redding, who had been thus far the most reckless and bloodthirsty tory of all, burst into the room, hurriedly exclaiming, —

"The people have risen in arms, and are pouring in upon us, by hundreds, from every direction! In five minutes this house will be surrounded, and we in their power. Let every man look to his own safety! I shall to mine," he added, rushing back down to the front door, where, instead of attempting to escape through the back way, as he might then have done, he began to shout, "Hurra for Congress!" and, "Down with the British court!" at the very top of his voice.

"I resign my commission," cried Chandler, jumping up in great trepidation. "Let it be distinctly understood," he repeated, raising his voice in his anxiety to be heard — "yes, et it be distinctly understood, that I have resigned my commission as judge of this court."

" D——n him! what does he mean by that?" muttered Gale, turning to Patterson.

" It means he is going to turn tail, as I always thought he would,—the cursed cowardly traitor!" replied the latter, gnashing his teeth. " But let him, and that pitiful poltroon of a Redding, go where they please. We will see to matters ourselves. I don't believe it is any thing more than a mere mob, who will scatter at the first fire. So follow me, Gale; and all the rest of ye, that aint afraid of your own shadows, follow me, and I'll soon know what can be done."

And, while lawyers and suitors were hastily snatching up their papers, and all were making a general rush for the door, in the universal panic which had seized them, the boastful sheriff, attended by his assistants and the tiger-tempered Gale, pushed his way down stairs, shaking his sword over his head, and shouting with all his might,—

" To arms! Every friend to the court and king, to arms! Stand to your guns there below, guards, and shoot down every rebel that attempts to enter!"

But, when he reached the front entrance, the spectacle which there greeted his eyes seemed to have an instant effect in cooling his military ardor. There, to his dismay, he beheld drawn up, within thirty paces of the door, an organized and well-armed body of more than three hundred men; while small detachments, constantly arriving, were falling in on the right and left, and extending the wings round the whole building. And as the discomfited loyalist ran his eye along the line of the broad-breasted and fierce-looking fellows before him, and recognized among them the Huntingtons, the Knights, the Stevenses, the Baileys, the Brighams, the Curtises, and other stanch and leading patriots, from nearly every town bordering on the Connecticut, and saw the determined look and the indignant flashing of their countenances, he at once read not only the entire overthrow of his party in this section of the country, but the individual peril in which he, and his abettors in the massacre, now stood before an outraged and excited populace.

" What ails your men, Squire Sheriff?" cried Barty Burt, now grown to a soldier in the ranks of the assailants, as he pointed tauntingly to the company of tory guards who had been stationed in the yard, but who now, sharing in the general panic, had thrown down their arms, and stood huddled together near the door; "why don't they pick up their shooting-irons, and blaze away at the ' d——d rebels,' as I think I heard you order, just now ? "

"And if that won't ditter do," exclaimed the well-known voice of Tom Dunning from another part of the ranks, '' suppose you ditter read another king's proclamation at us: no knowing but we might be ditter done for, entirely."

The sheriff waited to hear no more, but hastily retreated into the house, followed by a shout of derisive laughter; and his place was the next moment occupied by Chandler, who bustled forward to the steps, and, in a flustered, supplicatory manner, asked leave to address his "*respected fellow-citizens.*"

"Short speeches, judge!" impatiently cried Colonel Carpenter, who seemed, from his position on horseback among the troops and other appearances, to be chief in command—"short speeches, if any. We have come here on a business which neither long speeches nor smooth ones will prevent us from executing."

The judge, however, could not afford to take this as a repulse ; and, with this doubtful license, he went on to say. that on hearing, in the morning, as he did with astonishment and horror, of the unauthorized proceedings of last night, he had denounced the outrage, in an address at the opening of the court ; and not finding himself supported, he had resigned, and left his seat on the bench.

"And now," he added in conclusion, "being freed from the trammels of my oath of office, which have lately become so painful to me, I feel myself again one of the people, and stand ready to coöperate with them in any measure required by the public welfare."

A very faint and scattering shout of applause, in two or three places, mingled with hisses and murmurs in others, was the only response with which this address was received. But even with this equivocal testimony of public feeling towards him, this despicable functionary felt gratified. " I *am safe*," said he to himself, with a long-drawn breath, as he descended the steps, to watch an opportunity to mingle with the party with whom he was now especially anxious to be seen, and to whom he was ready to say, in the words of the satirist, —

> " I'm all submission, what you'd have me, make me;
> The only question is, sirs, will you take me ?"

At this moment a sash was thrown up, and the prisoner, Her riot, appeared at a window of the court-room above.

" I have been brought up here this morning," he said, shaking back his gray locks, and raising his stern, solemn voice to a pitch clearly audible to all in the grounds below — " I have been brought here from my dungeon to answer to the charge of a foul crime ; and both my accusers and triers, fleeing even before any one appeared to pursue, have left their places, having neither tried nor condemned me. But scorning to follow their example, I now appear, to submit myself for a verdict, to the rightful source of all power — the people."

" Neither will we condemn thee," cried Knowlton, pursuing the scriptura. thought of the other ; " if thy accusers and judges have left thee uncondemned, thou shalt not be condemned by us ; at least not by me, who have long had my opinions of the character of this prosecution."

" As also have I," responded Captain Wright. " I know something of the witnesses, on whom, it is said, they depended to convict father Herriot ; and I would not hang a dog on their testimony. I move, therefore, that we here pronounce a verdict of acquittal. Who says, ay ? "

" Ay ! " promptly responded a dozen voices ; and " Ay ! " the next instant rose in one loud, unanimous shout from the whole multitude.

" A thousand thanks to you, my friends, for your generous confidence in my innocence," returned the old man with emotion ; " and, thank God, your confidence is not misplaced. I was formerly guilty of much, which has cost me many bitter tears of repentance ; but there is no blood on *my* hands, and I will now return to my hermit hut, from which they dragged me, there to pray for the success of the good cause in which you are engaged, leaving to you what lesson shall be taught those Hamans who have filled these dungeons with the dying and wounded, now demanding your care."

The effect of the old man's closing hint was instantly visible on the multitude, who decided by acclamation to act upon it without delay ; and accordingly a score of resolute fellows were detached to proceed to the prisons, release their friends, and fill their places, for the present, with their murderous oppressors.

CHAPTER VIII.

" ——— right represt,
**Will leave with the deep earthquake's fierce unrest,
Then fling, with fiery strength, the mountain from its breast."**

WHEN the besieged tories, who were now mostly crowded together in the broad space on the lower floor, saw a column of their assailants entering the front door, and advancing upon them with levelled muskets to sacrifice them, as they supposed, on the spot, they were seized with a fresh and uncontrollable panic, and made such a tremendous rush for the back entrance, that the only sentry who happened at that moment to be there, was, in spite of all his threats to fire upon them, instantly borne down, or thrust aside, by the living torrent that now burst through the door; and before a force sufficient to stop them could reach the spot, numbers had escaped into the adjoining fields, where, scattering in different directions, they commenced their disorderly flight, with all the speed which their guilty terrors could lend them. The next moment, however, as the cry that the tories were escaping was raised, a hundred of their most fleet-footed opponents were seen leaping the fences into the fields, and giving chase to the frightened fugitives. A scene, in which the ludicrous, the novel, the wild, and the fearful, were strangely mingled, now ensued; for, although a strong guard still retained their places round the Court House, who, with the detachment that had entered as we have described, proceeded to take into custody the remaining tories and liberate the imprisoned, yet the main body of the revolutionists joined in the work of hunting down the flying enemy; those not only who had escaped from the Court House in the manner we have named, but all concerned in the massacre that could be found secreted or lurking about the village; while the exulting shouts of the victors as they overtook, seized, and brought to the ground the vanquished; the abject cries of the latter for quarter; the reports of muskets fired by pursuers over the heads of the pursued, to frighten them to surrender; the beating of drums, and the loud clamor of mingling voices, — all combined to swell the uproar and confusion of the exciting scene

" How like the ditter deuse these lawyers do scratch grav

el !" exclaimed Tom Dunning, as he singled out and gave chase to Stearns and Knights, who together were making their way across the fields, in the direction of the river, as if life and death hung on their speed. " Ha ! ha !" continued the tickled hunter, laughing so immoderately at the novel spectacle, as greatly to impede his own progress — " ha ! ha ! ha ! ha ! Why, I der den't believe but what they've got consciences, after all ! for what e'se could make their ditter drumsticks fly so ? "

But although the hunter, in thus indulging his merriment, suf-fered himself actually to lose ground in the race, yet he had no notion of relinquishing the chase, or losing the game ; for, con-scious of his own powers, and thinking lightly of those of the fugitives, he supposed, that, as soon as he chose to exert himself, he could easily make the race a short one, and as easily capture and lead them back in triumph ; and he began to think over the jokes he would crack at their expense on the way. But the un-seen event of the next moment showed him, to his vexation, that his inaction, and confidence in his own powers to remedy the consequences of it, had cost him all the anticipated pleasures of his expected victory. For scarcely had he commenced the pur-suit in earnest, when the fugitive lawyers reached the bank of the river, and at the very place too, as it provokingly happened, where his own log-canoe chanced to be moored, and hastily leap-ing into it, they managed with such dexterity and quickness, in handling the oars and cutting the fastenings, as to push off, and get fairly out of the reach of their pursuer, before he could gain the spot ; and his threat to fire at them, if they did not return, and the execution of that threat the next moment, which sent a bullet skipping over the water within a foot of the receding canoe, as he only intended, were all without effect in compelling the return of the panic-struck attorneys. And the balked pursuer had soon the mortification to see his crafty brace of intended captives and in safety on the opposite shore, which he had now no means of gaining, and disappear in the dark pine forest then lining the eastern bank of the Connecticut at this place.

" Outwitted, by ditter Judas !" exclaimed the hunter, in his vexation. " These lawyers, dog 'em ! they have so much of the Old Scratcher in 'em, that they will outdo a fellow at his own trade. However, I've done the new state some ditter service, I reckon, seeing I've fairly driven such a precious pair of 'em out of it." *

---

* Knights, who, unlike his companion, was no loyalist, appears to have become infected with the panic that had seized his loyal associates.

With this consolatory reflection, he now turned and retraced his steps towards the scene of action. While on his way thither, and soon after passing the rear of the building before described as the head-quarters of the tory leaders, his attention was arrested by the lamentable outcries of some one alternately bawling for help, and begging for mercy ; when, turning to the spot, he there beheld his associate, Barty Burt, astride the haughty owner of the mansion just named, who, with dress sadly soiled and disordered, was creeping on his hands and knees on the ground, towards his house, which, it appeared, he had nearly gained, when he was overtaken, thrown to the ground, and mounted by his agile and tormenting captor, who was now taking his whimsical revenge for former indignities, by compelling the fallen secretary, through the efficacy of a loaded pistol just wrenched from the latter's hand, to carry him on his back, in the manner above described.

"What the dogs are you ditter doing there, Bart ?" said Dunning, with a broad grin, as he came up and recognized the secretary in such a strange plight and attitude.

---

in common with the whole court party; and, though he had no cause for alarm, fled with those who escaped from the Court House, on this memorable occasion. It is probable, that owing to his supposed interest in the continuance of the court, and consequent unwillingness to coöperate in the measures on foot to overthrow it, he was purposely kept in ignorance of the movements of the revolutionists, and therefore taken wholly by surprise when the storm burst. At all events, his speedy return, immediate resumption of his professional duties at Brattleborough, and subsequent promotion to the bench, abundantly shows that he no less enjoyed the confidence of the American party than his two namesakes, and, we believe, relatives, whom we have named as present among the assailants, and who were afterwards officers in our revolutionary forces. An aged and distinguished early settler, to whom the author is indebted for many of the incidents he has here delineated, thus writes in relation to the particular one in question : —

"I have heard Judge Samuel Knights, who, as chief justice, presided in the Supreme Court from 1791 to 1793, describe the trepidation that seized them, when, after the massacre, and on the rising of the surrounding country, they came to learn the excited state of the populace. He related how he and another member of the bar (Stearns, I think, who was afterwards attorney secretary of Nova Scotia) hurried down to the river, and finding there a boat, (such as was used in those times for carrying seines or nets at the shad and salmon fishing grounds, which were frequent on both sides the river, below the Great Falls,) they paddled themselves across, and lay all day under a log in the pine forest opposite the town ; and, when night came, went to Parson Fessenden's, at Walpole, and obtained a horse, so that, by riding and tying, they got out of the country till the storm blew over, when Knights returned to Brattleborough."

G

" O, nuthin very desput; only showing Squire Brusn, here the differ between to-day and yesterday, that's all," replied Bart, kicking and spurring, like a boy on some broken-down horse " Get up, here! Gee! whoa, Dobbin! Kinder seems to me," he continued to his groaning prisoner—" kinder seems to me l heard somebody say, 'tother night, that Bart Burt wasn't above a jackass. Wonder if I aint above a jackass now? only his ears may need pulling and stretching a little," he added, suiting the action to the word.

" For God's sake, my good man," said Brush, turning imploringly to Dunning, " do relieve me from the clutches of this insatiate imp of hell. Let him shoot me, if he will; but don't leave me to be worried, and trod into the mud and splosh, like a dog, by the revengeful young savage. It is more than flesh and blood can bear."

" Well, now, squire, I wouldn't make such a tearing fuss about this little bit of a walloping, after what's happened, if I was you," said Bart. " There was our differ about who was the jackass, and sich like, that night, you know, which I kinder thought I might as well settle; and then, again, there was your good-by, yesterday; but may be I've done enough to make that square, too. So I don't care if I let you up, now, seeing as how Mr. Dunning has come to take care of your worship," added the speaker, springing nimbly a few paces aside, and facing about with presented pistol, as if to keep the other on good behavior.

" What can you want with me, sir?" said the disencumbered secretary to the hunter, after gaining his feet and shaking off the mud from his bedraggled garments.

" Ditter considerable," replied the other. " In the first place, the people want to see you back to the Court House, where you may ditter consider yourself invited to go, under my care. They there may have the first claim on you."

" Well, if I am a prisoner, let us go there, then," said the crestfallen loyalist, relinquishing, with bad grace, his hope of being allowed to escape. " But what do you mean by *first claim* on me?"

" Well, I ditter mean that I have another, when they get through with you."

" Explain yourself, sir."

" I will. You ditter know that your governor has offered a reward of fifty pounds for the ditter delivery of Ethan Allen for the gallows, under a law got through the York Assembly, principally by one Squire Brush. Well I aint a going to ditter fight old

Ethan's battles; for he can der do that himself. But you may ditter know, also, that Ethan has offered the same reward for the governor and you. Now, as we are ditter expecting Allen over here, in a few days, I was der thinking, I and Bart, here, might as well ditter deliver you up, and claim the money." *

So saying, the hunter, bidding the prisoner to follow, and Bart to bring up the rear, marched off in triumph to the Court House; and, having delivered over his charge to the guard at the prison doors, sallied out into the village in quest of further adventures Nor was he long in meeting with them. After gaining the street, he soon perceived a gathering and commotion nearly in front of the mansion whose owner he had just taken from the rear; and, on reaching the spot, he found a crowd collected round a sleigh, filled with gentlemen and ladies, which proved to be that of Peters and his company. It appeared that Haviland, who had remained at his quarters that forenoon, and had thus become apprised of the rising of the people sooner than the mass of his party, had instantly ordered the team to be harnessed, and every thing prepared for an immediate departure, as soon as Peters should arrive. And the latter, who was among those who broke away from the Court House after it was invested, having at length reached the house undiscovered, and adopted such disguise in dress as the time would permit, they had all jumped into the sleigh, (which could still be used better than any other vehicle,) and were rapidly driving from the yard, in an attempt to escape from the town, when they were recognized and detained by a party of the revolutionists. Haviland and Peters had already been seized and taken from the sleigh, and would have instantly been forced off to prison, but for the entreaties and distress of the females who refused to be conducted back to the house, or even to be separated from their protectors; Miss Haviland, especially, declaring that if her father must go to prison, she would go with him. This had produced a momentary delay, during which a sharp altercation had arisen, some being for taking the prisoners back to the house, there to be guarded, and others strongly insisting on dragging them off, at once, to jail. The latter, at length, appeared to prevail, and were on the point of forcing the

---

* Crean Brush, who procured himself to be elected from this county to the New York legislature, for several years, was believed to be the main mover of the act of outlawry against Ethan Allen and others. He certainly, as chairman of the committee on the subject, reported, and recommended the passage of, that notorious measure. [See Slade's State Papers.

adies, in spite of all their entreaties, from the sides of their
protectors, when a man came pushing his way through the
crowd : —

"For shame! shame! my friends," he cried; "you surely
would not molest innocent and defenceless females."

"I will tell you what it is, Harry Woodburn," responded one
of those who were for proceeding to active measures, "when
ladies attempt to stand between murderers and their deserts, they
must expect to be molested."

The circumstances of the case were then explained to Woodburn; when the crowd, who had been irritated by the threats and
arrogant behavior of the prisoners, at the outset, again began to
cry, "Away with them, women and all, if they will have it so —
away with them to prison!"

"Men, hear me!" exclaimed Woodburn, planting himself
between the ladies and the angry crowd. "You see this!" he
continued, holding up his bandaged and bl. od-stained arm: "the
wound was received in defending your cause; and I have but
this moment come from the felon's hol. where I passed the
night, for the part I took in the affray. Now, have I not earned
the right to be heard?"

"Ay, ay, certainly, Harry; go on!" responded several, while
the silence of the rest denoted a ready acquiescence in the
request.

"This, then, is what I would say," resumed the former.
"These ladies, who are doubtless anxious to escape from a scene
of strife which may not yet be ended, came from a distance,
under the care of this old gentleman, whose imprisonment would
not only take from them their protector, but deprive them, probably, of all present means of returning to their home. I propose,
therefore, to let him and them depart unmolested."

"If the ladies were all — but I don't know about letting this
old fellow off so easily," said one, exchanging doubtful glances
with those around him. "He is both tory and Yorker to the
eyes."

"Yes," urged another, "and who know but he was among the
murderers last night?"

"I have ascertained that he was not among the actors of last
night's outrage," replied Woodburn.

"Well," rejoined the former, "I know the other was — that
upper-crust tory by his side there, who was always too proud to
wear an old coat and hat, till he thought they might help him in
skulking away out of the reach of punishment."

'I know Peters was there, to my cost; and I had no notion of asking any exemption for him," returned Woodburn, with bitterness. "But this old gentleman, whatever may be his feelings, has committed none of those acts of violence, for which, only, I understand, our leaders intend to institute trials. Shall we not, then, let him and his ladies proceed, as I proposed?"

Receiving no direct answer to his appeal, the speaker now took two or three of the leading opposers aside, and, after conversing with them a few moments, returned, and announced to Haviland that he was at liberty to depart.

How well and wisely had he read the human heart, who penned the scriptural apothegm, "If thine enemy hunger, feed him; if he thirst, give him drink; for, in so doing, thou shalt heap coals of fire on his head"! Haviland, though by nature an honorable man, had yet suffered himself to enter deeply into the personal animosities of Peters towards Woodburn, which, with his political and aristocratic prejudices, had caused him to think of the young man only with feelings of contempt and bitterness. And when he witnessed the noble conduct of the latter, first in rescuing his daughter from the flood, and now so generously interposing in his behalf, it produced that struggle between pride and conscience, whose operation is so forcibly expressed by the sacred writer just quoted. And, although he could bring himself to acknowledge his obligations only by a formal and constrained bow, yet the conflicting and painful expressions that were seen flitting over his disturbed countenance, as he now returned to the sleigh, plainly told how effectually, and with what punished feelings, his enmity had been silenced. But not so with his single-minded and quickly and justly appreciating daughter. She had no prejudices to combat, no pride to conquer; and she, therefore, witnessed each new act of her deliverer with as much pleasure as gratitude — feelings which sought expression in no parade of words, it is true, but in the more meaning and eloquent language of the kindly tone and sweetly-beaming countenance. And, in her low-murmured, "Thank you — thank you for all," as Woodburn handed her to her seat in the vehicle, he felt a thousand fold repaid for all he had ventured for her sake; while the speaking smile, with which she the next moment turned to him, and nodded her adieu, left an impress on his heart destined never to be effaced.

While this was transpiring, Peters, who had been standing apart from the rest of his company, sullenly looking on, without uttering a word, except to bid Haviland go on without him, contrived, with-

9

ou exciting any suspicion of his design, to work himself by de
grees to the outer edge of the crowd, in the direction in which
the team was about to pass. And, as the sleigh, which was now
put in motion, approached him, he made a sudden feint of running
the opposite way; when, as the crowd were confusedly springing
forward to head him, he quickly tacked about, leaped into the
sleigh, and, snatching the reins and whip from Haviland's hands,
applied the lash so furiously, that the frantic horses bounded forward with a speed which carried the receding vehicle more than
fifty yards on its course, before the balked and confused throng
could recover themselves, and fairly comprehend what had happened. But the sharp, bitter shout of execrations, mingled with
cries for immediate pursuit, which now rose from the agitated
multitude, proclaimed at once their hatred of the haughty loyalist,
and their determination not to suffer him to escape from justice
And the next instant, a half dozen swift runners, led on by Dunning, shot out from the crowd, in the eager chase, like so many
arrows speeding to the mark. And, notwithstanding the supposed
advantages of horses over men in a race, and notwithstanding
the increased speed with which the fugitive team thundered along
over the half-bare and uneven ground, the pursued had scarcely
reached the end of a furlong, before the fleet and determined
hunter, still in advance of his companions, gained the side of the
sleigh, leaped up, pounced upon his cringing victim, and brought
him headlong to the ground, leaving Haviland to seize the relinquished reins, check the horses as he best could, and proceed on
his way unmolested.

" There! you ditter sneak of a runaway tory. You will now
go, I der rather calculate, where there's no ditter petticoats to
shelter you," said Dunning, raising the chapfallen Peters by the
collar, and drawing him along back, amidst the exulting shouts of
the revolutionists, by whom he and his friend Brush were then
forced away, in no very gentle manner, to join their fellow-pris-
oners, in the same dungeon where the victims of their last night's
outrage were so unfeelingly and so unwisely immured.

A detailed description of the various scenes which here succeeded, in the winding up of this local revolution, as it may justly
be denominated, would occupy too much space for the limits of
our tale, without evolving any further incident, having much
bearing on the destinies of those of its personages whose fortunes
we design to follow. We will now, therefore, sum up, in a few
words, the doings of the triumphant party, and, with a comment
or two of our own, dismiss the subject.

In the first place, all the supposed actors and abettors of the massacre within reach were seized and secured, excepting Redding and one or two others of a like character, who, by their activity in assisting to apprehend the fugitive comrades whom they had so meanly deserted, and their offers to give evidence against them, had purchased an exemption from punishment, and excepting also the Janus-faced Chandler, who, by his duplicity, had contributed more than any other man, perhaps, towards this catastrophe, but who now contrived to make even his iniquities count in his favor.* After this was effected, the victors, all but enough to constitute a safe guard, laid aside their arms, and resoved themselves into a sort of civil convention, to take measures for the trial of the prisoners by some mode, which, in the absence of all proper authorities, should answer for a legal process. And, as the first step in the matter, a jury of inquest, to sit on the dead body of French, was ordered, and a committee appointed to see to the empanelling of impartial men, and collect evidence and conduct the investigations to be had before them. All this being

---

* As the acts of this notorious personage, whose character we have been at considerable pains to ascertain, and accordingly portray, will have no further connection with our story, we cannot forbear, before dismissing him entirely, giving the reader a short account of his subsequent career, and singular end. Although, by his facility of accommodating his political principles to those of the majority, and his alacrity of tacking about, and mounting, like a squirrel on a wheel, so as to be found rising to the top in every revolution or counter-revolution of public sentiment, he thus adroitly managed to get appointed to some offices of minor importance, under the new state government, yet, becoming every year better and better understood, and consequently more and more distrusted, he finally sunk into utter insignificance and contempt; and, falling into pecuniary embarrassments, brought about by a long course of secret fraud in selling wild lands, of which he had no titles, he was confined for debt in the very building in which the massacre occurred; where, as if by the retribution of Heaven for the part he once there acted, he soon died, unhonored and unlamented. And, what is still more remarkable, his remains were strangely destined to be denied even the respect of a common burial. For some exasperated creditor having attached the body, and the neighbors, from a notion that prevailed at that time, supposing, that by removing the body for a public burial they would make themselves liable for his debts, suffered it to remain till it became too offensive to be endured, when, at the dark hour of midnight, a few individuals went silently to the prison, got the putrid mass into some rough box, and drew it on the ground to the fence of the neighboring burial-ground; and, having dug a norizontal trench under the fence, and a deep pit on the other side, pushed through and buried up all that remained of the once noted Chief Justice Chandler. An old, decayed oak stump, still standing, is the only object that marks the site of his grave.

duly accomplished, and the jury bringing in a verdict that the de
ceased came to his death by the discharges of muskets, in the
hands of Patterson, Gale. and others therein enumerated, all the
latter, thus designated as the murderers of the unfortunate young
man, were taken, and, under the authority of another order or
decree of the convention, marched off, under a strong guard, to
the jail in Northampton, some forty or fifty miles into the interior of Massachusetts, and there confined, to be tried for their lives
at the next court that should be holden in the county where the
offence was committed; while a less deeply implicated portion of
the prisoners were put under bonds to appear at the court to answer to the charges of manslaughter and assault, or made to undergo other punishments and restrictions immediately imposed by
the convention.* The actors in the outrage, who comprised nearly all the leading members of the British party in that part of the
Grants lying east of the mountains, having been thus summarily
disposed of, the people, now taking the government into their own
hands, and acting in primitive assembly, proceeded to reorganize
the county, by the appointment of new judges, and all the usual
subordinate officers, of their own principles, to adopt measures to
reduce to submission or drive away the remaining loyalists of the
county, and, finally, to declare themselves alike independent of
the government of Great Britain and of New York.

Thus terminated this memorable outbreak, which acquired
additional importance from the fact, that it resulted in the entire
subversion of British authority in this, the only section among the
Green Mountains where it ever gained a foothold. And not
small the praise, which, in view of the circumstances, should be
awarded to the hardy spirits by whom this miniature revolution
was achieved; for, so great was the power of patronage exercised
by this court, and the influence of those enjoying office or immu-
nities under it, — a great majority of whom were stanch, and the
rest tacit, supporters of the royal cause, — that, till the occurrence
of this sanguinary affair, it is evident the former had but little

---

* Among the different kinds of sentences imposed on the class of offenders here last named, was one dooming Judge Sabin to the limits of
his own farm, and making it lawful for any one catching him off of it to
kill him. And so deep was the public indignation against this inveterate
loyalist and supposed secret abettor of the massacre, that he was narrowly
watched for the chance of executing the penalty. An aged revolutionist,
from whom this fact was derived, stated that he had lain many a Sunday,
with a loaded rifle, in the woods near the judge's farm lines, to see if he
would not, when coming out to salt his sheep, stray over his limits. But
the old fellow, he said, was always too wary for him.

hope of being able to overthrow this petty local dynasty withou assistance from abroad. The aged survivors of that stormy period inform us, indeed, that but for the massacre of Westminster, it would have been difficult to predict whether the opening of the revolution, a few months afterwards, would have found, in the section in question, a whig or tory majority predominating. But that act of murder and madness, which the loyalists here, with the strange infatuation attending their doings almost every where else at the time, seemed destined to commit, as if to hasten their own overthrow, settled their doom.

> "It was the electric flame to fire the hearts
> Of a true people."

And while it opened the eyes of hundreds of the hitherto acquiescent, it armed the opposing with an energy and determination in their cause, which at once became irresistible; and when the war-note was subsequently sounded by such patriots as Benjamin Carpenter and his associates, it found a ready response in every glen and corner of the surrounding country, and the hardy settlers seized their arms, and, with the cry of *French and vengeance!* hastened away to the scenes of action at Lexington, Ticonderoga, and Bunker Hill.

We are aware that some historians have classed this affair among the difficulties and skirmishes growing out of what has usually been termed the New York controversy, while others have treated the subject in a manner which shows them to be doubtful in what light to place the transaction; and, for that reason apparently, they have slid over the matter in those general and ambiguous terms so often and reprehensibly indulged in by writers at a loss about facts, to conceal their own ignorance, or to avoid the responsibility of deciding the point at issue. But a careful examination of the subject has led us to the conclusion, that the affair in question had little or no connection, in reality, with the New York controversy, but that it was wholly of a revolutionary character. No resistance to the authority of New York had ever been previously made in this section of the Grants; nor did the opposers of this court, in any of their remonstrances, or other proceedings, either before or after the massacre, assign any reason for their doings which can be fairly construed into an objection to the jurisdiction of that province, as such; or any otherwise than that it had, up to that time, refused to adopt the resolves and recommendations of the Continental Congress. On the contrary, all their arguments are based on their duty and

9 *

determination of joining their revolting brethren in the other colo
nics, and, consequently, of resisting the longer continuance of
British authority among them.   Such, indeed, is the ground taken
by Dr. Jones, in his minute and authentic account of the
occurrence, in which he was, as we have made him in our illustrations, an actor.   And even the inscription on the tombstone of
the ill-fated French, written when the transaction, and all its
attendant circumstances, were fresh in the minds of all, sufficiently
proves, if further proof were necessary, that the version we have
given of the affair is identical with the one generally understood
and received at the time." *

It was this view of the occurrence which led us to occupy the
space we have devoted in attempting to illustrate it; for it be-
comes invested with a new interest and new importance, when it
is considered, as we think it must be, that here was enacted the
first scene of the great drama that followed; here was shed the
first blood, and here fell the first martyr, of the American revolution.

---

* The inscription here alluded to, which we insert as supporting our
position rather than as affording any new antiquarian curiosity to many
readers, is verbatim as follows : —

"In memory of William French, son of Mr. Nathaniel French,
Who was shot at Westminster March ye 13th 1775 by the hands
of Cruel Ministerial tools of George ye 3d, in the Court
House, at 11 o'clock at night, in the 22d year of his age.

" Here William French his Body lies
For murder his blood for vengeance cries
King George the third, his tory crew
Tha with a bawl his head shot threw
For liberty and his country's good
He lost his life and dearest blood."

CHAPTER IX.

"They sank till their fair land became a sty
Stygian with moral darkness. Heart and mind
Debased — dark passions rose, and with red eye,
Rushed to their revel; until Freedom, blind
And maniac, sought the rest the suicide would find."

THE traveller of the present day, as he enters the town of
Guilford, on the southern confines of Vermont, will soon be
struck with the peculiar appearance of many things around him.
Few or no traces of a primitive forest are to be seen, while its
place is supplied by a heavy second growth of woods, sixty or
seventy years old, in the midst of which the remains of old en-
closures and other indications of former habitations are not unfrequently observable. On the cleared farms, also, may often be
seen three or four different clumps of aged fruit-trees, scattered
about in the nooks and corners of the lot, and sometimes extending into the woods, in such a manner as to preclude the idea that
they could have been planted under any thing like the present
arrangements of the farm and its buildings. Near these old rel-
ics of former orchards may likewise generally be perceived some
levelled spot, remains of old chimneys, traces of cellars, or other
marks of dwellings long since removed, or fallen to decay.
These, with many other peculiarities, give to the whole town an
aspect nowhere else to be seen in Vermont, nor even, perhaps,
in any part of New England. And if the traveller be of a fanci-
ful turn, he will associate the place with the idea of some deserted
country, resettled by a new race of men ; and even if he be a
mere matter-of-fact man, he cannot fail to perceive that the town
must have been originally tenanted under a division of lands and
an order of things quite different from those now existing. And
either of these suppositions would be far better justified by the
facts than most of the speculations of modern tourists made in
their flying visits through the land, as will be seen by a recur-
rence to the early annals of this town, of which, for the purpose
of insuring a full understanding of some scenes here about to be
described, we must be permitted to give a brief outline.
The events connected with the first settlement of the town of
Guilford, which afterwards became so noted as the stronghold of

toryism and adherence to the New York supremacy, form a curious anomaly even in the anomalous history of Vermont. The territory comprising this township appears to have been granted, as early as 1754, to a company of about fifty persons, by a charter, which, unlike that of any other town, empowered the proprietors, in express terms, to govern themselves and regulate the concerns of their little community, by such laws as the majority should be pleased to enact, without being made amenable to any power under heaven, save that which might be exercised by the British Parliament. Being thus constituted a band of freemen and legislators, at the outset, they soon took possession of their chartered piece of wilderness, organized by the election of the proper officers of state, and assumed the title of an independent republic, which their charter, in fact, created, any control of the Parliament of England being as little to be apprehended, in their secluded retreat among the wilds of the Green Mountains, as that of the Great Mogul of Tartary. And as novel as was the idea of a republic at that early period, when " the divine right of kings " to govern all men was as little questioned as the divine right of Satan to afflict the pious Job of old, this enterprising little band of settlers, for many years, appear to have well sustained the character they had assumed, not only by carrying out, in all their public doings, that essential principle of a republic which makes the will of the majority supreme, but by the simplicity of their tastes and habits in private life, and their beautiful exemplification of the great law of love, that can only be fulfilled towards our neighbors by according to them equal rights and privileges with ourselves. At length, however, new doctrines began to prevail, and the independent character of our little republic was soon, in a good degree, forfeited ; and that, too, by the very means, it would seem, which had been taken to make it flourish and increase. It had been one of the conditions of the charter that every grantee should become an actual settler, and, within five years, clear and cultivate five acres of land, for every fifty purchased. And in accordance with this cunning policy for insuring the actual and rapid settlement of the place, the township had been laid out in fifty and one hundred acre lots, except the governor's right of five hundred acres, which his excellency of New Hampshire, in granting Vermont lands, never forgot to reserve for his own use, in every township, but which the proprietors generally contrived, as in this instance, to have set off on the highest mountain in town, considering it but respectful and fitting, as they used waggishly to observe, that so elevated a per sonage should be honored with the most elevated location. And the effect of this policy, together with the low prices at which the lands were put, and other inducements held out to draw in settlers, soon became visible in the rapid increase of the population, and consequent improvement of the town. So unexampled in these new settlements was its progress, indeed, in both the particulars we have just named, that within twenty years from the time when the sound of the axe was first heard in its woody limits, the inhabitants were found to number nearly three thousand; while fields were every where opened in the wilderness, and buildings raised in such neighborly contiguity, that the whole town presented the appearance of a continuous village. It is not very surprising, therefore, that, through such an influx of settlers, coming from all parts of the country, and including many interested and active partisans of the York jurisdiction, a majority should soon be obtained, who were induced to depart from the views of the first settlers respecting the independence of their community, and adopt the more fashionable form of subordinate government, which prevailed in all the towns around them. And accordingly we find them, at their annual meeting in 1772, voting the district of Guilford, as they termed it, to belong to the county of Cumberland and province of New York, and thereupon proceeding to reorganize the town, agreeably to the laws of that province. This change, however, does not appear to have been followed by any material alteration of their internal polity, or to have been productive of any great civil discord, till about the time of the opening of the American revolution; when the town became the prey of contending factions, of so fierce and lawless a character as to convert this once Arcadian abode of virtue, simplicity, and rural happiness, into a theatre of violence and social disorganization, which never, perhaps, found a parallel within the limits of order-loving New England. Sometimes the York party and tories, — for, in this town, it so happened that the two were identical, — and sometimes the whigs and friends of the new state of Vermont, were in the ascendant; while scenes of such disorder and outrage were constantly occurring between the belligerent parties, that his honor, Judge Lynch, for many years, appears to have been not the least among the potentates of this notable republic. Nor was order restored to the ill-starred town till after the close of the war; when every refractory spirit, whether tory or Yorker, was punished or awed into submission by the fiery energy of the iron-heeled Ethan Allen, who, then being relieved from the pursuit of more important game, came

:hundering down upon the town with his hundred Green Mountain Boys, proclaiming to the disaffected, with demonstrations which they well knew how to interpret, that the peaceable and instant submission of the place to the new authorities of the land should alone save it from being " *made as desolate as the cities of Sodom and Gomorrah.*"

It was a dark and gloomy day in April, and the sleety storm was beating, in fitful gusts, against the broken and creaking casements, and the disjointed, loose, and leaky covering of an old, dilapidated log-house, standing by the road-side, in one of the thousand little dales, which, with their corresponding hills, so beautifully diversify the face of the town we have been describing. But as comfortless as this miserable hut was, and as poor and insufficient a protection from the elements as it afforded, even for the healthy and robust, it was now the only shelter of a sick and destitute woman, the widowed mother of Harry Woodburn. The hand of her son's persecutor, as it not unfrequently is seen to occur in the history of human oppression, was destined to fall even more heavily on her than on him for whom the blow was designed. The minion officer, selected by Peters for the purpose, had no sooner received his warrants, than, faithful to the cruel instructions of his employer, he had repaired post-haste to the residence of the absent Woodburn, of which he was authorized to take possession, and, with insults and abuse, rudely thrust the lone and unprotected occupant out of doors, in despite of all her entreaties for mercy, or delay till her son should return, or even for one day, to give her an opportunity to find some shelter for her now houseless head. He then, with the aid of the three or four ruffian assistants enlisted to accompany him, threw all the furniture out of the windows or doors into the mud and snow beneath where the whole, consisting of crockery and glasses, now half broken by the fall, and beds, linen, kettles, chairs, tables, and the like, soon lay piled promiscuously together. Having thus driven the terrified and distressed woman from the comfortable abode which had formerly cost her and her deceased husband so many years of toil to erect and furnish, and having, to add to the wrong, either injured or destroyed the greater part of her little stock of goods, by the wanton or careless manner in which they had been removed, this brutal officer next proceeded to the barn, and by virtue of his *capias* for costs, seized the cow and oxen, the last remaining property of the wronged and ruined young man, which, after intrusting the present keeping and defence of the premises to two of his band, he drove away to another part of the town, to be sold at the post, as soon as the forms of the law, respecting notice of the sale, could be complied with. The poor widow, half distracted at being thus suddenly bereft of house and home, spent the remainder of the day in vainly endeavoring to procure some tenement into which she could remove with her furniture, or with so much of it as might yet be saved. On the next day, however, as a last resort, she obtained and accepted the present use of the deserted cabin we have described, situated but a short distance from the house from which she had been ejected. And into this comfortless place, after several days of incessant toil and exposure, she succeeded in getting her damaged furniture, but not till her exertions, combined with her anxieties and grief, had given rise to a malady which, though not at first very threatening, became, each subsequent day, more and more alarmingly developed in her overtasked system. In this situation she was found by her son, who, being entirely ignorant that any judgment had passed against him, and, consequently, little dreaming what was taking place at home, had remained at Westminster nearly a week after the massacre, attending the public meetings, which, as we have before intimated, followed that event; when he returned to Guilford, and, with feelings bordering on desperation, learned the extent of his misfortunes. But the bitterness of his feelings, as great as it was, at being stripped of all his property through such a series of wrongs, soon became wholly merged in anxiety and grief for his sick and sorrow-stricken parent, and in the exasperating thought that her sickness and suffering proceeded from the same source with his other injuries. And close and unremitting had been his attentions to her, until the day previous to the one on which we have introduced her to the reader; when he had been induced to leave for Brattleborough, or other more distant towns, to try to obtain money to redeem his stock, which was now about to be sold, and which was worth more than double the amount, as he had recently ascertained, of the execution on which it had been seized. On the morning after his departure, she had become so much worse that she was compelled to take to her bed, and despatch her only attendant for a doctor. That attendant was Barty Burt, who had come down from Westminster with Woodburn, and had been engaged by the latter to remain with his mother during his absence. Having thus glanced over the events which had occurred previously to the opening of this new scene of our story, we will now return to the point we left to make the digression.

Slowly, to the suffering invalid, rolled the sad hours away, as with thick and labored breathing, she lay tossing upon her rude couch, standing behind a blanket-screen, in one corner of her cheerless abode. Occasionally she would raise her fevered head from the pillow, and seem to listen to catch the sounds of expected footsteps, and her languid eye would turn anxiously towards the door; when, after thus exerting her senses in vain a few moments, she would sink back upon her bed, with a long-drawn, sighing groan, which told alike of disappointment and bodily anguish. At length, however, footsteps were heard approaching, the door opened, and Barty Burt stilly glided into the apartment, and approached the bedside of the sufferer.

"You have come at last, then," said she, lifting her dim eyes to meet the face of the other. "It seemed as if you never would arrive. But where is the doctor?"

"He will be on afore long, mistress; but I've had a time on't in getting round, I tell ye!" replied Bart.

"I am very sorry, if you have had any unexpected trouble on my account," meekly observed the invalid; "but what has befallen you?"

"O, nothin," answered the former — "nothin, at least, but what I was willing to bear for Harry's sake, who invited me home here till I got business, or for yours, who let me be. Though to be stopped and bothered, when one is going for the doctor, is worse than I ever thought of humans before. But it shows their character — dum 'em!"

"Did they really stop you, knowing your errand?"

"Yes, that they did, mistress. As I was going by the tavern, a mile or two up the road yonder, three or four of them torified Yorkers came out, and told me I couldn't go for the doctor, nor nowhere else, without a pass from one of their committee. So I had to post back more than half way, to Squire Ashcrafts, and there had to be questioned a long while before he would give me any pass at all. And then again, when I got to the doctor's, he said he wanted a pass, too; for he darsent go to see a whig woman without one, which I must go and get him from Squire Evans, another committee man. Well, finding there was no other way to get him started, I went, feeling all the time just between crying and fighting. And as soon as I got the bit of paper into the doctor's hands, I put for home, leaving him fixing to come horseback, which is the reason of my getting here first."

"These are, indeed dreadful times," sighed the widow. "But they cannot always remain; for, though God may chastise us n while for our sins, yet the rods of the oppressors will surely be broken."

"I'd rather see their necks broken," responded Bart, dryly "When we left Westminster, I thought, as much as co ld be, the tories were all used up; but I find 'em down here thicker than ever now, and as sarcy and spiteful as a nest of yellow jackets that, like them, have been routed in one place and got fixed in another. Blast their picturs, how I hate 'em!"

"That is not right, Barty. You should love your enemies. Evil wishes, towards those who injure us, are both wicked and foolish."

"I don't understand, mistress."

"Why, Barty, to love is to be happy, as far as circumstances will permit; and to hate is but to feel disquieted and miserable. So when we keep the command to love our enemies, we obtain a reward which often outbalances the evil they inflict on us, or, at least, enables us the better to bear it; while, on the contrary, when we hate those who injure us, we receive a double evil— the wrong they inflict, and the unhappiness created by the ex-ercise of our revengeful passions. Did you ever think of that, Barty?"

"No, mum; Harry talks kinder that way, sometimes; but I can't understand it, no how."

"With your means of moral instruction, perhaps it is not sur-prising that you should ot; so I will drop the subject, and ask you if you heard any thing of Harry, while you were gone."

"No, mistress; didn't see nobody that knew he was gone."

"O, when will he return? He has now been gone two long, long days; but I must not repine."

"Why, mistress, I kinder guess he'll be along to-night, unless so be he's met with considerable bother to get the money, or somethin. He must be here afore to-morrow afternoon, when the sale is, you know."

"Yes, I knew the sale was delayed till town meeting day, which is to-morrow, I believe; though for what reason they put t off I never heard. Harry felt so bitter about the affair, that I thought I would not disturb his feelings by making any allusions to the subject. But there appeared to be something about it tha, I didn't understand. Why didn't the sale take place last week, as first appointed?"

"For as good a reason as ever a tory officer had for doing any thing — or not doing any thing, may be, I should say — in the world," replied Bart with a knowing look.

" What was it ? "

" Why, when the day come, he couldn't find any cattle to sell.'

" What had become of them ? "

" Well, mistress, I don't know how much it is best to say about that, considering. But I shouldn't be surprised," continued the speaker, while a sly, roguish expression stole over his usually grave, impenetrable countenance, " that is, not much surprised, if it turned out that two or three of Harry's friends got the cattle out of the barn where they were keeping, one dark night, and driv 'em off into the woods, near the top of Governor's Mountain, and then backed up hay enough to keep 'em a spell ; while the company took turns, for a few days, in going a hunting over the mountain, so as to come round, once in a while, to fodder and see to the creters, for which old Bug-Horn paid in milk, on the spot. Now, mind, I haven't said I *knew* this was so, but was only kinder guessing at it ; for all that's really known about it — that is, out loud — is, that Fitch and his men found the cattle up there ; and the way they found them was by following up the trail made by the hay straws that some one, after a while, grew careless enough to scatter from his back-load along the path."

" Did my son have any hand in this affair ? " asked the widow, anxiously.

" No, mistress ; Harry is so kinder notional about some things, that we thought — that is, I guess some thought — it wasn't best to say any thing to him about the plan till his cattle were fairly saved."

" I am glad to hear it. I should rather see him deprived of his last penny than do a questionable act. We should never do wrong because others have done wrong to us."

" There is a differ between your think and mine, I see, mistress. If they did wrong in getting away Harry's cattle so, as every body knows they did, then the tother of that — getting them back again — must be right. But you needn't tell any body what I've said, mistress ; for they might, perhaps, have Bill Piper and me up, and try to make barglary out of it — or simony, I don't know but the law folks would call it — the breaking into a log-barn. But hush ! Somebody's coming. It is the doctor."

Doctor Soper, who now entered, was a small, pug-nosed, hubby man, of ostentatious manners, and high pretensions to skill and knowledge in his profession ; though, in fact, he was but a quack, and of that most dangerous class, too, who dip into books rather to acquire learned terms than to study principles. and who, consequently, as often as otherwise, are found " doctor-

.ng to a name," which chance has suggested, but which has little connection with the case which is engaging their attention.

"Ah, how do you find yourself, madam?" said the doctor, throwing off his dripping overcoat, and drawing up a chair towards the head of the patient's bed.

"Very ill, doctor," replied the other. "Not so much on ac count of the loss of strength, as yet, as the deeply-seated pain in the chest, which, for the last twenty-four hours, has caused me great suffering ; though, for the last half hour, not so severe."

"Indeed, madam! Well, now for the *diagnosis* of your disease. I pride myself on *diagnostics.* Your wrist, madam, if you please," said the doctor, proceeding to feel the pulse of his patient, with an air intended for a very professional one. "Tense — frequent — this pulse of yours, madam ; showing great irritability. Your tongue, now. Ay — rubric — dry and streaked ; usual *prognostics* of neuralgy. Pretty much made up my mind about your complaint coming along, madam, having learned from your lad here something of your troubles and fright on losing your home. And I was right, I see. It is *neuralgy* — decidedly a *neuralgy.*"

"What is that, doctor?"

"Always happy to explain, madam, so as to bring my meaning within the comprehension of common minds. *Neuralgy.* madam, is a derangement of the nerves. Your disease, precisely."

"Why, I am not at all nervous, sir," responded the patient, looking up in surprise.

"You may not think so, madam. Few do, in your case."

"And then, doctor, I have an intense inward fever," persisted the other, "and my lungs seem much affected."

"Nervous fever, madam," returned the doctor, too wise to be instructed, "and lungs sympathetically affected — that's all. Quiet and strengthen the nerves, and all will be right in a short time. I shall prescribe *Radix Rhei*, in small doses, *assafœtida*, *quinine*, and brandy bitters of my own preparing. These, with nourishing food, as soon as you can bear it, will speedily restore you, madam."

Having dealt out the prescribed medicines, calculated rather to increase than check the poor woman's malady, which was inflammation of the lungs, the self-satisfied doctor, swelling with his own importance, departed, leaving his patient now to contend with two evils, instead of one — a dangerous disease, and the more dangerous effects of a quack's prescription.

" What time is it now, Barty ? " asked the invalid, with a deep
sigh, as she awoke from a troubled slumber, into which she had
fallen after the doctor's departure.

" Why, don't know exactly, mistress," answered Bart, rousing
himself from the dreamy abstraction in which he had been indulging, as he sat looking into the decaying fire — " don't know,
exactly ; but it has got a considerable piece into the night. About
nine o'clock, guess ; may be more."

" Nine o'clock at night, and Harry not yet returned ! " sighed
the invalid. " Well, well, I will complain no more."

" Can I do any thing for you, mistress ? " asked her untutored
attendant, touched at the sad and despondent tone of the other.

" You may bring me in a pitcher of fresh, cold water, with
some ice in it, if you will, Barty," replied the former. " It seems
to me as if this inward heat was consuming my vitals, since I
took the doctor's medicines."

The youth, with noiseless step, then disappeared with his
pitcher, and, in a few moments, returned with it filled with water
and several pieces of clear, pure ice, which were heard dashing
against its sides.

" How grateful ! " said the sick woman, as she took from her
lips the wooden cup which had been filled and handed her by her
attendant, and from which she had eagerly drained nearly a pint
of the cooling beverage at a single draught. " There, now, set
the pitcher on the table yonder, and raise the largest piece of ice
up in sight, so, as I lie here, I can look at it. The mere sight
of it seems to do me good."

Another dreary hour rolled away in silence, which was broken
only by the restless motions and occasional suppressed groans
of the invalid within, and the wailing of the winds and the pattering of the rain against the windows without, when a slow,
heavy step was heard coming up to the house.

" That is he — that is his step ! " faintly exclaimed the sick
woman, partially raising herself in bed, and gazing eagerly
towards the door ; while her pain-contracted features were, for
the moment, smoothed by the smile of affection and pleasure that
now broke over them, like the faint electric illumining of a weeping cloud.

The quick ears of the afflicted mother had not deceived her.
The next instant Harry Woodburn entered the room, and, with a
gloomy, abstracted air, proceeded to divest himself of his wet
coat and muddy boots, without uttering a word, or bestowing any
thing more than a casual glance towards the bed, to which he

supposed his mother had just retired, as was usual with her, about this hour, and not suspecting that she was more indisposed than when he left her. But as he now turned and approached the fire, his eyes fell, for the first time, on her haggard features when, stopping short, with a look of surprise and lively concern, he exclaimed, —

"Mother! are you worse, mother?"

"Yes, Harry, I am very, very sick; and O, how glad I am that you are come."

For several moments he said nothing, but stood gazing at her with the distressed and stupefied air of one struggling to shut out painful apprehensions. At length, however, he aroused himself, and made a few hasty inquiries relative to her disorder, and what had been done for her; and, having been informed of all that had occurred in his absence, and now appearing fully to comprehend the danger of her situation, he sat down by her bedside, when his lip soon began to quiver, and his strong bosom heave with tumultuous emotions, while bitter tears flowed down his manly cheeks, as this crowning blow to his misfortunes was brought home to his feelings.

"Had they been content," he said, struggling hard, but vainly, to master his feelings — "had they but been content with robbing me of my property, I could have borne it; but to be the means, also, of murdering my only parent, is more than I can endure. God help me, or I shall go mad!"

"Do not — do not be so distressed, my son," said the mother, deeply touched at this exhibition of feeling, accompanied as it was with such a proof of filial affection in her idolized son, and anxious to soothe and divert his mind. "I shall recover, if God wills it. Let us, then, bow in resignation to his dispensations, and not disturb our feelings with unavailing regrets. Come, my dear son, cheer up, and tell me how you have succeeded in the object of your journey."

"No success," he replied, gloomily. "No; I have been running from town to town since yesterday morning, and have not been able to obtain a single dollar. So the cattle must go to satisfy the stolen judgment of that insatiable Peters."

At this moment the conversation was arrested by a low rap at the door, when, after the customary *walk in* had been pronounced by Woodburn, the door was gently opened, and a tall robust young man, with a frank, open countenance, hesitatingly entered.

"Good evening, folks," he said, in a suppressed tone.

didn't exactly know what to do about calling to-night, o. account of disturbing your mother, Harry; but wishing to know whether you had got home, and hear the news if you had, I thought I would venture to rap. What is going on up country?"

"Nothing very new, I believe, Mr. Piper."

"Well, what luck about the money, Harry?"

"None — none whatever."

"I am sorry for that. No, I won't lie, now; I am not sorry, Harry; and I will tell you why, hereafter. All I wanted to know to-night was, whether you had got the wherewith to redeem the cattle, to-morrow being the last chance for doing it, you know."

"Yes, I was aware of it, friend Piper; and many thanks for the interest you take in my misfortunes. But I cannot redeem he stock. It must go: nothing more can be done to save it."

"Well, I don't quite know about that, Harry. I don't know about standing by, and seeing a neighbor's property snatched away from him on such smuggled papers. But let that turn as it may, the subject brings to mind a certain circumstance, which I will name, after first asking a question; and that is, whether Peters has not been hung?"

"Peters hung? Why, no; the prisoners are not to be tried till the new court we have been appointing at Westminster holds its first session, some weeks hence. But why do you ask so strange a question?"

"Well, Harry, by way of answer, I will tell you the circumstance I alluded to, which was this: Last night, as I was crossing about town drumming up friends to attend the meeting to-morrow, seeing we are expecting a hard tussle, I met a man that I could have sworn was John Peters, if I had not known the fellow was close in Northampton jail; and as it was, I could swear it was his exact shape and appearance. Well, knowing it could not be him bodily, it soon struck me that they had been hanging off a parcel of them there, Peters among the rest, and that this was his ghost, kinder hovering about here to see if his affairs were fixed up to his liking."

"Your notion of a ghost, Piper, if you are serious about it, is all nonsense," said Woodburn, who had listened with lively interest to the singular story of the other. "Yes, that is nonsense; but it has brought to mind a rumor which reached Brattleborough yesterday, that all the prisoners at Northampton had been liberated by *habeas corpus* from the chief justice of New York, and were now at large. Although this was not credited, yet, if you saw Peters here last night, as I begin to fear, the story must have been true. And he appears here, at this time, for the double purpose of seeing, as you said, whether his orders have been carried into execution, and of being present to use his corrupting influence at town meeting to-morrow."

" Well, Harry, that's about what I meant; for I saw him sure enough, and knew, at once, that we had got to have him against us at town meeting, which makes our case rather doubtful. We felt quite sure, before this, of being able to carry a majority; and in that case, some of us counted on getting a vote to rescue your cattle, or, at least, putting them into the hands of our sheriff. * And either of these ways would be the means, we thought, of saving your property, and, at the same time, be a plaguy sight more lawful than any authority they have for selling them. But now there's no saying how it will go. I expect hot work there to-morrow; and that minds me to ask if you heard whether help from the towns up the river is coming down to join us on the occasion ? "

" Yes, Tom Dunning came down with me, and he informed me that several others were on the way."

" Good. Tom himself, in matter of managing, will be almost a match for Peters, whether ghost or no ghost. But where is he ? "

" He stopped back at the *Liberty Pole* tavern."

" All happens right, then. I am bound there myself. We are going to hold a little meeting at the Pole, after folks are to bed, to make up our plans and arrangements for to-morrow. You can't go, I suppose."

" No, I must not think of it."

" But you will be at town meeting to-morrow ? "

" Quite uncertain. In the first place, I ought not to leave my sick mother; and in the next, my feelings are in such a state of bitterness, that I dare hardly trust myself in such a scene, lest I should do that which would cost me months of painful regret. No, Piper, in mercy to a desperate man, let me keep away. But here is Bart to go, if he choose, both to-night and to-morrow."

" Bart is agreeable to that, if Harry and mistress don't want him," said the person just named, rousing up from the long-silent

---

* During the period of anarchy, change, and discord, in this distracted town, each of the belligerent parties had their sheriff, or constable, and other town officers, and would yield obedience to the officers of their opponents only on compulsion, though the officers of the majority were not generally resisted, except, perhaps, in matters purely political.

reverie in which he had been sitting before the fire apparently inattentive to the conversation of the others, which had been carried on in a low tone, at the opposite side of the room. "So here goes for the Pole to-night, and meeting to-morrow," he added, taking down his gun from the pegs on which it was suspended, near the ceiling above.

"What do you want to do with that, Bart?" asked Woodburn.

"I want it for lining to my coat," replied Bart. "If our coats had all been lined in that fashion, the first night there, at Westminster, we needn't have had to attend French's funeral, nor you been troubled about the papers they got out when you was in jail."

"Bravo, Bart. You see that my coat is not wanting of that kind of lining, don't you?" said Piper, throwing open his greatcoat and displaying a rifle, as the two now left the house together, on their way to the rendezvous of the liberty party.

CHAPTER X.

" Hurrah for Vermont ! hurrah for the new state of Vermont !
The victory is won, and the town is redeemed ! hurrah ! hurrah !"
Such were the sounds that rose and rung among the rafters of
the crowded old log Town House of Guilford, as, for the first
time for several years, a New Statesman and whig moderator was
declared elected by a majority of the suffrages of the freemen.
The next moment, the door was seen vomiting forth its throng of
excited victors, who, as they reached the open air, joined the
crowd eagerly awaiting the result at the entrance, and, with them,
renewed and reiterated the glad shout, till the distant hills responded in loud echoes to the roar of the stentorian voices of the triumphant party.

After a fortnight's active exertions on the part of each of the
opposing parties, in mustering and drilling their respective forces,
preparatory to the approaching contest, in which both were equally
confident of victory, though too sensible of the danger of losing
it to remit any effort, the voters had assembled at one o'clock in
the afternoon. After spending several hours in a disorderly and
wrangling debate, in relation to the qualification of voters, which
at last resulted in rejecting the test required by the charter, — that
of being a freeholder, — and in permitting every resident to vote, the
ballots had been taken for moderator, or chairman of the meeting,
when, as much to the dismay of the tories as the joy of their opponents, it was found that victory, in a majority of three, had
declared for the latter, who thereupon testified their exultation in
the uproarious manner we have described.

After a while, the noise and tumult within the house was sud
denly hushed, and the clear, deliberate tones of some new speaker
addressing the assembly, became audible to those without the
building ; while the attent and eager looks of those who stood lis
tening in the crowded pass-way, plainly evinced that some impor
tant and exciting subject had been introduced. At length the
voice ceased, and a new commotion ensued within.

" What new movement is that ? what is going on in there now,

Piper?" asked one standing near the door, as .ne young man came elbowing his way out of the house.

"Why, they are on Colonel Carpenter's resolution. Haven't none of you here been in there to hear it?" said Piper, turning to the querist and other political associates, standing near by.

"No; what is it about?" inquired several of the latter, with interest.

"The York Rule," answered Piper, with an animated air. "The colonel offered a resolve that we shake off the York government now, henceforth and forever. And this he backed with a speech which would have done you good to hear. He went into them, I tell you, like a thousand of brick; and not a single tory tongue of 'em all dare wag in trying to answer it. They are now beginning to vote on the resolution, which, if carried, the colonel intends to follow up by another, cutting up all British authority root and branch."

At this moment, they were joined by Tom Dunning, who came hurrying out of the house, and, taking Piper aside, said, —

"Do you ditter understand the plan of what's going on there, Piper, and the importance to you here, in Guilford, of carrying it?"

"Not fully, perhaps," answered Piper. "I didn't have a chance to talk with Carpenter and the other committee before this move was made, and don't understand why they did not urge on the election of the other town officers, as usual, after making a moderator, instead of getting up these resolutions."

"Der well, this is it; they are afraid to ditter try any of the town officers on so slim a majority, lest the tory candidates should have got some of our voters under their thumbs, by way of debts or other obligations, which they will der make use of to get their votes for them personally, but won't have 'em pledged for this."

"That is well thought of," responded Piper. "They have indeed got the screws on some I know of, and would so threaten 'em with prosecutions, that I'm fearful they would get 'em, sure enough. But what's the prospect about the resolutions?"

"Well, the colonel thinks, after what has ditter taken place at Westminster, that we can carry them; and if we can, it will pretty effectually tie 'em up, even if they got their officers. But we der don't mean to let 'em. For the plan is, that as soon as we've ditter carried the resolves, to dissolve the meeting without making any town officers at all, which we think can be carried by the same voters, and which if we can ditter

do it, with the resolves, will kill Fitch and his papers as dead as
a ditter dum smelt, and so save the property of Harry, and that
of all others in the same der situation."

"Good!" exclaimed Piper, with animation; "I see through
the move now; and we'll go at 'em, and whip 'em out on it; and
then if Fitch don't give up the cattle, we'll make him, by the
course we thought of taking, last night, in case we failed electing
our officers to-day, or of getting any vote on Harry's affair."

"Yes; but we must be ditter lively in getting in the voters
You and Bart go in and vote; and I will beat about the bush,
here, for more help, before I go in; for as they have just admitted
some to vote on a twenty hours' residence, — as I can ditter
swear they did, — I intend to vote myself, this time, and have all
those from my way der do the same," said the hunter, bustling
off to muster his forces.

Just as Dunning, who had collected a band of voters, without
much regard to their qualifications, was pushing into the house
at the head of his recruits, an outcry was raised within; and, the
next moment, Bart Burt was seen hastily emerging from the
crowd, followed by the kicks and cudgel-blows of the tories,
through whom he had been compelled, to save himself from a
rougher handling, to run the gauntlet to the door.

"What, in the name of der Tophet, is the meaning of that
ditter treatment, ye shameless lubbers?" sternly demanded the
hunter, shaking his stout beech cane over the heads of the fore
most of his opponents.

"He deserves it! He is an impostor! He tried to get in his
vote when he aint over eighteen years old!" shouted several
tory voices in reply.

"They let me vote last time without a word," said Bart, facing
round upon his foes, with a grin of spite and pain; "and so they
did John Stubbs and Jo Snelling, then and now too; and they
aint a day older than I be."

"Then we will der have you in, and vote too, if the ditter
divil stands at the door!" fiercely exclaimed the hunter.

"Let them prove he aint one and twenty," said one of the
same party. "He wasn't born in these parts, nor does he know
himself, I understand, where he was born, or how old he is; and
until they can prove him under age, I motion, blow high or blow
low, that we make them receive his vote."

"Aye, he shall vote! he shall vote!" shouted a dozen others. "They have admitted others under age, and they shall him,
whether or no! Let them live up to their own rules! Sauce for

goose is sauce for gander, the world over; they shall take him. they shall take him!"

A hasty consultation was now held, and a plan of operations for compelling the opposite party to admit Bart to the polls was soon digested. And, in pursuance of this plan, Bart, who was short and light of weight, was mounted astride the brawny shoulders of Dunning, while Piper, with his burly frame, was placed in front, with a stiff cudgel in hand, to act as the battering-ram or entering wedge to the crowd of tories, who had closed up the way with their bodies, obviously to prevent Bart, or any other whig, indeed, from again entering till the ballot-box was turned. Eight or ten stout, resolute young men were then selected and formed in column to bring up the rear, and give such an impetus to those before them as to force them forward in spite of all opposing obstacles, till they reached the voters' stand in the house.

"Ditter ready, boys?" now cried Dunning, firmly grasping Bart's legs, and glancing over his shoulders to his lusty little band of backers. "All ready there, behind, boys? Then go ahead, as if ditter Belzebub kicked ye an end!"

At the word, Piper, gathering himself up like a ram for a butting match, made a lunge head foremost into the recoiling ranks of the tories, and, borne irresistibly forward by the force of the rushing phalanx behind, overthrew, prostrated, and shoved aside, all before him, till the whole column gained the interior, and came to a halt before the ballot-box.

"I protest against that fellow's voting!" exclaimed Peters, approaching the stand as Bart, from his lofty seat on Dunning's shoulders, was about to put in his vote, which was a simple *yea*, written on a slip of paper, and handed up to him by some one stationed near the box to furnish the unsupplied. "I protest against such a glaring outrage! He is under age, and was very properly driven from the house."

"Prove it! prove it!" shouted several of Bart's friends.

"You can't do it," cried another, "and if you could, two of your party, who are under age, have voted already; 'tis a fact: deny it if you can!"

"In with it, Bart!" said Dunning, bending down to give the other a chance.

"Yes, in with it; for he shall vote!" responded the rest.

"He shall not vote!" vociferated Peters; "and if he attempts to do it; I'll blow his brains out!" he added, pulling out and levelling a pistol. Quick as thought, Bart threw open his over-coat, and, drawing from beneath it the light short gun there concealed, cocked, and brought it to his shoulder; while the threatening weapon of his foe was seen flying to a distant part of the room, from a sudden blow of Piper's cudgel, and its disarmed and nonplused owner slinking away out of the range of the suspicious-looking barrel still kept aimed at his head.

Amidst the loud cries of order, and the heated vociferations of both parties, now raised to condemn or defend the transaction, through the house, Bart, Dunning, and others of their company, who had not voted, now hastily deposited their votes, and retired unmolested.

Although the portion of the revolutionary party, whose movements we have been more particularly describing, acting on the supposed and probably actual frauds of their opponents, had thus secured Bart's vote. and the votes of two or three others, perhaps equally illegal, yet the event soon showed that their policy in so doing was a mistaken one, and calculated to defeat the very object they intended to promote; for, as will always be the result where one party attempts to adopt the wrongful measures of their opponents, the tories, now armed with the fact that they had detected the other party in a wrong more glaring, because more public, than any they had perpetrated, made use of the advantage with such effect as to bring over several, intending to support the resolutions, to change their intention, and go against them. And, in addition to this, by way of retaliating, and of making good at least all the ground lost by the questionable votes forced upon them, they brought forward every minor they could find approximating the size of a man, and boldly demanded their admittance to the polls. An opposition was, indeed, attempted to a measure so manifestly illegal, by the leaders of the other party; but they had become too much disarmed by the acts of their own partisans to produce any sensible effect; and their voices were soon drowned by the clamors of the tories, who now admitted the boys by acclamation. This, as will be anticipated, decided the contest. On counting the votes, the resolution was found to have been rejected by more than a dozen majority — a victory which the tories failed not to announce by shouts of exultation, which out-thundered those of their opponents in their late short-lived triumph. The friends of freedom, being thus caught in their own trap, or, at least, worsted by the indiscretion of their own friends, now pretty much yielded the contest: while the victorious Yorkers and tories had everything in their own way, electing their town officers, passing denunciatory and royal resolutions, and continuing their discussions unopposed till

11

It was nearly dark, when the meeting broke up in noisy confusion.

"Oyez! Oyez! Oyez!" was now heard crying the well-known voice of Constable Fitch, as he mounted a stump in the yard; while near by stood a gang of his confederates, hedging in Woodburn's cow and oxen, which the former had found the means to have on the spot, in readiness for the sale, the moment the assembly broke up. "Oyez! A cow and oxen, taken on execution, now about to be sold to the highest bidder, gentlemen. We will take the oxen first; as fine a yoke as ever drew plough Who will give us the first bid? Shan't dwell three minutes. Who bids, I say? One pound bid, gentlemen; one pound ten! one pound ten! and on Mr. Peters. Who bids higher?"

But, as rapid as had been the constable's movements, he did not, as he intended, take the friends of Woodburn by surprise. They had withdrawn from the meeting a short time before it dissolved, and met for consultation in the rear of the house, where, having arranged their plan of operations, they stood awaiting for the proper time to carry it into execution.

"There!" exclaimed Dunning, as the constable began to cry the sale in the manner we have just described — "there, that is ditter Fitch; he is at it! All ready, boys? You, Piper and Bart, with your vials of oil of vitriol in your sleeves, ready to uncork on to their ditter tails?"

"Ay, ay!"

"And your ditter snuff to throw into their eyes?"

"Yes, that, too."

"And your guns ditter cocked, and safe under your coats you that are to fire?"

"Ay, all right and ready — lead on!"

"Der well, but remember we ditter separate here, so as to come up on different sides of the crowd; and mind, don't let off your guns till the creatures begin to ditter grow uneasy and der snort and blow."

While Fitch was repeating the bids he had received for the oxen, and was about to knock them off to the highest bidder, which still chanced to be Peters, he was suddenly told to hold on, by several persons who had just at that moment made their appearance in different parts of the crowd, and who expressed their wish to bid, as soon as they could get up to examine the cattle. Owing to the duskiness, the faces of the new comers did not seem to be recognized by the tories, who unsuspectingly opened and admitted them to the stand. Quickly availing them selves of the opportunity, the former, among the foremost of whom were Piper and Bart, now crowded eagerly round the cattle, and, after rapidly passing their hands over the cow and each of the oxen a moment, and then stepping back, began to banter and bid. Not much time, however, was allowed them to do either; for the cattle, all at once, became unaccountably restless, at first backing and wheeling about in their confined space, and then wildly tossing up their heads, snuffing, and assuming the startled and furious appearance generally exhibited by this class of animals when about to make a desperate effort to break away.

At this critical juncture, the fierce flashes and stunning reports of a half dozen muskets burst over the heads of the startled and astonished company from various points on the outer edge of the crowd ; and the next instant the already maddened cattle, with loud snorts, leaping over or trampling down all in their way, broke through the living hedge of tories around them, and bounded off, with their tails thrown aloft, and bellowing in wild affright, in different directions, towards the woods, leaving the amazed and broken crowd jostling and pitching about with exclamations of surprise, groans of pain, volleys of oaths, and shouts of laughter, all mingled in Babel-like confusion.

" 'Tis all the work of the cursed rebels ! " exclaimed Peters, the first to rally and comprehend the affair. " Fitch ! " he added, pointing after the runaway cattle, " where the devil are your wits, that you don't order a pursuit ? "

" Yes, pursue and bring 'em back, instantly ! " screamed the constable, awaking from the stupor and confusion of ideas into which he seemed to have been thrown by the strange and unexpected occurrence. " Yes, 'tis an unlawful rescue — it's a conspiracy ! bring back the cattle ! seize the offenders, every one of 'em ! in the king's name I command ye."

Obedient to the call, the obsequious tories instantly rallied for the pursuit, and, breaking off into three distinct bands, eagerly set forward in the different directions taken by the fugitive cattle, then just disappearing over the distant swells, or in the borders of the woods. Dunning, Piper and Bart, who, in the mean while, had, unknown and unsuspected in the darkness and confusion, stood in the throng, keenly watching the result of their plan, no sooner heard the expected order of pursuit given, than, separating, like their opponents, and each joining a different band of the pursuers, they sprang in before the rest, and, by their superior alacrity and speed, soon succeeded in taking the lead and finally in completely distancing all others in the promiscuous chase. The tories, now soon wholly losing sight of their fleet and, as they still supposed, trusty guides in the pursuit, became, in a short time, confused and at fault respecting the courses to be taken; and, after hallooing and running about the woods and pastures at random, nearly an hour, without discovering any traces either of the lost cattle or the missing pursuers, at length came straggling back to the Town House, and, by way of saving their own credit, reported to Fitch, Peters, and the small party remaining there, that their swiftest runners were last seen nearly up with the cattle, and would soon be in with them, or that the creatures had been headed, and were on their way back, in another direction. On this, the company waited another hour; when, neither the cattle nor the expected pursuers appearing, they began to suspect something amiss; and the inquiries and investigations then put afoot soon resulted in the mortifying conviction, that the cattle had been overtaken and driven off by the same persons who previously had caused them to break away. Prompted by the enraged Peters, Fitch then offered a reward for the recovery of the cattle and the detection of those who had abducted them; when the company separated, to resume the search the next day. But although this was done, and the country scoured in every direction for several days, yet the search proved wholly fruitless. Not one of the cattle was to be found. Nor were the actors in the transaction, with any certainty, identified, though the absence of Piper and Bart, for some days after the event, caused them to be suspected and marked for punishment, when they should again appear abroad.

CHAPTER XI.

" Vital spark of heavenly flame!
    Quit, O quit this mortal frame!
    Trembling, hoping, lingering, flying,
    O the pain, the bliss of dying!
    Cease, fond nature! cease thy strife,
    And let me languish into life."

PERHAPS the nearest and dearest, as well as the most interesting tie of consanguity, is that existing between mother and son. Who has not witnessed the unfailing and unconquerable strength of a mother's love for the son of her heart and her vows, cleaving to its object through prosperity and through adversity, through honor and through shame, with a constancy which never wavers? And what son, especially after the thoughtlessness of youth has given place to the reflection of maturer years, and experience has taught him the insincerity and selfishness of the world — what son has not turned back and lingered, with the most grateful emotions. over the pleasing memories of a mother's care; pondered with the most heart-felt admiration over the deep, pure, and undying nature of a mother's love; realized more and more the priceless value of a sentiment so fraught with moral beauty, so exalted, so proof against all those considerations of self, those temptations of interest, before which all other ties are seen to give way, and, while thus realizing, found his yearning bosom oftener and oftener prompting him to exclaim with the poet,—

"Where'er I roam, whatever realms I see,
    My heart, untravelled, fondly turns to thee."

While the scenes of disorder and tumult we last described, and the similar ones that followed, were being enacted among the belligerent parties of this misgoverned town, the dutiful and sorrowing Woodburn was continuing his attendance on his sick mother, from whose bedside no call of business or of pleasure was suffered for a single hour to lure him. And well might he have done so, aside even from the dictates of filial duty; for she was a woman not only of unaffected piety, but of education

11 *   i

and intellect; and to her he had been mainly indebted for all
that was good and elevated in his character. She had emigrated
with her husband to this town, at an early period of its settlement,
from the vicinity of Boston, where the latter had become so much
straitened in his pecuniary circumstances, in consequence of
being surety for an improvident and luckless brother, that he
was induced, with the hope of bettering his fortunes, to gather
up the poor remnant of his property, and, with it, remove to the
New Hampshire Grant's, at that time the Eldorado most in vogue
among those seeking new countries. Here, having purchased
one of the best tracts of land in the place, he commenced the
slow and laborious process of clearing up a new farm. And this
Herculean task, which may well be considered the work of a
man's life, he had, after years of incessant toil and privation,
nearly succeeded in accomplishing, and begun to catch glimpses
of easier and brighter days; when he was taken away by disease,
leaving his property to his wife and son, an only child, then
drawing towards manhood. And nobly had that son discharged
the double duty which now devolved upon him, — that of becoming the stay and comforter of his widowed mother, and the
sole manager of the farm, their only dependence. For, while
discharging his filial duties in such a manner as to gain him the
reputation of being a pattern of a son, he not only kept good,
but, by his industry and enterprise, even improved, the property
to which he had thus succeeded. And he was fast surmounting
the difficulties of his situation, and making hopeful advances
towards a competence, when, in an evil hour, his flourishing
little establishment attracted the coveting eye of the unconscion-
able Peters, who, owning an adjoining farm, which would be
rendered much more salable by being united with Woodburn's,
undertook, at first, to wheedle the young man into a sale, or rather
an exchange of his valuable farm for another, or wild lands, at
false valuations and of doubtful titles. But, finding himself
wholly mistaken in the character of the person whom he thus
endeavored to overreach, and consequently failing in his attempt,
he next began to think of the quibbles of the law, as the means
of accomplishing his purpose. And having discovered some
slight irregularity in Woodburn's deed, to begin upon, he then
resorted to a trick quite fashionable among the corrupt speculators of those unsettled times — that of purchasing from some un
principled person, ready, for a small sum, to enter into the fraud,
a deed of prior date to that of the one to be defeated, with
descriptions of premises and references to suit the purchaser

the worthless assumed owner neither knowing nor caring what his deed might convey.   Having secretly procured a prior deed of Woodburn's farm in this manner, Peters could see but one obstacle now in the way of his success, which was the town records, embracing that of Woodburn's deed.   How was this to be disposed of?   A bold measure, which could be executed by his minions under political pretences, occurred to him ; and the result was, that part of the town record soon disappeared.   Peters then commenced an action against Woodburn, to eject him from his farm, the course and consequences of which are already known to the reader.

Spring had now come; but its bland and balmy breath brought no relief to the suffering widow.   From the hour she had been compelled to take to her bed, her disease, though sometimes lulled, or raging less fiercely than at other times, had never for a moment loosened its tenacious grasp.   And although her cheer-ful words, and meek, uncomplaining looks, had often misled her anxious son, or, at least, prevented him from despairing of her recovery, yet the dry, parched, red tongue, the daily return of the bright hectic spot, and the tense, hurrying and unvarying beat of the strained pulses, might have told him how certainly and rapidly the work of destruction was going on at the citadel of life, and better prepared him for the agonizing scene which was now to follow.

It was a calm and pleasant evening towards the close of April, and the low descending sun was shedding the mellow light of his parting beams over the joyful face of reanimating nature. The invalid, during all the fore part of the day, had suffered greatly from pain — that general and undefinable distress which is so frequently found to be the precursor of approaching disso-lution.   To this had succeeded a sort of lethargic sleep, from which it was not easy to arouse her, so that she could be made to take any notice of what was passing around her.   But now she awoke, clear and collected; and, glancing round the room, with a sort of pensive animation, met and answered the inquiring and solicitous look of her son with an affectionate smile.   Presently her wandering eye rested on some objects of the landscape, glimpses of which she had caught through one of the small patched windows of the room, and she faintly observed, —

"How pleasant it appears without !   Harry," she continued after a thoughtful pause, "could you take out that window before me ?   I feel a desire to look out once more on the green earth and breathe the sweet air of spring."

"Yes, mother," said the other, approaching the bed, with a surprised and hesitating air; "yes, I could easily do it, I presume; but would it be quite safe for you to be exposed to the evening air?"

"Yes, Harry; the time for the exercise of such cares is gone by. You need fear no more for me, now, my son," she replied in accents of tender sadness.

The son then, with a doubtful and troubled look, proceeded in silence to comply with the unexpected request; after which, he gently raised the head of the invalid, who, thereupon, gazed long and thoughtfully on the variegated landscape, which lay spread out in tranquil beauty beneath her dimly-kindling eye.

"How beautiful!" she at length feebly exclaimed, in a tone of melancholy rapture — "beautiful of itself, but more beautiful as the type of man's destiny after his body has mingled with the dust. The scene we here behold, my son, exhibits the resurrection of nature. In summer the foliage and blossom expands, in autumn the fruit is perfected, and in winter the visible part falls back to earth and perishes, leaving the hidden seed or germ to spring forth again into another life. So it has been, so it will be, with me. I have had my brief summer of life, my still briefer autumn, and now my winter of death is at hand, from which I trust to come forth into the more glorious spring of life eternal."

"Do not talk thus, mother," responded the son, greatly moved —"do not talk thus: you distress me. I trust you may yet recover. You certainly look brighter this evening; and I hope another day will find you still better."

"No, Harry, not better, as you mean. If I appear brighter, it is but the brightness of the last flashing up of the expiring taper. I feel that my time is come, and thanks to *Him* who has prepared my heart to hail the event as a relief and a blessing."

"O, my mother, my mother, how can I part with you?"

"My longer sojourn here, my son, would be of little benefit to others — even to you: my blessing is worth more than would be my further abiding: come and receive it."

The weeping son then knelt down at the bedside, and the mother laying her hand on his head, pronounced her blessing and a brief prayer for his earthly prosperity and eternal happiness.

For several minutes, the son, overcome by his emotions, remained kneeling, with his head, on which still languidly rested the emaciated hand of his dying mother, bowed upon the bedclothes, while the latter, sinking back exhausted on her pillow, closed her eyes, and seemed to be silently communing with herself. She soon, however, aroused herself, and observed, —

"My work is not yet quite done. I have a little more to say before the scene closes."

"Say on, mother," said the other, making an effort to calm himself, as he now rose, and, taking a seat near, wistfully rivetted his gaze on her pallid face. "If you are, indeed, about to leave me forever, withhold nothing you feel inclined to communicate ; for your dying counsels, my dear parent, will be received with pleasure and gratitude, and treasured up in heart and memory as the last, best lesson of one to whom I am under such countless obligations."

"You have ever acted the part of a dutiful son towards me, Harry ; and that is always a mother's best reward for her care and affection for her offspring. And I know not that I have aught now to say to you, by way of counsel for your future guidance, being willing to leave you to practise upon the principles I have endeavored to inculcate, and be to others what you have been to me. But it was not of that I intended to speak. I was about to name some facts connected with our early reverses, which, it being always unpleasant to recur to those scenes of trial, I think I have never told you, but which, I thought, it might, perhaps, some day avail you something to know. You have heard us casually speak, I presume, of your uncle Charles Woodburn ? "

"I have, mother."

"And you may also be aware that, through his misconduct, we were suddenly reduced from the easy competence we once enjoyed to poverty and distress."

"I have so understood it, but never knew what kind of misconduct it was that led to our misfortunes."

"It was imprudence in speculations, and profligacy in living, and not dishonesty, or any intentional wrong to us, as I ever believed ; though your father, in his desperation when the blow came, would listen to no extenuation, but drove him from his presence with bitter reproaches and accusations. But your uncle, before leaving the country, as he soon after did, sought an interview with me ; and, after deploring the misfortunes he had brought on my family as well as himself, solemnly pledged himself that he would, some day or other, more than compensate me or mine for all the losses he had occasioned us And this is the circumstance I wished to tell you ; for, though we never received any certain information of him, yet something tells me he still is alive, and has the means and disposition to fulfil his promise to you whenever you may find him, and he recognize you as the representative of his brother's family, of whose location here he probably was never apprised. I would suggest to you, therefore, the expediency of trying to trace him out, and, if you succeed in doing so, make yourself and your situation known to him; and, without preferring any claim, leave the result with Providence."

"Your suggestion, mother, shall not pass from me unheeded, nor shall I fail, in due time, to act upon it; but, at present, I know not if the last tie that binds me to this place should be severed — I know not but our down-trodden country may have the first claim on my services. Ever since the startling news of the massacre of Lexington reached us, a sense of the duty of devoting myself to her defence has pressed heavily and constantly on my mind. And but for the stronger claim which nature and my own feelings have given you, in your situation, to my presence and attention, I might, before this, have been with my shouldered musket on my way to the scene of action. But even in the event of your death, I should hesitate to obey the call if I knew I must do it without your sanction."

"I thank you, my son, for your affectionate deference; but you shall not go without my sanction. Having conjectured what might be your feelings at this dark hour of our country's peril, I was about to speak to you on the subject. Yes, Harry, if you think duty calls you to the field, in defence of a cause so just and righteous as ours, go. You will be under the care of the same Providence there as elsewhere. Go, and with a dying mother's blessing, and a prayer of faith for your safety and success, do battle manfully for the Heaven-favored side, till the oppressor be cast down, and the oppressed go free."

With a heart swelling with conflicting emotions, the young man looked up to reply, when his words were arrested on his lips, by the evident change that the countenance of the other had suddenly undergone. The unnatural animation, which she had exhibited during the conversation, had faded away. She lay listless and exhausted, with her eyes nearly closed, and her lips slightly moving in secret prayer.

"And now, Lord, what wait I for?" she at length audibly uttered. "But I am not to wait," she continued, in a firmer tone after a short pause. "The final moment is at hand! Farewell earth! farewell, my son! May Heaven's blessings rest on you — on all, and be the offences of all forgiven. Ah! the light of day

is facing; but O, that brighter light which opens those ange
forms, with smiling faces, which beckon me away! Ready! I
come!—I come!"

And thus,—

> "——— blessing and blest,
> In death she went smiling away
> To the heavenly bosom of rest."

CHAPTER XII

" Whene'er your case can be no worse
The desperate is the wiser course."

LATE in the afternoon, several days subsequent to the melancholy event described in the preceding chapter, a mingled company, of some dozens of persons, including several town officials,
were seen assembling at the Tory Tavern, in Guilford; the object
of which appearances seemed to indicate to be the holding of a
magistrates' court, to try an offender who had that morning been
arrested, and who now, in custody of Constable Fitch, was demurely sitting on a rude bench under an open window of the
room in which the trial was to be had, and in which the two justices composing the court had already seated themselves at a
table, in readiness, on their part, to commence proceedings. That
offender was no other than our humble friend, Barty Burt, who
had lucklessly fallen into one of the snares which had been set for
him and his suspected companions, round the country, in consequence of the part they had acted in spiriting away, in so strange
a manner, Woodburn's cattle, when about to be sold on town
meeting day. He and Piper, during the night following that
affair, after meeting Dunning at an appointed place, and giving
him charge of the cattle, which had been successfully pursued
and there collected, to be driven out of that part of the country
by the hunter, left town in different directions, to avoid the arrest
they anticipated, in case they remained ; Piper going down the
river in quest of some temporary employment till the storm blew
over, and Bart setting off on a fishing excursion to Marlboro' Pond,
situated in a then nearly unsettled section, about ten miles to the
north. Here Bart had pursued his sport unmolested, many days,
occasionally going out to Brattleborough to sell his fish and buy provisions, and considering himself in this secluded situation perfectly
safe from any search which might be made for him by the officers
of Guilford. But the reward offered by the constable for the apprehension of the offenders, who had been soon pretty well identified, had put all the tories in the town and vicinity on the watch
and the result was, that Bart had been seen, traced to his retreat
seized and brought back for trial.

Although Bart's general demeanor seemed to show a perfec indifference to the fate that now threatened him, yet the quick keen glances with which, under that show of indifference, he noted every movement of those into whose power he had fallen and the restlesness he exhibited when their eyes were not upor. him, gave token of no little inward perturbation. And it was not without reason that his apprehensions were excited ; he knew the character and disposition of the two tory justices whom he saw taking their seats to try him, and he rightly judged that he need not expect either mercy or justice at their hands. He had also detected one of the constable's minions, who had been despatched to the woods for the purpose, stealing slyly round into the horse-shed, on his return, with a half dozen formidable looking green beech rods ; and he was at no loss to decide for whose back they were intended, or by whose ruthless hand they were to be applied.

"You can't go that, Bart," he mentally exclaimed. "You must get away; so now put your best contrivances in motion, for I tell you it won't do for you to think of standing that pickle."

And as hopeless as, to all appearance, was any attempt to escape his captors, who stood round him with loaded pistols in their hands, Bart yet confidently counted on being able, in some way or other, to slip through their fingers, and avoid the fearful punishment which he knew was in store for him, if he remained many hours longer in their hands. To effect this, he looked for no aid from others; for experience had taught him the value of self-reliance. The whole life of this singular being, indeed, had been one which was peculiarly calculated to throw him on his own resources, sharpen his wits, and render him fertile in expedients. He had been a foundling, and knew no more of his parentage than a young ostrich, that springs from the deserted egg in the sand. He was left, when an infant, at the door of a poor mechanic, in Boston, by the name of Burt, and by him transferred to the almshouse, where he was called after the name of his finder, with the pet name of Barty, given him by his nurse. Here he was kept till he was four or five years old, when he was given to the Shakers, from whom he ran away at ten or twelve. From that time, the poor friendless boy became a wanderer through the interior country, generally remaining but a few months in a place, being driven from each successive home by misusage, or for want of profitable work for him to do, or, what was still oftener the case, perhaps, for playing off some trick to avenge the fancied or real insults he had received, till, after having been kicked about the world like a fcot-ball, cheated, abused, cowed in feeling, and become, in consequence, abject, uncouth and singular in manner and appearance, he at length reached the situation in the family of the haughty loyalist where we found him.

While Bart was thus uneasily revolving the matter of his present concern in his mind, and beginning to cast about him for some means of escape, the constable was called aside by those who had undertaken to manage the prosecution, for the purpose of holding with them a consultation, the purport of which, though carried on in a low tone, and at some distance, was soon gathered by the quick and practised ears of the prisoner. It appeared that the trial was being delayed in consequence of the absence of Peters, who was an important witness, and who unaccountably failed to make his appearance. And it being feared that he might have been waylaid, and detained on the road, by some band of the other party, to prevent him from testifying, as all knew he was anxious to do, it was settled that Fitch should start immediately in search of him to the house which he usually made his temporary quarters in another part of the town. Accordingy the constable, after putting the prisoner in charge of two stout fellows who were in his interest, with orders to guard him closely, and shoot him down the instant he should attempt to escape, set forth on his mission after Peters. Bart's countenance brightened when he saw the savage officer depart, for he believed the absence of the latter would greatly increase his chances of escape ; and in spite of all the threats he had received of being shot, he resolved to improve that absence in making the attempt, though the manner of doing so yet remained to be decided, by the circumstances which might occur.

In the mean time a trotting-match had been got up in the road in front of the tavern, by a small party who had been boasting of the speed and other qualities of their horses; and it being now understood that the trial was to be delayed till the constable' return, the whole company left the house, and went out to the road to witness the performance. Bart's keepers not being able, where they stood, to see and hear what was going on very distinctly, and being equally desirous with the rest to get a favorable stand for that purpose, after renewing the threat of shooting him, if he attempted to run away, took him along with them, and entered the line of spectators extended along the road. After a few trials among those who began the contest, several new competitors led on their horses and entered the lists. By this time most of the company began to take a lively interes in the performance, taking sides, and betting on the success of the different horses now put into the contest. The prisoner having, by this time, through dint of persevering in good humor and sociability, in return for the abusive epithets, by which all his attempts to converse were, for a while, received, succeeded, in a great measure, in disarming his keepers of the stern reserve and jealous distrust they at first exhibited towards him, he was soon permitted to talk freely, and offer, unrebuked, his opinions of the success of the various horses about to make a trial, which his previous observation and acquaintance with many of them, made during his residence in town the preceding year, enabled him to do with considerable sagacity. And his predictions being luckily fulfilled in several instances, and especially in one in which his most rigid keeper had been saved from losing, in a bet, which would have been made but for his timely cautions, Bart at length found himself on such a footing of confidence and good will with those whom he wished to conciliate, that he thought it would now do to commence operations for himself.

" I don't think much of such trotting, myself," said Bart, carelessly, as one of the contests afoot had just terminated ; " but there is one animal I notice here to-day, I should like to bet on."

" What horse is that ? " asked the keeper above designated.

" That dapple gray mare hitched over there in the corner of the cow-yard yonder," replied Bart, pointing to a small, long tailed pony, whose shabby coat of shedding and neglected hair greatly disguised the remarkable make of her limbs and other indications of strength and activity.

" That creature ! " exclaimed the other, contemptuously ; " why she aint bigger than a good-sized sheep. You may bet if you want to, and lose ; for there's not a horse on the ground but would beat her."

" Well, for all that, Mr. Sturges," responded Bart, banteringly, " I'll not take back what I've said about the nag. And to prove my earnest, I'll make you an offer ; I'll bet my gun, which you saw me hand the landlord for safe keeping when they brought me in — I'll bet my gun against your hat, I'll take that creature and out-trot you, with any hoss you may choose to bring on."

" Done ! " exclaimed Sturges ; " but you are contriving this up for a chance to get away, yo: scamp."

" What should I want to get away for ? " I haint done nothin : and there's a witness here that will swear to a thing or two for

me, when the trial comes on, guess you'll find ; besides, aint you
going to ride by my side, with a loaded pistol in your hand ? "

" Yes, and that aint all; I'll put a bullet through you the instant
you make the least move to be off."

" I'm agreed to that."

" Well, but will they let you take the colt for the march ? "

" Guess so ; I'll venture to take her.   The boy that rode her
here has cleared out down to the brook a fishing ; but I know
him, and think he wouldn't object."

" Who owns the colt ? "

" Old Turner did, last year, when I lived with him ; and the
boy is from that way, and borrowed her, likely."

" Then you have rode her, have you ? " asked Sturges, doubt
fully.

" Never rid her with any other hoss, but know she can tro
faster than any thing you can find here ; so you may as well
back out at once," answered Bart, with apparent indifference.

" Not by a jug-full, sir ; but I must look me up a horse, and fix
matters a little first ; and then, if it is thought safe for me to trust
you to ride, I'll go it," returned the other, with some hesitation.

Sturges then stepped aside with the other keeper, and, after
consulting with him a few moments, went forward and announced
to the company the bet offered by the prisoner, and his own
intention of accepting it, and indulging the fellow in a trial, if
they thought best, and would assist in measures to prevent the
possibility of his escape.   The proposal was received with shouts
of laughter by the tories ; and eager for the fun they expected to
see in so queer a contest, they agreed to be answerable for the
prisoner's safety, and urged on the performance.

The two keepers, now calling in others to take charge of the
prisoner, while they made their preparations, proceeded to arrange the company on both sides of the road, placing men at
short intervals along the whole line of the course, commencing
back about two hundred yards south of the tavern, and extending
'o the sign-post, which, standing on the edge of the beaten path
n front of the house, had been agreed on as the goal.   And not
satisfied with this precaution, they then procured four long, heavy,
spruce poles, and, extending them from fence to fence across the
enclosed road leading from the tavern yard northward, formed a
barricade five or six feet high, which, with the strong, high fences
on each side of the whole course, except at the starting-point,
where no danger was apprehended, seemed to cut off the prisoner,
even without being guarded, from all possible chance to escape

on horse back, as it was most feared he would do, after being allowed control of the reins.

"There, Bixby!" exclaimed Sturges, exultingly turning to his fellow-keeper, as they completed the barricade across the road beyond the goal — "there! I would defy the devil to jump over this barrier, or any of the fences on the way, as to that matter. So the little rebel will hardly escape us by running his horse from the ground, I fancy. But we must look out that he don't jump off at the end of the race, or before, and cut into the fields. You may therefore station yourself somewhere between this and the sign-post; and if he attempts to leap from his horse and run, as we fetch up here, shoot him down as you would a dog, and charge the blame to me or Fitch; either of us will bear it."

Having thus arranged every thing to his satisfaction, Sturges, ordering the pony we have described, and the horse he had selected for himself, to be brought on, then took charge of his prisoner and rival, and conducted him, with great show of mock dignity, and amidst a noisy and jeering troop of attendants, to the ground marked off for the place of starting, and now designated by the close line of men that had been stationed across the road to guard against the prisoner's escape in that direction. Bart, in the mean time, seemed perfectly indifferent to all these precautions of the tories, as well as the gibes and laughter which constantly greeted him on the way, and, on reaching the prescribed limit, quietly dropped down on the grass among the company, and awaited the coming of the horses with the greatest unconcern. The latter soon made their appearance on the ground, and were immediately led up and presented to their respective riders.

"Lightfoot!" exclaimed Bart, springing up to receive his chosen pony; "do you know me, Lightfoot?"

The animal instantly pricked up her ears, and responded by a sort of low, chuckling whinny, by rubbing her nose against his arm, and by other demonstrations of recognition and pleasure, which plainly showed the two to have been old acquaintances and friends. Bart then, stripping off the saddle and handing it to a boy to be carried back to the tavern, again went to the head of the pony, and, after patting her on her neck, repeated certain words in her ear, which seemed to produce the instant effect of arousing her spirit, and making her restless and impatient for a start. After going through these and other ceremonies of the kind, which seemed greatly to amuse the company, he mounted, reined up and announced himself ready for the signal.

12 *

After another delay, to indulge the company in the renewed shouts of laughter which were called forth by the ludicrous contrast now presented in the appearance of the oddly matched competitors, as the diminutive and shabby looking prisoner sat awkwardly mounted on his no less diminutive and shabby pony, by the side of the portly Sturges and his large and finely built horse, the signal was given, and the parties set forth amidst the encouraging hurrahs of the crowd. Their progress, for a while was nearly equal; and the pony, though very unskilfully managed by her seemingly raw and timid rider, continued to maintain her place by the side of the horse so fully, as to render the result of the contest extremely doubtful. But as they drew near the end of the course, and the horse, by the renewed incentives of his rider, began to gain on her, she suddenly flounced, broke into a gallop, shot by the horse, giving him a staggering kick in the chops as she passed, and, in spite of the apparent efforts of her rider, to bring her up at the goal, plunged on directly towards the fence that had been thrown across the road.

"Whoa! whoa!" cried Bart, in tones of distress and affright, still appearing to strain every nerve to hold in the ungovernable animal — "whoa! whoa! help, or I shall be thrown!"

"Help him there! stop her! seize her by the bits!" shouted Sturges, now riding up to the goal to claim the bet.

But the perverse pony, veering about among those approaching on either side to seize, or head her, with sundry monitory kicks thrown out sidewise towards them as she went, the next moment reached, and, with a tremendous leap, cleared the barricade, and landed safely with her rider in the open road on the other side. Here Bart hastily made another apparent attempt to rein her up; but rearing and spinning round on her heels, she again made a plunge forward, and set out in a keen run, making the ground smoke beneath her feet as she flew, with astonishing speed along the road; while her rider, grasping her mane with both hands, and swaying from side to side, as if hardly able to keep his seat at that, continued to bawl and screech, at every step, "Whoa! whoa! stop her! stop her!" with all his might.

The tories were so completely taken by surprise by these manœuvres, and the unexpected feat of leaping the barricade that Bart and his fleet pony were nearly a quarter of a mile off, before they sufficiently rallied from their astonishment and confusion to realize what had passed; and when they did, hearing his piteous cries for help, and expecting every moment to see him hurled headlong from his horse, they stood doubtfully looking at him and each other, several seconds longer, before they thought of following him. Sturges, however, now took the alarm, and, ordering the barricade to be thrown down, started off, with those who, like himself, happened to be mounted, n pursuit. By this time, the fugitive had passed over an intervening swell, which hid him from the view of the pursuers; and though their progress was rapid, yet, when they gained the top of the swell, which commanded a view of the road till it entered the woods, almost a half mile beyond, he was nowhere to be seen. But believing he must have gained the woods, they pushed on, in the vain pursuit, about a mile farther; when, meeting some towns-men, they ascertained that he had not passed in that direction. They then retraced their steps, carefully examining every by-path and open spot by the road-side, where any ordinary horse could be made to go; but making no discoveries, they concluded to return to the tavern for consultation; for they grew more and more puzzled to know what to make of the prisoner, or how to account for his mysterious escape, some affirming " he must have been in league with the devil, as no horse, in a natural state, could have leaped that barricade, or have gone off so like a streak of lightning after he was over it; and his strange doings with the pony, when he first met her, and the bluish appearance that attended him along the road as he went off, with such unnat-tural swiftness," were cited in confirmation. But when they reached the tavern, the prisoner, and every thing attending his escape, were for the time forgotten in the excitement occasioned by the more startling tidings just received. The constable had just arrived in great haste announcing that Peters had been way-laid, and found murdered in the road, and calling on all to turn out to arrest the unknown but suspected perpetrators of the horrid deed.

CHAPTER XIII.

———"despair itself grew strong
And vengeance fed its torch from wrong

ON the same day, and near the same hour, on which Bart so singularly and luckily effected his escape from his vindictive enemies, the bereft Woodburn left his lonely residence and walked to the graveyard, to shed another tear over the freshly-laid turf that covered the remains of his sainted mother. Here, as, standing over her grave, he reflected on the many excellences of her character, recalled the many acts of her kindness and love towards him, never before justly appreciated, and, at the same time, thought of the circumstances under which she had sickened and died, his tears flowed fast and bitterly. While he was still lingering near the sacred spot, immersed in these painful reflections, two ladies, from a neighboring cottage, came, unperceived by him, along the road leading by the graveyard; when the younger of the two, wholly unconscious that any one was within the enclosure, left the other to pass on to the next house, and entered the yard to amuse herself there till her companion returned. Now pausing to read an inscription, and now to pluck a wild violet, she slowly wandered towards that part of the yard where Woodburn, still screened from her view by a clump of intervening evergreens, was pensively reclining against a tomb stone in the vicinity of his mother's grave. And here, taking a turn round the shrubbery, she came suddenly upon him; and, stopping short in her course, she stood mute and confused before him, while her cheeks were mantled with a deep blush at the awkwardness of the position in which she unexpectedly found herself.

"Miss Haviland!" exclaimed Woodburn, looking up in equal surprise. "Excuse me if I am wrong, but, as little as I was expecting it, I think it is Miss Haviland whom I am addressing?"

"It is, sir," she replied, in a slightly tremulous voice; "but trust you will not think this an intentional intrusion."

"No intrusion, fair lady. You do not rightly interpret my

expression, which was one of surprise at seeing you here, when I had supposed you to be in another part of the country. When I last saw you, I supposed you on your return to Bennington."

" I was so at that time. But having recently come over with my father, who was journeying to Connecticut, I am now tarrying with a sister in this neighborhood till he returns. Your allusion to our parting, however, cannot but bring to mind the circumstances connected with our meeting, nor fail to admonish me of my great obligations to you, sir, which I have never before found a suitable opportunity of personally acknowledging. But be assured, Mr. Woodburn, I shall never forget that fearful hour; yet sooner far the hour, than the hand that snatched me from my seemingly inevitable doom."

" We both may have cause to remember the incidents attendant on that journey to Westminster, Miss Haviland; and I, though I did but a common duty in assisting you, shall remember them, on more accounts than one, I fear but too long."

" If you allude to your difficulties on that journey, and subsequently with one with whom we were in company, I can only say, sir, that I have heard of them, and all your consequent misfortunes, with the deepest regret, scarcely less on account of the author than the victim."

" I could have submitted to my pecuniary losses with a good degree of resignation ; but, when I think of the crowning act, and the consequences that followed it — when I look on that grave," continued the speaker, pointing to the fresh mound, with an effort to master his emotions, " it is hard to endure."

" Such misfortunes," responded Miss Haviland, visibly touched at his distress ; " such misfortunes, — injuries, perhaps, I should call them, — I am sensible, are not easily forgot'en ; and I have sometimes feared that it too often might be my fate to be associated with them in your mind."

" O, no, lady, no," said Woodburn, promptly ; " though it were better for my happiness, perhaps, if I could," he added, more gloomily ; " for who will care what may be the feelings of one who is now an outcast, without property, family, or friends ? "

" Think not thus of yourself, Mr. Woodburn," replied the other, while a scarcely perceptible tinge appeared on her fair cheek ; " feel not thus. You do to yourself, and I doubt not to many others, great injustice ; certainly to one who can only think of you with the warmest gratitude."

" O, if all were like you, Miss Haviland ! " returned Woodburn, with much feeling ; " so just, so generous, so pure, so

J

beautiful! But I have already said too much," he continued, checking himself. "I intended not to have intimated aught of the thoughts and feelings which have obtruded themselves upon me, even before I heard these kind expressions. And though what I have said cannot be recalled, yet I have no thought of pressing any questions upon you under the accidental advantage which your gratitude — other things being the same — might give me. I ask for no corresponding impressions — I expect none. Being aware of your position, as well as my own, I shall not drive you to the unpleasant task of repulsing me. I will repulse my self. I will conquer this new enemy, though planted in my own bosom, lest it prove more dangerous to my peace than the one with whom I have so vainly contended in another rivalry."

She raised her eyes with a look full of maidenly embarrassment, indeed, but with an expression more resembling that of sorrow than resentment, as she gently replied, —

"I feel additionally grateful to you, Mr. Woodburn, for your delicate and generous course under the circumstances in which, as you seem to be aware, I am placed. But as I now perceive my companion approaching in the road, you will excuse my departure."

"Certainly," said Woodburn; "and you will forgive what has been said by one who is so truly the prey of conflicting emotions?"

"O, yes, sir," she answered, looking up with a witching smile, as she bowed her adieu; "that is, I will when you do any thing *worthy* of my forgiveness."

Woodburn stood mutely gazing after his lovely visitor till her small and graceful figure, floating on in its devious course through the diversified grounds in almost fairy lightness, receded from his enraptured sight; when he turned away with a sigh to commune with himself, try to analyze his feelings, weigh consequences, give Reason her rightful sway, and follow her dictates. After a long and deep struggle with his feelings, he appeared to come to some determination, and, resolutely bringing down a foot on the ground, he exclaimed, —

"No, never! I will not give way to feelings which can only end in disappointment and mortification. Begone, enticing vision, begone! I will harbor you no longer." And under the impulse of his freshly-formed resolution, he abruptly left the spot, and hastened through the enclosure to take his way homeward. As he was about to pass out into the road, his attention was attracted by the barking of a small dog, that, having followed the ladies, and tarried behind on their return, seemed to be intent on dragging out something from under a broad, flat stone, lying in one corner of the graveyard. Feeling some inclination to know what discoveries the dog was making in a spot so unpromising of any game that would be likely to attract him, Woodburn walked to the spot; when he perceived the animal to be eagerly tugging away at some object, which presented the appearance of the corners of some old leather-bound book, buried beneath the stone. His curiosity being now excited, he stood by and patiently waited to see the result. In a few minutes the dog succeeded in dragging out the object in question, which proved to be an old record-book, or rather the remains of one, for a part of it had been converted by the mice into a nest, and the rest was mutilated and falling to pieces. Leaving the dog to pursue his object, which was now sufficiently explained, Woodburn gathered up the remains of the book and stepped aside to examine them. On beating off the dirt and opening the unmutilated parts, he soon, and to his great surprise, discovered it to be a volume of the town records; the very volume, the loss of which, as he believed, had caused his defeat in his lawsuit with Peters. And hurriedly running over the leaves, his eye, the next moment, fell on the record of his own deed, with the dates precisely as he had contended, and standing in a connection which would have proved the priority of his title, furnished him a complete defence, and saved him from ruin!

The previous suspicions of Woodburn, respecting the disappearance of these records through the agency of Peters, were now confirmed in the mind of the former, as certainly as if he had witnessed the act; and this aggravating discovery, coming as it did too late to be of any benefit to him, and at a moment, too, when his feelings, notwithstanding his recent declarations to Miss Haviland, and his subsequent resolves, were sore from the insidious workings of jealousy, and the revolting thought of the pretensions of his hated foe to her hand—this discovery, we say, wrought up his mind, already embittered to the last degree of endurance, to a state little short of absolute frenzy. And clinching the fragments of the book, which contained the proof of the black transaction, in one hand, and flourishing the heavy oak cane he had with him in the other, he rushed out of the enclosure, and, with a disturbed air and hurrying step, took his way towards his desolate home, resolved, that in case he found, as he feared, that all chance of legal redress had passed by, he would, at least, unsparingly make use of the means, now in his power, in trumpeting the villainy of Peters to the world.

In this state of exasperation, after proceeding a short distance he unexpectedly and unfortunately encountered the very object of his pent indignation, the haughty and hated Peters, who, on horseback, was coming up a cross-road on his way to the Tory Tavern, where, as the reader has been already apprised, his tools and partisans were anxiously awaiting his arrival.

" Ha! here?   Then he shall be the first to hear it," muttered Woodburn, as with a flashing eye he suddenly turned and sternly confronted the other in his path.

" What now, sir? " said Peters, reigning up with a look of surprise not unmingled with uneasiness.

" I will tell you what, now, sir," replied Woodburn, in a voice quivering with suppressed passion ; " your frauds are exposed! Here are the remains of those very records you or your tools purloined to enable you to accomplish your unhallowed triumph over me, and now just found buried in yonder graveyard ! "

"Away, sir ! " exclaimed Peters, recovering his usual assurance. " I know nothing of your crazy jargon : stand aside and let me pass."

" Not till you have looked at the proof of what I assert, or acknowledged its correctness," persisted the other, extending his cane before the horse with his right hand, and thrusting forward the open book with his left.   " Here it is ; here is the record of my deed — dates and all, as I and you, too, sir, well knew them to be.   Look at it, sir, and restore me my property, or confess yourself a villain ! "

At this juncture Peters, who had covertly reversed the loaded whip he carried in his hand that he might strike more effectually, suddenly rose in his stirrups, and aimed a furious blow at the head of his accuser.   But as sudden and unexpected as was the dastardly movement, Woodburn threw up his cane in time to arrest and parry the descending implement, when, quick as thought, he paid back the intended blow with a force, of which, in the madness of the moment, he was little conscious, full on the exposed head of his antagonist, who, curling like a struck bullock beneath the fearful stroke, rolled heavily from his saddle to the ground. The exclamation of triumph that rose to the lips of the victor died in his throat, as he took a second glance at the motionless form and corpse-like aspect of the victim ; and, recoiling a step, he stood aghast at the thought of what he had done.   After standing a minute with his eyes rivetted on the face of his prostrate foe Woodburn, arousing himself, hurried forward, and, raising the head, chafed the temples and wrists a moment, and then felt for me pulse, when, finding no signs of life, he suddenly relinquished his hold, and with a look of horror and unutterable distress, hastily fled from the spot, muttering as he went, "A murderer!—to crown the host of misfortunes—a murderer!"

Soon striking off into a deep glade, diverging from the public way, he continued his course, with a rapid step and troubled brow, on through the woods and back pastures, till he gained, unobserved, the rear of his own cabin, when, entering, he threw himself into a chair, and, burying his face in his hands, sat many minutes motionless and silent, apparently engaged in deep and anxious thought. At length, he arose with a more composed look, and proceeded to make up a pack of his wardrobe, with such valuables as could be conveniently carried, including his mother's Bible. He then fitted his pack to his shoulders, took down his gun and ammunition, and, throwing a sorrowful farewell glance round the lonely apartment, left the house, and bent his course for the woods, in a northerly direction.

After travelling in the woods and unfrequented fields about two miles, he came in sight of the point of intersection between the road near which he had been holding his course, and a road coming into it from the central parts of the town. Here, concluding to pause till the approaching darkness should more perfectly screen him, before going out into the main thoroughfare leading up the Connecticut, he sat down on a log within the border of the woods, and again gave way to the remorseful feelings and moody reflections that still painfully oppressed him. His meditations, however, were soon disturbed by the quick, heavy tread of some animal, which seemed to be approaching in the woods, at no great distance behind him. Instantly peering out through the thicket in which he had ensconced himself, he soon, to his great surprise, descried a horseman descending a difficult ledge, leaping old windfalls, and making his way through all the opposing obstacles of the forest with wonderful facility, directly towards the spot where he stood concealed in the thicket. Knowing that whatever might be the object of the person approaching, it would be his wisest course to remain in his covert, from which he could not move unobserved, and his curiosity being excited by the appearance of a horseman in a spot that would have scarcely been deemed passable for a wild deer, he kept his stand; and continued to regard the advancing figure with the most lively interest. But owing to the thickness of the now full-leaved undergrowth, and the duskiness that by this time had gathered in the forest, he could only catch occasional

13

glimpses of either horse or rider, which enabled him to as
tain nothing more than that they both were quite diminutive, and
as it struck him, rather oddly accoutred. They continued to
advance directly towards him till within fifty yards of his covert,
when the horse, in emerging from a clump of bushes, which still
enveloped the rider, stopped short, and, looking keenly into the
thicket, gave a quick, significant snort.

" What's in the wind now, Lightfoot ? " said the rider to his
horse, as, parting the obstructing foliage with his hands, he thrust
out his head, and disclosed to the surprised and gratified Woodburn the well-known visage of his trusty friend, Barty Burt.

" This is, indeed, unexpected, Bart," said Woodburn, stepping
out into plain view.

" Harry ! " exclaimed the other, agreeably surprised in turn;
" but are you sure there are no more of you there in the bush ? "
he added, with a cautious glance at the thicket.

" Yes, I am alone here," answered the former.

" Well, I vags now ! " resumed Bart, drawing a long breath,
and riding forward — " I vags, if I didn't begin to feel rather ticklish when Lightfoot give me that hint to look out for snakes, just
now. But the case aint quite what it might have been, considering."

" Considering what ? "

" I know."

" Of course you do, as well as what brought you here with a
horse, in so strange a place for a horseback excursion."

" Just so, Harry ; same as you know what brought *you* here
with a *pack* on your back, in so queer a route for a journey, when
a smooth road is so near you."

Well knowing Bart's peculiarities, and that it would be useless
to try to draw from him the secret of his appearance here until
he chose to reveal it, Woodburn, while the other dismounted and
told his pony to be cropping the bushes in the mean time, related
all that had transpired between himself and the victim of his
deeply regretted paroxysm of passion, adding, at the close of his
gloomy and self-accusing recital, —

" I first thought, after reaching my house, that I would return
and give myself up to the authorities ; but knowing, whether
Peters should live or die, that I should be a doomed man in this
part of the country, I at length brought myself, perhaps wrongly,
to try to get out of it undiscovered. And I have now set my
course for Boston, to join those there gathering for the approaching struggle for liberty. And Heaven knows with what pleasure
I shall now sacrifice my life in her battles."

" Good! that's grand!" warmly responded Bart, who had
listened to the other with many a *whew!* of surprise at his ac
companying expressions of self-condemnation for killing an antag·
onist who struck the first blow — " that's grand! Here is what
goes with you, Harry ; for, between us here, I and Lightfoot are
clipping it from a predicament, as well as you."

" So I suspected. But what is it? Let us have *your* story
now."

" Well, Harry, in the first place, do you know this critter I call
Lightfoot ? "

" No ; at least I don't now remember to have noticed the animal before."

" Well, it is the colt old skin-flint Turner cheated me out of,
last year."

" I think you told me something about it, but don't recollect
the particulars ; though I had then no doubt, I believe, but the old
man wronged you, as I understood you worked very hard for him
through the season."

" I did, like a niggar — cause he promised to give me this colt,
then a little snubby three-year-old, for my summer's work, if I
would stay and work well for him, which I did, as I said. Well,
supposing the colt was to be mine, without any mistake, I made a
sight of her, named her Lightfoot, fed her, got her as tame as a
dog, then trained her to understand certain words and signs,
which I at last got her to obey ; and whether it was to trot, run,
or jump fences, she would do it as no other critter could. But
just as I had got her to mind and love *me*, as I did *her*, my time
was out ; and I went to settle off matters with the old man, and
tell him I was going to take her off with me, when — rot his pic-
tur! — he pretended he had forgot all about his promise to let me
have her, and forbid my touching her, saying he had paid me all
I earnt in the old clothes which he urged on to me, against my
will, and which were not worth one week's work, as true as the
book, Harry. Well, I couldn't help crying, to be cheated so,
and, what was worse, to lose Lightfoot. But it did no good. I
had to come away without her, or any other pay ; and, from that
time, I haven't seen her till to-day."

" But you have not now stole and run away with her, I trust
Bart ? "

" No ; she run away with me," replied Bart, roguishly, as I
can prove ; for I hollered *whoa* all the time, as loud as I could
yell."

" But how came you mounted upon her at all ? "

" Well, Harry, that brings me to the worst and best part of my story, all in one ; and here goes for it."

Bart, in his own peculiar manner, then related, with great ac curacy, the particulars of his arrest and escape from the tories, as we have already described them in the preceding chapter, merely explaining, in addition, that Lightfoot well understood the game, and knew she was to obey the signs he secretly gave her with his feet and hands, however loud he, or others, might cry *whoa* or any of the terms usually addressed to horses. He then pro ceeded : —

" Well, you see, as soon as I got over the hill, out of sight, I looked out for a hard, stony place, where Lightfoot couldn't be tracked ; and, soon finding one, I leaped her over the fence, and made full speed for the woods, which I luckily reached jest in time to wheel round in safety, and see them thundering along by, in the road, after me. I then took it leisurely off in this direction, contriving to keep mostly in the woods, where I had learnt Lightfoot, in riding after the cows, last summer, to be as much at home in as in the road."

" And what do you propose to do with this horse now ? " asked Woodburn.

" Take her along with me, to be sure, Harry."

" And so make yourself, in law, a horse-thief, eh ? Do you expect me to join company with such a character ? "

" Well, now, Harry, I didn't expect the like of that from you, any how," observed Bart, evidently touched at the remark. " The creature is honestly mine ; and I supposed I had a right to get what was mine away, if I could, without going to law, which would help me about as much as it has you, I reckon. But sup posing that to be law which aint right and justice, and so make me out a thief, as you say, how much boot could I afford to give you, Harry, to swap predicaments with me ? You have just called yourself a murderer, which you aint, and me a horse-thief, which *I* aint, any more than you the other. Now, how will you swap characters ? "

" Bart, you have silenced me. Injustice and oppression have made us both outlaws, but not intentionally wrong-doers. Let us still abstain from all intentional wrong, however trifling. And that leads me to observe, that whatever justification you may have for taking away the horse, you probably have none for car rying off the bridle."

" There you are out again, Harry. That bridle, which queerly happened to be put on Lightfoot to-day, (as if it was kinder ordered I should get the beast,) is the very one I bought last fall, to take her off with; but being so worked up, when I left, I forgot to bring it away."

"Upon my word, Bart, you are successful to-day in making defences."

"Always mean to be able to do so, Harry. Nobody has any honest claims on me in Guilford, now, nor I any on them. I leave 'em with every thing squared, according to my religion."

"Except in the matter of your gun, which you leave — no exactly won by your opponent — behind you; do you not?"

"They are welcome to it; much good may it do 'em. It has gone pretty much where I calkerlated to get it off — among those who used me the worst; though I'd some rather it had gone to Fitch, who hunts some, and would be sure to try it."

"That is queer reasoning, Bart."

"Well, there is a head and tail to it, for all that, Harry."

"What are they?"

"Why, the head, or cause, is, that the last time I shot the piece, I overloaded it, being for black ducks, and the charge raised a seam, in a flaw underside the barrel, which I could blow through. And the tail, or consequence, is, that the next man who shoots it will wish he'd never seen it, I reckon."

"Ah, Bart, Bart, your religion, as you term it, is a strange one! But let us now dismiss the past, and think of the future. If you join me for the army, what do you propose to do with your horse — sell her?"

"Sell her?" why, I'd as soon sell my daddy, if I had one. No, we'll keep her between us. You, and Tom Dunning, and Lightfoot are the only friends I have in the world, Harry; and I want we should kinder stick together. So I've been thinking up the plan, that we ride and tie, or keep along together and foot it by turns, to-night, till we get to Westminster, when we will beat up Dunning, and leave Lightfoot with him, who can take her to some of his sly places over the mountain, and have her kept for us. Then, if one of us gets killed, or any thing, so as never to come back, let the other take her; and if both fail to come, then let Tom have her for his own."

And Bart's plan being adopted, our two humble, friendless, and nearly penniless adventurers left the wood, and entering the northern road, set forth on their destination, Woodburn first mounting the pony and keeping some hundred yards in advance, and Bart forming the rear-guard, under the agreement that the latter, on hearing any sounds of pursuit, should utter

13 *

the cry of the raccoon, when both were to plunge into the woods, and remain till the danger had passed by.

After travelling in this manner, and at a rapid rate, about two hours, without encountering any thing to excite their apprehensions or delay their progress, they entered a long reach of unbroken forest, which neither of them remembered ever to have passed through. But not being able to conceive where they could have turned off from the river road, which was their intended route, they continued to move doubtingly onwards some miles farther, till the increasing obstructions and narrowness of the path, together with the absence of the settlements which they knew they must have found before this time on the road up the Connecticut, fully convinced Woodburn they had lost their way. And he was on the point of proposing to retrace their steps, when, descrying a light some distance ahead, emanating, as he supposed, from the hut of a new settler, he at once concluded to push on towards it, for the purpose of making inquiries of the occupants to ascertain their situation. In making for the light, of which, for a while, only feeble and occasional glimmerings could be obtained through the dense foliage that overhung the devious path, they at length came to an apparently well-cultivated opening, containing about a dozen acres, on one side of which stood a small, snug-looking stone house, built against or near a boldly projecting ledge of rocks. As they approached the house, their attention was arrested by the loud and earnest voice of a man within, engaged, evidently, in prayer. Concluding that the man was at his family evening devotions, which they had no thought of disturbing, they left the horse at a little distance from the house, and silently drawing near to the door, paused and reverently listened. A confused recollection of the supplicant's voice, together with his deep and fervid tones, his bold language, and especially the subject that seemed then mostly to engross his thoughts, at once awakened the interest and rivetted the attention of Woodburn. The great burden of his soul was, obviously, the political condition of his country. And, after vividly painting the many wrongs she had suffered from her haughty oppressors, and warmly setting forth her claims to divine assistance, he broke forth, in conclusion,—

"My country! O my injured, oppressed, and down-trodden country! shall the cry of thy wrongs go up in vain to Heaven? Will not the God of battles hear and help thee, in this the hour of thy peril and of thy need? O, wilt thou not, Lord, extend thy mighty arm in her defence? O, teach the proud Britons, now thronging our shores — teach them, scoffing Goliahs as they are, that there are young Davids in our land! O, bring their counsels to nought! Scatter their fleets by thy tempests at sea, and destroy their armies on land! Sweep them off by bullet and plague! and — and " — suddenly checking himself, he meekly added, " and save their souls; and this, Lord, is all that in con-science I can ask for them. Amen."

Woodburn now gently rapped at the door, which, after a sligh: pause, was opened, and Herriot, the late prisoner of the royal court, stood before him.

" If this is Harry Woodburn," he said, after scrutinizing the other's features a moment, " he is very welcome to my hut. But you are not alone ? " he added, glancing towards Bart, who stood several paces in the background.

" No," replied Woodburn; " I have in company a young man whom you may, perhaps, recollect as the messenger that appeared several times at the grate of our prison at Westminster, to bring us news of the progress of the rising."

' Ah, yes, well do I recollect that goodly youth, and have ever since taken a peculiar interest in him. Invite him in. All this is opportune, very — very," said Herriot, leading the way into the house.

After the recluse had ushered his guests into the principal room of his very simply furnished house, of which he and a servant boy, of perhaps fifteen, were the only inmates, he turned to Wood-burn, and said, —

" As my retreat here in the woods, and the road that leads to it, are known to so few, I conclude that your young friend here, Mr. Woodburn, acted as your guide on the occasion."

" O, no," replied the other; " we had lost our way, having left the river road inadvertently, and were about to turn back, when, catching a glimpse of your light, we came on to make inquiries. We neither of us knew when we struck into the road leading hither."

" Do you agree to that statement, without any qualification, master Bart ? " asked the recluse, with a doubting and slightly puzzled air.

" Well, some of it, I reckon," answered Bart, with a look of droll gravity.

" Why, you told me, sir," responded Woodburn, rather sharply " that you had never travelled this road before."

" No more I hadn't," replied Bart, composedly; " but I didn't say I didn't know where it turned off, for Tom Dunning told me that."

" Bart," said Woodburn, seriously, " though I am not sorry to nave fallen in with father Herriot, yet, as between you and me, this needs explanation. It looks as if you purposely led me astray."

" Well now, Harry, no offence, I hope. The thing was kinder agreed on, somehow, that you should come this way, when you left Guilford, which was understood would happen soon. If I hadn't fell in with you as I did, it was my notion to take Lightfoot here, or at Dunning's, and then go back and skulk there somewheres till you was ready to come; but finding you and things all coming so handy like, when we got to where the road turned off, I thought I'd let you follow me into it, if you would, and say nothing till we got here."

" I am still perfectly at a loss how to understand all this, Bart · and I sti.. wish you would more fully explain it."

" I will take that task upon myself; for I suppose I am somewhat in the secret respecting the little plot of your friends," said Herriot, going to a chest, and bringing forward a small bag of money. " This has been deposited with me for your use and benefit. It is the price of your cow and oxen, sold by Dunning to a drover from Rhode Island. The sum is, I believe, about fifty dollars, which I now deliver you, as your own unquestionable property."

In the explanation that now ensued, it appeared that the cattle, which had been rescued by the friends of Woodburn, without his privity, lest the scruples it was feared he might entertain should lead him to interfere with the plan, were taken that night to the retreat of Herriot, who was made acquainted with the whole transaction; and that the next day, while Dunning went up the river in search of a purchaser, the other, who was not without his scruples, also, about sanctioning the procedure, repaired to lawyer Knights for his opinion on the subject. And the latter, having been confidentially let into the secret, and given it as his decided opinion that the judgment, to satisfy which the cattle had been seized, was an illegal and void one, and that the cattle so seized might rightfully be taken for the owner, without legal process if found out of the hands of the officer, the recluse returned and actively coöperated with the hunter; the result of which was, that a purchaser was soon found, who paid the money for the stock and immediately drove it from the country.

This, to Woodburn, was an unexpected development. And now, after hearing the explanation of Herriot, being satisfied of the propriety of the course so generously taken by his friends in

his behalf, he gratefully received the money; and, in turn, while
Bart and the servant were out caring for the pony, he confidentially disclosed to the recluse the painful occurrence of the afternoon which had led to his sudden flight from home, and his
determination of immediately joining the army, concluding by
giving the particulars of Bart's arrest and singular escape from
the tories.

"You have acted wisely, Mr. Woodburn," observed Herriot
after listening with deep interest to the recital. "Peters may yet
recover; but should he not, I do not view the act in so criminal
a light as that in which you yourself have placed it. And in the
absence of all intention of killing the man, I feel very clear that
it is not a deed meriting the punishment you would be likely to
receive, if you had put your fate into the hands of the corrupted
witnesses who would probably have been brought against you.
Yes, you have acted wisely in leaving that wicked Babel of toryism, and nobly in devoting yourself to the cause of your bleeding
country. My blessing and prayers will attend you and your
young friend, to whom, I trust, you will act the friend and adviser
he will doubtless need. But come, Harry," he added, taking up a
light, and making a sign for the other to follow him, "some new
notions have come into my head since I became acquainted with
you and your young friend, at Westminster, and knowing of no
two persons in whom I take greater interest, I have concluded to
impart something to you in confidence."

So saying, he led the way into the cellar, the bottom of which
was flagged over with stones of various shapes and sizes; when
pointing to a broad, flat stone lying near the centre of the room,
he asked Woodburn to raise it. Wondering what could be the
object of so unexpected a request, the latter, with considerable
effort, succeeded in raising the stone to an upright position, and
in so doing brought to view two small iron-bound casks, standing
in a cavity beneath, and labelled, in large inky letters, "Printer's
Type."

"Printing, then, was formerly your trade?" said Woodburn,
inquiringly, perceiving the other not inclined to be the first to
speak.

"Well, that is a respectable calling, is it not?" said the other,
evasively.

"Certainly," replied Woodburn; "but I had not looked for
any immediate use for such implements in this new settlement."

"The contents of those casks, nevertheless, are of more value
than you may think them, Harry, and may soon be needed for

.he public, in the times now at hand. But what wish to say to you is, in the first place, that you are not to divulge what you have seen to any one but your young friend, and not to him unless you are satisfied he can be trusted, or you are about to die. And, in the second place, if you hear of my death, both of you are to come here, take possession of these casks, and divide the contents equally between you as your own. I have now no relative that will appear to claim them. You will also find, enclosed in one of the casks, certain documents, which I have recently deposited there, explaining my wishes, as well as some secrets of my life connected with discoveries lately made by me, tha' interest others besides myself. This you, or the survivor of you two, if one should die, will do in case I am taken away. And even if I continue to live, my designs will probably not be altered and I shall wish to see you both again when you are permitted to return to your old homes. And still further, I would say, that should you be in want at any time, and will apply to me, I will dispose of enough of this property to supply your necessities. Now replace the stone, and let us return to the room above."

Woodburn knew not what to make of all this mystery, or affected mystery, as he believed it. But knowing the singularities of the man, he forebore to ask any questions, and they left the cellar in silence. Soon after they had returned, Bart and the servant came in; when a frugal meal was set before the travellers. And while the latter were occupied in partaking their repast, the recluse procured his writing materials, and penning a brief letter, presented it to Woodburn, saying, "There is a letter of introduction to a former friend of mine, who, I understand, is appointed to an important command in the army now mustering at Cambridge. It may be of service to you. And now," he added, as his guests rose to depart — " now, my young friends and fellow-sufferers from oppression, go — deserve well of your country, and desert her not till the British Dagons are all leveled to the dust, which may God speedily grant. Amen."

In a few minutes more, our adventurers were on their way. And being now invigorated, both in body and mind, by what had occurred during their call at the retreat of their mysterious friend, they pressed on so rapidly, for the next three or four hours, that they arrived at Dunning's cabin, in Westminster, just as the first faint flush of daylight appeared in the east. Here luckily finding the hunter already astir, cooking his breakfast, preparatory to any early start on some new excursion, they joined him in his delicious meal, which consisted of the rich steaks of a salmon caught the preceding evening. And having finished their breakfast, and made the contemplated arrangement with Dunning, to take charge of Lightfoot, their now common favorite, the last-named person set them across the Connecticut in his log canoe; when, looking back from the woody shore of the New Hampshire side, they bade a long farewell to the Green Mountains, whose tall, blue peaks were then beginning to grow bright in the rays of the rising sun, and resolutely plunged into the dark recesses before them.

VOLUME II.

THE RANGERS;

OR,

THE TORY'S DAUGHTER.

CHAPTER I.

"We owe no allegiance, we bow to no throne;
Our ruler is law, and the law is our own;
Our leaders themselves are our own fellow-men,
Who can handle the sword, the scythe, or the pen."

VERMONT was ushered into political existence midst storm and tempest. We speak both metaphorically and literally; for it is a curious historical fact, that her constitution, the result of the first regular movement ever made by her people towards an independent civil government, was adopted during the darkest period of the revolution, at an hour of commotion and alarm, when the tempest of war was actually bursting over her borders and threatening her entire subversion. And, as if to make the event the more remarkable, the adoption took place amidst a memorable thunder-storm, but for the happening of which, at that particular juncture, as will soon appear, that important political measure must have been postponed to a future period, and a period, too, when the measure, probably, would have been defeated, and the blessings of an independent government forever lost, owing to the dissensions, which, as soon as the common danger was over, New York and New Hampshire combined to scatter among her people. The whole history of the settlement and organization of the state, indeed, exhibits a striking anomaly, when viewed with that of any other state in the Union. She may emphatically be called the offspring of war and controversy The long and fierce dispute for her territory between the colonies above named had sown her soil with dragon teeth, which at length sprang up in a crop of hardy, determined, and liberty-loving men, who, instead of joining either of the contending parties, soon resolved to take a stand for themselves against both. And that stand, when taken, they maintained with a spirit and success, to which, considering the discouragements, difficulties, and dangers they were constantly compelled to encounter, history furnishes but few parallels. But although every step of her progress, from the felling of the first tree in her dark wilderness to her final reception into the sisterhood of the states, was marked by the severest trials, yet the summer of 1777 — the period to which the remainder of our tale refers — was, for her, far the most gloomy and portentous. And still it was a period in which she filled the brightest page of her history, and, at the same time, did more than in any other year towards insuring her subsequent happy destiny.

In the beginning of this eventful year, the people of Vermont, by their delegates in formal convention assembled, had declared themselves independent —

"Independent of all save the mercies of God,"

as the poet, who has furnished us the heading of this chapter, and who has so strikingly embodied the feelings of those he describes, has significantly expressed it. And having taken measures for publishing their declaration to the world, the convention closed their proceedings by appointing a committee, selected as combining the most happily an acquaintance with form and precedent with a knowledge of the ways and wants of the people, to draft a constitution to be submitted to a new convention, which the people were invited to call for that purpose. In response to that call, a new convention assembled at Windsor, in the month of July following, and proceeded, with that diligence and scrupulous regard to the employment of their time for which the early public bodies of this state were so noted, to take into consideration the important instrument now submitted to them as a proper basis on which to erect the superstructure of a civil government, suited to the genius and necessities of an industrious and frugal people — a people who, though keenly jealous of their individual rights, and exceedingly restive under all foreign authority, had yet declared their willingness, and even their wish, to receive and obey a system of legal restraints, if it could be one of their own imposing. For five days, from rising to setting sun, this convention employed the best energies of their practical and enlightened minds in discussing and amending the document before them. But their labors for the present, if not forever, had well nigh been lost, for, soon after they had assembled, on the sixth day of their session, and while they were intently listening to the reading of the instrument for the last time before taking a final vote on its adoption their proceedings were suddenly brought to a stand by the alarming news, loudly proclaimed by a herald, who appeared on his foam-covered horse before their open door, that Ticonderoga, the supposed impregnable barrier of frontier defence, had fallen, and our scattered troops were flying in every direction before a formidable British army, that was sweeping, unopposed, along the western border of the state, flanked by a horde of merciless savages, from whose fearful irruptions not a dwelling on that side of the mountains would probably be spared!

This intelligence, so unexpected and so startling, too nearly concerned the members of the convention, not only as patriots, but as men, to permit their entire exemption from the general consternation and dismay which were every where spreading around them; and many a staid heart among them secretly trembled for the fate of the near and dear ones left at homes in which the red tomahawk might, even at that very moment, be busy at its work of death; while the bosoms of all were burning to be freed from their present duties, that they might seize the sword or musket and fly to the relief of their endangered families, or mingle in the common defence against the haughty invaders of their soil. Any further proceedings with the subject on hand, at such a moment, were soon perceived to be utterly impossible; and a majority of the members began to press eagerly for an immediate adjournment. But while a few of their number, sharing less than the rest in the general agitation, or being more deeply impressed with the importance of accomplishing, at this time, an object now so nearly attained, were attempting to resist the current, and prevent any action on the motion to adjourn, till time was gained for reflection, an unwonted darkness, as if by the special interposition of Providence, suddenly fell upon the earth. The lightnings began to gleam through the dark and threatening masses of cloud that had enveloped the sky, and the long, deep roll of thunder was heard in different quarters of the heavens, giving warning of the severe and protracted tempest which soon burst over

1 *

them with a fury that precluded all thought of venturing abroad. The prospect of being thus confined to the place for some hours, and perhaps the whole day, taking from those moving it all inducement for an immediate adjournment, they now began to take a cooler view of their situation; and soon, by common consent the business on hand was resumed. The reading of the constitution was finished; and, while the storm was still howling around, and the thunders breaking over them, that instrument was adopted, and became the supreme law of the land.*

One thing more remained to be done; and that was, to constitute a provisiona. government to act till the one pointed out by the constitution just adopted could be established. This was now effected by the appointment of that small body of men since known as the *Old Council of Safety* of Vermont, and noted alike for the remarkable powers with which they were clothed, and the remarkable manner in which those powers were exercised: for, from the nature of the case, and the emergency in which these men were called to act, they were almost necessarily invested with the extraordinary combination of legislative, judicial, and executive power. But this power, absolute and dictatorial as it was, they never abused or exercised but for the public good; and in this they were cheerfully sustained by the people, who felt that they were thus not only sustaining the cause of freedom, but the laws which were of their own providing, and which they were anxious should be obeyed.

To that unique assembly, of whose origin we have been speaking, we propose next to introduce the reader. In obedience to an order of the convention, issued at the moment of its hasty dissolution, near the close of the memorable day before described, the different members of this newly-appointed body, many of whom, it is believed, were also members of the one just dissolved, had promptly convened at Arlington. But finding themselves here endangered by the near vicinity of the enemy, they had adjourned into the more interior town of Manchester, within whose barricade of mountains they could proceed with their deliberations with little fear of interruption. And here, conscious that the eyes of all were turned anxiously upon them, in the expectation that they would provide for the safety of the infant

---

* Through inadvertence arising out of the unsettled state of the times, or design among the leaders who might have fears for the result, the constitution was never submitted to the people for their ratification or rejection; but, no questions ever being raised on account of this informality it was acquiesced in as valid and binding.

state, whose destinies had been committed to their hands, they commenced the worse than Egyptian task devolving on them — that of making adequate provisions for the public defence, while the means were almost wholly wanting; for with scarcely the visible means in the whole settlement, in its then exhausted and unsettled condition, of raising and supporting a single company of soldiers, they were expected to raise an army. Without the shadow of a public treasury, without any credit as a state, and without the power of taxing the people, — which, by the constitution just adopted, could only be done by the legislature not yet called, — they were required to do that for which half a million of money might be needed. Such were the difficulties by which they were met at the outset — difficulties which, to men of ordinary stamina and mental resources, would have been insurmountable. But these were not men of ordinary stamina, either moral or mental. They had been selected by the representatives of the people for the qualities which would fit them to guide the helm of state in this difficult and alarming crisis. And, unshrinkingly proceeding to the discharge of their high responsibilities, they soon evinced, by their conduct, that the confidence reposed in them had not been misplaced; for the glorious results of the field of Bennington, and the incessant and harassing warfare on the flanks of the enemy which both preceded and followed that event, and which drew forth from its despairing leader his best apology for his defeat and surrender, were, far more than is generally supposed, the fruits of the combined energy and talents of that unequalled little band of patriots and statesmen.* But the particular time we have chosen for lifting the curtain from their secret proceedings was at the darkest and most disheartening hour they were doomed to experience, and before the united mind of their body had been brought to bear on any measure which afforded a reasonable promise of auspicious results. The army of Burgoyne was then hovering on their borders in its most menacing attitude. Marauding parties were daily penetrating the interior, and plundering and capturing the defenceless inhabitants, while each day brought the unwelcome news of the defection of individuals who

---

* A finer tribute of praise to the Green Mountain Boys could scarcely have been given, than the one involved in Burgoyne's letter to Lord Germain, written about the time of the battle of Bennington, in which he says, "The Hampshire Grants, a country unpeopled, and almost unknown, in the last war, now abounds in the most active and the most rebellious race of men on the continent, and hangs like a gathering storm on my left."

had openly gone off to swell the ranks of the victorious enemy to whose alarming progress scarcely a show of resistance had yet been interposed. Nor was this the end of the chapter of trials and discouragements that awaited the council. Another blow was to be added, more calculated than all to test their firmness and bring home to their bosoms a sense of the perils of the crisis, and the necessity of immediate action, unless they should conclude to yield at once to the current of destiny which seemed to be setting so strongly against them. But let us present the mortifying and disgraceful event, to which we last alluded, in another form, in which the historic pen, that thus far in this chapter has only been employed, may be legitimately aided by the pencil of fancy, while we bring the leading individuals of this body to view, and sketch the details of a scene as truthful in outline as it was important in result.

The long summer day was drawing to a close. It had been thus far spent by the council, as had been the several preceding days of their session, in discussing the subject of the ways and means of doing something to avert the doom that hung over their seemingly devoted state. But up to this hour their deliberations had been wholly fruitless. Project after project for the means of raising military forces had been brought forward and discussed; and each in turn had been thought to be impracticable, and had been consequently abandoned, till, wearied with their unavailing labors, and discouraged at the dubious prospect before them, they now began to think of giving up business for the day, when the door-keeper, with unwonted haste and an agitated manner, entered the room, and announced to the astonished members of the council the alarming tidings that one of their own body, and, until that day, an active participator in their discussions, had proved a Judas, and was now, with a band of his recreant neighbors, on his way to the British camp. The news fell like a thunder-clap on the council, producing, at first, a sensation not often witnessed in so grave an assemblage. But no formal comments were offered; and, after the commotion had subsided, all sunk into a thoughtful silence, which we will improve by our promised introduction to the reader of the leading members of the council.

Separated from the rest by a sort of enclosure composed of tables strung across one end of the apartment, which was a large upper room of an inn, hastily fitted up for the occasion, conspicuously sat the president of the council, the venerable Thomas Chittenden, the wise, the prudent, and the good, who was to Vermont what Washington was to the Union; and who, though not possessing dazzling greatness, had yet that rare combination of moral and intellectual qualities which was more fortunate for him — good sense, great discretion, firmness, honesty of purpose, benevolence, and unvarying equanimity of temper, united with a modest and pleasing address. And by the long and continued exercise of this golden mean of qualities, he was destined to leave behind him an honest, enduring fame — a memorial of good deeds and useful every-day examples, to be remembered and quoted, both in the domestic circle and in the public assembly, when the far superior brilliancy of many a contemporary had passed away and been forgotten. He was now something over fifty; but so fine were his physical endowments, and so temperate and regular had been his habits, that time had scarcely left a trace on his manly brow; and his fair and well-moulded features had almost the freshness of youth. And notwithstanding the unpretending simplicity of his deportment, and the extreme plainness of his dress, the large arm-chair, in which he now reclined, furnished probably by some considerate matron of the neighborhood for his special convenience, could not have found, in the broad land, an occupant who would have filled it with more native dignity, or one better fitted to restrain by courteous firmness, and by tact guide into safe and appropriate fields of action, the less disciplined and more fiery spirits of the body over which he presided.

Let us now take a glance at the more prominent members of this notable little band of public conservators. Here, immersed in thought, sat, side by side, like brothers, as they were, the two Fays, those intelligent, enterprising, and persevering friends of freedom and state independence. And there sat the two Robinsons, alike patriotic, and active, or able, according to the different spheres of action in which they were about to be distinguished — one in the tented field, and the other on the bench and in the national councils. In another place was seen the short, thick-set form of the uncompromising Matthew Lyon, the Irish refugee, who was willing to be sold to pay his passage to America, for the sake of getting out of the despotic moral atmosphere of the old world, into one where his broad chest, as he was wont to say, could expand freely, and where his bold spirit could soar unclogged by the trammels of legitimacy. In his eagle eye, in every lineament of his clear, ardent, and fearless countenance, indeed, might be read the promise of what he was to become — the stern democrat, and the well-known champion of the whole right and the largest liberty. In contrast to him, near by was seen the tall, commanding form, and the firm and thoughtful countenance, of Benjamin Carpenter, who had just arrived, with pack and cane, from Guilford, from which he had that day come on foot by a route designated by marked trees, through the mountain wilderness, nearly thirty miles in extent. Farther on, and seated before an open window, was Thomas Rowley, the first poet of the Green Mountains. He was here because he was a public favorite, a trusty patriot, and something of a statesman. But, like most other poets, he was not without his peculiarities of temperament, as might have been seen by his manner and movements even in this staid assembly ; for, as if disgusted with a tedious and profitless debate, and determined also not long to be troubled by the disconcerting news just announced, he had now evidently cast these cares from his mind, to indulge in the more congenial employment of gazing out upon the landscape, over which his kindling eye might have been seen to wander, till it rested, in rapture, on the broad empurpled side and bright summit of the lofty Equinox Mountain, whose contrasted magnificence was growing every moment more striking and beautiful in the beams of the low-descending sun. On the opposite side of the room stood the mild and gentlemanly Nathan Clark, the future speaker of the first legislature of Vermont ; and by his side, the dark and rough-featured Gideon Olin, an embryo member of Congess, was leaning against the wall, with a countenance of mingled sternness and gloom.

By the side of one of the tables, in front of the president, might also have been seen the stout, burly frame, and the matter-of-fact and business-like countenance, of Paul Spooner, engaged in writing a despatch. And as the last, though not as the least, among the strongly-contrasted characters of this assembly of whom we propose to take note, let us turn to the youthful secretary of the council, Ira Allen. So much the junior of his colleagues was he, indeed, that a spectator might well have wondered how he came to be selected as one of such a sage and elderly body of councillors. But those who procured his appointment knew full well why they had done so ; and his history thenceforward was destined to prove a continued justification of their high opinion of him. He was of an active, mercurial turn, and, as might have been seen, was not inclined to remain long in one place or posture. He had now thrown aside his rapid pen, and, with a quick, light step and deeply-cogitating air, was traversing back and forth the open space between his table, in front of the president, and the closed door of the apartment

Both in form and feature, he was one of the handsomest men of his day; while a mind at once versatile, clear, and penetrating, with perceptions as quick as light, was stamped on his Grecian brow, or found a livelier expression in his lucid black eyes and other lineaments of his strikingly intellectual countenance. Such as he appeared for the first time on the stage of public action was the noted Ira Allen, whose true history, when written, will show him to have been, either secretly or openly, the originator, or successful prosecutor, of more important political measures, affecting the interests and independence of the state, and the issue of the war in the Northern Department, than any other individual in Vermont, making him, with the many peculiar traits of character he possessed, one of the most remarkable men of the times in which he so conspicuously figured.

"I have finished, Mr. President," said Spooner, now breaking the gloomy silence which had, for an unusual interval, pervaded the assembly — "I have finished the despatch, suggested by your honor, requiring the attendance of the absent member from the east side of the mountain — General Bayley. And having put it into the form of a familiar letter, I have ventured to enlarge somewhat on our perplexing situation, especially in the matter of the miserable Squire Spencer, whose treasonable desertion I little dreamed, when I commenced writing, I should have the mortification of announcing." *

"That is well," responded the president; "and we must look up some suitable messenger to convey it to its destination. But I had hoped to forward, by the same hand, the despatch requesting the aid and coöperation of New Hampshire, which has been deferred till some definite action of our own should enable us to inform the council of that state what we of the Grants propose to do ourselves towards the object for which we invoke their assistance. This they will doubtless consider essential to be known, before listening to our call, as otherwise they will not know whether they will find among us more friends to assist than enemies to impede them. But what can we now tell them? I

---

* The original letter from Paul Spooner to General Jacob Bayley, of Newbury, written in council, requiring the attendance of the latter, and informing him of Spencer's defection, and the gloomy situation of affairs, is still preserved, and affords, notwithstanding the disheartening news it communicates, a striking proof of the determination of that body to struggle on to the last against the mountain of difficulties which, at this dark crisis, seemed to lie before them.

will submit to you, gentlemen of the council," he continued, in
a kindly expostulating tone — " I will submit to your good sense
and patriotism, whether it is not now time to adopt some decided
course to be pursued.   We must not be disheartened by a few
untoward circumstances.   Providence not unfrequently frowns on
us for our own good.   And who shall say, in the present instance,
that our deliberations have not been wisely and kindly rendered
of no effect till after Spencer's desertion, since, had we adopted
a plan of operations while he was here, the whole of it, by this
time, had been in the possession of the British general ?   But be
that as it may, the event of this man's apostasy, of itself, instead
of making us timid and irresolute in action, should but render us
more prompt and decided.   The people, as we all feel painfully
conscious, I presume, expect much from us.   Shall we disappoint
them in every thing ?   Because we cannot consistently do all
that may be expected, shall we resolve to do nothing ?   I have
listened to your objections to levying a general tax upon the people, as the means of raising a military force ; and, with you, I
consider them valid ; for to infringe the constitution, just adopted,
by an arbitrary taxation, would be setting a dangerous precedent,
and one which would come with a bad grace from those of us
here who helped to adopt it.   No ; we must resort to other means.
We can, if we will, borrow, pledging ourselves as individuals,
with such others as we may find willing to stand sponsors with
us, that the state shall hereafter pay the debt ; or we may resort
to voluntary contributions.   I am aware the people are unable to
contribute much.   I am aware that a great portion of the inhabitants have been driven from their homes, and are now living on
the hospitality of the rest.   But for all this, the people can and
will cheerfully contribute something — more, I think, than we
should be willing to require of them.   I have ten head of cattle,
which can be spared for the emergency.   But am I more patriotic
than you, and hundreds of others in the settlement ?   My wife
has a valuable gold necklace.   Hint to her to-day that it is needed
for the public service, and, my word for it, to-morrow you will
find it in the treasury of freedom.   But is my wife any more
public-spirited than yours and many others among us ?   Gentlemen, I await your propositions."

During this moderate, but really well-timed and effective appeal of the president, drooping heads began to be raised, perplexed and desponding countenances grew brighter, and by the
time he had closed, several speakers were on their feet, eager to
respond.

"Mr. Carpenter has the floor, I think, gentlemen," said the president.

"I rose," said Carpenter, "but to give my hearty response to the sentiments of the chair. It *is* time, *high* time, for some definite and decided action. Less talking and more action shall henceforth be *my* motto. I have not now, it is true, any digested proposition to present to the council; but I soon will have one, unless others are offered; for, in this emergency, it is little short of a crime to dally any longer."

"Ay, action! action!" responded several voices.

"A soon let it be, then," said Rowley, the next rising to speak. "If it be true, as has been urged, Mr. President, that we cannot raise money by general assessment without exceeding our powers and disaffecting the people, and that we must depend on voluntary contribution, which receivers, appointed for the purpose, may more appropriately gather in than ourselves, why are we needed here? I will, therefore, make a proposition, which, while it will be obnoxious to none of the objections brought against other plans of defence, will give gentlemen as much action as they want. I propose, Mr. President, that each of us here, before any more of us run away to the enemy, seize a standard, repair singly to the different hamlets among our mountains, cause the summoning drum to beat for volunteers, and lead them, when obtained, to do battle in person with this Jupiter Olympus of a British general, who has so nearly annihilated the country by proclamation."

"Tom Rowley all over! but a gallant push nevertheless," vivaciously exclaimed Samuel Robinson, in an under tone. "And yet, Mr. President," he continued, dropping the jocose, and now rising to speak in form—"and yet, if our colleague's spirited proposal could be carried into effect, and men be found to volunteer under such military leaders as most of us would make,—or if the different towns, as has been suggested by others, would order out the militia on our requisition,—even then, it appears to me, we should raise a permanent and regularly enlisted force, to serve a rallying point or nucleus for the militia, or our patriotic friend's army of volunteers. I therefore move, as I was about to do when others claimed the floor—I move the raising of a regular force, however small our means may compel us to make it; and as the smallest to be thought of, I will name one company of one hundred men, to be raised and supported by one of the methods suggested by the president."

"And I," said Clark, promptly rising—"and I, believing we

may venture to go a little higher than that, I propose, we have to raise two companies of sixty men each."

" No, No !" cried several voices ; " one company.   Means can be found for no more than one."

" Yes, yes !   the larger number first, Mr. President !   I go for two companies," cried others.

" And I go for neither, Mr. President ! " said Ira Allen stopping short in his walk, and turning to the chair.   " For] believe the council, on a little reflection, will conclude to do something more worthy of the character of the Green Mountain Boys, than the raising of the paltry force which even the bes' of these propositions involves.   And I doubt not the means of so doing may be soon and abundantly supplied, without infringing the constitution or distressing the people.   And I therefore move, sir, that this council resolve to raise a full regiment of men, forthwith appoint their officers, and take such prompt and speedy measures for their enlistment, that, within one week every glen in Vermont shall resound with the stir of military preparation."

" Chimerical ! " said one, who, in common with the rest of the council, seemed to hear, with much surprise, a proposition of this magnitude so confidently offered, when the doubt appeared to be whether even the comparatively trifling one of Clark would be adopted.

" Impossible, utterly impossible to raise pay for half of them," responded several others.

" Don't let us say that till we are compelled to do so," said the patriotic Carpenter, in an encouraging tone.   " This proposition jumps so well with my wishes, that I would not see it hastily abandoned.   For, although I confess I do not pretend to see where the requisite means are to come from, yet some new light, in this respect, may break in upon us by another day.   And could we but see our way clear to sustain this proposition, we should feel like men again."

" Amen to all that," responded Clark.   And as the hour for adjournment has now arrived, I move that our young colleague, who offered this proposition with so much confidence in the discovery of a way to carry it into execution, and who is said to be very fertile in expedients, be appointed a committee to devise the ways and means of paying the bounties and wages of the regiment he proposes to raise ; and that he make his report to the council by sunrise to-morrow morning."

" Second that motion, Mr. President " cried Lyon, in his usual full, determined tone of voice and strong Irish accent. "I go for the whole of Mr. Allen's proposition, means or no means. But the means can, must, and shall be found, sir! We will put the gentleman's brains under the screws to-night," he continued, jocosely turning to Allen; "and if he appears here in the morning empty-handed, he ought to be expelled from the council. Ay, and I'll move it, too, by the two bulls that redeemed me!" *

"I accept the terms," replied Allen, bowing pleasantly to the former. "Give me a room by myself, pen, ink, paper, and a lamp, and I will abide the condition."

"For your lamp, Mr. Allen, as your task is to discover money where there is none, I advise you to borrow the wonderful lamp of Aladin," gayly added Rowley, as the question was put, and carried; and the council, in a half-serious, half-sportive mood, broke up, and separated for the night.

At sunrise, the next morning, as had been proposed, the council punctually assembled to receive the promised report of their committee. Most of them, from having lodged in the same house, were aware that Allen had spent the whole of the intervening time on the business which had been committed to his charge; for, hour after hour, during that important night, they had heard the sound of his footsteps, as he continued to walk his solitary chamber, intensely revolving in his teeming mind the vexed question, upon the decision of which he felt the last chance of making a successful stand against the invaders of the state would probably depend. And this and the expectation, which had somehow been generally raised, that he would present some feasible plan for carrying out his proposals, the character of which no one could conjecture, caused his appearance to be awaited with no little curiosity and solicitude. They were not left long in suspense; for scarcely had the president called the council to order, before Allen came in, holding in his hand an

---

* Matthew Lyon, who very soon became much noted as a leading partisan in the legislature of Vermont, and subsequently more so as member of congress from Kentucky, having, as before intimated, been sold to pay his passage from Ireland to Connecticut, where he landed, was afterwards redeemed by the payment of a pair of bulls to the purchaser, by a gentleman of that state, for whom he was permitted to labor, at liberal wages, till this novel kind of indebtedness was cancelled. And as this bold and singular man entered upon his series of life as a successful freeman, he was fond of boasting of the ready manner in which he became one, while the expression, "by the two bulls that redeemed me," became his favorite oath on all occasions.

open sheet of paper, to which, as the yet un.lried .ah e·o▪ ed. m had just committed the result of his night's labor.

"Is the committee, appointed at adjournment last ev·· ·r⸵ p/o pared to make his report ?" asked the president.

"Fully, your honor," promptly responded Allen, who ⌐·· ⸴ :· ingly then rose and said, —

"My report, Mr. President, consists of two parts. The first comprises the nomination of a list of officers, from colonel to subaltern, for a regiment, to be styled *The Rangers*. The second part involves the subject more particularly committed to me, and proposes the means of raising and supporting them. As the first will be useless unless the second is adopted, I will submit it without present reading, and proceed at once with the second and more important proposition, which, after a long and patien: consideration of every argument for and against the measure, I have concluded to recommend to the council, as the best and most effectual means of securing the desired end. And that proposition, for the sake of convenience, as regards the action of the council on the principle involved, I have thrown into the form of the following resolution : —

"Resolved, That by specific decree of this council, and under regulations hereafter to be made, the estates, both real and personal, of all those who have been, or hereafter may be, identified as tories, aiders and abettors of the enemy, within this state, be confiscated for the military defence thereof; and that so much of said estates as may be needed for the payment of the bounties and wages of the regiment now proposed to be raised, be forthwith seized, and within ten days sold at the post, for that purpose, by the officers appointed by this council to execute its orders and decrees in that behalf."

The speaker, without offering any further remark in explana tion or defence of the measure he had reported, resumed his seat, and calmly awaited the expression of the council. But they were taken by such complete surprise by a proposition at that time so entirely new in the colonies, so bold and so startling in its character, that, for many minutes, not a word or whisper was heard through the hushed assembly, whose bowed heads and working countenances showed how deeply their minds were engaged in trying to grapple with the momentous subject, upon which thei· action ·a· t..·s unexpectedly required. At length, however, low murmu.s of doubt or disapproval began to be heard; and soon the expressions, "*unprecedented step !*" — "*doubtful policy !*" and "*injury to the cause*" became dis.

tinguishable among the over-prudent in different parts of the room,
when Matthew Lyon sprang to his feet, and, bringing his broad
palms together with a loud slap, exultingly exclaimed, —

"The child is born, Mr. President! My head has been in a
continual fog, every hour since we convened, till the present mo
ment; and I could see no way by which we could even begin to
do all that the exigency required, without running against law, or
distressing the people. But now, thank God, I can see my way
out. I can now see, at a glance, how all can be speedily and
righteously accomplished. I can already see a regiment of our
brave mountaineers in arms before me, as the certain fruits of this
bold, bright thought of our sagacious and intrepid young colleague.
Unprecedented step is it? It may be so with us timid republicans
but is it so with our enemies, who are this moment threatening to
crush us, because we object to receive their law and precedent?
How were they to obtain the lands of the half of Vermont, which,
it is said, they recently offered the lion-hearted Ethan Allen, if he
would join them, but by confiscating *our* estates? What has become of the estates of those in their own country, who, like ourselves, have rebelled against their government? From time
immemorial they have been confiscated. Can they complain
then, at our following a precedent of their own setting? Can they
complain because *we* adopt a measure, which, in case we are vanquished, they will not be slow to visit on *our* estates, to say nothing
of our necks? Can these recreant rascals themselves, who have
left their property among us, and gone off to help fasten this very
government upon us, complain at our doing what they will be the
first to recommend to be done to us, if their side prevails? Where,
then, is the doubtful policy of our anticipating them in this measure, any more than in seizing one of their loaded guns in battle,
and turning it against them? Injury to the cause, will it be? —
Will it injure our cause here, where men are daily deserting to
the British, in belief that we shall not dare touch their property
to strike a blow that will deter *all* the wavering, and most others
of any property, from leaving us hereafter? Will it injure our
cause here to have a regiment of regular troops, who will, perhaps, draw into the field four times their number, in volunteers?
If this be an injury, Mr. President, I only wish we may have a
few more of them; for, with a half dozen such injuries, by the
two bulls, we would rout Burgoyne's whole army in a fortnight.
Yes, Mr. President, this measure must go; for it promises every
thing to cause, and threatens nothing that honest patriots need

fear, and had I a hundred tongues, they should all wag a good stiff ay for its adoption."

"A bold meas.are, boldly advocated!" next spoke Carpenter. "But as bold as it is, Mr. President, I rise not to condemn it, but rather to say, that I am determined to meet it fairly, and without fear; and if, when I get cool enough to trust myself to make a decision, the objections to it appear no more formidable than they now do, I will give it my hearty support."

"If the public should call this a desperate remedy, they must recollect that it is almost our only one," remarked Olin, in his cool, quiet manner. "Nothing venture, nothing have;—let us go for it who dare!"

"Let us *oppose* it who dare!" warmly responded Lyon. "The measure will be a popular one; and let it once be known among the people, as I promise gentlemen it shall be, that this proposition was considerately recommended to us by a committee we appointed for the purpose — let this be known, and who among us has nerve enough to stem the storm of popular indignation that wil. burst on his head, for the timid and cowardly policy which led him to go against it?"

"Vermont," added Rowley — "Veimont was the first to show her sister states the way to take a British fort; let her also be the first to teach them the secret of making tories bear their proportion of the buidens of the war. I am already prepared to give the measure my support, Mr. President."

Almost every member, in turn, now threw in a few observations. The doubts and fears of the more cautious and wavering gradually gave way; and it soon became evident that the measure had found too much favor with the council to be resisted. Lyon, with his rough and pithy eloquence, had broken the ice of timidity at the right moment; and he and the originator of the measure, at first the only unhesitating members of the assembly, perceiving the gathering current in its favor, now warmly followed up their advantage; and, within two hours from its introduction, the resolution was adopted. This was immediately followed by the passage of the decree named in the resolution, specifying the names of those thus far fairly identified as openly espousing the British cause in Vermont, and declaring their estates forfeited to its use. Allen's proposal to raise a regiment of rangers was then, as a matter of course, unanimously carried, and the officers he had nominated were, with a few alterations, as unanimously appointed. All were now animated with a new spirit. Hope and confidence had taken the pace of doubt and despondency in their bosoms

and the remainder of the day was spent in carrying out the details
of their plan, which all agreed should now be put into execution
with the greatest possible promptitude and secrecy. In this, as
soon as the different appointments, made necessary for the execution of the decree, were completed by the united action of the
council, all the members, individually, took an active part. And
for many hours, they might have been seen sitting round the tables, silently and intently engaged with their pens; some in draft-
ing despatches to be sent to New Hampshire and Massachusetts,
some in writing confidential letters, unfolding their plans and asking the co-operation of the leading men in the different parts of
their own state, and some in making out commissions for the
military officers, or the commissioners and other officers of confiscation, while others were out, scattering themselves about
town, warily and cautiously inquiring out prompt and trusty messengers, to be despatched, as soon as it was dark, simultaneously
and post-haste, to convey these important missives to their different destinations round the country. And all being accomplished,
— the blow struck, and the machinery put in motion, — the
council concluded to adjourn, to meet again in a few days at
Bennington, the interim to be spent by them in repairing to their
respective spheres of influence among the people, and there
taking an active part in defending and explaining their measures, and assisting to carry them into operation.

Such was the origin of those temporary tribunals in Vermont,
subsequently termed courts of confiscation, which formed a prominent feature in her early history, and which furnished, it is believed, the first example of the exercise of this extraordinary
power ever known in the United Colonies during the revolutionary struggle. And whatever may have been the effects of this
retributive policy in other states, its results here were salutary
and important. It put an immediate stop to any further espousing
of British interests, especially among men of property, while,
within the astonishingly short space of fifteen days, it brought a
regiment of men into the field, well armed and prepared for instant service, — thus securing those advantages to the defenders
of liberty, in the peculiar posture of their affairs in which it was
introduced, and giving that impetus to their military operations,
without which the brilliant successes that marked the ensuing
campaign in Vermont could never have been obtained. Of this
there can scarcely be a doubt. And scarcely less doubt can
there be, that the important measure in question would not have
been brought forward and adopted at the crisis, in which alone

the advantages it then secured could have been derived from it but for its sole projector, the sagacious, scheming, and fearless Ira Allen.

Speculative writers have often amused themselves in tracing great events to small causes. And in this they have oftentimes so wonderfully succeeded, as to show, beyond the power of man to refute, some of the most trivial circumstances of life, considered by themselves, to have caused the revolutions of empires. Were we to make out an instance of this character, to be added to the many other remarkable ones which have been noted by the curious, it should be done by tracing the independence of America to the measure which Allen so boldly projected, as he walked his lonely chamber, on the eventful night we have described. The independence of the colonies was, at that dark crisis, balancing, as on a pivot; and the success of Burgoyne must seemingly have turned the scale against us. The success of Burgoyne, at the same time, hung on a pivot also; and the victory of Bennington, with all its numberless direct and indirect consequences, as now seems generally conceded, turned the scale of his fortunes, when his success, otherwise, could scarcely have been doubtful. But the victory of Bennington would never have been achieved but for the decided and energetic movement of Vermont, which alone secured the coöperation of New Hampshire, or, at least, insured victory, when, otherwise, no battle would have been hazarded. And that essential movement of Vermont would never have been made but for the bold and characteristic project of Ira Allen.

All this, to be sure, is but supposition; but who can gainsay its truthfulness?

CHAPTER II.

" Say what is woman's heart? — a thing
Where all the deepest feelings spring;
And what its love? — a ceaseless stream,
A changeless star — an endless dream —
A smiling flower, that will not die —
A beauty and a mystery ! "

WHILE the scenes last described were occurring at Manchester, in the Council of Safety, whose secret and unforeseen action was about to be felt in the remotest corners of the state, an athletic, well-formed, though plainly-dressed young man, whose fortunes, in common with those of hundreds around him, were suddenly and unexpectedly to be affected by the movements of that body, might have been seen, in the evening twilight, moving, with slow and apparently hesitating steps, across a new-mown field, towards a neat and commodious dwelling, situated on the main road leading from the town just named, to the south, and near where it entered the then fast increasing little village of Bennington. Though he wore no regular military uniform, or arms that were visible, yet there was that in his gait, manner, and general appearance, which indicated the recent occupation of a soldier, while the natural cast of his bold, manly features, and the clear, calm, and steady expression of his fine countenance, all combined to show him a man of coolness and courage ; and that, consequently, the seeming timidity and indecision of his present movements were attributable to some passing doubts respecting the issue of the business on hand, or other causes of a similar character, rather than any general want of firmness and resolution. After advancing within a stone's throw of the house, he turned into a clump of small trees, which, extending along the outer border of an unenclosed garden to the north of the establishment, had concealed his approach ; and here taking a position that commanded a view of the front and rear entrances of the house, he seemed to await some expected event, with manifestations of considerable uneasiness and solicitude. In a few moments, a slight stir, as of company taking leave, was heard in the front part of the house ; and very soon a fashionably-dressed personage

of a somewhat swaggering deportment, accompanied with many
of those supercilious airs with which the colonial loyalists of
the times often thought to dignify their carriage among despised
republicans, made his appearance in the yard, where, equipped
for riding, stood a stout, well-conditioned horse, which he approached and led out some distance into the road, preparatory to
mounting. He then paused, and, with a hasty glance around
him, covertly drew forth, from a concealed girdle apparently, a
pair of good-sized pistols, and carefully examined their flints and
priming; after which he replaced them, and, vaulting into his
saddle, rode leisurely away along the road leading northward.
In the mean time, the person first described retained his position
within his leafy concealment, where, unseen himself, he had seen
and watched from the first, with keen interest, all the movements
of the other, whom, at length, he seemed to recognize, with
recollections which caused him to recoil, and his whole countenance to contract and darken with angry and disquieting emotions. He was not allowed much time, however, for indulging
his disturbed feelings; for scarcely had the object of his annoyance disappeared, before his attention was attracted by a slight
rustling sound somewhere within the garden; when, turning his
head, the frown that had gathered on his brow suddenly gave
place to a look of joyful animation, as his eager eye caught a
glimpse of the light, fluttering drapery of a female, who, with
soft, rapid tread, was gliding along the outer edge of the screening shrubbery towards him. The next instant he was at her
side, ardently grasping her half-proffered hand, and tenderly
gazing into her sweetly-confused countenance.

"How grateful," he began, after a broken salutation — "how
grateful I should be for this obliging attention to the note I sent
you, soliciting a meeting which ——"

"Which my gallant preserver of old will be pretty sure to
misconstrue, I fear me," interrupted the maiden, with a half-
murmured, sportive laugh.

"No, Miss Haviland," he replied, too intent on a serious
demonstration of his feelings to respond in the same spirit — "no,
I am not so presuming; nor do I wish to count on the former
service, which you so magnify, and which has induced you, perhaps, to grant this interview."

"In part, I confess," was the answer to this implied question.

"I suspected — I feared so," he rejoined, despondingly. "Would
to Heaven you could have acted entirely aside from that motive,
and then I might have found cause to hope. But now," he

added, with suppressed emotion — "now —— But O, how can I harbor the chilling thought of being doomed to love without a return! Say, fairest and best, must this indeed be so?"

The downcast look and the quick-heaving bosom were the only reply; and the impassioned lover, gathering courage even from these uncertain indications, proceeded: —

"Years, eventful years, have passed away, my dear Miss Haviland, since your face, like some unexpected vision, first greeted my sight, and its image, at the same moment, as a thing not to be resisted, sunk deep into my heart. And there, from that hour to this, it has constantly remained — remained in spite of all my attempts to exclude it; for I struggled hard to banish it, as I had so much reason to do. You were the daughter of wealth and prosperity — I the son of poverty and misfortune; and, what was more revolting to my pride, you were found with my political opponents — my oppressors — nay, in the closest connection, apparently, with my bitterest foe. But with all the aid which these thoughts and associations were calculated to lend me, I struggled in vain. And when I was driven, poor, sorrowing, and desperate, from my home, by the wrongs and insults of this same man, of whose position towards you I was not left in doubt, I carried that image with me. It would not be eradicated; it would not even fade; but became more deeply impressed, and grew more and more vivid with time and change. In the stirring scenes of military life into which I then entered, — in the hour of battle, the exhausting march, the horrors of a prisonship, the perilous escape, and the lone wanderings through the wilderness, till I again reached the soil of freedom, — in all these, the impress remained unweakened, constantly presenting itself to my thoughts by day, and shaping my dreams by night. And it was this, when, on my return, I came into this quarter, where I had learned our scattered troops were rallying, and where I found myself near you — it was this that brought me to your father's dwelling — it was this, which, in spite of the coldness of my reception by all but yourself, urged me to the repeated visit, in which I was driven with insults from your house."

"Not by me, Mr. Woodburn," interposed the fair listener, in kindly and earnest tones — "not by me, nor by my consent or sanctioning. And it was mainly to show you this that I was induced to grant your request for this, on my part, I fear, imprudent meeting. No! O, no, sir, I have never forgotten — I can never forget — to whom I am indebted for my life; and gratitude as well as respect for his general character, will ever forbid

aught but kind and courteous treatment at my hands. And I hope
you will make some allowance for my father, who feels so
strongly that the people, whose cause you espouse, are criminally
wrong."

"I do make an allowance," responded Woodburn —"great
allowance for his imbittered state of mind towards the defenders
of the American cause; but does that fully accour for the
course he pursues towards me?"

"To be frank with you, sir, it does not," she replied, after
some hesitation. "There are those often with my father, who
are not backward in fanning his prejudices, and perhaps in instigating the undeserved treatment you have received. I may be
unwise in saying this; but justice to all, it appears to me, requires
that you should be apprised of it. You will not surely make use
of this to embroil us?"

"Certainly not; but what you communicate is hardly news to
me. I well understand that the principal one of those to whom
you allude is no other than the person who just rode away from
your house."

"You saw him, then? I am thankful you did not come in
collision with him; for he is a man you must avoid. Yes, that
was indeed Colonel Peters."

Colonel Peters! Colonel, did you call him? Has he, then,
actually joined the British forces, and received a commission for
such a post in their army?"

"Yes; but I had supposed this was known, else I might have
hesitated to disclose it, lest his frequent visits here might implicate
my father, who, I hope, may be induced to remain neutral in this
unhappy contest."

"Fear not. fair friend. No advantage shall be taken of this,
through my means, to the injury of your father. But, tell me,
does that officious adviser of your father still urge a suit, and
plead an engagement, of which, I have inferred, you would not be
sorry to be relieved?"

"He does," answered the maiden, sadly — "he does urge a
suit, and insist on an engagement, of which he knows I wish to be
relieved."

"Why should he do this?"

"Perhaps he counts on the effect of events to reconcile me —
events which he seems to expect will shortly happen — the complete triumph of his cause, the disgrace, banishment, or death of
its opposers, and his own elevation thereby to stations which, he
thinks, no woman will refuse to share with him. He counts

much also, probably, on the aiding influence of my father, who feels warmly interested in his success, and believes with the other that he, who is so loyal, while so many of his standing are otherwise, cannot fail of reaping a brilliant harvest of rewards, which, with the connection they propose, will reflect lustre on our family."

"Then it does not occur to them," said Woodburn, with a smile at this specimen of that loyal air-castle building in which the tories of the revolution seemed to have so extravagantly indulged — "it does not occur to them that it is even *possible* these splendid schemes may fail, in the failure of their cause in this country, which has thus, in anticipation, been parcelled out into dukedoms and lordships, to reward its sanguine adherents?"

"One would think not, from their conversation on the subject," replied the other.

"And what thinks *she*, whom they would have so much *interested* in this great issue?" asked Woodburn, encouraged to the question by the manner and tone of her last remark. "Has it never occurred to *her* mind that their cause, as strong as they deem it, is destined to fail; that even this vaunting army, which hangs so menacingly on our borders, may be swept away by the vengeance of a wronged, an insulted, and now aroused people; and that this despised people have right and Heaven on their side; and by the blessings of that Heaven, while they do battle in the consciousness of that right, will yet triumph, and become an independent nation, to which even her present haughty foe will do reverence?"

"It has," replied the maiden, warmly and with emphasis — "it has, Mr. Woodburn; and — why should I attempt to conceal it? — and I have wished — for I could not help it, though against the feelings, and, perhaps, the best interests of a generally kind parent — I have long secretly wished, and even prayed, for your success; because I could not stifle the conviction of the truth of what you assert respecting the wrongs of the American people, and the justice of their cause."

"Sabrey Haviland," exclaimed the surprised and delighted lover, "as long as I have respected and loved you, I have never till this moment, known you — never half appreciated the worth of your character!"

"What you may appreciate highly, sir, others may as highly condemn," she meekly responded. "I have said more to you than I have ever expressed to human being; and I may be wrong — wrong in saying it to you — wrong in saying it or believing it at all."

" Wrong? O, no, no, noble girl!" he rejoined, with increasing animation; " no, you are not wrong; you are right — right in your convictions, right in the wish, the prayer, and the declaration. Men will honor your honest independence, exercised against so much to bias and prejudice, so much to tempt and dazzle you; and Heaven will approve and bless you. But with such sentiments," he added, in tenderly expostulating accents — " with such sentiments, dear lady, will you doom me to plead my heart's cause in vain? Will you still adhere to a lover active in the work of oppression which you condemn, and reject his rival, equally active in the cause you approve and pray for?"

" I see my error, Mr. Woodburn," she replied, with an air of self-reproach and of slightly-offended pride, which, however, gave way to kindly tones, as she proceeded; " I have unintentionally helped you to an argument, while I am constrained to decide that no argument, so long as I stand in my present position, must prevail with me. Do not, then, O, do not press me with questions like these. You know not the extent of my perplexities, and I may not explain. Besides, are these the times to engage in such affairs, when the next hour may lead to an eternal separation, or place our respective destines as wide as the poles asunder?"

" But will you not allow me even to hope for the future?" still persisted the lover.

" Why should I bid you tantalize yourself with hopes so likely to prove futile, when nobler thoughts should engross you? Look, Mr. Woodburn," she said, pointing, with charming enthusiasm, towards the distant summits of Manchester, then beginning to be dimly visible in the rays of the rising moon, "cast your eyes northward! Beneath yon blue mountains is gathered the council of your people. There also rolls the recruiting drum of your brave Warner, who needs men like you; or if, as you intimated, you are waiting to engage in a different corps, which your council is expected to raise, would not your attendance there be more worthily bestowed, than in adding to the perplexities of one already so thickly surrounded with difficulties, and one who, to your suit, cannot say yea, while she would be pained to say nay?"

" Cruel girl, but noble in your cruelty!" exclaimed Woodburn, with mingled disappointment and admiration. " I will forbear to press my suit for the present, but not forever. I will heed the lesson of patriotism you have given me, but only to remember my fair prompter with deeper devotion."

" Hark!" said the other, starting; "I hear my father's chiding voice in the house inquiring for me. I must go. Adieu, Mr.

Woodburn. With this tendered hand of friendship and gratitude,
adieu."

"If it must be so, my precious, my beautiful one, farewell to
you, also."

Lips uttered no more, but the mute pause that followed, while
eye met eye, and hand lingered in hand, was not meaningless
The fond lover was not permitted, however, to prolong the entran
cing moment, which, as the slightly-returned pressure of the small
white hand, closely imprisoned in his own, told him, had not been
reluctantly vouchsafed him; for, quickly arousing herself, the
maiden broke from his clinging grasp, and tripped silently away,
leaving him gazing after her retreating form, and listening to the
soft and decreasing sounds of her light footsteps upon the grass,
till the jar of the closing door, to which she had directed her
devious course, made him feel that he was alone, and that the
charm of the place was gone.

With a sigh, he turned from the spot, and soon gained the
highway; when, taking the direction in which his rival and foe
had departed, he walked musingly onward, heedless alike of the
cool and balmly air of the evening, or the quietly reposing beauties which the light of a full moon, now beginning to peer over
the eastern hills, was gradually unfolding around him, and intent
only on the dreamy images with which love and his new-fledged
hope seemed conspiring for a while to amuse his willing mind
At length, however, a quickened pace, a firmer tread, and a
prouder bearing, showed that a different and less peaceful train
of thought was springing up within.

"So this evil genius of mine, it seems," he muttered, "who
forever appears in my path to snatch from me every prize I so
my heart on, is secretly an officer in the British service, com
missioned, probably, to head a regiment of tories, whom he is now
by his false statements and delusive promises, attempting to gather
from the weak and wavering of our overawed people. This
must be instantly made known. Heavens! what effrontery!—
to be playing the spy under the garb of pretended neutrality, and
seducing away the deluded men under our very noses, to lead
them back to fall with fire and sword on their kindred and neighbors! And I am to be the particular object of his vengeance, I presume, from the significant hint she gave me to avoid him. Avoid
him! He shall be spared much trouble to find me if that is what
he wants. He is now the country's foe, and lawful game with me.
I would that I could meet him to-night — yes, this night; and if I
thought I could overtake him — stay, why can't this be done?—

only three miles start, probably, and on a moderate trot; while my horse is a fleet one, and — and — we will try it."

By this time he had reached a log house, and barn of the same materials, which formed a small opening on the left side of the road, and which was the residence of a recently-married and here settled friend, in whose care he had left his horse before proceeding, as on the lady's account he did, through the adjoining wood and Haviland's broad fields beyond, to the clandestine interview with her that we have described. And now turning in towards this rude establishment, he hastily proceeded, without calling at the house, directly to the barn, that was partially enclosed by one of those close-laid, high, pole fences which the settlers usually constructed round their barns to protect their flocks against the depredations of wild beasts. Within this strong enclosure, the owner's cattle, consisting of a pair of oxen, cow, and two or three young creatures of the same species, were now quietly chewing their cuds, with those occasional wheezing grunts, which with them seem so indicative of animal enjoyment; while in one corner stood the horse of which Woodburn was in quest — a little model of a creature, of a lively, attent appearance, as now particularly manifested by a low, earnest, recognizing whinny, and by instantly starting off, in a sort of half trot towards the bars of the enclosure, as her master came up on the other side.

" Yes, yes, Lightfoot, you shall go now, and as fast as you desire, this time," responded the latter, throwing himself over the bars, and patting the animal on the neck, as he passed on to the barn for his saddle and bridle.

To equip his willing steed, examine the trusty pistols, which, like his foe, he carried about his person, let down, pass through, and replace the bars, occupied him but a moment, and he was about springing into his saddle, when he was hailed from the house.

" Halloo, there, Woodburn, is that you ? " exclaimed a cheerly voice, as a stout-built, crank, honest-looking young man, without hat or coat, came out of the door, and with a free and careless air made his way towards the other; " but what is your hurry? Nothing unpleasant has befallen you in your affair over yonder, that makes you feel like being off in this sly and hasty manner, has there ? "

" No, Risdon, not quite so bad as that yet," replied Woodburn, taking all in good part.

" How much better, then ? Come, Harry, I have taken stones enough out of your path, and thrown them into that of your rival there, to earn a candid answer to such a question."

"True, sir; but you ask more than I am permitted to know myself. I can neither get accepted nor rejected. She, however has given me fresh reason to admire her. She is no common girl, friend Risdon."

"There is not a finer or fairer in all the Green Mountains; bu what is that fresh reason you name?"

"The discovery that at heart she is warmly with us in the good cause"

"That is, you hope, and therefore believe so, eh?"

"I have a much better reason than that, sir, for my assertion. S.ie has, within this hour, told me so herself."

"Ah! Well, then, it is indeed so; for Sabrey Haviland never uttered aught but perfect truth and sincerity in all her life. Why, God bless her for her spunk and independence, living and visiting, as she mostly has, from a child, in that circle of high-toned and bitter tories. And it argues well for your suit, too, Woodburn, which till now I have considered rather an unpromising one; for it tells me that she will struggle hard to get free from the fetters which Peters and her father have fastened on her, and by which, counting on her high sense of the sacredness of all promises and contracts, they suppose have secured her beyond the least fear of escape."

"Do you allude to any thing other than the mere consent which she formerly gave to Peters's proposals of marriage, and which, I had supposed, constituted the only engagement existing between them?"

"Yes, a far stronger case, which I have learned by way of my wife, since I last conversed with you on the subject."

"Ah! What is it?" eagerly demanded the lover.

"Why as I gathered it, the case was this," answered the other. "The old man, as well as Peters, you know, must always do things, if possible, after the English custom; and both thinking more of property than women, they got up a regularly-written marriage contract, or settlement, by which one bound himself to give the other his daughter, with such and such a dowry, and the other to marry the daughter, and settle such and such sums on her and her heirs, all to be void in case the marriage fell through by fault of the girl. But to provide against this, they made another part to the instrument for her to sign, in which they made her solemnly promise and covenant to marry Peters, and none else; otherwise she was to forfeit her birthright in her father's estate This they somehow or other at last induced her to sign and seal thus binding herself hand and foot forever, with but one single advantage, which, it seems, she had the wit to get added to the

3 *

contract before she would sign it; and that was, that the time of fulfilling the contract, or day of the marriage, was to be left to her."

"What a detestable conspiracy for a father to enter into against the rightful liberty and happiness of a daughter!" exclaimed Woodburn, after a pause, during which surprise and indignation kept him silent. "That, then, explains the hints she has several times thrown out to me respecting some peculiar trials and difficulties to which she was subjected. But was she of age when she signed that paper?"

"No; but she probably, in her great scrupulousness, would long nesitate to break the engagement on account of that, or the fraudulent means they doubtless used to draw her into the shameful affair. Nevertheless, I would persevere. Her right to stave off the fellow, with her known wish to get rid of him, may yet procure her an honorable release; or she may be brought to take a different view about the binding nature of a promise obtained under such circumstances; or, as a last resort, that paper may be got out of his possession by some scheme or other. So I think you will worst him in the long run, in spite of his present advantages of the father's help, his own wealth, and ——"

"And his recent promotion," interrupted Woodburn, "which is to be the stepping-stone to the dukedom of Vermont, the reward for betraying his country, and the glittering bait, which, in anticipation, is already held out to this besieged, but bravely resisting, girl!"

"What do you mean, Woodburn?" bluntly said the other, in surprise.

"I mean," replied the former, "that Peters has lately received a colonel's commission in the British service, and is even now secretly but actively engaged, I suspect, in trying to seduce the people with British gold, and raise troops among us to coöperate with Burgoyne."

"You astonish me. Why, the hypocritical rascal has been giving out word about here, that, as he had friends and interests on both sides, he had concluded to remain neutral! Are you sure you have been correctly informed?"

"Quite sure. But while you may conjecture the source of my information, remember that it is to work no injury to the family of my informer."

"Ay, I understand, now — 'tis true, then; and you are correct, too, in your suspicions about his present movements. That will account for the existence of the hard dollars that have so strange ly made their appearance about here within a few days. But will he be suffered to prosecute his plans here among us? What better is he than a spy?"

" Nothing."

" He must be nabbed, then; and we will let him find his duke's coronet in a crow's nest, on the limb of some old hemlock, to which we will soon have him dangling in the air, unless our authorities wish to give him a more respectable gallows. What say you to that, Harry?"

" That you are not the first to think of it — that is, so far as to have him captured. He rode away from Haviland's in this direction, and at a moderate pace, just as I, unperceived by him, reached there, about an hour ago, on his way, doubtless, to one of the tory haunts in Manchester. My mare has a fleet foot, Risdon; so you now understand why I was in a hurry to be off, don't you?"

" I do; but Heavens! Woodburn, you are not going to give chase alone?"

" Yes; no horse but mine probably could overtake him before he reaches his associates; besides, since it was hinted to me that he would seek my life I am willing to give him a chance to take it, where neither he nor I shall have help or witness."

"Are you armed?"

" With dirk and pistols, as he only is."

"A rather hazardous push, Harry. But go, and God prosper you to take him, and with him that mischievous document. And one thing more: if you live to reach Manchester, tell that Council of Safety, that if they don't do something soon, we, the people, will set up for ourselves in war-making. I, for one, don't believe I can keep my hands off my rifle three days longer."

"Ay, ay," said Woodburn, springing into his saddle. "And now, Lightfoot, here is a loose rein for you. Go!" he added, striking with his heels the body, and with his hands the mane of the impatient animal, that, at these well-understood signs, gave an irregular plunge or two ahead, and then shot off like an arrow up the road.

CHAPTER III.

" What heroes from the woodland sprung,
　　When, through the fresh-awakened land,
The thrilling cry of freedom rung,
And to the work of warfare strung
　　The yeoman's iron hand ! "

LEAVING Woodburn to the hot and eager pursuit that patriotism and private animosity had prompted him to undertake, we will now precede him a few miles on the road, for the purpose of introducing and accompanying another old acquaintance, who was also destined to become an actor in the wild and stirring adventures of the night.

Near the southern confines of Manchester, about nine o'clock, the same evening, a youth of the probable age of twenty, of a sandy complexion, and of a rather slight, but evidently tough, wiry frame, with a short rifle on his shoulder, and powder-horn and ball-pouch slung at his back, was making his solitary way on foot along the main road towards the town just mentioned. As he now reached the Batenkill, where the stream, here first beginning to find a more peaceful flow, after its headlong descent from the Green Mountains, intersected the road, he suddenly paused and began to muse, with the air of one who has been struck by some new thought tending to divert him from his settled purposes ; and, slowly passing on to the bridge, which, after the rude construction of the times, had been thrown across the river at this place, he took a seat on one of the side-timbers, or binders, as they were usually termed, and, in accordance with an old and inveterate habit, generated probably by the peculiar circumstances of his early life, began to commune with himself aloud.

" I wonder what this new business is they want you should do Bart ? Harry said it was a secret matter when he handed over he paper," he continued, pulling out and abstractedly unrolling a small wad of white paper, " a kinder private commission, or something, which he would explain about, after I had gone and got his letter to the girl, as he met me on my way back But why don't he meet me fore this time ? It's pesky strange he should hang back in a woman affair so! Why, he would go—like enough has gone — but then how could he miss me? O Lord, Bart, what a stupid pup! He passed you when you was napping it in the bushes at that cool spring! I'll bet my old hat on't! Well, we shan't see much more of him to-night, likely, seeing it is love he's doing, and such a moon as this holds the candle; and we may as well be trying to find out this business without him. So let's be digging out what the paper says. Harry and the rest of 'em don't know I can read writing; but I can, when driv to it; though I think we won't let 'em know that, Bart; for no knowing what cunning things we may find out if they don't mistrust it. Now let's look. Why, I can see as plain as day!" he added, holding up the writing to the bright moonlight, and beginning to spell out the well-known bold and distinct characters of the secretary of the council, as follows:—

"To BARTHOLOMEW BURT:—
"You are hereby appointed by the Council of Safety to go through this and the neighboring towns, bordering on the British line of march; to spy out the resorts of the tories; to mark and identify all inimical persons; to gain all the information that can be obtained respecting the movements of the enemy at large; and make report, from time to time, to this council or some field officer of our line.
"IRA ALLEN, *Secretary.*" *

"Good! grand!" exclaimed the excited soliloquist, starting up and snapping his fingers in high glee. "This will be a great thing for you, Bart. Yes, and then how gentlemanly and respectful-like it sounds to be called Bartholomew, in that way! Bart, we'll go it for them; and have a touch of the trade this very night, if you please. But where shall we begin? Let's see, now. Why, there's old mother Rose's haunt up the great road here, where, I do think, she must hatch out tories, same as a hen does chickens, they are so thick about there. Then there's

* Those who may doubt the probability that such a commission would be issued by this body, would do well to consult that part of the journal of their proceedings, at this period, which has been preserved and published, in which will be found several similar ones, to serve as specimens of the many contained in the part that was lost, and to show how searching were the operations of these vigilant guardians of the cause of liberty in Vermont, and how various the instruments they made use of to effect their objects.

M

Josh Rose courting that up and a coming sort of girl you saw
at Howard's t'other day, when you called with Harry for a
drink of water.   Now wouldn't the fellow be apt to let out secrets there that we could get hold of, and put us on some good
scent ?   Ah ! that's it; so now up the river for Howard's, as a
beginning, hit or miss, Bart."

While this singular genius is proceeding on his proposed destination, in the hope of accomplishing something to show himself
worthy of the curious trust that had been so unexpectedly reposed in him, we will occupy the breathing spot, thus afforded
in our narrative, in apprising the reader, more definitely than
we have yet done, of the main incidents that had marked the
checkered fortunes of the two adventurers whom we have now
again brought upon the scene of action, since we left them.

When Woodburn and Bart left the state, under the circumstances described in the closing chapters of our first volume, they
proceeded directly to Cambridge, where the revolutionary army
was then gathering for the siege of Boston, enlisted, for two
years, into the continental service ; and actively participated in
all the most important movements of the army in the campaign
that immediately succeeded.   They were at Bunker Hill, on that
memorable day of fire and blood, so glorious for the yeoman
patriots of New England, and so fearful for her foes, —

> " When first, as at Thermopylæ,
>   The battle shout of freemen rose ;
> Firm as their mountains, and as free,
>   They nobly braved encountering foes."

And in the following autumn, they, in the same company, in
which Woodburn, for bravery and good conduct, had been made
a subaltern officer, marched with that division of the army which
Arnold, with almost unequalled energy and fortitude, and amidst
privation and suffering untold, led through the snow-clad wilderness of morass and mountain, to the distant Quebec.   And
there, in the onset, in which the high-souled Montgomery fell,
they were together cut off from their company and made prisoners ; when, after having, for nearly a year and a half, endured the
sufferings of a British prison-ship, they together escaped at Halifax,
wandered, half naked and starving, through the seemingly interminable forests of Brunswick and Maine, to the American settlements, and finally reached home ; not there, however, long
to repose, but soon to repair, with yet unbroken spirit, to the
new scene of action, at which their countrymen were beginning

to rally to meet the formidable invasion of the hitherto victorious
Burgoyne.

We will now resume the thread of our narrative. A walk
of twenty or thirty minutes brought Bart to the log tenement of
Howard, who was a soldier in the continental service, now absent
on duty, having left his house and business in charge of his wife
a woman no less noted, in her neighborhood, for energy in con
ducting her domestic affairs, than for the patriotic spirit with
which she espoused the American cause. She and her daughter,
a rustic beauty of eighteen, of keen perceptions, and even rare
good sense, when her frolicsome disposition would allow her to
exercise it, were now the only permanent inmates of this secluded
cabin, which consisted of but two rooms, with a front entrance
leading through an entry into either of them, and another door at
the end of the house opening into the one usually occupied by
the family as both sitting-room and kitchen.

"A light in both rooms, by the pipers!" exclaimed Bart, as,
after having cautiously approached, he paused to reconnoitre the
house. "The fellow is there at his traps, as sure as a gun!
Now what's to be done, Bart? 'Twon't do to go in and show
yourself, and have that torified scamp carry away word that you
are mousing round the country nights, will it? No, but I'll tell
you what, if it want for the name of sneaking and evesdropping,
we would creep round back of the room where they be, and hark
through the cracks; like enough get a peep, and so learn something. But such things they expected of you, didn't they, Bart?
Must be so, I think. Then suppose we throw the name and
blame of it on the council, and try it, mister?"

Taking a wide sweep round the house, Bart soon approached
that part of it, on the back side, in which he rightly conjectured
the young people were sitting; and gliding up to the wall with
steps as noiseless as those of a mousing fox, he discovered a
crevice between the logs, from which the moss calking had fallen
out so as to permit a small pencil of light to escape. Guided by
this, he quickly gained, after applying his eye to the aperture, a
distinct view of the couple within, and was enabled, at the same
time, to catch every word of their variously modulated conversation. They were seated at different sides of a light-stand, on
which a candle was burning, she assiduously engaged, to all
appearance, with her needle on some light sewing work, and he
no less diligently, with his penknife, on a pine chip, which he
was essaying to shape into a human profile, that of his mistress,
as might be surmised from the sly glances with which he seemed

occasionally to scan her features. Though now dressed in his
smartest fustian, he yet appeared awkward and ill at ease:
while the timid and hesitating air, with which he seemed to
regard his fair companion, indicated much conscious uncertainty
respecting the place he might hold in her affections. She, on
the contrary, seemed quite self-possessed, and wore the air of
one not particularly solicitous about pleasing, which gave her as
much advantage over him in her manner as she obviously possessed in her person ; for, besides a good form and a wholesome
roseate bloom, she had one of those polyglot countenances which
seem almost to supersede the necessity of speaking — a trait she
very prettily exhibited while listening to the forced hints and in-
nuendoes of her lover's conversation, as she occasionally lifted her
head, now with a blush, now with a smile, and now with a frown,
that caused his eyes to drop to the floor as quick as those of a
rebuked schoolboy. Thus far, she had not opened her lips ; but
now, as her suitor, turning in his chair, brought a hitherto shaded
arm into view, and displayed upon his sleeve a common brass
pin, (usually denominated in those days the Canada pin, as this
article, then almost excluded from the toilet by the war, rarely
found its way into this section except through the intercourse of
the tories with that province,) her attention was suddenly excited ;
and turning a sharp and searching look upon him, she said, —

" Where have you been lately, Josh ? "

" Why ? " he replied, evidently surprised at the question and
manner of the girl.

" That, sir," she responded, significantly pointing to the pin.
' Such articles don't get here but in one way, in these hard
times, which compel us to put up with thorns for pins, and
half tories for beaux," she added, with a meaning and roguish
look.

" Won't you accept it, Vine ? " he said, obviously disconcerted,
but pretending not to understand her allusions.

" Not unless you tell me honestly how you got it, sir," she
replied, decisively.

" O, picked it up somewhere ; don't remember now," he evasively answered.

" That, now, is a thumper, I know," she rejoined, with a pretty
toss of the head. " But you don't put me off so. The fact is
Josh, I suspect you have been among the tories to-day. Now be
honest, and tell me, sir."

And for the next ten minutes the determined girl plied her
reluctant and perplexed companion, by all the means which her

ingenuity could invent, to accomplish her object; teasing, coaxing and threatening by turns, till, being unable to resist any longer, he replied,—

"Well, I will tell you; and it can't do any hurt either, for they will all be out of reach before morning."

"Who will be out of reach?" eagerly demanded the other.

"The men that my brother Samuel enlisted. You knew he had got a captain's commission in General Burgoyne's army, I 'spose."

"We heard so; but has Captain Samuel Rose been in town to-day?"

"Yes; for I may as well tell the whole, now I've begun. The captain has been all day at the house of brother Asa Rose, who lives out of the way, there, in the woods, over beyond the great road, you know. Well, he had agreed to meet all he had enlisted in this section there at sunset, and lead them off to the British camp, after people were abed. I was there just before dark, and saw them; sixteen in all, besides the captain, all armed and equipped, and he in full uniform; and he looks complete in it, too, I tell you."

"But what was you among them there for?"

"O, I wanted to see Sam, and bid him good-by, you know, as he was going off, never to come back, for aught I knew; that was all, upon honor, now."

"Perhaps it was; but one thing I wish you to understand, Josh Rose, and that is, if you take up for that side of the question, openly or secretly, your visits here——"

"O, I shan't; no notion on't, not the least in the world; so don't worry; though candidly, Vine, I don't believe it's much use for your folks to think of standing out any longer. Why, hundreds are joining the British every day, and what will be left, in a short time, can do nothing towards stopping such an army as Burgoyne's."

"What are left will be apt to try it, I think, sir."

The subject was now dropped; and the girl, after a thoughtful pause, commenced on a theme more agreeable to her suitor, and for a short time, was unusually sociable and gracious; when she rose, and, carelessly remarking she must be excused a moment, left the room, and passed out through the front door, with noise enough in opening and closing it to leave the other in no doubt as to the direction of her exit.

"Well, Bart, what do you think of that?" whispered our listener to himself, as now, on the departure of the girl from the room, he withdrew from his peeping-hole. "Now, I pretend to say, I wouldn't take a gold guinea for what we have got through that crack, nor two either, if our legs will carry us to the village and rally help quick enough to have that batch of tories nabbed before they are off. But let's jest edge along against the mother's room, and see if there is any discovery to be made there, before we start."

Being equally fortunate in finding an opening into the room to which his attention was now directed, Bart cautiously peered in; when his eye soon fell on the solitary occupant, a fine, resolute-looking matron, quietly employed in knitting by the light of a torch stuck in one of the stone jambs of the broad fireplace. He, however, had scarcely time to note these circumstances before the door was softly opened, and the girl who had just left the other room entered on tiptoe, and whispered in her mother's ear something that seemed to produce an instant effect on the hitherto sedate and listless countenance of the latter; for, starting to her feet, she stood gazing at the other with a flashing eye, and listening with the keenest interest, as some further particu-'ars were added to the communication.

"Are you sure he was not fooling you?" said the mother.

"Very sure," replied the daughter, significantly holding up the Canada pin.

"Well, Vine," rejoined the former, with the air of one whose resolution is taken, "you whip back to your post the same way you came; and see that you keep him here till — say about mid-night," she added, exchanging a meaning glance with the daugh-ter, whose hand was already on the latch to depart.

No sooner had the intermingling tones of conversation in the other room apprised the woman that her daughter had there joined the unsuspecting suitor, than, hastily seizing bonnet and shawl, she noiselessly left the house and glided out into the road. After hesitating a moment here, respecting the course she should take, apparently, she made up to the log-fence enclosing an adjoining field, threw herself over it with the lightness of a boy, and, strik-ing off directly west, almost flew over the ground till she reached the boundaries of their little opening; when she fearlessly plunged into the dark and pathless recesses of the wood lying between her and the main road, to which she was evidently directing her course.

"There! just as I told you," muttered Bart, who, inwardly vexed that the secret he had been hugging, as exclusively his own should be shared by another, for fear measures might be taken to deprive him of the sole honor and profit he had promised himself of communicating it, had been jealously noting what had occurred. "Just as I told, Bart; the old woman has got your story, and there she goes, streaming off with it, like the house afire, for the great road, through woods, swamp, and all! Well, it's too late to try to stop her now, to save her the trouble of going, cause you'd frighten her, likely; besides, she'd find out you'd been listening. But we'll follow and keep track of her; may be she'll get lost, and we can cut by her; or may be we can seem to come kinder accidentally on her, and contrive to get employed to do her errand, and so let her go back."

With this resolution, he immediately gave chase; and by occasionally pausing, after entering the forest, to listen to the rustling of her garments as the intrepid woman rushed through the tangled thickets on her way, or the cracking of dry twigs under her rapid tread, he was enabled to trace her course and keep within hearing distance, though not without exertions which drew forth many an exclamation of surprise at the speed with which, at such a time and place, she got over the ground. At length, they both reached the opening on the other side of the forest opposite to a good-sized house on the main road.

"I vags," exclaimed Bart, pausing and wiping the perspiration from his face with his sleeve, as he emerged from the wood, "if the perlite Frenchman, they tell of, who thought women had no legs, had followed this one through a mile-swamp at the rate she has gone, he would think a little different about the matter, I guess. But never mind the tramp, Bart, but still keep your eye on her. There she goes smack into that house over yonder, which is — let's see, now — Why, that is Major Ormsbee's, who, I remember now, Harry told me, was her brother. Well, Bart, seeing you are fairly beat in this business, let's work along over into the road against the house, and see what comes of it."

Scarcely had Bart gained his proposed situation in a nook of the fence, before the major, followed by his son, came bustling out into the yard.

"Jock!" he said, hastily turning to his son, "you run to the barn, and saddle and bring out my horse, while I slip over to Captain Barney's. But who have we here?" he added, espying and approaching Bart. "Who are you, friend?"

"Well, you may call me any thing but a tory and I won't complain, major."

"That's right. O, I believe I know you now — the comical chap I have seen with Woodburn, at Warner's encampment

All right. Glad you happen here just at this time — we have business on hand."

"I know it."

"Know it! how? You didn't come with my sister?"

"No; after her; but got at the wrinkle about the gang down yonder before she did; and am now on my way to the council, or the camp, with the news."

"That I propose to do myself. I have a fleet horse, and it will be best I should go with the news myself. Besides, I wish to put you, with the few others I can raise hereabouts, on the track at once. You shall lose nothing by it; so turn in here, and go with me."

Content with this assurance of an officer known to be in the confidence of the council, and quite willing to make one in the expected affray, Bart cheerfully complied. And the two hurried on to the house the major had named; where, fortunately, they found not only the owner, but another fearless patriot, by the name of Purdy, to both of whom the news just received was communicated; when a hasty plan was devised among them for the capture of Captain Rose and his band of recruits, who, it was supposed, had not yet left the neighborhood, even if they had started from their place of rendezvous.

The dwelling of Asa Rose, which had been selected by the tory captain as a secluded and safe rallying-point for his band, was situated in the wood, about three fourths of a mile west of the main road, and the residence, thereon, of the old widow Rose, who has been already mentioned, and who was the mother of a hopeful brood of either open or secret loyalists, as their father, an extensive land-owner, who died about the beginning of the war, was before them. This old establishment of the Rose family, well known through the country as the harboring-place of the disaffected, was a little over a mile from the bridge over the river, at the south, and about half that distance from the residence of Major Ormsbee, at the north, where our handful of spirited friends were now rallying; while from the road, about half way between the two, diverged the path, which wound round south-westerly to Asa Rose's, and from which the tories were expected to emerge on their way out of the neighborhood.

"Here comes Jock with my horse," said the major, taking the reins from the boy, a sturdy youth of sixteen, who had not forgotten to bring his gun with him. "Well, captain," he continued, leaping into his saddle, "you understand the arrange ment; three of you to take the path to their rendezvous, one to go on to old mother Rose's, and, if they ar there, give the signal : the long howl of a dog, remember; bu if they are not there, to join the rest, and scout round, watch and delay them ; while I, on my way, start out Pettibone and others, and send them directly through the woods to Asa Rose's to get into the rear All understand, do you ? "

" Ay, ay, major."

" Well, then, God prosper you all, till I can get on with a platoon of Warner's boys for the rescue."

So saying, the major dashed off at full speed towards the village ; while Barney and his men, with no less spirit, hurried on to their respective destinations, in the opposite direction. The place where the latter were to separate being soon reached, appearances examined, and no discoveries made, the captain, with Purdy and young Ormsbee, struck off from the road, and proceeded cautiously along the bushy outskirts of the path before mentioned as leading to the supposed rendezvous, leaving to Bart the task of going on and reconnoitring the old establishment on the main road, at which, it was believed, the tories would be sure to call, on their way out, to take a last treat from mother Rose's ever-ready bottle, and perhaps some provisions from her cupboard, to invigorate them for their long night march to the British camp. A short walk now brought Bart in close vicinity to the house he was appointed to reconnoitre ; when, gliding silently along under cover of the fences, tall weeds, and other screening objects, he quickly made a circuit round the buildings, contriving, as he did so, to peer into the barns, sheds, and even into most of the rooms of the capacious old dwelling. He perceived, however, no indications of the presence of any but females about the establishment ; though, from the movements of these, and especially those of the old woman, who was busily engaged in cutting up large quantities of bread and cheese, and in replenishing her junk bottles, he became satisfied that the company, of whom he was in search, were shortly expected. Having made these observations, he retired from the house, crossed over the road into the opposite field, and was marking out a course for himself through the wood, which would intersect the path taken by his companions, and enable him to join them somewhere near the tory rendezvous, when his ear caught the clattering of horse-hoofs, approaching, at a furious pace, up the road from the south, And so rapid was the advance of the coming horseman, that Bart had scarcely time to gain the covert of a clump of shrubbery

4 *

standing by the fence, over against the house, before the former made his appearance, and, turning into the yard, galloped up to an open window, and addressed a hasty inquiry to the mistress of the house ; when, hardly waiting for the negative reply that appeared to be given, he suddenly wheeled about, and, regaining the road, pursued his course with renewed speed.

"Why !" exclaimed Bart in surprise, as he caught a view of the man's features ; " as sure as a gun, it is Harry's old troubler, that he thought he'd killed once, and felt so guilty about it, till ne heard he didn't. But what can the fellow be up to here, in such a hurry, just at this time ? Don't like the looks on't, exactly. Bart, hasn't this tall tory got wind of our movement, somehow, and come on to warn the gang, that, not finding here, he has gone to meet ? Let's be off and try to trace him. But hark ! Do you hear that ? Another coming from the same quarter ! yes, and scratching gravel too, like Mars, I should think, by the way his horse's feet strike the ground ! Here he comes ! What ' it is, by mighty — it's Harry and Lightfoot in full chase ! Go it, Lightfoot ! Catch him, Harry ! Stuboy ! stuboy !" he added, in low, eager shouts of exultation, as the recognized horseman passed, like a flash, by his place of concealment.

Springing forward to a small elevation in the field, which commanded a broken view of the road to the path before described, and even a small portion of the latter, Bart tasked both eye and ear to the utmost, in trying to trace the dimly-discerned forms of the receding horsemen, now obviously but a short distance asunder, his object being to ascertain whether Peters would keep on in the main road, or, as he suspected his intention to be, strike into the path to Asa Rose's, and try to reach the tories before he should be overtaken. For one moment, in which he lost sight of both pursuer and pursued, Bart stood in doubt ; but the next, the changing direction of the still audible sounds, and the slight glimmerings of the sparks from the horse's hoofs, now seen extending out in a line nearly at right angles to the course they had been pursuing, sufficiently apprised him that his suspicions were correct. Waiting, therefore, no longer than to ascertain this, he turned and plunged into the wood on his left ; and taking the course he had already decided on for joining his companions, and being now incited to his utmost exertions of speed by his anxiety to reach the other road in time to warn Woodburn of the trap into which his antagonist was doubtless intending to draw him at the tory rend zvous, or to be ready to lend any needed assistance in case o 'ollision took place between them before

reaching it, he made his way through the opposing obstacles of
the thickets with a rapidity, probably, that a wild Indian could
not have equalled, till he suddenly found himself in the path
of which he was in quest, within a few rods of the small opening
where stood the suspected log-tenement of Asa Rose. His first
act now was to stoop down and examine the soft ground in the
road, to ascertain whether Peters and his pursuer had passed the
place. A moment's inspection, however, confirming him in the
negative, he rose and bent a listening ear in the direction of their
expected appearance ; but no sounds reached him indicative of
their approach. While standing here in doubt respecting the
course next to be pursued, his attention was attracted by a commotion at the house ; when, stepping forward towards the edge
of the opening, he caught a glimpse of the whole body of the
tories, with their leader at their head, just leaving the house and
moving silently, and with a quick step, in the road towards him.
Stealing softly away from his post of observation, he retreated
rapidly along the path, some hundred yards into the wood ; when
he fortunately encountered Barney and his two men, to whom
he hastily communicated all the discoveries he had made since
he left them.

Fearing, from the non-appearance of Peters and his pursuer,
of whom, strangely, nothing had yet been seen or heard, that
the former had given the latter the slip in some by-path, which
would enable him to reach the tories in the rear, or otherwise
apprise them of the danger of proceeding, Barney instantly
adopted the bold resolution of attempting the immediate capture
of the whole band by stratagem, trusting to the firmness and
ingenuity of himself and his men to keep, or get them forward,
till the expected reënforcement should arrive.

" We must multiply ourselves, and then act according to circumstances," he said, after apprising his men of his project, which
they eagerly seconded.

" I will multiply into a platoon of ten, and be their orderly,
if you will let me have my own way in the managing of 'em,
captain," said Bart, entering with great spirit into a plan in which
his peculiarities so well fitted him for taking a leading part.

" Well, then," replied the other, " take a station in the bushes
five or six rods ahead ; the rest of us will take our coverts here,
on different sides of the road. You must all act for yourselves,
and on the hints of the moment ; but I will take the lead, and
give you such clews as the case may require."

Scarcely had this fearless little band settled themselves in their

respective stations, before the tories, marching in close Indi a
file, made their appearance, and came forward wholly unsus₁ i-
cious of danger. They were permitted to advance unmolested
till they were nearly all between the two points of ambush;
when Captain Barney, stepping partly out from his concealment
presented his gun, and exclaimed, —

" Stand ! Surrender, or die ! "

" Halt ! " cried the surprised, though not frightened, tory ₋ap-
tain, who was not only a fine-looking, but cool and capable
young officer — " halt, till we see what all this means."

" You will soon find out what it means, unless you surrender,"
rejoined Barney, in a bold and confident tone. " I give you one
minute to decide.   Attention there ! " he continued, as if addressing a numerous band of concealed forces — " attention there,
right, left, and front platoons ! Every man at his station and
ready for the word ! "

Purdy and Ormsbee now made a simultaneous movement in
the bushes, on the different sides of the road, by stepping about,
hitting their guns against the trees, and thrusting out the muzzles
at various openings towards the enemy ; while, at the same time,
the clicking sounds, as of the irregular cocking of a dozen muskets, with as many distinct movements of men, apparently, were
heard in the direction of Bart's concealment in front.

" Stand to your arms ! " exclaimed Rose, to his men, who now
began to show signs of fear and uneasiness.

" Don't all take aim at the captain, you fools ! " shouted Bart,
from his covert, to his men of straw ; " don't do that, I tell
you ! There's enough of 'em to furnish each of you a separate
mark, nearly. There, that looks more like it ! All cocked and
ready ? "

" Hold up there, Sergeant Burt ! " cried Barney ; " don't fire
yet. Let us spare their lives if we can. Purdy," he continued,
turning to the man concealed on his right, " you may give the
signal, now, for the reserve platoons, in front and rear, to advance, and close up on the road. The minute is nearly out, and
I perceive we have got to make a demonstration before they will
surrender."

The signal howl was then accordingly given, and, to the great
joy of the assailants, immediately answered by Pettibone, who,
having reached his destination in the rear of the house, and seen
the tories decamping, was now, with another man, cautiously
advancing towards the scene of action in the wood ; while nearly
at the same moment, as it strangely happened, the sharp reports

of three pistols, fired in quick succession, rang through .he 'orest a short distance on the road to the north. The noise of fire-arms which, to the assailants, portended a rencounter between Peters and Woodburn, and filled them with anxiety for the fate of the latter, was taken by the tories as an answer of the signal from the pretended corps in front, and so completed their dismay that some of them threw down their arms, and began to cry out for quarter.

"The minute is out ; shall we fire, Captain Barney ? " ex· claimed Bart, in a tone of impatience.

"Your answer, Captain Rose," sternly demanded Barney –- "your answer this instant, or ——— "

"I yield," said the reluctant tory leader. " We surrender our· selves prisoners of war."

"'Tis well, sir," responded the former. " Lay down your arms, then, here in the road, advance twenty paces, and wait further orders."

While this order, which was thus given for the double purpose of enabling the victors to get between the tories and their guns, and to give time for Pettibone and his associate to come up, was being carried into effect, Bart, who had been burning with impatience for a chance to go to the assistance of his endangered friend, Woodburn, slunk noiselessly from his post, and made his way, with all possible speed, towards the spot from whence the noise of the firing appeared to proceed.

But let us now return to note the issue between the belligerent horsemen. Woodburn having come in sight of his antagonist soon after crossing the river, and the latter then taking the alarm, the chase had proceeded, as witnessed by Bart, till the parties struck into the by-road leading to the tory rendezvous ; when the former, concluding that Peters would not have turned in here without the expectation of finding friends and defenders near, now redoubled his exertions to overtake him, and bring on an encounter while it would have to be decided by individual prowess, and before his foe should reach assistance to render the pursuit futile or dangerous. But notwithstanding his efforts, he soon lost sight of the other in the short turns of the winding and thickly-embowered path which they soon entered. Expecting, however, that the next turn in the road would reveal the object of his pursuit, he dashed ahead some distance ; when, becoming satisfied that his antagonist had given him the slip by riding out of the road into some nook or side-path in the wood, he retraced his way nearly to the opening, vainly endeavoring to discover the concealment of the fugitive. Vexed and disappointed at being thus balked, Woodburn was on the point of giving up the chase when he caught a glimpse of the other, emerging from a thicket into the road, not a hundred yards distant, and setting off on a gallop in the direction first taken. Incited to fresh exertion, Woodburn now shot forward after his flying foe with a velocity which none but a horse trained to the rough paths of the wood could equal, and which, consequently, soon brought the parties in close vicinity of each other. Peters, now seeing no further chance to escape, suddenly pulled out a pistol, and, turning in his saddle, discharged it at Woodburn, who, wholly unharmed by the badly-aimed instrument, instantly returned the fire. The bullet of the latter, grazing the person of the former, entered the head of his startled and rearing horse, just back of the ears, and, after two or three fearful plunges onward, brought him to the ground. Leaping from his falling horse, the desperate loyalist gained his feet and discharged another pistol at Woodburn; when, perceiving his opponent still unhurt, and about to make a rush upon him, he leaped over the body of his dying horse, still floundering in the edge of the bushes, and, in the noise thus occasioned, and in the screening smoke of his own fire, made good his escape into the forest.

" Come back, miscreant! coward! " shouted Woodburn, dismounting, and leaping forward to the place where the other had disappeared — " come back, and decide your fate or mine."

But the new-made tory colonel, who was more a coward from conscience than nature, in the present instance, perhaps, did not see fit to accept the challenge for a further personal combat. And Woodburn, judging that any attempt to pursue him in the woods would be useless, reluctantly gave up the chase, and turned to go back to his horse; when Bart, running up and peering an instant at the dying horse and then at his friend, rushed by the latter, and, throwing himself on the neck of his loved pony, fell to hugging and fondling her in an ecstasy of delight.

" O Lightfoot! Lightfoot! " he exclaimed; " lucky divil that you are, not now to be sprawling and kicking, like your tory brother there in the bushes! Yes, that you are, Lightfoot; and you shall have an oat-supper to-night that would make a horse laugh, for catching up with the rapscallion."

" Bart! " said Woodburn, in surprise; " how did you get wind of this? But no matter. You have come too late."

" Know it — couldn't help it, though — had other fish to fry first, that musn't cool. Captain Rose and sixteen other tory prisoners are on the road here, just below.'

"Prisoners! how? By whom taken?"

"O, Captain Barney, and Bart, and I, and Mr Stratagem and one or two others"

"What, only three or four of you to seventeen?"

"No; I was a flanking party of ten in the bushes, and sergeant of 'em — cocked all their guns for 'em, by cocking and uncocking my own — talked for 'em all, out of seven corners of my mouth at once, and kept 'em from firing till the word, you know. We heard your firing, and called you the front-guard; and — and we took 'em — every dog of 'em."

"Bravoes! and no fool of an exploit on your part neither, Bart, if all this is so. But are the prisoners secured? Had we not better hasten to join the escort?"

"No, two or three more came up just as I left, and there's enough now to manage in that quarter; but the advance-guard here must be kept up till we get 'em out to the great road, lest the sneaks slink away into the woods as they pass along the road and slip through our fingers as your smart trooper did just now. Let's see — about eight strong we will have this guard, I guess. I will be rank and file, and you shall be the officer. Come, mount! They'll be poking their heads along in sight in a moment. Ay, there they come! Advance-guard!" he now added, in a loud, commanding tone, as the slow tread of the prisoners, advancing along the devious and closely-embowered path, became audible —" advance-guard! Attention the whole! Prepare to march! — march!"

And accordingly he then, as Woodburn mounted and rode slowly on behind, commenced the enactment of his assumed part, always keeping within hearing, but never within distinct view, of the prisoners; now jabbering in as many voices as the most expert ventriloquist, and now sternly commanding, "*Silence in the ranks!*" -- now getting up a seeming scuffle among his men, and now driving them, with thwacks and curses, to their places; and now again softening his tones and cracking jokes with his men, — Smith, Johnson, &c., — who, in as many different tones, were heard to return various sharp and comical retorts, which raised shouts of laughter and made the forest ring with the sham merriment And thus he proceeded, to the secret amusement of the victors all of whom perfectly understood the artifice, till they emerged from the woods into the open grounds on the main road, when they were met by Major Ormsbee with a small detachment of regular soldiers. The tories were then, for the first time, permitted to know the smallness of the force that had captured them

when, amidst showers of gibes and shouts of laughter, at their ex
pense, from the Green Mountain Boys, the chapfallen creatures
were wheeled into the main road, and hurried on at a lively pace
to the village of Manchester, to be kept as prisoners of war, or
tried as spies, as the higher authorities there should see fit to
decide.*

"Captain Woodburn!" exclaimed the clear, animated voice
of one coming out of the door of the honored tavern before
described, in the village of Manchester, as the person thus
addressed, who had just arrived with those escorting the prisoners,
was describing the capture to a crowd gathered round him in the
yard — "Captain Woodburn, your most obedient! I am glad my
patience in waiting for your arrival is rewarded by the good news
which Powell, our landlord here, has just told us you bring. But
come, sir, a word in your ear, if you please."

Woodburn turned and confronted the bright and smiling countenance of Ira Allen, who was beckoning him from the crowd.

"Certainly, Mr. Allen; but why honor me with that appellation?" responded the former, stepping aside with the ardent young
secretary.

"Because I have the warrant for so doing in my pocket — a
captain's commission for you, my dear sir, if you will believe me."

"Indeed!"

"Yes, we have done something in the council at last worth
talking about — voted to raise a regiment of Rangers forthwith,
and appointed all the commissioned officers, Samuel Herrick heading the list as colonel."

---

* This band of tories were, the next day after their capture, marched to
Arlington, where the question was raised, and sharply discussed, whether
they should be considered as prisoners of war, or tried as spies, the latter
being insisted on by Mathew Lyon, and some others of the more bold and
ardent friends of the American cause, who declared that Captain Rose, at
least, should be tried and hung as a spy. A jury, however, — Eli Pettibone,
Esq., presiding as civil magistrate, — was allowed the prisoner; when, more
probably, from sympathy for the manly but misguided young officer, whom
they had known as a pleasant neighbor, than from want of proof, he was
acquitted as a spy, and, with the rest of his band, removed to Northampton
jail as prisoner of war. Considerable favor, also, seems to have been extended to the other brothers, some of whom married into whig families,
through whose influence, it is said, they retained their estates, none of the
extensive Rose property being confiscated, except that of Captain Samuel
Rose, which is now the residence of the Hon. J. S. Pettibone, from whom
these particulars have been obtained, his father being one of the captors
and his uncle the magistrate, above named.

"A gallant fellow, who will honor the post. But how about the means of paying and supporting such a force? You lately held taxing the people, without their consent, too bold a measure, I thought."

"We did, but have nevertheless adopted a bolder one."

"What is it?"

"Decreed the confiscation of the estates of the tories, appointed the necessary officers to execute the decree, and despatched messengers to them with commissions, instructions, and with orders to put the machine immediately into motion. By to-morrow nigh many of those on our black list will —— "

"Your black list?"

"Yes, already mostly made out for operations. But what is there to startle you in that?"

"Nothing; and yet I cannot forbear asking if that list includes one in whose family you may guess I feel some interest."

"I fear so, and regret that the proofs are so strong as to require it."

"Could not action in that case be deferred? An angel is pleading with him to remain neutral."

"If she were a whig angel, Woodburn, I know not —— "

"She is, she is — firmly, devotedly."

"Indeed! Well, for your sake, Woodburn, I am glad of it. And as the political hue of petticoats has already been permitted to have an influence, in some instances of the kind, in making up the list, it may have in this case. But the old man's enmity to our cause is so notorious, that I fear his estate must go, though the daughter, if she prove true, will not be forgotten on the question of a future restoration of her share of the property. But I am neglecting my chief business with you. We have fixed your present destination for the other side of the mountain, where among your old acquaintances, it was thought, you could raise a company most expeditiously."

"But where is the money to come from to pay my recruits? Even in case these estates are sold, who among us, these times has money to purchase them?"

"The answer to that question involves a secret which is known to but a few of us, and which must not be further revealed. Suffice it that there is yet among us abundance of money, besides the British gold that is beginning to be scattered along our border, to meet our present requirements. You will be supplied in season."

"I am content, and ready to depart."

" How soon can you start ? "

" This hour, if necessary."

" Retire, then, and obtain a few hours' sleep; but be off before day. Here are your commission and instructions, by which you will see that your subalterns are to be of your own appointing. Good-night, and God speed you on your way. Remember that we expect much of you, and that I stand voucher for your good conduct. And remember, also, my dear fellow," added the speaker, in a low, confidential tone, " that the interests of your fair friend could not be in better keeping."

" You have laid me under deep obligations to you, Mr. Allen for all this," began Woodburn, with grateful emotion.

" Yes, to do well; but not a word of thanks will I hear. So off with you to your rest. Begone, sir ! " said Allen, pushing the other away, with that winning smile and kindly playful manner, with which he ever so wonderfully contrived to gain the hearts and control the actions of all whom he wished to make friends

CHAPTER IV.

"It is not much the world can give
With all its subtle art ;
And gold and rank are not the things
To satisfy the heart."

THE day foll:wing the occurrences noted in the preceding chapter was an eventful one to the Haviland family, developing circumstances calculated to hasten the crisis to which the conflicting feelings and conduct of the father and daughter had been for some time silently tending, and to give a new turn to their respective destinies.

It was late in the afternoon. No event had thus far during the day occurred to mar the usual tranquillity of the family ; and Haviland, yet uninformed of the untoward affair which befell his party the last evening at Manchester, and little dreaming of the bold and decisive measures adopted by the Council of Safety, was seated at a table in his usual sitting-room, examining, with a satisfied and triumphant air, a map of New York, on which he was tracing out the intended route of the British army in its hitherto victorious way from the St. Lawrence to Albany. At length he began to muse aloud, partly to himself, apparently, and partly to his daughter, who, with a pensive brow, was seated at an open window in the same room, quietly engaged with her needle-work.

" As soon as General Burgoyne can clear the road of the trees and other obstructions, with which the rebels, in their impotent spite, have filled it, so that he can move on to the Hudson, how that grand army will sweep away the feeble and undisciplined bands that may venture to oppose its victorious march! And when a junction of the British armies is formed at Albany, what can this infatuated people think of doing then ? With the north completely cut off from the south, as will then be the case, what can these two sections, which together can hardly raise a respectable force, do, when thus divided and prevented from all concer' and coöperation ? Ay, what will they do then ? Come, Sabrey,' he added, turning with an exulting air to his daughter, " perhaps

you, who appear to have so high an opinion of rebel prowess —
perhaps you can answer the question?"

"I may be better prepared to answer the question, perhaps,
when I see the junction you anticipate really effected. Burgoyne
has not reached Albany yet," replied the other, with playful significance.

"Be sure not; but what is to prevent nim? What force car
the rebels oppose that he will not scatter like chaff before the
wind? None! I tell you, girl, their doom is sealed!"

"It might be, if they would consent to let you fight their battles
for them, father. But the battle which they are preparing to
give Burgoyne they will choose to fight themselves, I imagine.
A few Bunker Hill lessons, on his way, might materially alter the
general's prospects."

"Bunker Hill? Pooh! Why, we routed them even there,
behind their breastworks. Besides, we never had so fine an
army as this in the field before. I only wish I was as sure of
some good commission in Burgoyne's army, as I am that he wil·
march triumphantly through to Albany, and thus bring this un
natural war to a close."

"Would you think of going into that army, father, shoulc
you receive such an appointment?" asked the daughter, in a tone
of surprise and expostulation.

"Why, I should be proud to be there, Sabrey, in an army
that contains so much of the first talents and chivalry of England."

At this stage of the conversation, a man rode up to the door,
and, dismounting and entering the house, handed to Mr. Haviland,
after inquiring his name, a gorgeously-sealed packet.

Haviland, after examining the seal a moment, bowed low to
the stranger, and inquiringly observed, —

"From General Burgoyne, I believe?"

The messenger, nodding in the affirmative, and saying he was
directed to wait for an answer, the former broke open the
missive, and found in it, by singular coincidence, an answer to
the prayer he had a few moments before indirectly uttered a
commission, or appointment in the commissary department of
the British army. After perusing the paper a second time, he
turned, and, with a consequential air, handed it to his daughter,
whose countenance instantly fell as she glanced over the suspected
contents.

"You cannot seriously think of accepting this appointment,
father," she said, with a look of concern; "you cannot think of

.eaving your quiet and comfortable home, and engaging, at your age, in the fatigues and dangers of the camp?"

"Why not, Sabrey?" replied the other, reprovingly. "From my knowledge of the country, I can be of great use in procuring the supplies which the army will need, as the general doubtless foresaw; and I consider it my duty to the king to lend my feeble aid when called. The post is not, it is true, a very high one; but it is honorable and lucrative, and I shall accept it."

If this is Miss Sabrey Haviland, I have a letter for her also,' here interposed the messenger, rising and presenting the letter in question.

Sabrey broke open the proffered letter, which proved to be from her friend Miss McRea, and ran thus:—

"You remember your promise, Sabrey, to visit me the first opportunity. That opportunity now occurs. Captain Jones and other friends have presented your father's name at head-quarters for promotion; and he has now, I am informed, received an appointment. If he accepts, as I am sure he will, I hope you will accompany him, and remain with me. I have just received one of those letters so precious to me: he says the army will prob-ably move on to Fort Edward next week, the obstructions in the road being now mostly removed; so that, by the time you arrive, I shall probably be enabled to introduce you to the beau-tiful and accomplished ladies of whom he has so much to say,— such as the Countess of Reidesel, Lady Harriet Ackland, and others, who accompany their husbands in the campaign. But you will perhaps say that he is interested in praising these ladies for the love and heroism which prompt them to brave such fatigues and dangers for the sake of their lords, since he is warmly urging me to consent to an immediate union, that I may follow their example. He says, in his last letter,—and I think truly,—that I cannot long remain where I am, in a section which he evidently anticipates, will soon become a frightful scene of strife and bloodshed; and that I must therefore go away with my friends, and leave him, perhaps forever, or put myself under his protection in the army. And he seems hurt that I hesitate in a choice of the alternatives. On the other hand, my connections and friends here think it would be little short of madness in me to yield to my lover's proposal. The people about here are greatly alarmed at the expected approach of the British army, which is known to be accompanied by a large body of Indians. Many are already removing and nearly all preparing to go

5 *

The crisis hastens, and yet I am undecided. Prudence points one way, love the other. What shall I do? O Sabrey what shall I do? Should you come on with your father, I think I should feel a confidence in going with you to the British encampment. Come then, my friend, come quickly; for I feel as if I could not go without friends, and especially a female friend, to accompany me; while, at the same time, I feel as if some irresistible destiny would compel me to the attempt. And yet why should I hesitate to take any step which *he* advises? Why refuse to share with him any dangers which *he* may encounter? And why should my anticipations of the future, which have ever, till recently, during my happy intimacy with Mr. Jones, been so bright and blissful, be clouded now? I know not; I know not why it should be so; but lately my bosom has become disturbed by strange misgivings, and my mind perplexed by dark and undefined apprehensions. I must not, however, indulge them; and your presence, I know, would entirely dissipate them. I repeat, therefore, come, and that quickly. Adieu.

" Yours, truly,   JANE McREA."

The messenger in waiting, having been invited into another room to partake of some refreshment, and the father and daughter being thus left again by themselves, the latter now handed the other for his perusal the affectionate but too truly boding letter of her fated friend.

"And what answer do you intend to return to this kind and pressing invitation of your friend, Sabrey?" asked Haviland, after attentively reading the epistle.

"That I do not think it advisable to accept it, at this time, father," answered the girl.

"Why not advisable?" asked the other, in a censorious tone. "I see nothing to object to in the step, going, as you will, under the protection of a father; while it will introduce you to a circle which few American girls can ever reach."

"I feel quite willing to forego the honor of such an introduction," coolly returned the daughter. "And were it otherwise, the very letter that brings me the invitations unfolds enough to deter me from the undertaking."

"You wholly mistake your friend's meaning," responded the former. "Her apprehensions are merely the natural effect of maiden timidity. I think, as her lover seems to do, that the safest place for her is with the British army. So I think it will be for you; for I know not what punishment will be inflicted on

these settlements for their rebellious and treasonable con:uct
And it is my wish to separate myself and family from them, before the day of reckoning arrives. I shall, therefore, expect you
to attend me."

As the daughter was about to reply a domestic came in and
announced the arrival of Colonel Peters ; and the latter, the next
moment, with a dark and sullen brow, unceremoniously entered
the apartment. He did not, however, deign immediately to unfold the cause of his evident ill-humor, but contented himself
with listening to the news, which the elated Haviland was prompt
to impart in relation to his own promotion, the invitation received
by his daughter to accompany him to the army or its vicinity,
and his thus far rejected advice to her to accede to the proposal.
The cold countenance of Peters brightened with selfish delight
at the recital ; for in the old gentleman's appointment, his determination to accept it, and his intention of taking his daughter
with him, if she could be so persuaded, the former saw the triumph of his machinations to involve the family inextricably in
the royal cause. But that triumph would not be complete, unless
the daughter, whose predilections for Woodburn and the American cause were more than suspected, could be kept within the
scope of loyal influence. He therefore secretly resolved that,
if her father left the settlement to join the army, she should not
be left behind, but should be induced or compelled to accompany
him. He consequently was not slow to add his advice and en
treaties to those of the father. This he did for a while with
some show of respect and kindness ; but finding her still im-
movable, he at length became irritated, and assumed a tone of
dictation so inconsistent with the natural delicacy of a lover, that
she declined any further conversation with him on the subject.

" Where will you go, perverse and blinded girl ? " now interposed the father, reproachfully. " You would not stay here alone
and unprotected, would you ? "

" I should not hesitate to do so on account of any molestation
which *American* troops would offer me," replied Sabrey, with a
gnificant emphasis on the word American. " And should others
approach, I would go to my connections on the other side of the
mountains."

" Miss Haviland may have her private reasons for wishing to
remain in this section of the country," said Peters, with an ill-
suppressed sneer, turning to the father.

" Will you please explain your meaning, sir ? " demanded the
girl with spirit

" I mean," replied Peters, " that she who wou,d hold clandes
tine meetings with one whom her father has seen fit to eject from
his house, might see the advantage of remaining where her inter-
views could be enjoyed without molestation."

" Sabrey Haviland, is that true ? " asked the old gentleman
with a gathering frown.

" She will hardly deny, I think," said Peters, " that the fellow
was here soon after I left last night. At all events, he was seen
to leave the premises in pursuit of me. By whom he was informed of the direction I took, I know not ; but I know he overtook me, beset me like a ruffian, and shot my horse by a ball
intended for the rider."

" Is all that true, I repeat ? " again fiercely demanded Haviland
of his daughter, in a burst of rage.

But without deigning one word of reply either to the insulting in-
sinuations of Peters, or the angry and ill-timed demand of her
father, Sabrey, with cheeks glowing with offended delicacy and just
indignation, rose from her seat, and was about to leave the apartment, when her step was arrested by the altered voice of her
father, who, quickly becoming sensible of the harshness of his
conduct from its visible effects, now spoke to her in a softened
and more expostulatory tone.

" Surely, Sabrey, you are not going to deny my right, as a
parent, to question you, or at least ask you for an explanation
respecting charges which have the appearance of involving your
character ? "

" I might not," said she, coolly, but respectfully ; " and indeed, I should not, at another time, have refused to answer your
question so far as I could, however harshly it was put to me ;
but I must still decline to do so in *this* presence ! " she added,
glancing towards the abashed Peters, with an air of scorn to
which her usually serene and benignant countenance never before, perhaps, gave expression.

" Perhaps, Miss Haviland," said Peters, stung by the remark
and manner of the other, and now rallying for the revenge to which
such minds are prone to resort — " perhaps Miss Haviland, on
a little more reflection, may be willing to acknowledge that I,
also, am not wholly without a right to ask for an explanation in
an affair which she seems to admit requires one."

" I am not aware, sir," promptly responded the maiden, so
much aroused by the cool arrogance of the other, as to forget her
determination to hold no more conversation with him —" I am
not aware, sir, of having admitted any necessity of an explanation

And had I done so, I should be very far from acknowledging your right to require it of me."

"It is possible," rejoined the former in the same strain — "it is possible Miss Haviland may be willing to qualify her last remark a little, when she is reminded of the existence of a certain marriage contract, to which she voluntarily became a party."

"I need no prompting to make me mindful of that evidence of my youthful indiscretion, sir," responded Miss Haviland; "nor should I be likely to forget the particular provisions of an instrument, the thought of which has cost me, as my entreaties to be released from it should have apprised you, so many painful regrets. But, while mindful of all this, I have yet to be informed of the provision which, till the contract is consummated, gives you any control over my actions, or right to require me to account for or explain them."

"If the instrument, which I have somewhere about me, I believe," replied the other, with his usual cold indifference, as he took the document from his pocket, and began, with a business-like air, to glance over the contents — "if the instrument does not express, or rather if it is not admitted to presuppose and give me, any of the rights I have named till it is consummated, then it is time that I should insist on its consummation, which, as few others would have done, I have so long forborne to urge."

"I perfectly agree with Colonel Peters," interposed Mr. Haviland, catching at the last suggestion in his growing alarm for the success of his favorite scheme, which the unexpected state of feeling here displayed taught him might be endangered, if not speedily consummated. "I perfectly agree with him, that this business has already been sufficiently delayed; and I think, as the family is now about to break up, that the final ceremony had better be performed before we go, or, at the farthest, when we reach the army, where, as Sabrey would perhaps prefer, it might take place at the same time as that of her friend, who is similarly situated."

"You forget," said the maiden, now freshly aroused at this combined attempt to make her forego her last remaining privilege in the abhorrent negotiation — "you both forget that the very instrument, by which you claim to dispose of my hand, expressly leaves to me, and to me only, the right and privilege of deciding upon the time for that ceremony, by which you would now, it seems, so summarily consummate your unmanly scheme. And thank Heaven!" she continued, turning to the nonplused suitor

with an air of decision and fearlessness which the excitement of
insulted feeling could only have given her — "thank Heaven, i
had the forethought to insist on a privilege now so precious to
me; for let me assure you, sir, that distant will be the day when
I shall fix on a time for consummating a contract, wrung from
girlish inexperience, to gratify selfish ambition or mistaken views
in the first place, and now claimed to hold me like a sold article
of merchandise, for the use and control of one whose feelings,
principles, and whole character are every way uncongenial with
my own."

"What! — how!" exclaimed the irritated and evidently aston
ished Haviland, who, in his obtuseness, even now, could not perceive what objection his daughter could have to a match esteemed
by him so advantageous. "What can this mean? Why, the
girl must be demented! You to decide on the time! Why,
reasonable time is all that was meant by that, if it is not so expressed!"

"That is all; nothing more," eagerly chimed in Peters.

"If a part of the instrument is to be construed differently from
what is expressed, and as you choose, why not other parts, and as
I choose?" calmly asked the unmoved girl. "If so, then its
power to bind me shall cease with this hour."

"What folly!" again exclaimed the old gentleman, balked and
chafing worse than before. "Why, don't the infatuated girl know
that, to say nothing about losing prospects which no other young
lady in the country would reject — that by marrying any other
man, she will forfeit her birthright in my estate, and make herself, as she will deserve to be, a beggar?"

"I have no thought of marrying any other man while in my
present embarrassing position," quickly retorted the former, with
an offended air. "But should I wish to do so, I should hardly be
deterred from it by either of the considerations you have just
named, I think. And, indeed, if the mercenary and ambitious
motives, which you would have actuate me, were alone to be my
guide in such a step, I could see but little temptation for the sacrifice in the honors and wealth which are so much to depend on a
triumph that, for all your boasts, I believe will never be accomplished; while the failure, if the same justice is meted out to you
which you seem to be meditating for others, will leave you with
a branded name, and no estate here to give or withhold."

"Silence! audacious girl," exclaimed the baffled loyalist, unable longer to endure the calm but scorching rebuke involved in
the reply of his daughter. "I will listen to no more of your

railings. This comes of being allowed to mingle with an ignorant, rebellious populace. But that evil shall, at least, be remedied. You will attend me to the army, where, I trust, your eyes may soon be opened to your folly."

"You may perhaps compel me to go, sir," responded the still unawed maiden; "but if you do so, let me warn you against all hope of thereby rendering my feelings less repugnant to the scheme we have been discussing, or of changing my views of the cause in which you are about to embark; for I will now openly declare, what I have often before left you to infer, that I have no sympathies for those who come to oppress and enslave my country; nor will I ever aid or sanction their ignoble purposes — not even to the withholding any intelligence I may gain of their movements, which may avert disaster or peril from our struggling people."

"Hurrah for the tory's daughter!" now burst on the ears of the astonished group, from a band of armed men standing immediately beneath the open but thickly vine-clad windows without, whither, it seemed, they had approached unperceived, and thus become unintentional listeners to the last part of the foregoing dialogue, which they were still hesitating to break in upon, when their admiration of the heroic girl's declarations led to the irrepressible burst of applause just mentioned — "Hurrah for the tory's daughter! She shall be remembered for that!"

The party within instantly rose to their feet at so strange and unexpected a salutation. Peters, aware, from the experience of the last night, that his capture was sought, was the first, as might be expected, to take the alarm. With a hasty step towards the window, and an equally hasty glance through the screening foliage at the new-comers, he hurriedly retreated through a door leading to the rear of the house. Haviland, scarcely less alarmed, though having no conception of the main object of the visit, advanced, with evident perturbation, to the front door, when he was met at the threshold by the secretary of the Council of Safety, who, bowing politely, proceeded to apologize for the noisy outbreak of his attendants, which, contrary to his wishes, he said, had been made to announce his arrival.

"Attendants, sir?" exclaimed Haviland, casting a flurried glance at the file of soldiers in the yard — "attendants — armed men led up here to my door? Who are they? What is their business, and yours, sir? This affair needs explanation, sir."

"Well, sir, if so, I am here to give it," composedly replied Allen. "But, as you appear somewhat agitated, let us walk in and talk over the matter calmly."

Mechanically complying with the suggestion, Haviland turns and led the way into the room, where his daughter still stood, mutely awaiting the development; when the secretary, after bowing with marked respect to Miss Haviland, with whom, it appeared, he was slightly acquainted, resumed, —

"The Council of Safety, sir, having determined on defending the state to the last extremity, in the present crisis, have perceived, with deep regret, that there are those in our midst who hesitate not either to take up arms against their countrymen, or, what is no better, secretly to aid the enemy, and harbor and conceal in their houses hostile emissaries, trying to seduce our people. And not perceiving the policy or justice of longer permitting their cause thus to be endangered, the council have decided on a measure for promptly remedying the evil — a measure which they had less hesitation in adopting, as they believed, from the repeated threats of the loyalists, they would only be anticipating their opponents by inflicting penalties, that, in case of the conquest of this country, will be visited on themselves. They have passed a solemn decree, sir, to confiscate, for the public use, all the estates of both of the classes of loyalists I have named, among one of which, at least, they have abundant proof, I regret to say, to warrant them in classing Esquire Haviland. And they direct me to permit him to take one of the horses, lately his own, and depart, with the least possible delay, for the British camp, where, they think, he more properly belongs.'

The arrogant loyalist, who had hitherto looked upon the Council of Safety with utter contempt for either their powers or their efficiency, was now perfectly thunderstruck at the announcement of so bold and unexpected a measure; and, for some moments, his mouth seemed wholly sealed against any remonstrance to a step which, not for public good, but for his own aggrandizement, he was conscious of intending to recommend to the British government in relation to the estates of the leading rebels, and especially those of the treasonable body by whom, as had just been so truthfully told him, his selfish designs had now been anticipated. Soon rallying, however, he wrathfully muttered, —

"They dare not do it; their audacity will not carry them to that length. But if they do," he continued, with louder and more menacing tones — "if they do attempt to carry out their plundering purposes, I will bring down upon them, within eight and forty hours, a British force that will give them enough to do to take care of themselves and their *own* property, without meddling with that of others."

' That is what we supposed you would be glad to do, in any case," quietly responded Allen. " It but swells the proof against you, and goes to confirm the justice of the decree."

" O, do not say any more, father," interposed Miss Haviland, with much feeling. " Do not, I beg of you, further and more inextricably involve yourself. You know how gladly I would have saved you from this; how often warned you of the consequences of persisting in your course. Perhaps it is not too late to retract, even now. Who knows but the council, who have done this but from a sense of duty to their country, and with no ill will against you personally, may yet be induced, if you will send in a pledge of neutrality, to reverse their sentence as regards you, and still leave you in possession of your property and a quiet home? I myself, feeble girl as I am, would go before them to intercede for you; and perhaps this gentleman would assist me," she added, with an appealing glance to Allen.

" Most gladly," replied the latter, touched at the magnanimity of the girl, in her distress — " most gladly, and with great hope of success."

" Do you hear that, father? " said the other, eagerly; " do you hear what I feel — I know — may yet be done for you? Then do not reject my petition, but retract, and give up your intention of joining these invaders of your country."

" No," replied the old gentleman, after a moment of apparent wavering — " no, never! Let the plunderers take possession of my estate here for the short time they will be enabled to hold it, if they will. To-morrow morning I start for the British camp."

" It is as I feared," observed Allen, turning to the daughter; " but your efforts to rescue your father, Miss Haviland, and the noble stand you have taken on this occasion and before, are, let me assure you, appreciated by myself, and will not fail to be so by those of more controlling influence. And although this property will, in a few days, be sold by those duly appointed, and now here to guard and dispose of it, yet the government, which has the power to confiscate, will have the power to restore; and I have no fears that your own interests will eventually be made to suffer by a measure which may now appear as harsh to you as it appeared necessary to the upright and patriotic men who felt themselves constrained to adopt it. In this you may trust, I think, as regards the future. As for the present, I am only empowered to offer you an asylum in some friendly family of the neighborhood, with ample means of support, or, if you prefer, a safe coveyance, with a female attendant, should you desire ft, to any family in a more distant part of the state."

"My daughter will probably go with me, sir," said Haviland, resentfully.

"No, father," said the girl, firmly; "that army is no proper place for a young lady and especially one of my views. I shall, for the present, go into the family of our neighbor Risdon ; but in a few days, I will gratefully accept of Mr. Allen's offer of a conveyance, and, as I proposed to you a short time ago, go to my connections on the other side of the mountains."

"Your wishes will be attended to in this or any other respect as soon as you shall please to signify them, Miss Haviland," said the secretary, as, bowing a respectful adieu, he now departed with part of his armed attendants, for other and similar visits which remained to be accomplished that night among the unsuspecting tories of that vicinity.

Within an hour or two after the departure of Allen, or as soon as the growing darkness would enable a skulker to approach unseen, a man, who was of the latter description evidently, might have been discovered slowly and cautiously making a circuit round the house, but at so respectable distance from it as to escape the observation of the guard now stationed at three or four commanding points about the premises. When he had reached a point nearly opposite to the back door, he ventured up to the border of the intervening garden, and gave a low, significant whistle. After a momentary silence, a slight rustling was heard in a thick patch of corn occupying a portion of the garden, and Peters, who, it will be recollected, passed out in this direction, and who, perceiving his retreat cut off by men already posted in the fields, had here lain concealed till now, cautiously emerged from his covert, and came forward to the spot where the other stood awaiting his approach.

"Well, Redding," said Peters, in a low voice, as he came up: "when I asked you this morning to come here to Haviland's to-night to see me, before I went to the army, I didn't exactly expect you would have to call me out of a corn patch to receive my orders. But how came you to know or suspect I was here? You have not ventured in there, I take it?" he added, leading the way into the field, which the guard had now left.

"No," replied the other; "I caught a glimpse of the fellows in the yard as I came in sight, and, mistrusting what was to pay from what I had just heard of their movements this fore 100n in Manchester, and other towns thereabouts I struck off at pasture, where I luckily encountered the old squire, who walked out there, after the leader of the gang had left and who told me of your concealment, and all."

"Yes, he came to the back door, here, the first chance he could get, to see if I had escaped, when, contriving to apprise him where I was, I had got a moment's talk with him just before But what have you heard about their movements in other places to-day ? "

"Why, I met Asa Rose going post-haste to warn our friends in this direction to be on their guard. He says they have seized on the estates of all the Rose family, and every other leading loyal-ist, as far as they could hear, in all that section ; and, in several instances, put the owners themselves under guard. What do you say to all that, colonel ? "

"Glad of it. Though an act of lawlessness and audacity which I did not once dream of their attempting, and which, even now, they will not dare to carry out, should they have time to do so before their brief career is arrested, yet I am glad the rebel fools have done it ; for, between you and me, Redding, I have had my doubts whether the British government, which is ever too merciful, would take their estates from them, when we come to subdue them, as you know we have talked ; but now vengeance will be swift and certain. Their estates will all be seized and given to the deserving."

"Ay, that's it ! " exclaimed the perfidious minion, with a chuckle of satisfaction ; " it will give us our revenge, and at the same time supply us with the needful. I have a good many scores to settle with the people about here ; and I know of the farm of a certain rebel that I shall ask for my share, as I think I justly may, seeing how active I've been this summer.

"Yes, yes," replied Peters, rather impatiently ; " but there must be no more wavering and turning with you. What you ask you must earn, remember."

"You see if I don't ! only name what you would have me do, colonel ! " eagerly responded the other.

"Well, I will now," said the former, coming to a halt. " Yes, as we are, by this time, fairly out of reach and hearing of these foiled rebels, who have so kindly yielded me a pass through this side of their watch, thinking, doubtless, that I could not have been in the house when they surrounded it, but should be there this evening — yes, I will give you my orders now, which will em-brace a fresh item or two above what I intended before some of the occurrences o' this afternoon. Well, in the first place, you are to proceed to Castleton, and join the northern company there collected and ready for operations at the Remington rendezvous. You will then become the guide and assistant of the leader of that force, which is to move on to some secret and safe place, 'o be selected by you (as you know the localities, and the leader don't) in the woods near the Twenty Mile Encampment, where, acting as the advanced corps of our planned expedition to the Connecticut by that route, they will remain concealed as much as possible, till further orders, watching all movements of the rebels, and drawing in every trusty loyalist that can be approached. And mark me, Redding, while there, or elsewhere, remember, that accursed Woodburn is a doomed man, and is to be taken, if found, and kept for my disposal. And I have another order, which must be left still more to your especial management. Haviland's daughter, with whom you know, I suppose, how I am situated, has got some dangerous notions into her head, and, refusing to hear to her father, who wishes her to go with him to the army, has determined to go to her relatives, over the mountain, in a carriage the rebels have promised to provide her. She will be along that road, probably, soon after you get to your rendezvous. She must be stopped, and conducted, with good treatment, mind you, back, through some secret route, to the British camp, where her father, though he knows nothing of my plan, will be glad to receive and keep her. And now I will be off to my horse, which I luckily left at the house of a friend, on the cross road, about a mile to the west of us."

" Will you go far on your journey to-night ? "

" About seven miles, to the house of another friend, where I am to be joined by the squire in the morning, and, with him, proceed directly to the army."

" How soon are we to hear from you ? "

" Within ten days, or sooner. I shall, with all possible despatch, organize and prepare the force designed for the purpose ; when I shall sweep on through Arlington and Manchester, and, after teaching them a few lessons in that quarter, proceed at once to join you. There ! you now know all ; go, and remember that secrecy and vengeance are the watchwords."

" Ay, ay; I am your man for all that, colonel," responded the heartless tool, as the two now separated to depart on their different destinations.

CHAPTER V.

"What nearer foe is lurking in the glade? —
But joy! Columbia's friends are trampling through the st ade!"

ONE of the earliest and most noted of the houses of public entertainment in Vermont was that of Captain John Coffin, situated in the north part of Cavendish, on the old military road, cut out in the French wars, by the energetic General Amherst, with a regiment of New Hampshire Boys, and extending from Number Four, as Charleston on the Connecticut was then called, to the fortresses on Lake Champlain. This tavern, at the time of the revolution, being on the very outskirts of the settlements on the east side of the Green Mountains, was long the general resort of the soldier and the common wayfarer for rest and refreshment. before and after passing over the long and dreary route of mountain wilderness lying between the eastern and western settlements of the state. And to the soldier, especially, it was a favorite haven; the more so, doubtless, from the congenial character of its frank, fearless, patriotic, but blunt and unpolished landlord, whose substantial cheer and hearty welcome, money or no money usually caused him to be looked upon as a friend, as well as a good entertainer. To this then widely-known establishment we will now repair, to note the occurrences next to be related in the progress of our story.

On a dark and cloudy afternoon, about ten days after the events related in the last chapter, a company of five persons were assembled in the rudely finished bar-room of the inn just described. Of these, three were strangers, or pretended strangers, to the house and each other; having dropped in at different intervals during the afternoon. Of the two others, one was the landlord, whose burly frame, rough, open features, and fear-nought countenance need have left none in doubt of either the physical or moral traits which experience proved he possessed. The other, a somewhat tall, thin, gaunt man, of a weather-beaten visage, and a sort of sly, scrutinizing look, was an old acquaintance of the reader. As of old, his large powder-horn and ball-pouch were slung under his left arm, and his long, heavy rifle, standing by

6 *   O

his side, was resting on the sill of the open window, beneath which he had seated himself, so as to enable him to note wha' might be passing without as well as within. The manner in which the latter and the landlord occasionally exchanged glances, implied a previous and familiar acquaintance, the usual manifestations of which seemed to be repressed by the presence of the three guests first named, who were evidently objects of the secret suspicion of the former. But all this, for some time, might have passed unheeded by any but close observers; for few remarks, and those of the briefest and most common-place kind, were offered; and an inclination for silence and reserve was manifest among the company.

A circumstance at length occurred, however, which quickly awakened the landlord from his apparent apathy, and brought some of the leading characteristics of the man at once into view. A very large and powerfully-made black dog, which belonged to the house, had just marched into the room, and laid down to sleep in the middle of the floor; when one of the strangers, whom we have noticed, in returning from the bar, where he had been for a drink of water, trod on the animal's tail, either through accident or design — probably the latter; — at least the landlord seemed to suspect so; for his countenance instantly flashed with indignation, and, turning abruptly to the aggressor, he said, —

"What was that done for, sir?"

"Done for?" replied the other, indifferently. "Why, it was done because the dog was in my way. If he don't want his tail trod on, he must keep out from under foot; that's all."

"Well, sir," rejoined the former, in no gentle tones, "I don't know who you are; but whether whig or tory, gentle or simple, I shall just take the liberty to tell you, that if I was sure you did that intentionally, I would pull your ears for you; for, if any living being has a good right to remain undisturbed, and do as he likes in this house, it is that dog. Roarer, come here, my old friend," he added, turning to fondle the creature, that now, dropping the menacing attitude he had assumed towards the aggressing stranger, came up and thrust his huge snout into his master's lap "Yes, old fellow, while I live, you shall never want a friend to avenge your wrongs, though I have to fight a regiment to do it! And aint I right in that, Dunning?" he still further remarked, turning to the hunter.

"Der yes, if needful," replied the latter; "but the ditter dog. I'm thinking, would ask no favors, if you would give him leave to der do his own work on meddlers."

"O, that wouldn't do, you know, Tom," rejoined the former, "for, if I but said the word, Roarer would tear him in shoe-strings, as quick as you could say Jack Roberson! No I'll settle the hash myself. And I am now ready to hear the fellow's explanation," he added, again turning sternly to the aggressor.

But the last-named questionable personage, not relishing the course matters were taking, now, in a subdued and altered tone promptly disclaimed any intention of touching the dog, and expressed his regret at what had happened,

"O, that's enough," said Coffin, instantly cooling off. "All right now, Roarer. You may lie down again, sir," he continued, waving away the dog, that had faced round, and still stood suspiciously eyeing the offender. "Yes, that's enough; we'll call the matter settled. But by way of explaining to you, who are strangers, what I have said about that dog's claims to my friendship and protection, I must tell you a story, which will show you how much the noble creature is deserving at my hands.

"Six years ago, the seventh day of last March, as I was returning from the settlements on Otter Creek, a distance of from twenty to thirty miles, through the then entire wilderness, with the snow nearly five feet deep on a level, and the weather so cold and stormy, that I was compelled to travel with great-coat on, as well as snow-shoes, I undertook to cross one of the ponds in Plymouth on the ice, which I supposed perfectly sound and safe for any thing that could be got on to it. But for some reason or other, there seemed to have been one place, concealed from view by the snow, so thin and spongy, that the moment I stepped upon it, I went down some feet below the surface into the water, while the snow and broken ice at once closed over me. And although I succeeded in forcing my way up through the slush, and getting my head above water, yet I soon found it, hampered as I was with snow-shoes and great-coat, impossible to get out. As sure as I tried to raise myself by the treacherous support at the sides, so sure was it to give way, and precipitate me back into the water. But still I struggled on, till chilled to the vitals, so benumbed that I could scarcely move a limb, and growing weaker and weaker at every effort, I could do no more; and I saw myself gradually sinking for the last time. O heavens! who can describe my sensations — who conceive the thousand thoughts that flashed through my mind at that horrible moment! But just as I was on the point of giving up in despair, I caught a glimpse of my dog (that had taken a circuit wide from me after some game) coming on to the pond. I raised one faint shout — it was all I could do, — and, though nearly a half mile off, he heard it, and came on, with monstrous bounds, to the spot. In a moment he was there; and, after giving me one look, — I can never forget that look, — he slid down to the very verge of the hole to try to assist me. With a struggle, I made out to raise one hand out of the water within his reach. He seized the cuff of my coat, and, drawing back with the seeming strength of a draught-horse, he, with one pull, brought me half out of the water. With a desperate effort on my part, and another on his, the next instant I was lying helpless, but safe, on the ice, while the dog fairly howled aloud for joy! I said safe; for as hopeless as some might have viewed my situation, even then, wet, benumbed, nearly dead with cold and exhaustion, and many miles from any human help or habitation, as I was, yet rallying every energy I had left me, and rolling, kicking, and pawing, to put my blood in motion, and regain the use of my limbs, I soon got on to my feet; when, seizing my gun, that I had hurled aside as I went down, I made for a dry tree in sight, fired into a spot of spunk I luckily found on one side of it, kindled a fire, warmed and dried myself, set forward again, and reached home that night; but with feelings towards that dog, sir, that I can never know towards any other created being — not even, in some respects, towards my wife and children. Yes, sir; I will not only fight, but, if need be, die for him."

While the captain was relating his oft-told but truthful adventure with his justly-prized dog, the quick eye of Dunning caught, through the window, a glimpse of a recognized form, approaching in the road from the east; and slipping out unnoticed from the room, he beckoned the approaching personage round the corner of the house, and when safely out of the hearing and observation of those in the bar-room, he turned to the other, and said, —

"Der devil 's in the wind, Captain Harry!"

"How so? Have you discovered the suspected rendezvous?"

"Der yes; and more too."

"Indeed! where is it?"

"Ditter deep in the thickets, on the west side of the pond nearest the great road over the mountains."

"Ah, ha! but their numbers? any more, probably, than the small club we supposed?"

"Der double, and then the d'tter double of that, if it don' make more than twenty."

"Yo surprise me, Dunning. Are you sure?"

Sure as that I am der talking to Captain Woodburn.'

"Impossible! It must be some secret meeting of the disaf
fected in this quarter."

"Der not that, but a regularly armed force, and, with the ditter
exception of two or three about-home tories, may be, a'l strange
faces, including a sprinkling of red skins, brought along with
them for ditter decency's sake, I suppose."

"But how could such a force get so far into the interior un
detected? How dare they venture on so hazardous a movement? and what can be their designs in so doing?"

"Der here is something that ditter tells a rather loud story about
that; at least, as to the matter of intentions," said the hunter,
by way of reply, taking a crumpled paper from his cap and
handing it to the other.

Woodburn took the paper, and eagerly ran over its contents;
which to his astonishment he found to be a copy of an order from
General Burgoyne to Colonel Peters, detailing the plan of an
expedition, to be conducted by the latter, with one hundred loyalists and a company of Indians, by way of the head waters of
Otter Creek, across the mountains to Connecticut River, where
this force was to be joined by the loyal troops from Rhode
Island, and directing him " to scour the country, levy contributions, take hostages, make prisoners of all civil and military
officers acting under Congress, collect horses, and, after proceeding down the river as far as Brattleborough, return to the
great road to Albany." *

"How did this get into your hands, Dunning?" demanded
the surprised and excited officer, as soon as he had mastered the
contents.

"Der well, having crept along near the edge of the pond
within ten or twelve rods of their camp, I was lying in the bushes
for discoveries; when ditter one of 'em — their leader, I suppose
— came down to the pond, for observation, likely; and, while

---

* The document here quoted was brought to General Stark on his
advance through Vermont; and there can be but little doubt of its
genuineness; as it afterwards came out, in the trial of Burgoyne, in the
British Parliament, that such an expedition was actually started, but
subsequently changed for that of Bennington How considerable a portion of the whole intended force penetrated into the interior is not ascertained. But we have the authority of the oldest inhabitants for asserting,
that a portion of his force did cross over the mountains, and some of
them even reached Springfield; when, owing to the unexpected movements they found going on among the people, and the rumored advance
of Stark, all, who were not taken, speedily decamped.

peering up and down the shore, a gust of wind blew his hat off into the water. But though he regained his ditter hat and disappeared, I soon saw a piece of white paper blowing along in the water towards me. After a while, it reached the sort of point where I was, and lodging against a bush, I secured it, and found it this same thing. What do you think of it, captain?"

" Why, it unfolds a plan too bold for credence."

" Not too bold for *my* ditter credence, captain."

" Then you think it no feint?"

" Der no, sir, but a regular bred expedition, which they mean to push as soon as more force arrives. I have been ditter watching things a little since I got at this wrinkle. They have spies out in every direction. 'Tis not an hour since I espied a fellow peering from the corner of the woods up yonder, who, I think, must be that treacherous ditter devil, David Redding; and there are three now in the bar-room of the same kidney."

" Ah! well, all this may be. Such an expedition may have been set afoot at the instigation of such fellows as Spencer, who, having left the Council of Safety before any thing was done, and while its distracted counsels seemed to preclude all prospect that any thing would be done for the defence of the state. Ay, that is it; and little dreaming of what has since transpired, Peters, who is probably behind, with the main force, has sent forward this as a sort of pioneer corps, who, coming over a route now mostly deserted by our people, have penetrated here nearly to the Twenty Mile Encampment, without once suspecting what is going on through the rest of the state. But that is a secret, which, thanks to the prompt patriotism shown by our young men in enlisting, we shall now soon be able to teach them; for my company is already nearly full; and, if you have notified the recruits you enlisted, Sergeant Dunning, they will all be here for mustering by to-morrow night."

" All done, as in der duty bound, captain; and six of my men said they would be here this evening."

" Indeed! there will be almost enough of us, if your six recruits all get in, to make a pounce upon this nest of vipers to-night. Let's see; six — you, myself, and Captain Coffin, and ——"

" And der Bart, if he comes; ditter don't you expect him along here to-night?"

" I do. Miss Haviland, according to the letter of Mr. Allen, who wrote some days ago, to apprise me of her coming, would have started, I calculate, this morning; and Bart, whom I immediately despatched to act as her guard on the way, will of

course come with her. They will probably arrive before long,
now — unless ——" and the speaker suddenly paused at the
new and startling thought that now seemed to occur to him.

"Unless," said Dunning, guessing the thoughts of the other
and taking up the supposition — "unless beset by some of this
crew, who are ordered to take prisoners and hostages. But der
stay; didn't I catch the glimmer of a distant horseman then?"
he continued, pointing along the partially wooded road to the
west. "There! that was a clearer view; and, by the ditter
darting kind of gait of the horse, I should think it might be
Lightfoot, and the short rider the critter we've been talking
about."

The hunter's eye had not misled him; for in a few minutes
the horseman emerged from the forest into open view, and confirmed the conjecture that had just been made respecting his
identity. As he neared the house, perceiving Woodburn and
Dunning beckoning to him from behind the buildings, he threw
himself from his saddle, leaped over the fence, and approached
them.

"The news, sir? What is it? Speak!" eagerly exclaimed
Woodburn, as Bart, with a downcast and troubled look, drew
near.

"Bad as need to be, consarn it!" replied the latter, with an
air of mingled vexation and self-reproach. "But I couldn't
help it."

"Help what? What has happened? Where is the lady?"
rapidly asked the alarmed and impatient lover.

"Taken prisoner by the tories, as I guessed 'em. She and
Vine Howard, that come with her, and the boy that drove 'em."

"How? when? where?"

"Why, as we were coming down this side the mountain, and
when nearly to the bottom, five or six fellows, with guns, rushed
out of the bush, seized the horse, pulled out the women, and
hurried them off with two of their number into the woods towards the pond; while the rest made a push to take me, who
was riding just behind. But firing a pistol in their faces, and
giving Lightfoot my stiffest sign, we dashed through or over
them, and escaped, with their bullets whistling after us, one
after another, till we were out of reach."

"These ladies shall be rescued before I sleep, or I will perish
in the attempt," said Woodburn, with stern emphasis. "Let us
arm and set forward immediately with the best force we can
raise.'

" There is a thing or two to be ditter done first, it strikes me,'
observed Dunning, with his usual coolness; " that is, if we don'
want enemies both before and behind us, on the way."

" What is that, Dunning ? "

" Secure those three chaps in the bar-room, or they'll be ditter
sure either to be on our heels, or get there before us to raise the
alarm of our coming."

" Are they armed, think you ? "

" With ditter knives only, I'm thinking — their guns may have
been left in the point of woods yonder, in charge of the spy I
named, who, now I ditter think on't, ought to be taken about the
same time, for fear of some secret signal being given."

The suggestions of Dunning, who, as the reader will already
have inferred, had been made a sergeant in Woodburn's company
of Rangers, were at once approved by his superior, who accordingly, as the first step, despatched him and Bart to the woods,
where the man conjectured to be in charge of the arms of his
comrades was supposed to be concealed.   After waiting till the
two others might have had time to gain the woods in question,
Woodburn left his stand, and, passing round to the front of the
house, boldly marched into the bar-room, where the three suspected personages still sat listening to the stories with which the
landlord, who suspected what was in progress, seemed intent on
amusing them.   They, however, now seemed suddenly to lose
all interest in the recital going on, and, after exchanging uneasy
and significant glances, simultaneously rose to depart.

" You are my prisoners, gentlemen," said Woodburn, stepping
before them and presenting a cocked pistol.

For a moment, the surprised tories stood mute in alarm and
doubt, alternately glancing from their armed opponent to the
landlord, and from the latter to the door and windows, as if
weighing the chances and means of escape.   But, the next instant,
two of them suddenly turned, and drawing and flourishing their
knives behind them, sprang for the open windows, with the inten
tion of leaping through them.

"At 'em, Roarer ! " exclaimed Coffin, seizing one escaping tory
by the leg, and hurling him back with stunning effect upon the
floor.

The dog was but little behind his master in drawing back, by
a grip in his clothes, the other to the floor, where he was glad to
lie without offering further resistance to the grim and growling
conqueror standing over him.   The third, in the mean while, not
daring to stir lest a worse fate should befall him, standing as he

was directly before the muzzle of Woodburn's pistol, and seeing the situation of his comrades, immediately submitted; when all, giving up their concealed arms, now quietly yielded themselves as prisoners.

In a few minutes after the surrender of the tories, their guns were brought in by Dunning and Bart, who found them at the suspected place, though the traitor, Redding, whom they identified, had just taken the alarm, and was seen retreating over a distant knoll as they came up to the spot.

The prisoners being left in charge of the landlord's oldest boy, who was armed for the purpose, and the dog Roarer, the rest of the company now retired to another part of the house, to devise measures for the rescue of the fair captives, for which a preliminary step only had as yet been taken. Having at length fixed on the plan of operations which they believed most promising of auspicious results, they immediately commenced their hasty preparations for the bold adventure. And Dunning's six recruits luckily arriving in season, the whole company, now consisting of ten resolute woodsmen, and led on by a man fully resolved to succeed or perish, set forward, a little after sunset, for the scene of action, which was several miles distant from the tavern. According to the plan that had been adopted, two men were to proceed to the eastern shore of the pond, take a log canoe, and, under cover of the darkness, row silently over to some point beyond, but near the tory encampment; and, after making what discoveries they could respecting the situation of the captives, lie in ambush and await the operations of the rest of the company, who were to proceed round by the road, enter the woods, and gain a post on the other side of the encampment, and, by a feigned attack, draw off the tories, and thus afford the former a favorable moment to rush from their concealment and release the captives. And if they found this impracticable, they were then to shout aloud the watchword, *To the rescue!* when both parties of the assailants were to make an earnest and desperate onset on the foe. Dunning and Bart, from their known sagacity and skill as woodsmen and coolness and intrepidity in action, were the two men selected to undertake the more difficult and hazardous part first mentioned.

After a rapid and silent march of about an hour, the company reached the vicinity of the pond, just as the last suffusions of an obscured twilight disappeared in the west, and halted a few minutes, that the different parts of the plan might be repeated and clearly understood by all before separating

7

" Remember the arrangement, boys," said Woodburn, address
ing Dunning and Bart, in a voice which betrayed the intense solicitude he felt in the event at issue. " Recollect the first and main
object is to release and get off the ladies, and if this can be done
within the hour we will give you for the purpose, as it possibly
may be, before we make any demonstrations in front, so much
the better ; if not, proceed in the manner agreed on. And may
Heaven favor the innocent, whose cause, remember, is mostly in
your hands."

With this the company separated, and each party proceeded to
their different destinations. We will follow the two intrusted with
the most difficult part of the enterprise.

CHAPTER VI.

———— " The first that hears
Shall be the first to bleed."

THE hunter, followed by his young comrade, now leaving the
rest of the band to proceed to their contemplated stand by the
main road, struck off into the woods to the right, and, with silent
and rapid steps, led the way to the south-eastern shore of the
pond. Here finding, as he seemed to have expected, a capacious
canoe, dug out from the trunk of some huge pine, he drew it forth
from its concealment, beneath a mass of fallen trees projecting
over the bank, and, bidding Bart enter with the oars, and placing
one knee on the stern, with a grasp on the sides, gave a push
with his foot from the shore, which sent his rude craft surging out
far into the open expanse of water before him. Before applying
the oars, however, and while the canoe continued to move under
the impulse it had thus received, its occupants employed themselves in bending their heads to the water, and listening for any
sounds that might indicate the presence of others abroad on the
pond. The night, as it was yet moonless, and as the sky was
overclouded, was consequently a dark one; and the adventurers
could distinguish little else but the dark outlines of the Green
Mountains, that rose high in the western heavens, casting, by their
huge shadows, an impenetrable pall of darkness over the intervening space beneath, from which not a sound rose to the ear,
save an occasional short croak of some waterfowl, or the low,
sullen dash of the waters along the shores.

" Nothing out on the pond, guess, but loons, ducks, and sich
like," quietly observed Bart, raising himself from his listening
attitude ; " nor can I make out any sounds from the nest of 'em
you say there is over on the shore yonder. Ma'be they've pulled
up stakes and are off with their traps, the wimin folks and all —
shouldn't wonder, single bit."

" Now I reason a little ditter different," replied the sergeant.
" They may be getting oneasy and suspicious, because their spies
we took there at Coffin's don't return ; and so keep still, and put
out their fires, lest the absent ones be dogged back, and their rendezvous thus discovered ; but I der don't believe the company

would clear out till they knew what become of them. They are still there, I'm apt to think; so we will now put forward — first up north a piece, on this side, and then across and down to a little cove there is near their encampment."

So saying, Dunning took up one of the oars, and, with long vigorous, but noiseless strokes, sent the boat rapidly ahead; while the other took a position most favorable for a lookout. In this manner, and taking turns at the oar, they soon, by the course they had marked out for themselves, reached the western side of the pond, and, heading round, moved cautiously along the shore towards the hostile encampment.

"Ah! there! one — two — yes, three camp fires, I can der catch glimmers of occasionally," softly exclaimed Dunning, rising up in the boat, and peering ahead for observation. "I was right — the ditter rapscallions are there, snug in their quarters, but had wit enough to build their fires behind logs, or something, so as not to be seen from 'tother side. We are within the ditter matter of three hundred yards of 'em, now; so carefully, Bart, and don't let your oar graze the boat, or any thing, to give out the least sound; for they've ears, it's der probable, as well as we."

A short time now sufficed to bring them to the small cove, at which the hunter had proposed to land. Here, under the screen of an impervious tangle of brushwood and fallen tree tops, which intervened between them and the foe, they drew up their boat on to the shore. They then, after taking off their shoes, which they left in the canoe, carefully crawled up the bank, passed round the thicket, and paused to listen. The sounds of voices conversing in low tones in one spot, the slow steps of a sentinel in another, and the snoring of some hard sleeper in a third, were soon detected by the quick ears of the anxious listeners.

"As I thought," whispered Dunning, putting his mouth close to the ear of the other: "the head ones are ditter suspicious and watchful; but we must try what can be done — at least to find the spot where they've put the gals. There's a ditter old shanty I used to camp in, about fifty yards ahead; and as that is probably the best they've got, I've been thinking they may have cooped 'em in there. Suppose you, who are lightest and smallest, creep forward to it, for ditter discoveries. I will follow half way, and wait."

Without demurring to the suggestion, Bart immediately set forward, on his hands and knees, in the direction indicated by his companion. Carefully removing every dry twig and leaf from each place where he wished to bear his weight, and moving as noiseessly as the preying cat along the ground, he made his way on ward till he had gone far enough, as he judged, to reach the expected shanty ; when he paused to listen and reconnoitre. But now all seemed perfectly still. Not the slightest sound of any kind reached his ears ; while it had, in some unaccountable manner, suddenly become so pitchy dark that he could not distinguish a single object before him. And he began to feel confused and doubtful about proceeding, when, by the action of those secret and undefinable sympathies, perhaps, by which, it is said, we sometimes become apprised of the presence of others before we are informed by the senses, he all at once became impressed with the idea that some person was near him. He therefore strained his senses to the utmost in trying to discover what objects might be before or around him ; but all, for a while, to no purpose. In a short time, however, his ear caught the sound of a deep sigh, the softness of which told him it came from a female, within a few feet of him. With a palpitating heart, he now doubtfully attempted to move forward, when he suddenly perceived his head on the point of coming in contact with some broad, high obstacle, which seemed to rise like a wall before him. Surprised, and still more confused than before, he retreated a few paces, and looked upward, to try to make out the nature of the obstacle before him ; when he discovered it to be the backside of the very shanty of which he was in search. The strange darkness, which had so suddenly overshadowed him, and which was caused by the obstruction of the skylight by this rude structure, being now explained, and every thing made clear to his mind, he cautiously moved round towards the front of the shanty, to find the entrance, no longer doubting that those he sought were within. On reaching the front corner, so as to enable him to peer round it on that side, he soon made out the entrance ; but directly across it, to his disappointment, he discovered the half-recumbent form of a man, with a musket leaning on his shoulder. After a few hurried observations, in which he discovered, by the decaying fires before them several other shanties or tents among the trees, a few rods in front, Bart again slunk back to the spot he had just left, and was about to retrace his way to his companion, when a new thought occurred to him, and, moving up to the back of the shanty, which was formed by broad pieces of thick bark standing slantingly against a pole supported by crotches, and, placing his mouth to a crack, softly whispered the names of the captives, and turned his ear to the spot to catch the hoped-for response. For the first moment, all was still · but the next, the catching of a long-sus

7 *

pended breath, and even, as he thought, the rapid beatings of a
fluttering bosom, became audible.   Presently a slight movement,
as of a cautiously changed posture, was heard within ; and the
next instant a pair of soft lips came in contact with his ear at the
crevice, articulating, in sounds scarcely above the slightest mur-
mur of the air, —

" Who speaks my name ? "

' Bart," replied the other.   " You know what I'm after.   Can
one of the barks between us be removed without alarming your
keeper ? "

" I fear — but he seems asleep — try it," was the measured and
hesitating reply.

After slightly essaying several of the pieces of the bark he wished
to remove, he at length commenced operations at the bottom of
one of them, and gently forcing it aside, inch by inch, in a short
time effected an opening sufficient, as he judged, for the egress
of the captives, and that too, he felt confident, without attracting
the attention of the dozing guard.

" Now feel your way out ; and, without stirring a twig or leaf
creep on after me," whispered Bart.

And receding a few paces from the opening, he paused to
await the result.   In a moment he had the satisfaction of perceiving a female form slowly emerging from the narrow passage
into the open air without.

Supposing her companion to be immediately behind, he now,
with a whispered word of encouragement, led the way from the
spot.   With frequent pauses, both to assure himself that he was
followed by his charge, and to listen for any stir among the foe
that should indicate a discovery of the escape, he continued to
creep forward till he encountered Dunning, when, the latter taking the lead, they all moved on, one after another, in the same
cautious manner as before, and soon reached the landing in safety ;
but as they emerged from the bushes, and the hunter turned to
congratulate the ladies on their escape, it was now, for the first
time, discovered that but one of them was present.

" Bart, how is this ? ditter tell me — where is the other ? " demanded Dunning, in a tone of disappointment and vexation.

But Bart, equally disappointed and perplexed, was mute ; and
the lady, who proved to be Miss Howard, replied, —

" Miss Haviland, if not retaken, is now wandering in the woods."

" Der wandering in ditter woods. and you not with her ? "
again demanded the former with an air of mingled surprise and
reproach.

" Yes sir, but I did not intend to desert her," promptly replied
the girl. " Perceiving we were not watched very closely by the
man they put over us, she and I had thought of a plan of escaping
into the woods and getting round into the road. And while he was
talking with another, that he had stepped forward a little ways to
meet, we slipped out undiscovered, and gained a thicket ; when
finding I had left my shawl, I, contrary to Miss Haviland's advice,
I will own, ventured back to get it, and was detected, just as I was
leaving the shanty a second time, and her absence discovered.
This made a stir among them, and they ordered off scouts after
her along the pond towards the road, which was the way I pointed
when they were threatening me if I didn't tell. But she must
have heard all and escaped."

" Escaped ! ditter deuse of an escape that ; for a woman to
get out into a forest full of Indians in search of her," replied the
still unreconciled hunter. " But what course has she der taken,
think ye, gal ? "

" The one we planned, likely ; and that was, to take a wide
sweep round their camp, gain the road, and make for the tavern,
which she said was not far off," replied the other.

" Well," said Dunning, in a more mollified tone, " though der
dogs is in the luck, to be sure, yet half a loaf is better than none.
We must save what we have got ; so into the canoe there with
ye, gal ; and you, Bart, take her across, der find Harry, whom I'd
ditter rather you would meet first, and tell him you have left me
this side to go in search of the other, who, if found, can most
likely be got to the road as well the way she set out as this, in the
shape things now stand."

Although this conversation scarcely occupied a minute, and
although, while the hunter was yet speaking, Bart and his fair
friend were in their respective positions in the boat, which instantly
shot out silently and swiftly into the pond, under the vigorous push
given it by the former, yet the event showed that they had been
none too speedy in their movements ; for, at that instant, a sudden bustle in the tory encampment, which was quickly followed
by the confused sounds of voices making rapid inquiries and
giving orders, together with the stealthy tread of approaching
footsteps, apprised the fugitives that not only was their escape
discovered, but probably also the direction they had taken.

" Der narve it, narve it, Bart ! The ditter divils are after ye !"
shouted the hunter, hastily retreating from the shore and disappearing in the nearest thicket.

And scarcely had he gained a covert before his place was

occupied by four or five of the enemy, who came rushing down to the water; when, discovering the receding boat, then not fifty yards distant, the acting leader of the band fiercely exclaimed " Put about there instantly, and come ashore, or we'll fire and kill every person in the boat ! "

" O, but you'll kill us if we come back," replied Bart, splashing round his oar as if turning the boat, which in fact was going swiftly ahead.

" No, we won't," responded the leader, deceived by the apparent simplicity of the reply ; " but be quick, or we fire ! "

" Well, seeing you aint going to hurt us," said the former, carelessly, while at the same time directing, in a whisper, the girl to throw herself close on the bottom of the canoe, he silently, but with all his might, bent himself to the oar.

" Why," said the leader, after a short and doubtful pause, as he peered out in the darkness at the dimly-seen boat — " why, aint the fellow still moving ahead? He is, confound him : fire ! "

" Let drive, then ! " sung out Bart, with the greatest *sang froid*, as he hastily cast himself down in the boat.

The next instant several bullets struck the boat, or whistled over it, as the fierce flashings and deafening reports of as many exploding muskets burst from the shore with startling effect on the darkness and silence of night.

" I vown ! but that an't so bad shooting as might be, in the dark so," exclaimed Bart, hastily springing up and seizing his oar. " They are more at the business than I thought 'em ; and we may as well be a little further off afore they have time to load and fire agin, guess," he added, suddenly changing the direction of the boat from the course it had been taking, and plying the oar with an energy which showed rather less indifference to his proximity to the hostile marksmen behind him than his words might seem to imply.

The tories, in the mean while, who had foolishly all discharged their pieces at once, fell to loading again as fast as was possible for them to do in the dark. But before any of them was ready to fire, the last traces of the fugitive boat had vanished from their view.

They were, however, after giving vent to their vexation in a volley of curses upon the fellow who had thus outwitted them, in getting beyond controlling distance, preparing to fire again, at random, in the direction in which the canoe was last seen moving, when their attention was suddenly arrested by firing in the woods r short distance to the south, which seemed to be an exchange of snots between their pickets and some enemy assailing them from that direction. They therefore hurried back to their companions, and with them ra ied to make a stand against the force which all supposed was about to storm their encampment. But to their agreeable disappointment, though an occasional shot continued to be directed towards them by persons who seemed to be lurking in the distant thickets, no tangible force made its appearance for the firing which had so alarmed them, and caused them to call in all their scouts within hearing, and make every preparation for a desperate resistance, was, as the reader will have already imagined, but the feint made by Woodburn's party, who, hearing the reports of the guns discharged at the escaping canoe, and partly divining the cause, had advanced from their concealment, and begun to make the diversion agreed on at the outset. But not receiving the signal promised, in case help was needed, and feeling doubtful how to act, most of them fell back, and ceased operations, till Bart, who had, in the mean time, reached the shore, and, with the fearless girl he had released, hastened round to their post, arrived and informed them of all that had occurred. On receiving this aggravating intelligence, Woodburn, now almost frantic with disappointment and anxiety, instantly withdrew to the road with all his band, except two left to keep the enemy in a state of alarm ; when they all, including even the heroic Vine Howard, immediately scattered in different directions through the dark forest in anxious search for the luckless Miss Haviland, to whom we will now return, for the purpose of following her in the wild and perillous adventures she was destined to encounter on that eventful night.

P

CHAPTER VII

"Unshrinking from the storm,
  Well have ye borne your part,
With woman's fragile form,
  But more than manhood's heart." — *Whittier*

THE observation is no less true than trite, that no one knows till he has tried it, what he can do or endure. And as just as is the remark in a general application, it is, we apprehend, more strikingly so when applied to the gentler sex; for, from the position they occupy in social life, their powers of action or endurance are so seldom fully put to the test, that they are generally far less conscious than men of what deeds they might accomplish or what degree of suffering they might endure, in emergencies calculated to call forth the highest energies of their physical and moral natures. And if there be any disparity between the number of heroes and heroines in the world, such emergencies as we have named are only wanting, we believe, to make up any deficiency that may be found in the latter.

When Miss Haviland ascertained that her too venturous companion had been intercepted and retaken, in the manner mentioned in the preceding chapter, she for a moment greatly hesitated whether to return and yield herself again to her captors, or persevere in her attempt to escape. But, beginning to suspect the true source of the present misfortune, which, if her suspicions were just, pointed only at herself, and thinking that her escape would soon lead to the voluntary release of her companion, she quickly decided on the latter alternative, and glided noiselessly away into the depths of the forest.

After proceeding in a direct course from the camp to such a distance as should preclude the possibility that any ordinary sound made in walking through the woods would reach her captors, unless they were in actual pursuit behind, of which her often strained senses had as yet given her no evidence, she turned short to the south, and, in pursuance of the hasty plan formed by herself and companion at the outset, now made her way, as fast as the darkness and the usual obstacles of the woods would permit, towards the road, her only guide being the parallel swells of land, which, running north and south, rose, as she had luckily noticed before dark, in successive lifts up the mountain to the west. Still hearing no sounds of pursuit, she began to entertain strong hopes that she should be permitted to reach the road unmolested. In this, however, she was doomed to be disappointed; for, in a short time, a cracking, as of dry twigs under the tread of some one stealthily advancing, arrested her attention, and brought her to a stand. Fortunately, no part of her dress was sufficiently light-colored to betray her. And, having nothing to fear from this, and believing that, by placing herself in close contact with some natural object, she might still have a good chance to be passed undetected, she glided to the nearest tree, and, placing her back to the side opposite to the suspected foe, awaited his approach in breathless silence. Presently he came up, and, after pausing a moment within a few yards of her, apparently to listen and reconnoitre, he passed by so near as to graze the bark of the tree behind which she stood, and moved care-lessly on some distance before again pausing to repeat his *re-connoissance.* She drew a long-breath; but, before she dared move from her stand, the sounds of other approaching feet reached her ears. And soon two more men, evidently on the same search, passed by her, at different distances to the east, and, like the first one, bent their courses northward. After waiting till all sound of their receding steps had wholly died away, she again moved forward, and soon had the satisfaction of finding herself in the road, but a short distance from the spot where, a few hours before, she and her attendant had been captured. It remained now to get beyond the tory encampment. Could she be permit-ted to pass down the mountain, in the road, but a half mile, she might then consider the danger mostly over, and proceed on to the tavern in comparative safety. And, though aware that this portion of the way might be scarcely less dangerous than any she had passed over, yet, tempted by the facility with which it could be accomplished in the road, she resolved to make the attempt, and accordingly, with a guarded but rapid step, began to move down the sloping way before her. But she had proceeded but a short distance, when she was startled by the loud report of fire-arms in the direction of the tory encampment, which, as already described, were, just at that moment, being discharged at the escaping canoe. While pausing in doubt at the meaning of this unexpected outbreak, the random firing of Woodburn's party which we noted as soon following that of the tories, now burst from the forest a little before her on the left, and greatly in creased her perplexity. Suddenly conceiving the idea, from these circumstances, that the tories had been assailed in their rear, and were now retreating towards her, and this notion being the next moment confirmed by the glimpses she caught of a dark form emerging from the bushes on the left, whom she mistook for a foe, she hastily turned and fled, in agitation and alarm, into the opposite forest bordering the road on the south, having thus approached within a few rods of the very men who were in search of her, and thus unconsciously eluded their friendly grasp. Though intending soon to turn her course eastward, so as to come out again into the road at such a point as should place her beyond any danger of a recapture, yet, urged by her fears lest her foes should cross the road and overtake her, she pressed on so far into the depths of the woods, that when she paused to change her course, she became confused and doubtful respecting the direction she should take to regain the road in the manner she had proposed. She had now no further knowledge of the make of the land, or the situation of the hills, by which she could be guided. But at length, fixing on a course which she thought most likely to be the right one, she again set forward, slowly picking her way through the swampy and tangled tract of forest into which she seemed now to have entered. In this manner she pursued her dubious course onward nearly an hour, every moment expecting that the next would bring her out into the road. At length she fell in with a small stream, which she rightly judged to be one of the brooks running into Black River, and which, from what she knew of the course of that river, she supposed would lead nearly in the direction she sought to go. But on stooping down to feel the current, she, to her great surprise, found it running in a course directly opposite from what she expected. Scarcely knowing now which way to direct her steps, she passed over the stream, and, with a sense of desolation, growing out of the thought that she was lost in the depths of the wilderness, which she had never before experienced, wandered on, and on, for several of the successive hours of that dark and dismal night. At last she came to the top of a high swell, where, the new aspect presented in the slope of the forest before her naturally causing her to pause, she dropped down upon an old mossy log to rest her worn and wearied frame, and try to collect her confused and scattered faculties. While here endeavoring to rally her sinking spirits, and compose her thoughts so as to look more coolly on her situation, she began to discern, through the openings of the foliage, the dark outlines of a high mountain, rising, at the distance of two or three miles, directly in front of her. It now occurred to her that, like other persons lost in the woods, of whom she had heard, she might have been, all this time, wandering in a circle, and that the mountain before her might be the very one she supposed she had left far behind her, west of the tory encampment. If this supposition should prove correct, the long-sought road must lie somewhere between her and the mountain in view, and a little more perseverance in that direction would consequently put an end to those perplexities which were now becoming more painful and dread than any sensations she had experienced from the pursuit of her enemies. Encouraged by the gleam of hope which this thought imparted to her almost despairing mind, she started up, and again nerved herself for the task of meeting the many difficulties which she knew, at the best, yet remained to be overcome. It had, by this time, in consequence of a scattering of the clouds, or the rising of a waning moon, become perceptibly lighter, and, for the next hour, her progress was much more direct and easy. By this time, she came to a spot in the forest which was sufficiently open to give her another and fairer view of the mountain she had been approaching. She looked upon its dark sides a moment, and the pleasant delusion under which she had been laboring wholly vanished from her mind. She saw it could not be the mountain she had hoped to find it, nor indeed any she had ever seen; and she again gave herself up as lost, perhaps, irretrievably lost, far away and deep in the dark recesses of a howling wilderness, from which she might never be extricated. And yet her usual firmness did not wholly forsake her. " *Is not your life of more value than many sparrows* in the sight of Him who careth for all?" she mentally exclaimed; and she was calmed and comforted by the ready affirmative which her faith responded.

While casting about her in doubt respecting the next step to be taken, she discovered traces of what was evidently once an imperfect road, or path, which seemed to extend through a partial opening towards the mountain. Thinking it might possibly lead to some human habitation, or at least to some place preferable to the open forest for rest and shelter till the return of daylight, she resolved to follow it. As she proceeded on, she began to detect marks of the woodman's or hunter's axe in the trees, here entirely cut down, and there girdled, or denuded of their bark as high as the hand could reach. These indications of the former presence of men appeared to grow more frequent as she went on; and at length she came out into a small opening in the forest in the midst of which stood a roughly-constructed log-house, or shanty, with a regularly-formed bark roof still standing. The remains of smaller and less durable shanties were also visible in the vicinity of the former.*

With a cautious and hesitating step, Miss Haviland drew near to this rude structure, and at once perceived, by the appearance of the unguarded loop-hole window, and the open entrance, before which the untrodden wild weeds were growing, that it was untenanted. Approaching still nearer, and peering into the window, she discovered, in one corner of the deserted apartment, a comfortable-looking bed, composed of branches of the hemlock, which she rightly concluded had been collected and used by hunters, who occasionally made the place their quarters for the night. Immediately concluding to avail herself of the advantages which this shelter and primitive couch seemed to promise for obtaining the rest her exhausted system so much needed, she entered, and, throwing herself down on the soft and yielding boughs, soon surrendered herself to the influence of the grateful repose, and fell asleep. She was soon, however, awakened — by what she knew not, unless by the feeling of uneasiness and apprehension, by which she now found herself unaccountably agitated. She had heard, or read, of those mysterious intimations, by which, it is said, we sometimes instinctively become apprised of impending danger, when there is no apparent cause for apprehension, and when reason utters no warning. If such instances ever in reality occurred, this might be one of them ; or the impression might have been unconsciously received from actual sounds, which came from foes now secretly lurking near, and which, as it is known often to be the case, had fallen on her slumbering ear, and disturbed and troubled, without fully awakening her. But whatever the cause of the strange foreboding, the effect soon became too strong and exciting to permit her longer to remain passive. And she arose to examine the apartment, and see what precautions could be taken to render it more safe against the intrusion of enemies, whether they should come in the shape of men or wild beasts. On approaching the entrance, she discovered, standing by the side of it against the wall

---

* Colonel Hawks, while traversing the wilderness of Vermont, in the French wars, with a regular force, among whom was the then Captain John Stark, once encamped near the foot of the mountain, in the south part of Cavendish, where the incident we are narrating is supposed to have occurred. The mountain still bears the name of Hawks's Mountain, and the traces of the encampment, it is said, are still visible.

a sort of rough door made of long cuts of thick bark, confined by withes to two cross-pieces, and intended, evidently, as there were no contrivances for hanging it, to be set up against the entrance on the inside as a barrier against the cold, or the un-welcome intrusion of any thing from without. But it had become so water-soaked and heavy, and the end on which it stood so firmly set in the ground, that she found, on making the attempt, her strength unequal to the task of removing it. And she turned away to look for other means of protecting herself from danger. Casting her eyes upward, she perceived, lying loose on the beams, or rather poles, extending across the room above, several long pieces of bark, which had been left there, probably, when the roof, of the same material, was constructed. And it immedi-ately occurred to her, that, if she could mount this loft, she might so dispose of herself there as to escape the observation of any human intruders, and, at the same time, be out of reach of any wild beasts that should enter the room below. Accordingly, going to one corner, she began to mount by stepping on the pro-jecting sides of the logs in the two converging walls, and soon succeeded in reaching the loft, and forming, from the bark, a piece of flooring sufficiently strong and broad to bear her weight and screen her person from observation. Upon this she extended herself, face downwards, with her eyes placed to a small aperture, to enable her to see what might happen in the room below, and silently, but with highly excited expectation, awaited the event. But what event did she expect? She could not tell; and yet she was wholly unable to divest herself of the continually in-truding idea that something fearful was about to occur; and impelled by the singular apprehension, she could not help listen-ing for sounds which might herald the approaching evil. For some time, however, no sounds reached her ears, except those low, mingled murmurs which are peculiar to the forest in the stillness of night. But at length her quickened organs were greeted by some noise which she knew was not a fancied one; and the next moment the sound of human footsteps became dis-tinctly audible. Presently she heard voices at the door, and then saw two dark forms cautiously entering the room below. After walking around the apartment and thrusting the muzzles of their guns into corners, with the apparent purpose of ascertaining whether any one was concealed within, they approached the pile of boughs before described, and gave vent to their satisfaction at finding so good a bed, in a short, guttural ugh! which proclaimed them, to the trembling listener above, to be Indians, and of those.

doubtless, who had been sent out in pursuit of her. They then proceeded to draw up the old door and barricade the entrance after which they set their guns against the wall, and camped down on the bed in the corner.

It would be difficult to describe the sensations with which the hapless girl witnessed what had occurred ; and these, with the fear of what might still be in store for her, nearly filled the measure of her distress and perplexity; for although she had thus far escaped observation, and although she soon had the satisfaction of knowing, by the heavy and measured breathing which reached her ears, that her foes had sunk into a deep sleep, yet how was she, even now, to avoid falling into their merciless hands ? Should she attempt to descend and escape through the window, could she effect her purpose without being heard and detected ? She feared not. And should she remain in her present situation till daylight, would her terrible visitors then awaken and depart without discovering her ? This alternative appeared to her even less promising than the other. And yet one of the two courses must be adopted. Which should it be ? While anxiously reflecting on the subject, fresh noises in the woods arrested her attention. These were also the sounds of footsteps, but evidently not those of any human prowler. With a light, quick pat, pat, pat, the animal came up to the door, paused, and snuffed the air through the crevices. He then moved along to the window, reared himself on his hind legs, thrust in his nose, and after giving two or three quick, eager snuffs there also, withdrew, and trotted off, at a moderate pace, a short distance into the forest, where he appeared to come to a sudden halt. The next moment, the long, unearthly howl of a wolf rose shrill and tremulous from the spot, and died slowly away, in strange, wild cadences, among the echoing mountains around. Sabrey instinctively shuddered at the fearful sound, but instantly turned her attention to the sleeping Indians, whom she expected to hear rousing up and rushing out with their guns after the insidious prowler. But they, to her surprise, snored on, unconscious of the danger. The howl was soon repeated, when short, faint responses, in the same shrill, savage modulations, became audible in every direction in the surrounding forest. These answering cries, growing more distinct and loud every moment, in their evident approach to the spot where the first signal howl was given, now fully apprised the agitated listener of the fearful character of the scene which was likely soon to occur beneath or around her. In an incredibly short space of time, the gathering troop of famished monsters seemed to be arriving and arranging themselves under their invoking leader to be led on to the promised prey. And soon the trampling of multitudinous feet evinced that they were in motion and cautiously advancing towards the house. The next moment, they all appeared to have assembled under the window, and paused as if to plan the mode of attack. After a brief interval, in which no sounds could be distinguished but the low, suppressed snuffling of the troop for the scented prey, a large wolf leaped up into the narrow aperture paused a second and then quickly thrusting his balanced body forward, dropped noiselessly down on the ground floor within. Another, and another, and another, followed in rapid succession, till more than half a score of the gaunt, grim monsters had landed inside, and silently arranged themselves in a row before the bed of their intended victims, who still strangely slept on. One more fearful pause succeeded, in which the greedy band seemed to be eagerly eyeing the fated sleepers, and marking out portions of their bodies for the deadly gripe; when suddenly springing forward, they all fiercely pounced upon the victims, and, with the seeming noise of a thousand wrangling fiends, mingled with the sharp, short, half-stifled screeches of human agony, that were heard in the hideous din, seized, throttled, and tore them, limb from limb, to pieces, and bore off the dissevered parts, munching and snarling, to different corners of the room. The noise now for a short time subsided, and nothing was heard but the low, broken growls of the cannibal troop, as they busily craunched the bones, and tore the flesh on which they were raking their horrid feast. Then followed the fierce and noisy encounters for the decreasing fragments, till none were left worth contending for.

At this juncture, two of the half-glutted but still ravenous gang, relinquishing the well-picked bones on which they had been aboring, rose, and, advancing into the middle of the room, stood a moment listlessly viewing the operations of the rest; when they suddenly started, and, turning slowly round and round, began busily to snuff the air, and throw their noses upward in search of some fresh game that appeared now to have struck their keen olfactories. The affrighted maiden, who had been witnessing this hideous scene from her hitherto unsuspected concealment above, with blood curdling in horror at the sights and sounds that reached her recoiling senses, now shuddered in fresh alarm; for she but too well understood what this new and fearfully-significant movement of the wolves portended. And, instinctively withdrawing her face from her loop-hole of observation, she hastily

8 *

d.ew nerse.f up in the middle of her frail support, so as to be a
far as possible out of the reach of her expected assailants. Bu
they at once detected the slight sounds occasioned by her move
ment, and, now guided by two senses instead of one, instantly
began to gnash their teeth, and, with wild howls, to leap upwar
after their newly-discovered prey. And although her position
was more than seven feet from the ground,—a height which,
might be supposed, could not have been reached by this class of ar ·
imals in a perpendicular leap,—yet so desperate had the presen
gang become by the taste of human blood, that they soon, in their
determined and constantly-repeated efforts, began to strike and
seize the beams with their teeth, by which they would hung sus·
pended a moment, and then drop back again to the ground fo
another trial. The terrified maiden now gave herself up as los'
and tried to quell the tumult of her frenzied feelings, that she
might meet her approaching fate, as dreadful as it was, with
calmness and resignation. But the terrific noise of her maddened
assailants, as they leaped up, snapping, snarling, and howling, in
demoniac chorus, and made nearer and nearer approaches every
moment to her person, once more aroused her natural instinct for ·
self-preservation ; and she arose, and, standing upon her feet,
involuntarily bent over one end of her support to catch a view
of what was passing below.

In withdrawing her shrinking gaze from the fiercely upheaving
heads and fiery eyeballs which there greeted her, she espied the
guns of the Indians still standing against the wall, almost directly
beneath her, with the muzzles extending upward within the reach
of her arm. With the rapid process of thought which danger is
known often to beget, a new plan of deliverance, suggested by
the discovery just made, was instantly formed and digested in
her mind. And in its pursuance, she drew a white handkerchief
from her pocket, and, hastily folding it together, threw it down to
the farthest corner of the room below. As she had anticipated,
the whole gang rushed after it. And instantly seizing the opportunity thus afforded to execute her design, she hastily balanced
herself on the edge of the bark the most nearly over the guns,
reached down her arm, grasped one of the muzzles, and drew
up the heavy weapon, just in time to escape the baffled brutes as
they came bounding back, with redoubled howls of rage and dis·
appointment, to the spot. Too much accustomed, in the new
settlement in which she had been mostly reared, to the sight are
even handling of fire-arms not to know how to use them, she
cocked the piece, and, again advancing to the edge of her pla

form, pointed down into the thickest of the infuriated pack, and fired. One wild, piercing yelp followed the deafening explosion, and, the next instant, all the survivors of the hushed and frightened gang were heard scrambling through the window, and scattering and fleeing off with desperate speed into the surrounding forest. With the last sounds of the retreating steps of the wolves, and with the relief which a returning sense of safety brought to the over-wrought feelings of the maiden, all her strength gave way, and, sinking down, weak and helpless as an infant, she sobbed out, in the broken murmurs of an overflowing heart, her gratitude to Heaven for her deliverance from the horrid death from which she had so narrowly escaped. For a while she could only tremble and weep; but at length the violence of her emotions began gradually to subside, exhausted nature would be cheated no longer, and she sunk into slumber, too sound, happily, to permit her to dream over the fearful scenes of the past.

When she awoke, it was broad daylight, and all was quiet within, while without the birds were chanting their morning melodies. At first she could scarcely believe that the scene she had passed through was not the distempered imaginings of some frightful dream. But there, on the blood-stained floor beneath her, lay the carcass of a dead wolf, and the scattered bones of the slain Indians, to attest the dreadful reality. Hastening down from the loft into the room, and averting her eyes from the revolting spectacle, she hurried forward with a shudder to the door, effected an opening sufficient for her egress, and rushed out into the open air, of which she now drew a long, grateful inhalation, more expressive than words of the deep sense of inward pleasure she experienced in being freed from this den of horrors.

Believing that, by the advantages daylight would now afford her, she might be able to retrace her way to the road, she immediately sought out and entered the old path by which she had approached the cabin; and this serving to indicate the general course she must pursue to accomplish her purpose, she followed it back to the end, and then passed on through the forest in the same direction. She had proceeded but a short distance, however, before she was startled by the unexpected appearance of a man advancing through the thick intervening undergrowth directly towards her. As she was about to strike out obliquely into the forest to avoid him, her steps were arrested by his voice calling out to her.

"Don't be alarmed at a friend, young lady," he said, in a plausible manner, as he came forward and stopped at a respectful distance—"don't be alarmed at my appearance at all; for you are the one, I take it, that we are searching for. It is Miss Haviland, is it not?"

"Yes, s.r," replied the latter, looking doubtfully at the man whom she thought she had somewhere before seen — "yes, that is my name; but as there may be both friends and foes out in search of me, you will excuse me for saying that I do not know to which of these you belong."

"True, true," said the other, in a wheedling tone — "true; I don't blame you for being a little cautious. So I must tell you that, living in these parts, and being acquainted with Captain Woodburn, I volunteered, when I heard you were lost last night, to go with the rest in search of you. And being now so lucky as to find you, I will conduct you out to Coffin's — four or five miles from this, I suppose — where your friends are anxiously waiting to see or get word of you."

Although our heroine was not exactly pleased with the manner and countenance of the man, yet the charm of the name of Woodburn, to whom he had so artfully referred, restored her confidence, and she at once and thankfully accepted of his prof-fered guidance, little suspecting that she had yielded herself to the most subtle of her foes — the deceitful and treacherous David Redding!

CHAPTER VIII

" Then marched the brave from rocky steep,
From mountain river, swift and cold.
The borders of the stormy deep,
The vales where gathered waters sleep,
Sent up the strong and bold." — *Bryant*

THE bold and decisive measures of the Council of Safety had
by this time begun to manifest themselves in results little anticipated by the adherents of the royal cause in Vermont. The
latter, emboldened both by the presence of a powerful British
army on their borders, and the doubts and difficulties which, for
a while, were known to have embarrassed and rendered ineffectual
the deliberations of their opponents, had become so assured and
confident of an easy conquest, that in some sections they proceeded openly in the work of enlistment, and in others pushed
forward their parties into the very heart of the interior, before
perceiving their error ; while, by their representations at head-
quarters, they completely deceived Burgoyne and his advisers
respecting the true state of feeling that animated the bosoms of
the great mass of the people — a fact made abundantly evident,
not only by the subsequent confessions of that general, but by all
his operations at the time, and especially that of the short-sighted
expedition, which we have before shown him to have planned and
set afoot, under Peters, to the Connecticut River. It was no wonder, therefore, that when they now suddenly discovered the whole
state in motion — armed men springing up in every glen, nook,
and corner of the Green Mountains, and concentrating to join
another no less unexpected, and no less formidable force, which
was understood to be rapidly advancing from New Hampshire —
it was no wonder they were taken wholly by surprise, and slunk
silently away to their retreats, or immediately fled to the British
army, whom they still neglected to undeceive.

It was about one week subsequent to the events last recited ;
and the interim had been marked with little, as far as immediately
concerned the action of our story, and those of its personages to
whom we must now return — with very little to which pen can do
justice, except what the reader's imagination probably has already
anticipated ; for though thrilling events may be described with a

good degree of adequacy, there are yet certain states of high wrought feeling that language can never but feebly portray. The search for the lost maiden, on the eventful night of her capture and escape, had been, as the reader will have inferred, as vain and fruitless as it was agonizing to her lover, and anxious to all. The renewal of the search next day, till afternoon, had been no better rewarded. More force having then arrived, the tory encampment was assailed, but found empty of occupants, who had, some hours before, scattered and fled. Still unwilling to relinquish his object, Woodburn, with a small party of his friends, continued his efforts in wider ranges through the forest, which, on the third morning, brought him to the cabin in which her most fearful trials had occurred ; when the dead wolf, the remnants of the slain Indians, not yet wholly carried off by the foxes or returning wolves, the guns, the torn and blood-stained earth, and, above all, the white shreds of some part of female apparel, discolored and scattered round the room, told a tale, that, in spite of the entreaties of his sympathizing friends, who deemed the evidence not yet wholly conclusive, drove the appalled lover, in a frenzy of grief and horror, from the dreadful scene.

It was about a week, as we have said, after that night of adventure and excitement. Three companies of the newly-enlisted regiment of Rangers, embracing all the recruits yet raised on the east side of the mountains, were paraded in the road before Coffin's tavern, while their officers were standing listless on the grass in front, and occasionally throwing inquiring glances along the road to the east, as if awaiting some expected arrival from that quarter. At length Woodburn, on whose brow rested an air of gloomy sternness, advanced, and calling his sergeant and scout-master, Dunning, to his side, in a low tone, imparted to him some private order or suggestion ; when the latter, beckoning from the ranks his and the reader's old acquaintance, Bill Piper, who was also a subaltern in the same company, the two laid aside their guns and equipments, and proceeded leisurely down the road, the way in which the attention of all seemed directed. After proceeding about a quarter of a mile, they came to a turn in the road, which, now becoming invisible from the tavern, led down a long hill, and entered an extended piece of woods nearly another quarter of a mile distant.

" Well," said Dunning, here pausing and casting his eyes forward to the woods, " they der don't seem to make their appearance yet. I ditter think they must have halted there by the brook to drink and rest a little so we wil' stop at this point, where we

can see both ways ; and when the troops begin to show themselves, we'll then give the signal."

With this, they threw themselves down in the cool shade of a
tree by the way side, and, for a while, yielded themselves to that
listless, dreamy mood, which reclining in the shade, after exercise, on a warm day, almost invariably induces.

"Dunning," said Piper, at length rousing up a little, and drawing from his pocket a well-filled leathern purse, which he carelessly chinked against his upraised knee, by way of preliminary
—"Dunning, it is a mystery to me where all this stuff comes
from. Six weeks ago, it was thought there were scarcely a thousand hard dollars, except what was in tory families, in all the
Grants. Now, there must be well on to that sum even in our own
company, every recruit having been paid his bounty and month's
advance pay, in silver or gold, on the spot. Where does it come
from ? "

" From the sales of the der tory estates, of which they have
been making a clean sweep, you know," replied the other.

" Yes, yes, we all know that, I suppose ; but where do the pur-
chasers of these estates get the money to buy with ? " rejoined
the former.

" I never ditter catechized them about it," said the hunter,
evasively.

" Nor I," remarked Piper ; " but I have lately heard a curious
story about the matter. They say there has been a sort of home-
spun-looking old fellow, that nobody seems to know, following the
commissioners of sales round, from place to place, with an old
horse and cart, seemingly loaded with wooden ware, or some such
kind of gear, for peddling ; and that he has bid off a great part
of all the farms, and stock on them, which have been sold, paying down for them on the spot in hard money, which they say he
carries about with him tied up in old stockings, and hid away in
his load of trumpery. Some mistrust he is a Jew ; and some are
afraid he is a British agent, not only buying up farms, but also the
Council of Safety, who are also strangely full of money these
days."

" That last would prove a rather ditter tough bargain for him
and his masters, I reckon," responded the hunter, dryly.

" Yes, that is all nonsense, no doubt," observed Piper. " But
still it is a mystery to my mind, how money, that a short time
ago was so scarce, should now all at once be so plenty ; and that
was the reason I raised the question before you, who generally
know pretty near what is going on among our head men, and
who, I thought likely, could easily explain this secret."

" No,' said the other; ' no, Bill ; there might be der trouble about that. When a stat secret falls into my ears, it is not so easy to get it out of my mouth. I've got an impediment in my ditter speech, you know,' he added, with a slight twinkle of the eye.

" Your mouth goes off well enough on some public matters, I find," remarked Piper, with an air fluctuating between a miff and a laugh.

" Der yes, to say, for instance, that the decree to confiscate and sell the tory estates was a ditter righteous one — has worked like a charm — called out the rusty dollars from their hiding-places thick as der bumblebees in June — ditter drove off the blue devils from among the people, and raised a regiment of men in less than three weeks ! "

" Ah ! and a fine regiment, too, it will be. I long to see it all brought together, for I don't know a tenth of them — men or officers — not even our colonel."

" Herrick ? Well, I can't der quite s y I should know him now ; but he is a ditter go-ahead fellow, who loves the smell of gunpowder nearly as well as Seth Warner himself, whose pupil he is in the trade. We shall have the pleasure of seeing him in a few minutes, probably, as Coffin told me he passed along here night before last, on the way to *Number Four*, to come on with Stark. *That* may be told without ditter mischief."

" And so may another thing, perhaps, which I should like to know, Dunning."

" Der what is that, Bill ? "

" Why, you know that Bart, the night after we discovered the place where we supposed the girl was destroyed, disappeared, and has not been here since. Where have they sent him, and what after ? "

" Piper, you are as brave as a lion, and as strong as a horse, ter doubtless ; but your tongue may ditter need training, for all that Still, as you mean right, and will probably learn to bridle hat unruly member only by practice, I will, for once, put you to he trial. Bart has gone a spy to the British camp. Though Harry, in his despair, would for a while believe nothing but that she was der dead, or worse, yet, as I and others, putting all things together, hoped and reasoned ditter different, in part, and thought she might not have been killed there, but retaken ; and, for fear of pursuit, hurried off directly to the British, he concluded to despatch Bart to his friend Allen, of the Council, to take advice, and then proceed, in some disguise or other, right into the

ion's den — ascertain whether the girl was there — and, after
ditter learning what he could about the enemy's movements, return
with the news."

"Well, I'll be chunked if the project wan't a bold one! But
if any creature on earth can carry it out, it is Bart; and he will,
unless they get word from this quarter that such a fellow is among
them. Ah! I now see the need of a close mouth on the subject,
and will keep one, thanking you kindly, Dunning, for your caution and confidence."

"It will be all right, I presume, Bill, now you perceive Bart's
neck may depend on your ditter discretion. But who have we
there?" added the speaker, pointing down the road towards the
woods.

While Dunning and Piper were thus engrossed in conversation,
two men, on foot, had emerged from the woods and approached
within a hundred yards, before attracting the attention of the former. They were without coats, or in their shirt sleeves, as, in
common parlance, is the phrase for such undress; and, having
handkerchiefs tied round their heads, and carrying in their
hands rough sticks, picked up by the way-side, for canes, they presented an appearance, as they leisurely came along up the
ascending road, with occasional glances back towards the woods,
that left Dunning and his companion wholly in doubt, while
attempting to decide who or what they were.

"Now, who knows," said the wary hunter, "but they may be
der tory spies, hanging round the skirts of Stark's army, and
intending soon to be off cross-lots to the British, to report his progress. I'll ditter banter them a little, at all hazards, before we
let 'em pass."

But as the strangers drew near, their appearance grew less and
less like that of the ordinary footpads for whom they had been
taken; and there was something in their bearing which considerably shook, though it did not wholly alter, the hunter's intention
to banter them. One was a strongly-built, broad-chested man,
with a high head, hardy brown features, and a countenance betokening much cool energy and decision of character. The other
was rather less stocky, and slightly taller, of quicker motions, but
withal a prompt, resolute-looking person.

"Well, my friends," said the former, coming up and pausing
before the expectant Rangers, with an air that seemed to challenge
conversation, "this is Coffin's tavern here ahead, I suppose. Will
the captain be pleased, think ye, to see a little company about
this time?"

"Der yes," replied Dunning, eyeing the speaker with a cui.-
ous, half doubtful and half quizzing expression. "Yes, if of the
right sort, he wont ditter cry, I reckon. But the captain is sometimes rather particular — for instance, if you should happen to
be tories ——"

"Tories! — do we look like tories?" demanded the former
glancing to his companion with a droll, surprised look.

"Why der no," replied the hunter, a little abashed, "I ditter
think not."

"Well, I had hoped not," rejoined the man. "But who are
you, my friend — one of the Green Mountain Boys, that we hear
so much about?"

"Not far from the mark, sergeant, or commissary, or whatever
is your ditter title; for you belong to the army that's at hand, I
take it?" said Dunning.

"O, yes," briskly returned the other, again looking at his companion, and joining him in a merry laugh. "Yes, I am one of
them, and mean to have a hand in stirring up Burgoyne, when
we reach him, I assure you."

"That's right, commissary!" exclaimed Dunning. "You are
a der chap of some pluck, I'll warrant it. I begin to ditter like
you. What shall I call your name, friend?"

"My name is John Stark, if you will allow," replied the stranger, with an amused look.

"John Stark? Why, that's your der general's name!" said
the hunter, incredulously. "Come, come, friend, you are ditter
gumming me. I have seen John Stark — Captain Stark, that was
then — now general — the same that was bought back by our
folks for a white pony — ditter dog cheap, too, as the British
will find, before he is der done with them, or I mistake the
amount of fight that's in the critter, amazingly." *

"Thank you, sir!" heartily exclaimed the former, now evidently as much gratified as amused at what he heard. "In behalf of that same John Stark, I thank you, sir, for your good
opinion of him. But where, my good fellow," he continued, with

---

* When General Stark was exposed for sale in Montreal, by the Indians, by whom he had been captured in the French war, and some of
his countrymen were trying in vain to make his savage master set a price
on him, an English gentleman happened to ride by on a handsome white
pony, which so greatly struck the Indian's fancy, that, pointing after the
coveted animal, he exclaimed, "Ah! ugh! me take that you get him."
Whereupon the gentleman was followed, the pony purchased, and, with
it, the captive Stark redeemed.

a look of lively interest, "where did you ever fall in with Captain Stark ?"

"Why, in the old war, when he der marched through here with Colonel Hawk, I ditter acted as the colonel's guide over the mountains to Otter Creek. Stark, as I've said, was one of the captains, though I wasn't much with him, to be sure," replied the hunter, becoming more doubtful and puzzled every moment, at the turn matters were taking

"Ah ! yes, yes, — our hunter guide on that rough march ! I remember now. Well, well, the fault is not wholly on one side after all !" said the other, musingly.

"Der — der — ditter how ? der — ditter —" began Dunning opening his eyes with an uneasy stare.

"This is General Stark, my boys," here quickly interposed the other gentleman. "I see by your badges that you belong to the Rangers. I am your colonel, Herrick, and this the general himself, who, by way of relief from a long ride in the saddle, threw off his uniform, like myself, down in the woods yonder, and walked on, while the troops were halting to refresh a moment, and recover from the effects of their march in this scalding heat, before they made their appearance at your rendezvous. They will now be on the move shortly."

"Der — der — ditter —" cried the confused hunter, rising hurriedly to his feet, and lifting his cap, in a tremor of respectful deprecation, before the general, while his tongue began to trip and fly in the vain attempt to get out an apology — "der — der — ditter — ditter — ditter —"

"Never mind, my brave fellow !" exclaimed Stark, with a hearty slap on the other's shoulder ; "never mind a mistake so naturally growing out of our unmilitary guise. No offence, even had your remarks been less pleasant. But you, sir ! — why, you have paid me the greatest compliment I ever had in my life !"

"No — no offence whatever to either of us," added Herrick "But yonder come the columns of our friends and helpers from New Hampshire. If you are here to give notice of their approach, as I suppose, make the signal, and back to your post. And here, general," he continued, pointing to two fine-looking and gayly caparisoned horses, now led up by waiters, with the coats, swords, sashes, and great military cocked hats of the denuded officers swinging on their arms — "here, general, come our horses and uniforms. Let us rig up before a worse mistake shall befall us."

With a curious mixture of chagrin and gratification at what had just occurred, the two Rangers now made the appointed signal, and

hurried back to join their companions in arms at the tavern. And
in a few minutes, the fine little brigade of the hardy and resolute
New Hampshire Boys, headed by their intrepid leader, now
equipped in imposing regimentals, and mounted on his curvetting
charger, came pouring along the plain in all the pomp of martial
array, and were received by the customary military salutes, and
the reiterated cheers of their congenial welcomers of the Green
Mountains.

The hour that succeeded was a bustling and a joyous one.
The greetings, the introductions, the mutual compliments for deeds
done at Ticonderoga and Bunker Hill, and the merry jokes given
and taken, as the mingling forces partook of the good cheer prepared for the whole at the expense of the public or patriotic individuals, together with the strong community of feeling that agitated their bosoms in view of a common object to be accomplished, and common dangers to be encountered, — all combined
to render the scene one of no ordinary interest and animation. At
length, the drums of the different companies began to beat to arms,
and the soldiers were seen gathering at their respective stands, preparatory to the march of the combined forces across the mountains.

At this juncture, a single horseman came galloping along the
road from the west ; and, the next moment, Ira Allen, the active
and untiring secretary of the Council of Safety, with a countenance betokening good or exciting news, rode up to the door;
and, throwing himself from the saddle, turned to receive the
greetings of his acquaintances gathering round him.   With a significant look and gesture to Woodburn to follow, he led the way
to an unoccupied room, at length found in the crowded tavern.

" What news do you bring, Mr. Allen ? " said Woodburn, with
an effort at calmness, as soon as the two were by themselves.

" That which will scatter the blackest part of that cloud on
your brow, I trust, my dear fellow," replied Allen, with an animated and exulting air.   " Here, look at this ! " he added, pulling
out and presenting a small and closely-folded letter.

With trembling eagerness, Woodburn seized the missive, and,
with a glance at the well-known hand of the superscription, " To
Captain Woodburn, or Mr. Allen, of the Council," opened it, and
read as follows : —

" I am at the British head-quarters — not exactly a prisoner
but evidently a closely-watched personage, having reached here
with my captors, after a forced and fatiguing journey, which
however, was not made unpleasant by any disrespectful treat

ment. Although the party, to whom I became a prisoner, have been frightened back or recalled, and the expedition, of which they were the advance, given up, yet I think it my duty to say that another, and much more formidable one, is in agitation against Bennington. I hope our people will be prepared for it. and show these haughty Britons that they do not deserve the name of the undisciplined rabble of poltroons and cowards by which I here daily hear them branded.   S. II."

We will not attempt to describe the emotions of Woodburn on the occasion. But the letter disclosed that which involved more momentous interests than those merely that concerned the individual feelings of a lover. And it was soon concluded to lay it before General Stark, who, with Colonel Herrick, was then called in, the letter shown, and all the attending circumstances, past and present, so far as concerned the public to know, fully explained.

Mean while the troops were drawn up, in marching order, before the tavern, and stood wondering why their general did not appear, or, at least, give order for the column to move onward.

At length, however, the long expected leader, attended by those with whom he had been in consultation, made his appearance at the door, and ordered the horses of those who were to travel mounted to be led forward.

" 'There's something more than common on John Stark's mind," whispered a tall New Hampshire Boy, to his fellow in the ranks. " See how his eyes snap ! I am an old neighbor of his, you know, and can read him like a. book. I shouldn't be surprised if we heard from him soon ; for he an't one of those that like to keep chawing on a thing that makes him feel, but wants to out with it, and always will, unless he has good reason for a close mouth Yes, I'll bet a goose we hear from him before we start."

The speaker had conjectured rightly. Stark was heard to say to Allen, —

" Mount and ride along against the centre there, sir, where you can best be heard. We must have it ; for, besides preparing their minds for what they probably must soon meet, it will make a battle cry for your boys and mine as potent, for aught we can tell, as was the name of Joan of Arc among the Frenchmen.

The officers, with Allen, then sprung into their saddles ; and as the latter reached his allotted post, and faced round to the lines, the general commanded attention, and added, —

" My men, let me introduce you to Mr. Allen, the patriotic secretary of the Vermont Council of Safety, and say that I hold myself voucher for the truth of what he shall tell you. Listen to his communication."

The secretary, now bowing respectfully to the attentive and already prepossessed ranks before him, began by saying that among the recreant few of any note in the Green Mountains, who had basely deserted their country and joined the enemy, there was one who had a daughter of whom he was wholly unworthy. The speaker then proceeded to relate Miss Haviland's noble stand for the American cause, from which she was not to be allured or driven by all the inducements and menaces held out by a tory father and lover, both of whom had received royal commissions — her absolute refusal to go with them, on their late departure for the British army, and her more recent capture and abduction, while on her way to her friends, by the probable instigation of the rejected lover, and with the connivance, perhaps, of the father; all of which was concluded by reading the letter just received, 't was added, by a trusty messenger, who had gone in disguise to the enemy's camp to receive it, and who had now returned to keep open the important communication.

"Men of New Hampshire!" now cried Stark, in a loud, animated voice, as with flashing eyes he glanced over the throng of upturned and excited faces before him, "is it any wonder the Green Mountain Boys are so gallant and brave in fighting for their wives and sweethearts, when such is a specimen? Will you join them in defence of their homes and country, and help fulfil this matchless girl's expectations when we meet that taunting foe at Bennington, as by God's favor we will? If so, then let it now be told in three cheers for *the good cause,* and as many more as you please for *The Tory's Daughter!*"

The next instant, as the bidden drummers brought their sticks to the bounding parchment of their instruments with blows that seemingly would have thrown their arms from their shoulders, a thousand men were seen leaping wildly into the air, and giving their patriotic response in a round of cheers that rent the ringing heavens above, and shook the startled wilderness for miles around them.

"Order in the ranks!" at length broke in the deep, stern voice of the general, as the last cheer was dying away. "Prepare to march! March!"

And the excited troops could scarcely be kept in their places as, with the stirring strains of lively fife and rattling drum, they were rushing and pouring along on their way to the seat of war

CHAPTER IX.

"In dreams the haughty Briton bore
The trophies of a conqueror."

THE scene of our story changes to the vicinity of the Hudson, to which the eyes of millions were now turned as the theatre of approaching events, on which hung, perhaps, the great issue of the American revolution. Although both parties seemed to look upon the matter at stake as one of immense magnitude, yet far different were the views and feelings which, at this time, pervaded the two opposing armies. The British, flushed by their successes, and confident in that strength before which every opposing obstacle had thus far given way, were looking down with little other than absolute contempt on the American forces in their front, believing them wholly incapable, either from numbers or courage, of opposing any serious resistance to their march, when they chose to move forward. And here thus lay their proud and infatuated chief for weeks, dreaming of coronets, frittering away the time in feasting with his officers, and indulging himself and them in all the follies which characterized their gay and licentious camp. On the other hand, the Americans, deeply sensible of the consequence of suffering their enemies to effect their contemplated junction at Albany, were vigilant, active, and determined. Though firmly resolved to dispute the way of the invader to the death when they must, they yet preferred, for a while, the policy of embarrassing and impeding him, rather than openly exposing themselves to his attacks. Whole brigades were therefore employed in the work of destroying the bridges, blocking up the roads with fallen trees, and putting every possible obstruction in the way of his advance, so that his delay, where he now lay at Fort Ann, might be protracted till a sufficient force could be gathered to meet him with a more reasonable hope of success.

And every hour that hope waxed stronger and stronger. Every day brought fresh accessions of strength to their self-devoted bands, and every gale wafted to their gladdened ears the sounds of the warlike preparations of an aroused and indignant people gathering from afar to the rescue ; and hey began to breathe more freely while they thought, as with trembling solicitude they still did, of the fearful meeting that must now soon follow.

At the time which we have selected for opening the scene that forms the next connecting link in the chain of our tale although the road had been at length opened, and a few detachments thrown forward to the Hudson, the main part of the British army still lay at Fort Ann ; where their long lines of tents, marked, at intervals, by the colors of the different regiments flying from their slender flagstaffs, were now seen stretching, a city of canvas, over the plain. A little apart from this imposing array stood a small number of dwelling-houses of different sizes, irregularly scattered along on both sides of the road towards the south, over the largest of which floated the broad British flag, proclaiming it the head-quarters of the commander-in-chief. The next, in size and commodiousness, among these various structures, — all now occupied by the general officers and other favored personages of the army, — was a large, low farm-house, which the intermingling devices of the British and Hanoverian flags, conspicuously displayed from the roof, denoted to be the quarters of General Reidesel, suite, and well-known family. This last building seemed now to be the principal point of attraction. Gayly dressed officers and ladies were seen entering the doors, or standing inside at the open windows ; while the sounds of the familiar greetings, lively sallies, and merry laughter of the assembled and assembling company, sufficiently indicated the convivial character of the scene about to be enacted within. Let us enter. Around a long and richly-furnished table, in the principal apartment, were just seated those who deemed themselves the *élite* of that boastful army. Its notorious chief, the weak and wise, vain-glorious and energetic Burgoyne, occupied the post of honor, at the head, and the fair hostess, the amiable, learned, and vivacious Countess of Reidesel, the foot of the table ; while, at the sides, were ranged, according to the prevailing notions of precedence, the variously-ranked individuals composing the rest of the company, among whom, with other officers of less note, were Generals Reidesel and Frazier, Major Ackland and his devoted wife, together with several Americans, including the elated Esquire Haviland and his beautiful daughter. The latter, who, sorely against her inclinations, had been prevailed on, or rather constrained, by her father to attend him to the entertainment, was seated by the side of Lady Ackland, to whom she seemed shrinkingly to cling as a sort of shield against the fierce glances she was compelled to encounter from the eyes of those whom it was there counted treason to repulse.

The feast proceeded. With the constant bandying of compliment, joke, and repartee, among the merry and self-satisfied lordlings who assumed the right of engrossing the conversation, course after course came and passed in rapid succession, till a sufficient variety of viands and other substantial esculents had)een served to warrant the introduction of the lighter delicacies of the dessert. But still there seemed to be a saving of appetite, a looking for some expected dish that had not yet made its appearance, on the part of several of the guests, and especially on that of the pompous votary of Mars, who had been installed master of the ceremonies, and who at length ventured to say, —

" I had looked, my lady hostess, to have seen, ere this, among your many other delectables, the fulfilment of your ladyship's promise gracing the table, in the shape of the blackbird pie, wherewith we were to be regaled, at your entertainment, if your polite note of invitation was rightly read and interpreted."

" O, the blackbird pie ! " replied the countess, with a sprightly air and a charming touch of the German brogue. " I was waiting to be reminded of that ; for there is a condition, which I wish to propose to your excellency, before the promised extra can make its appearance."

" Ah ! What is that, my incomparable cateress ? " asked the former.

" Why, only that you carve and serve the pie to the company yourself, mon general," archly replied the countess.

" A challenge to your chivalry, general, which no true knight can refuse to accept," cried Frazier and others.

" I yield me, and accede to the condition," said Burgoyne, gracefully waving his jewelled hand, and joining in the general laugh.

" It is well," said the countess, with a finely-assumed air of mock gravity, as she raised her exquisite little table bell, which now, under her rapidly-plied fingers, sent its sharp jingle through the house.

The next moment, a liveried servant, whose countenance seemed slyly gleaming with some suppressed merriment, was seen advancing with a broad, deep dish, tastefully crowned by the swelling crust of snow-white pastry, which tightly enclosed the supposed contents beneath.

At a motion of the indicating finger of the hostess, the tempting d.sh was brought forward, and carefully placed on the table before the many-titled carver, amid a shower of compliments to the distinguished artificer of so fine an edible structure, from him and many others of the admiring company. The general now rose, and, intent only on a dexterous performance of the duties of his new vocation, gave a preliminary flourish of knife and fork, and dashed into the middle of the pie ; when lo ! through the rent thus made in the imprisoning crust, out flew half a score of live blackbirds, which, fluttering up and scattering over the dodging heads of the astonished guests, made for the open win-dows, and escaped, with loud chirping cries, to their native meadows !   At first, a slight exclamation from the gentlemen, a half shriek from the ladies, then a momentary pause, and then one universal burst of uproarious laughter, followed this strange *dénouement* of the little plot of the playful countess.   She, it appeared, had engaged a fowler to bring her a couple of dozens of blackbirds, which, by a net, he had taken, and brought to her alive ; when, keeping part as they were, she contrived up the scheme to amuse and surprise her guests here described, and, slaying the rest, made of them a veritable pie, that was now brought forward, and partaken, with great gusto, by the delighted company.

At length the cloth was removed, and the table replenished with bottles and glasses.   Then followed the usual round of toasts — " the health of the king," — " the invincibility of British arms," — " success to the present expedition," — and, with many a deriding epithet, " confusion to the rebels and their ragged army."

" Fill, gentlemen," said Burgoyne, after the subjects above named had been sufficiently exhausted — " fill up your glasses once more ; for, in descanting on the public responsibilities and glory of the soldier, let us not be unmindful of those private felici-ties which are to reward his prowess.   I give you," he added, with a significant glance at our heroine — " I give you, ladies and gentlemen, the health and happiness of our two loyal American officers, Colonel Peters and Captain Jones, the prospective bride-grooms of the double wedding of to-morrow, extremely regretting that *both* of the fair participants of the happy occasion, instead of one, are not here to give the beautiful response of their blushes to the sentiment."

As the lively applause with which this toast was received and drank was subsiding, the ladies, to the great relief of the aston ished and confused Miss Haviland, now rose and retired to another apartment.   Here, pleading some excuse for an imme diate departure, Sabrey hurried out through a back way, and escaped unperceived to her father's quarters, a small adjoining cottage, where she had lodged since his arrival in camp, and where she now secluded herself, to endeavour to fathom the plot which the unexpected and unwarranted announcement just indirectly made, together with some other circumstances of recent occurrence, plainly told was in progress to insnare her.

But it may here be necessary, for a clear understanding of some things which have preceded, and others which may follow, to revert briefly to the experience of the luckless maiden since placed in her present uncongenial and embarrassing position.

When Miss Haviland, on the termination of her compulsory journey, arrived at the outposts of the British army, she was conducted, by the order of some one evidently apprised of her coming immediately to her father's quarters. The old gentleman, at the somewhat awkward meeting that now took place between them, seemed both surprised and gratified at seeing her there; and though his manner betrayed a sort of guilty embarrassment arising, perhaps, from the consciousness of his former harshness to her, he yet at once, and pointedly, disclaimed having had any agency in her abduction, which he laid to the chances of war; to which, he contended, her perverse and unadvised conduct had been the means of exposing her. Peters, also, who soon made his appearance, joined in the disclaimer; and tendering some empty apologies for what had happened, which, he said, grew out of the mistake of a subordinate officer in construing an order in relation to taking hostages from the enemy, in certain cases, offered to convey her back, if she chose it, as soon as found consistent with her safety. The offer, however, was never repeated; and his own conduct very soon belied his assertions, and convinced her of the truth of her suspicions from the first, that he was the sole instigator of the outrage she had received, and that it was still his purpose to detain her and keep her in a position which would enable him the more effectually to prosecute his designs; for although in the few formal calls he continued to make at the house, he never pressed his suit, but seemed rather to avoid the subject, as if determined to afford her no opportunity to repeat her former refusals, she yet quickly perceived that he was busy at his intrigues to bring about, by the agency of others, and by secret management, what by himself, or by any open and honorable means, he despaired of accomplishing. All this, from day to day, unfolded itself in the renewed importunities and reproaches of her father, the added entreaties of Jones, the lover of Miss McRea, then soon expected in the British camp to be married, in the reports which had been put in circulation to place her in a false light,—that of a perverse and coquettish girl,— in the efforts made to force her into social parties, where the opinions of all were obviously forestalled, and especially in the contrived introductions she was compelled to undergo to those who had evidently been enlisted as intercessors, among whom were some whose ambiguous conduct often greatly annoyed, and, at times, even filled her bosom with perplexity and alarm.

Such was the position of the unhappy girl at the time of her reluctant attendance as one of the guests of the merry party we have described. Although annoyed, sickened, and disgusted at what she had daily witnessed, and vexed and indignant at the contemptible artifices and intrigues of Peters, which, however intended, were beginning to be the means of exposing her to new trials, yet, till what took place at that party, she had entertained no serious apprehension that any attempt would be made to coerce her into a marriage which she had so decidedly repudiated.

But the announcement which had just been so strangely made coming as it did from so powerful a personage, and one, at the same time, whose equivocal behavior, when she had casually met him, had excited her deepest aversion, now gave her to understand that such an attempt was indeed about to be made by the assumed arbiters of her fate, and that her resistance to the contemplated scheme, should she be able to make one against the overawing influence that was about to be brought to bear upon her, and even her acquiescence, she feared, was to be followed by persecutions, from the thought of which she shrunk with dismay. She might have taken that announcement, perhaps, as a mere *ruse*, as in part it really was, got up to place her in a predicament in which most females would yield rather than become the principal actor in the scene that would follow further resistance ; or she might have viewed the whole as a contemptible fabrication, but for a circumstance of that morning's occurrence. Captain Jones had called and apprised her that he was about sending an escort to Fort Edward for his betrothed, informed her that the next morning was appointed for his wedding, and concluded by making his last appeal to induce her to consent to be united to Peters at the same time.

And it was this occurrence, in connection with the former, that had so thoroughly alarmed her.

While pondering on the means and chances of escaping the threatened destiny, she perceived from her window that the company at Reidesel's had broken up, and were scattering to their respective quarters. And presently her father entered her room, and after announcing that he had been honored by the commander-in-chief with a mission to Skenesboro', from which he should not be able to return till late at night, presented her a sealed billet, and immediately departed. With a trembling hand she opened the suspected missive and read, —

"Miss Haviland will pardon the mistake involved in the sentiment delivered at Lady Reidesel's table. Its author, however, cannot but think that the full arrangement which he had supposed to have been already settled may still be effected in season. And he therefore proposes, if Miss H. will permit, a call for friendly intercession, at twilight this evening."

With a flushed and flashing countenance the offended maiden instantly sprang to her feet, and paced the room several minutes in silent agitation. Her naturally mild spirit was at length evidently aroused for some decided action ; and the manner in which it was to be commenced appeared soon to be determined in her mind.

"Ay, and the step, as bold as it may be, shall first be taken," she said, as, preparing to leave the house, her burning thoughts began to press for utterance. "Ay, if it will not avail me, in bringing aid to escape from this den of iniquity, or protection to remain, it shall, at least, serve as a proclamation of villany, which shal' yet be heard in every house and hamlet of the American people !"

The next moment she was in the street ; and, with hurried step, making her way to General Reidesel's quarters. Instantly seeking a private interview with the readily assenting countess, she frankly and without reserve told the whole story of her wrongs, and implored assistance in escaping the toils that had been spread for her, or, at least, the protecting shield of an influence which should enable her to withstand them. And the effect of her forceful recital soon showed her that she had not over-estimated the discernment and magnanimity of the noble lady she was addressing.

"Well, that is right, my bonny rebel, as they call you !" said the countess, encouragingly. "And it is the spirit in a woman which I like, and which I will have no hand in repressing. Yes, I see clearly, now, what I half suspected before — the man who had you brought here, where he could more surely noose you, is repugnant even to the misery ; and some of those he has been fool enough to enlist as intercessors, are still more dreaded. Ah ' wicked, wicked Briton! But, do you know, he is king here and that it is treason to talk, and worse treason to try to hwari him?"

"I have greatly feared so, my lady."

"What, then, do you propose to do, wherein I could befriend you?"

"Leave the army before night."

"Have you a carriage at command, and a protector?"

"I have, strictly speaking, neither, madam."

"Then how can you go?"

"On foot, and alone, unless I chance to engage one to attend me in the character of a servant."

"You are a brave one, my young lady. But they will be likely to detain you at the outposts."

"I had supposed so, and therefore came here with the hope that, after you had heard my story, you might be moved to prevail on your husband to give me a pass."

"O girl, girl! No, no, he would not dare to do it, after finding out the cause, which he must first know," exclaimed the lady, in a tone of kindly remonstrance. "He would dare do no such thing. But I would, in such a case; indeed I would! And, stay, let me see!" she continued, rising and opening the general's desk. "Here are several passes which he keeps for occasions of hurry, all signed off and ready, except inserting the name of the bearer. O, what shall I do? I am tempted to write your name in one, and trust to your honor and shrewdness to shield me, in case of your failure, from exposure and blame."

"Will your hand-writing be acknowledged, madam?"

"O, yes, I don't hesitate on that account; for I often fill up the general's passes under his direction."

"O, then, dear madam, as I know you would do by a daughter, do by me — trust to my discretion, and hesitate no longer."

The good-hearted countess soon yielded, and our heroine, with tears of gratitude, mutely imprinted a farewell kiss on her cheek, and departed with the coveted pass in her pocket.

When Miss Haviland reached her chamber, she seated herself by an open, but partially curtained window, where, unseen herself, she could easily note what was passing in the street below, to which her attention seemed somewhat anxiously directed. She had been but a few minutes at her post of observation, before she was apprised, by the hooting of boys, and the gibes and laughter of the idling soldiers, with whom the street, at this hour, was commonly thronged, that some unusual spectacle was approach-

ing. And peering forward through the folds of the curtains, she
beheld, amidst a slowly-advancing crowd, a meanly clad, simple
looking country youth wearing a ragged broad-brim, and mounted
on an unsightly, donkey-like beast, whose long tail and mane
were stuck full of briers, and whose hair, lying in every direction,
seemed besmeared with mange and dirt; all combining to give
both horse and rider a most ungainly and poverty-struck appearance. The fellow was trying to peddle apples, which he
carried in an old pair of panniers swung across his pony's back
and which seemed to be bought mostly by the boys, who with
them were pelting him and his cringing pony, to the great mirth
of the bystanders. While the crowd, and the object of their attention, were thus engaged, at a little distance, an officer, who was
passing, paused near the house, and, calling a couple of soldiers
to his side, said to them, —

"Keep your eyes on that fellow with the scurvy pony yonder,
and if you notice any thing suspicious in his movements, arrest
him. It appears to me I have seen him in almost too many
places to-day."

An expression of concern passed over Sabrey's countenance,
as she heard these words, and she gave an involuntary glance to
the object thus pointed out, who, as she thought from his appearance, had also heard the order himself, or at least guessed its
import. But instead of making off, as she expected, he spurred
up his pony, and, coming directly up to the officer, asked him,
with an air of confiding simplicity, to buy some of his apples,
which he said were "eny most ripe, and grand for pies."

"Who are you, fellow?" said the officer, without heeding the
other's request.

"Who I be? I am Jo Wilkins. But aint you going to buy
some of the apples?" persisted the former.

"Blast your apples!" impatiently replied the officer; "that
is not what I want of you. Where do you live?"

"Up in the edge of Arlington, when I'm tu hum — next house
to uncle Jake's great burnt piece there, you know," answered
the other; "but these ap —— "

"Whom are you for? King or Congress?" interrupted the
officer.

"Who be Congus? I don't know him," said the former, with
a doubtful stare.

"Well, then, whom do you fight for?" resumed the somewhat
mollified officer.

"Don't fight for nobody tu our house, — cause dad's a
Quaker — but then if you'd buy —— "

"Yes, yes; but you must tell me honestly, what you came here for to-day, and who sent you, my lad?"

"Why, dad sent me to sell the apples, 'cause he wants the money to buy some rye with. But I've been all round, and aint sell'd half, they kept bothering me so. And now its time to go hum, and nobody won't buy 'em!" said the speaker, with a doleful tone, and evident signs of snivelling.

"Well, well, my honest lad," responded the commiserating and now satisfied officer; don't mind it — nobody wants to harm you. There is half a crown to pay you for my part of the bothering.

"Why, you going to buy 'em all?" eagerly asked the other, as, with a grin of delight, he clutched the precious metal.

"No, no," said the former, kindly. "I don't wish for any of your apples — they are too green, though they may do for cooking. You would be most likely to sell them in some of these houses."

"Well, now, I vown! I never thought of that! jest's likely's not I mought, you!" exclaimed the fellow, brightening up. "Good mind to go right straight into this ere house and try it — will, by golly!" he added, leaping nimbly from his pony, swinging his panniers on his arm, and hurrying off round for the back door.

"Don't molest the poor simpleton any more, but disperse to your quarters," said the officer, now waving his ratan to the scattering crowd, and resuming his walk up the street.

Waiting no longer than to hear this order, and see that it was about to be obeyed by the crowd, Sabrey hurried down to the kitchen, where she encountered the object of her solicitude standing within the door, holding up the half crown between the fingers of one hand, and snapping those of the other, with a look that needed no interpreting.

"Your disguise, Bart," said the maiden, looking at the other with a smile — "your disguise is so perfect, or rather, the new character, in which you this time appear, has been so well acted, that had it not been the afternoon you set for your third appearance, I should have never known you. I think you make a better Quaker boy than you did a crazy man last time, or buffoon and tumbler the first one. But what have you been able to gather, to-day?"

"Pretty much all that's afoot, guess. The movement on Bennington is begun. Peters's corps of tories and Indians have gone on to Cambridge; and he, who is off to the lake, to-day, to consult with Skene and others about the expedition, is to follow some time to-morrow, as is the German regiment picked out for the service. Got at it all, think ? "

" Nearly. It is the plan, however, I understand, that when the stores are secured at Bennington, the troops are to proceed to Manchester, make prisoners of all the Council of Safety, and others of the principal men whom they can find, and return through Arlington."

" They've got to get there, first, guess, and then catch 'em afterwards. But have you fixed out a letter about that and other things, ready for me to take? I'm aching to be off with the news."

" No, Bart. I have just discovered plots to entrap me that have made me resolve to die before I will remain here any longer My old persecutor, and others a thousand times more powerful, are in league against me."

" The girl that killed the wolf would stand the racket against big bugs and all, rather guess, if she tried it. Don't know, though, being about woman matters so."

" Ay, sir, to a woman there are human monsters more terrible than all the wolves of the forest. And I am determined on attempting to escape from this place without another hour's delay ; with you, if you will permit."

" Yes, glad to go into it; and by Captain Harry's request, I was a going to propose the same thing myself, even without your new reasons. But this getting you off before dark, which you name, may be rather ticklish, miss. How did you think to manage it ? "

" Look at this, sir ! " said Sabrey, exhibiting her permit by way of reply. " Signed by a man whose authority, I think, will not be questioned, and allowing me, with my servant, to pass through the lines to my friends in the country. I engage you to act as that servant, Bart."

" I vags, now if that aint lucky ! " exclaimed the former, with glistening eyes. " Yes, lucky enough, whether it come by ploughing with heifers or steers. But let's see a bit, though. How will my turning servant to a lady, all at once, tally with the stories I've been telling, — that is, till we get beyond all who heard 'em ? Don't know about that. But look here, miss ! " he added, beckoning the other to the window. " Do you see that tall old pine, standing alone, nearly in a line with the road, a mile or so off there, at the south ? "

" Yes, very clearly."

10 *　　　R

" Well, that tree, which is beyond, and out of sight of the last
pickets, stands near a house where a widow woman lives, who
washes fine clothes for some of the officers, but wants to keep in
with all sides, and so asks no questions and tells no stories.   My
saddle and fixings are hard by there, in the bushes.   Now, suppose I go on there alone, and be scrubbing up Lightfoot, and
feeding her with these apples, to pay her for playing Quaker so
well.   Can you get on to that place by the help of the pass, and
tell straight stories, if questioned, about your servant being at the
wash-woman's, fixing things ? "

" If you think it wisest, as it may be, I will try, and be there
within an hour, if not detained.   If I am, do not desert me, Bart,
but return to this kitchen at dusk."

" Agreed!   But you'll go it without the ifs, I reckon," said
Bart, swinging his panniers to his shoulder, and departing with
full confidence in his ability to effect an escape perilous to
them both, but made much more so to him by the new charge he
had so cheerfu ly undertaken.

CHAPTER X.

"But a gloom fell o'er their way,
A fearful wail went by'

FORTUNATELY for Miss Haviland, all those who had beer.
enlisted to act as spies upon her movements happened; that
afternoon, to be absent, or busily engaged in a quarter of the
encampment from which all view of her proposed path of escape
was intercepted by intervening buildings. Much to her relief,
therefore, on setting out on her perilous journey, she was permitted to pass forward through the street unquestioned, and without
exciting any particular observation. And when she arrived at
the outpost, the soldier on duty, with a bare glance at her offered
pass, respectfully motioned her to proceed on her way. A short
walk then brought her to the house to which she had been
directed ; and here, finding every thing in readiness, she immediately mounted the now strangely-improved pony, and, with her
trusty attendant on foot, set forward, at a quick pace, in the main
road leading from the lake to Fort Edward. Their way was now
mostly through a deep forest, and over a road which every where
exhibited evidence with what perseverance and skill the Americans had labored to destroy and block it up, and with what in-
credible exertions it had been reopened by their opponents, wholly
untaught in the easiest modes of accomplishing the Herculean
task. In some places, long causeys over miry morasses had
been entirely torn up, and every log of which they were composed
drawn off beyond the means of recovery ; and, in others, streams
had been dammed up, causing extensive overflows, or turned from
their natural channels, and thus made to wash out impassable
gulfs. Every bridge had disappeared, and all the surrounding
timber rendered useless for constructing more ; while, for mile
after mile, one continued mass of gnarled and crooked trees,
here pitched together in seemingly inextricable tangles, and there
piled mountains high, had been felled into the road, which even
now had scarcely been made passable by the toiling thousands
who, for weeks, had been employed upon it. In consequence
of this, and the time spent in making circuits round in the woods

to avoid parties of the enemy, who were seasonably discovered by the wary guide to be still at work, in several places, in trying to improve some of the worst portions of the road, the progress of our heroine was slow and tedious. And it was not till after a dreary and fatiguing ride of several hours, that she and her attendant began to emerge into the more open country bordering the Hudson.

"Now, miss," said Bart, falling in by the side of the maiden, and speaking in a low, cautionary tone — "now we are coming out on to the river, and at a spot that I feel kinder shyish of."

"On what account, Bart?" asked the other, with a glance of concern.

"Well, it's for a reason I have, and then one or two more on top of that," replied the former, with his usual indirectness. "In the first place, it is a sort of a torified neighborhood about there, which may hold those more likely to mistrust and snap us up, than the regular-built enemy, who may, some of 'em, be there too, likely; as a regiment, or so, have already gone on, by this same road, to Fort Edward, which is not a great ways beyond."

"Is there no way to avoid going through the place?" asked Sabrey.

"That is what I'm thinking about," replied Bart, musing. "But one thing is certain, you must be got somewhere, and a little reconnoitring be done, before we try to go through or round the pesky place. Now, here on the left is a pine thicket, that reaches along, and comes to a point, very near this Sandy Hill place, as they call it; and by entering the woods, and keeping on in a line with the road, we both might gain a spot, in that point, where we could safely see enough of what is going on there to judge of the rest."

"I am unacquainted with the locality, and the character of the inhabitants, and shall, therefore, be wholly guided by you," responded Sabrey, reining up in compliance with the motions, rather than the words, of the other. "But what means have you had of ascertaining what you suggest respecting the place?"

"Why, I came this route the last spying trip I made," replied the former; "and being afoot — crazy folks don't ride, you know — I kinder naturally kept going back and forward, and calling at places on the road to inquire for swamp angels, or blue dogs I had lost, or some sich-like whimseys, till I managed to find out who and what lived in most every house, all the way to Ben

nington. It is a tory concern of a place, and a sort of rendezvous for those running away from our parts. One fellow, of the
last sort, came plaguy nigh knowing me ; and would, forzino
if I hadn't suddenly gone into a fit, to screw my features out
of his acquaintance. Yes, we may as well be turning in here, I
am thinking."

In accordance with the plan just suggested, Miss Haviland now
turned her willing steed, and plunged directly into the dark forest
bordering the road on the left. Here following her guide, who
kept some rods in advance to select and point out the places
affording the most feasible route through the thick undergrowth,
she slowly, and with no little personal inconvenience, made her
way forward in the proposed direction, till she at length succeeded in reaching the desired station, which was the top of a low,
woody bluff, commanding, from some portions of it, a near and
distinct view of the hamlet, in the opening below, of which the
intended *reconnoissance* was to be made. Bart, now assisting
the maiden to dismount, and directing her attention to a mossy
hillock at hand, as an eligible seat or bed for resting herself,
turned the pony loose to crop the bushes, and disappeared to
commence his observations. In a few minutes he returned, and,
having reported the discovery of a safe and easy route for passing to the east of the public road, as far as it might be necessary
to avoid it, proceeded to reconnoitre the houses below. And
taking a well-screened seat on a log, lying on the verge of the
bluff, he looked long and intently.

" Well, sir, what discoveries are you making there ? " at length
asked Sabrey, wondering at his prolonged silence.

" Why, nothing very alarming, be sure," replied the other.
" The place looks as if it was deserted, except one house ; but
there's something going on about that which I don't somehow
seem to understand. Suppose you throw a few of those ever-
green vines near you over your head and shoulders, to prevent
your dress from attracting notice, and come here to help me read
out the puzzle."

In compliance with the unexpected suggestion, the maiden
instantly rose, and, preparing herself, as directed, cautiously
advanced and seated herself at his side. The road they had
recently quitted was in plain view, a little distance to the right,
and continued distinctly visible as it swept round towards the
broad Hudson, whose tranquil surface was gleaming with the
reflected brightness of the low-descending sun. On each side
of the road, till it disappeared over a distant swell, were scat-

tered, at irregular intervals, the dwellings to which allusion has been made. Among the nearest and most respectable of these, stood, in a retired situation considerably to the east of the highway, the house presenting the questionable appearances to which Bart's attention had been directed. On one side of the spacious yard or lawn, in front of this building, stood, tied to a post, and impatiently pawing the ground, a noble-looking horse, equipped with a richly-caparisoned side-saddle ; while near by, under the fence, sat, patiently smoking their pipes, three Indians, one of whom, as was evident by their contrasted bearing and accoutrements, was a chief, and the other two his attendants. Near the principal entrance was drawn up a two-horse team, having the appearance of awaiting the reception of persons about to depart on some journey. At length the family, consisting evidently of father, mother, and their children, slowly, and in seeming mournful silence, issued from the door, and approached the wagon, when the former, lifting the latter into the seats, again turned an anxious look towards the house, and, with his companion whose handkerchief was frequently applied to her eyes, stood lingering and hesitating, as if reluctant to part with some object of their solicitude still remaining behind. Presently the agitated couple returned to the door, and, with gestures of grief and supplication, appeared to be making a last appeal to one standing just within the entrance, whose partially disclosed form, and white fluttering decorations, proclaimed her to be a gayly-dressed female.

"It acts some like a funeral there," observed Bart, doubtfully ; "but then those Indians, that seem to be waiting for some one — and that horse with the lady's saddle on him, which they appear to have the care of, and which looks, by the trim, like a British a-my horse — and —— "

"Bart, do you know who lives there ? " interrupted Sabrey, with a sudden start.

"A tory," replied the other ; "but not a fighting one, I gathered. That's him and his wife standing before the door, I take it. His name is Me — something."

"Merciful Heaven ! " exclaimed Sabrey. "I understand it all now. That lady, in the door, is dressed for her wedding — those before her are her brother and sister-in-law, pleading with her to go with them, instead of taking the questionable step she is evidently meditating. O, that I dared rush down to the side of her well-judging friends, and join them in dissuading her from listening to the ill-timed summons of her lover, and especially from going with such an escort as the infatuated man appears to have sent for her!"

Although Miss Haviland was wholly unprepared for here finding the residence of her friend, Jane McRea, which she had supposed to be in another and more distant locality, yet her quick perceptions, in combining the past and present circumstances, had not misled her. It was, indeed, that lovely and hapless girl, passing through the last trial she was destined ever to be conscious of undergoing, — that of the distracting conflict of emotions produced by being now finally compelled to decide between the behests of prudence and of love, — between the advice and entreaties of confessedly kind and judicious relatives, and the opposing counsels and impassioned importunities of an idolized lover. Deeply and anxiously, that afternoon, had the thought of her situation engrossed the mind of our heroine, who both expected and dreaded to meet her on the way — expected, because her coming had been announced; and dreaded, not only on account of the pain it would occasion to witness her disappointment, and resist her entreaties, but also on account of the danger of the unintentional betrayal which would be likely to attend a meeting with that guileless creature of the affections and her probable escort. And it was now with the mingled emotions naturally called up by the associations of former friendship, the contrast between the circumstances of the past and present, together with fears and anxieties for the future, that Sabrey, after a few brief explanations to her attendant, resumed her observations of the scene before her, which, she hoped, might still result in the triumph of wisdom over the delusive pleadings of love.

At length, she who had now become the principal object of solicitude in the family group, to which the attention of our concealed spectators had been directed, followed, with slow and hesitating steps, her still importuning friends into the yard, where, in her bridal robes of vestal white, and with her rich profusion of bright and wavy tresses hanging like a golden cloud over her shoulders, she stood at once a vision of loveliness and an object of commiseration. Again and again did those friends appear to renew their entreaties, at which the agitated girl seemed sometimes to waver, and at others to reply only with her tears; till at length the former, evidently wearied with their fruitless attempts, and despairing of success, ascended their vehicle, and drove off at a rapid pace, along the road to the south, without turning their heads to look behind them. Once, as she stood, like one bound by some fatal spell to the spot, wistfully gazing after the receding

wagon, a momentary relenting appeared to come over the
wretched maiden. She irresolutely ran forward a few paces,
and, imploringly stretching forth her white arms, uttered a faint,
sobbing cry of, "*Come back! O, come back!*" But the late appeal,
which would have so gladdened the hearts of those for whom it
was intended, was destined to be unheeded. The cry was lost in
the din of their rattling wheels, as they urged on their horses, as
if anxious to escape from the painful scene. And the poor girl,
dropping her arms, and turning hopelessly away to a small tree
near by, leaned against the trunk for support, and, for a while,
seemed to yield herself wholly a prey to the wild grief which
now burst forth from the dreadful conflict of emotions that was
rending her distracted bosom. At length she appeared to be
slowly regaining her self-possession, and now soon fully arousing
herself, she advanced towards the Indians, and, by signs, signified
her readiness to attend them. With eager alacrity, the horse was
led up for her to the door-step; when, lightly throwing herself
into the saddle, she immediately set forth along the road to
the north, preceded by the chief, and followed by his dusky
assistants.

"Well, the poor thing has settled it at last," observed Bart, drawing a long breath. "But I aint so sure that those red characters,
who appear to feel so crank at having got her started, will be
allowed to get far with their prize, without seeing trouble."

"Why, sir?" asked Sabrey, wiping away the sympathetic tears
that had started to her cheeks at what she had been witnessing —
"why do you make such a remark?"

"Well, it may not amount to any thing, be sure," replied
the other. "But having had one eye on the lookout, during
this affair at the house, I noticed, a while ago, some five or six
scouts, slying along on the other bank of the river, over there,
and crossing in a boat, and entering the woods on this side. By
their appearance, I think they must be Continentals from our
army below; and if it is these Indians they have been spying
out, and are after, they will waylay them along here somewhere,
likely."

"O, if they could but take her from these creatures, and send
her to her friends!" said the former, with emotion.

"Yes, but I hope they won't attempt it," said Bart; "for if
these Redskins, who are probably to have a smart price for getting
her safe to camp, should find themselves about to be robbed of
her, there's no telling what they would do."

At this juncture, their attention was arrested by the sounds of footsteps approaching in the road from the north; and, the next moment, a second party of Indians, headed by a tall, fierce looking chief, emerged into view, and advanced nearly to the edge of the woods; when the chief, beholding the other party coming on with their charge, suddenly halted, and stood awaiting their approach, with an air of doubt and disappointment, and with looks that plainly bespoke his jealous fears of losing the reward, which, it appeared, the short-sighted lover, in his impatience at the delay that had occurred, had offered him also to bring off his betrothed. The bold and arrogant air of the newly-arrived party, standing in the middle of the road, and seemingly intending to dispute the path, caused the others, as they now came up, to pause, as if for parley or explanation; when a fierce and angry debate arose between the rival chiefs, in which the new comer, with dark scowls and menacing gestures, demanded the exclusive possession of the lady, which the other, at first mildly, and then in a tone of defiance, persisted in refusing. At length the latter, under the pretence of wishing to obtain water, but with the real object, probably, of avoiding a collision till some compromise could be effected, approached the alarmed maiden, and led her horse out into a little opening in the bushes on the left, where a cool and inviting spring was seen bursting from beneath the wide-spreading roots of a stately pine-tree standing in the background; and here leaving her under the shade of the tree, still sitting on her horse, he and his attendants gathered round the spring for the purpose of quenching their thirst. At this instant, white streams of smoke, followed by the startling reports of muskets, suddenly burst from a neighboring thicket, and the band of concealed scouts, with challenging hurrahs, were seen springing from their coverts, and rapidly gliding from tree to tree towards the spot. The astonished and unprepared Indians, who had escaped death only by the distance from which the missiles of their assailants had been discharged upon them, all, with one accord, slunk instantly away into the surrounding bushes.

Scarcely had they disappeared, however, before the tall chief, whose ill-omened appearance and conduct we have noted, again darted out into the opening; when, with a quick, wild glance around him, and a yell of fiendish triumph, he rapidly whirled his arm aloft, and, the next instant, the glittering tomahawk was seen, like a shooting gleam of light, swiftly speeding its way on its death-doing errand.

One solitary, piercing shriek, suddenly cut short, and sinking into an appalling groan, rose from the fatal spot; while the white robes of the victim, like the ruffled pinions of some suddenly struck bird, came fluttering to the ground. The deed was done and the spirit of the beauteous and unfortunate Jane McRea had left its mangled tenement and fled forever ! *

A momentary pause ensued ; when, amidst the intermingling shouts and cries of murder and vengeance, that now burst from both scouts and Indians, the fiend-like perpetrator of the foul deed, who had been seen to leap forward towards his fallen victim with his scalping-knife, bounded back into the road, and, there holding up and shaking the gory trophy at his rival, immediately plunged into the forest and disappeared. The next moment a detachment of British cavalry, who had been sent out to intercept the scouts, came thundering down the road, and put an end to the tumult. Turning away in horror from the spot, now made dangerous by the presence of the British, who, on seeing what was done, and learning the facts, soon began to scatter in all directions after the murderer, Miss Haviland and her guide hastily resumed their journey by the route which the latter had discovered for avoiding the road, and which they pursued till dark, when, arriving at the house of a family in the interest of the American cause, they found a comfortable shelter for the night, and the repose so much needed to counteract the effect of the agitating events of the day on our heroine, and fortify her for the trials yet in store for her.

---

* From the various published accounts of the massacre of Miss McRea, we have followed, in our illustrations of that melancholy tragedy, as far as our limits and plan permitted us to carry them, the one deemed by us the most probable. By way of finishing the details of the horrible scene, however, it may be proper here to state, that Captain Jones, the strangely infatuated lover, having despatched, for the reward of a barrel of rum, one party of Indians after her, and then a second one, for the same reward, had started to meet her, when, encountering the murderer with the scalp, which he recognized by the peculiar color and length of the hair, he hastened, in a state bordering on absolute distraction, to the fatal scene. A British officer, with a few attendants, had, in the mean time, removed the corpse to a wagon by the road side, and was guarding it, when the lover arrived to claim it. But his lamentations were so terrible, and his conduct so frantic, that it was deemed advisable to remove him, and bury the remains from his sight. From that hour, the bereaved lover was an altered and ruined man. And he died soon after, as there is every reason to believe, of a broken heart.

CHAPTER XI.

"Still on? Have not the forest gloom,
The taunt of foes, the threatened doom,
Shaken thy courage yet?"

THE indefatigable Bart, after seeing the object of his greatest
solicitude in safety for the night, that of his next, his loved
Lightfoot, well stabled and fed, and, lastly, his own wants supplied,
determined, with his usual caution and forethought, on making a
little tour of observation to Fort Edward, now some miles in the
rear, for the purpose of gathering what new intelligence could
be gained respecting the movements of the enemy, which might
both enhance the value of his budget of news to carry home,
and enable him to shape his course more understandingly and
safely on the morrow. Accordingly, in the new disguise of a
barefooted, bareheaded, coatless farmer's boy, with a basket of
green corn to sell for roasting slung on his arm, he proceeded
on foot to the recently-established rendezvous of the enemy at
the place above named, and boldly entered their encampment.
Here he soon made discoveries that filled him with uneasiness,
and, finally, those which thoroughly alarmed him for his own
and the safety of his charge. The whole camp was in a state
of bustle and commotion. Colonel Baum, in anticipation of the
time fixed for his march, had just arrived with his appointed
force, and was intending, after allowing his troops a short
respite, to press immediately forward that night on the contemplated expedition. Bands of painted Indians, who had also arrived from the main army since dark, were feasting and drinking
in grim revelry, or enacting the frightful war-dance, on the outskirts of the encampment. Parties of tories were constantly
coming in from the surrounding towns, receiving arms, and departing to their different allotted stations, to act as pickets to the
force about to advance, or as scouts to scour the country along
the road to the south. And at last, to crown all, Peters and
Haviland, with a small number of attendants, all bearing, on
their bespattered persons, evidence of hard and rapid travelling,
rode hurriedly into camp, and announced that a dangerous spy

had, that afternoon, been at the head-quarters of the main arm.y audaciously abducted a young lady, and with her escaped in this direction, for the arrest of whom a handsome reward should be paid.

"It is time you and I was jogging, Bart," muttered the unsus-pected personage within hearing, who deemed himself not the least interested in this unexpected announcement, as he gradually edged himself out of the camp, and made his way, with unusua. haste, back to his quarters for the night.

Scarcely had the first faint suffusions of morning light begun to be distinguishable in the chambers of the east, before the well-recruited Lightfoot stood pawing at the door, as if impatient to receive and bear off her precious burden from the scene of danger. In a few minutes, the fair fugitive, in answer to the summons of her vigilant attendant, came forth, evidently refreshed by her repose, and, in a good measure, recovered from the shock occasioned by the sad and fearful spectacles of yesterday. Without any allusions to the startling discoveries he had made since they parted for the night, other than the quiet remark that he had ascertained that it might not be wholly safe for them to proceed any longer in the main road, Bart assisted the lady to mount, and led the way on their now doubly difficult and haz-ardous flight. Striking off obliquely to the left, into a partially cleared pine plain, and then, after thus proceeding a while, again turning to the right, they directed their course forward in a line parallel to the great thoroughfare to the south, but at a sufficient distance from it to insure them against the observation of all who might be passing therein, or scouting along its borders. And on on, now through open fields, and now through dense forests, now through splashy pools, or rapid rivers, and now over sharp pitches or deep ravines, now in cross-roads or cow-paths, and now in trackless thickets, now over fenny moors, and now along the rocky declivities of mountains, — on, on, did they pursue their toilsome and weary way through the seemingly interminable hours of all the first half of that eventful day.

At length, however, believing themselves many miles beyond the rendezvous of Peters's corps, who were understood to have been selected as the pioneers of the expedition, they emerged from the woods, and fell into the main road leading up the winding Walloomscoik to the village of Bennington. Greatly rejoiced that, at last, she could be permitted to travel in a smooth road with some assurance of safety, and encouraged by the prospect of soon reaching the friends and acquaintance of her old neighborhood, from whom she was confident of a cordial welcome, our heroine now rode on with lightened feelings and renewed spirits. But she soon perceived, by the manner of her guide, as he examined the appearances of the road, as he went on, and occasionally cast uneasy glances before and behind him, that he did not consider it yet time to rejoice. And soon he stopped short, and observed, —

"'There are too many tracks in this road for my liking, and not of the right kind to read well, either."

"I hope you will indulge in no unnecessary alarms, Bart,' said the other, reluctant to leave the road, as she supposed he was about to advise. "You, who yesterday manifested little uneasiness, to-day, when we are farther removed from danger, have appeared extremely cautious and apprehensive, I have thought. Why such a change, while the reverse would seem so much more rational ? "

" Well, miss, the question is not so onnatural as it might be, I reckon," replied the former ; " and I have been expecting you'd wonder some why I led you on such a jaunt as we've had. But the fact was, your chance of getting off has been a little scaly, to-day, to say nothing of the shadow of a rope that's been round my own neck in the mean time."

"I cannot comprehend you, Bart," said the maiden, with a look of surprise and concern.

" Spose so ; for I have held in, cause I thought I wouldn't worry your mind till needful, which it may be now ; so I'll tell you the whole kink," replied Bart, proceeding to relate his last night's discoveries, and then adding. —

" Now a party of the enemy — for I saw a moccason track just now, and none on our side would be in such company as that means — a party of 'em have gone on before us ; and my notion is, that we strike off through this bushy pasture to the left."

" Let us do so, then, if such is our situation, and that without a moment's delay," cried Sabrey, in alarm at the unexpected disclosure.

" Well, perhaps it an't best to fret about it, jest at this minute," responded the imperturbable guide — " I kinder want to make an observation or two, before we start," he added, ascending an elevation near by, which commanded a view of the road both ways for a considerable distance.

After glancing along the road in front, a moment, he turned and bent his searching gaze in the other direction, where he

11 *

soon appeared to discover something that both interested and disturbed him.

"It is, by Herod! it is the whole main body, Germans and all, at their rations, within a mile of us, and their pickets on the move in this direction!" he at length exclaimed, hastily quitting his post of observation.

Hurrying down to the side of the startled maiden, he sprang to the nearest length of the fence, here enclosing the road, and grappling, with main strength, the topmost of the heavy poles of which it was composed, soon effected a breach sufficiently low to allow the horse to leap over without endangering the seat of the rider.

'Here, go it, Lightfoot! gently! there you are! Now off with ye, as if the divil was at your heels!" cried Bart, as the horse, with her fair burden, dashed lightly through the breach, and cantered off in the direction indicated by the finger of her master.

Pausing to replace the fence, lest the opening should attract the notice of those coming on behind, Bart rapidly followed, and, in another minute, the fugitives were safely screened from observation by the thick foliage of the different clumps of bushes, which they managed to keep between them and the road they had just quitted.

"There is a house," said Bart, musingly, after they had proceeded a while in silence — "there is a house about half a mile ahead, and nearly the same distance from the great road, with woods between, which is a place I called at when I came down, and which I had been all along calculating to turn off to, for a short stop, as we might shape our course to do now, if not somewhat risky."

"A little rest and refreshment would certainly be very acceptable," said the other, "if it could be safely obtained. Who lives there?"

"Well, some folks"

"Loyalists?"

"Tories, d'ye mean? No, not by a jug full."

"Who are they, then, sir?"

"The man," said Bart, glancing up to his wondering companion, with an odd air of shyness, as he provokingly persisted in his evasions — "the man is one of Warner's sergeants, and a sort of relation to somebody that I thought likely would be visiting at his house by this time. And — and I guess we'll venture there, considering," he added, suddenly dashing some distance ahead, under pretence of pointing out the way

After winding their course a while among the variously grouped little thickets that studded the old pasture, they at length entered a tall forest of maple, which the incisions in the trees, together with the marks of an old boiling-place, that they soon reached, proclaimed to be the sugar orchard, belonging, probably, to the establishment they were seeking. And, now falling into a beaten path, they soon perceived, by the glimpses of an opening which they occasionally caught through the trees, that they were drawing near to the object of their search. The serpentine course of the path, however, and the undergrowth, so thick as to be nearly impervious to the sight, prevented any direct view of the opening; and they passed on without any very exact notions of propinquity till a sudden turn of the path brought them unexpectedly to the edge of the wood, and in full view of the house, not a hundred yards distant; when, to their astonishment and dismay, they beheld the place in possession of a large party of the enemy. Bart instantly caught the bridle, and was turning the horse for the purpose of fleeing back into the forest, when five or six armed men sprang out from the bushes behind and around them, cutting off their retreat in every direction. And the next moment they were prisoners to the minions of the vindictive Peters.

Bart's quick eye had told him, at a glance, that there was no chance for him to escape ; and, before his natural looks could be noted, he had become transformed into a lout of so stolid and inoffensive an appearance, that his captors seemed greatly disappointed, and evidently entertained doubts whether he could be the one they supposed they were about to secure. And it was not till his pale and trembling fellow-prisoner had been conducted off on her horse some rods, that they could make him seem to comprehend that he was a prisoner, and must go with them. He then burst out into a piteous fit of weeping, and, passively receiving the kicks and cuffs of his keepers to get him in motion, went bawling along, like a whipped schoolboy, towards the house.

"I thought 'twould be jes so!" he exclaimed, between his sobs and outcries. "I most knowed when that man hired father to have me go to show the woman the way — I most knowed she was running away, and would get me into some scrape. Then the man, like enough, had done something, so he darsent go any furder with her. And now they'll lay it al. to me — boo-hoo i oo-oo-oo!"

"Conduct the lady into the house!" said the officer in command, as the prisoners were led into the yard — "conduct her into the house, and set a guard round it, till orders can be got from the colonel. And as to this bawling devil," he continued, turning with a scrutinizing, but somewhat staggered look, to the blubbering Bart, "take him to the barn, where I just noticed some good cords, bind him hand and foot, and guard him closely. He will make less noise within an hour from now, I fancy."

"But, your honor," began one of the scouts who had brought in the prisoners ——

"Yes, yes," interrupted the other, "I have just been informed of his pretences; but there's an even chance that he is shamming, and the fellow we want, after all. Do as I have ordered."

Bart was now led into the open barn, which stood facing the yard, and projecting in the rear over a steep bank, making from the floor, on the back side, that was also open, a perpendicular fall of nearly a dozen feet. He was then ordered to sit down in the middle of the floor, when two of the half dozen keepers who had him in charge, with many a half taunting, half pitying joke at his doleful whimpering, carelessly proceeded to prepare the cords for binding him, while the rest laid aside their guns, and went searching about the barn for eggs, all, notwithstanding the caution of their commander, being evidently so much impressed with the idea of his innocence as to disarm them of the vigilance usually exercised on such occasions. At this juncture, just as the two men, one standing before and the other behind him, were in the act of stooping to take his legs and arms, Bart started to his feet with the suddenness of thought, and giving the one in his rear a paralyzing kick in the pit of his stomach, grappled round the legs of the other, and, bearing him, in spite of all his struggles, across the floor, leaped with him from the verge to the earth below. Managing to keep uppermost in the descent, Bart, as the man struck heavily on the ground, leaped unhurt from the senseless body, and, with the speed of a wild deer, made his way to the nearest point of woods, which he fortunately reached just in time to avoid the volley of bullets that was sent after him by the rallying guard from whom he had so strangely escaped. While he balked tories, in the general commotion that now ensued, were giving vent to their rage and mortification, in cursing one another and the more particular object of their wrath, whom they concluded it was useless to pursue, a long, shrill whistle was heard issuing from another point of the forest, to which it was thought the escaped prisoner could not have had time to pass round. Scarcely had the sound died away, when a movement, accompanied by a low snorting, was heard in the high-fenced cow-yard, into which Lightfoot had been turned for safe keeping. The whistle was soon repeated, and the next moment the sagacious animal was seen rearing herself nearly upright in the air, and then, with a prodigious leap, throwing herself over the fence into the field beyond. Although the tories, for a while, as little comprehended this movement of the pony, as they did, at first, that of her master, yet they raised the alarm that the horse had broken away; and a dozen men threw down their guns, and ran out into the field to head her, but, dashing at and through them, like a mad Fury, she bounded off at full speed, and soon disappeared in the woods in the direction in which the whistling had been heard, leaving the baffled pursuers and their associates now fully to perceive how completely they had all been outwitted and outdone by both horse and master.

Much of our happiness is the result of contrast. A slight alleviation, unexpectedly springing out of a disheartening misfortune, not unfrequently affords a comparative pleasure more keenly appreciated than unalloyed blessings arising out of the ordinary circumstances of life. The pleasure of Miss Haviland was equalled only by her surprise, when, on entering the house, she found her former fellow-prisoner, the sprightly and fearless Vine Howard, a transient but favored inmate, whose presence here now fully explained the enigmatical language of Bart, on the way, while it soon raised a shrewd suspicion of the cause of the awkward shyness he had exhibited in making his partial and roundabout revelations. Their mutual salutations, inquiries, and explanations, had scarcely been exchanged, before they were called to the window by an outcry and commotion among the tories without; when they had the unspeakable satisfaction of witnessing the escape of Bart, for whose situation and fate they had both, from different causes, felt the deepest commiseration and the most gloomy apprehensions.

" Now, " said the animated Vine, as she turned exultingly away from the gratifying scene that had opened by the escape of Bart, and closed by that of his pony — " now, Sabrey, if they will let you remain here till dark, I will see what *I* can do towards effecting *your* escape, which, to be candid about it, I mainly came here to favor. But whether you escape, remain, or are dragged back to the British camp, I will not this time be separated from *you.*"

The proffered assistance of the spirited girl, however, at least so far as related to the contemplated attempt to escape by night, was not destined to be called in requisition. In a short time, a messenger was seen to arrive; upon which the whole party of

S

tories commenced preparations for an immediate departure. Presently a closely covered vehicle, drawn by one horse, appeared coming from the main road, and approaching the door. The next moment, the officer, whom we have already noted, entered the house, and told Miss Haviland she was required to depart.

"This young lady attends me, if I am compelled to go, sir," said Sabrey, firmly, pointing to Vine, who instantly advanced and locked her arm within that of the former, by way of confirming the assertion.

"Such are not my orders," responded the officer, with an air of slight perplexity.

"Then I go not with you alive, sir," said Miss Haviland, with calm determination.

"Nor will I be separated from *her*, by you, while *I* am living," added Vine, with no less spirit.

"Well, well, ladies, you must have your own way, I suppose But be prompt; the carriage waits for you," replied the officer, stepping back to the door.

In a few minutes more, the ladies presented themselves at the door, and, without accepting the offered assistance of their sum moner, entered the unoccupied vehicle, which was now immediately put in motion, and conducted on in the rear of the main column of the tories, who had already commenced their march towards the great road. As they emerged from the short piece of forest through which their way now led, the exciting spectacle of a large body of troops, moving in military array along the road, accompanied by the hum of mingling voices, the steady tramp of men and horses, the rattling of tumbrels, and the heavy rumbling of artillery, unexpectedly burst upon the senses of the startled maidens. Baum's select and finely-equipped regiment of Germans and British occupied the front, and Peter's motley corps of tories and Indians the rear of the long-extended column. As the head of the detachment in possession of the fair prisoners reached the road, they came to a halt, when, after waiting till the corps to which they belonged had nostly passed by, they, to the agreeable disappointment of the girls, turned in, and moved on with the rest towards that little anticipated scene of defeat and death from which so few of them were destined to return.

"By this time," observed Vine to her thoughtful companion after they had concluded the remarks which the novelty of their situation naturally elicited — "by this time, Bart, at the rate he will be likely to ride, has nearly reached Bennington, now less than ten miles distant; and in another hour after, if the news he carries has the effect on our army there that I anticipate from what I learned when I came down, these fellows will be met on the way by a force which they cannot be expecting to see. Can they, do you suppose?"

"I think not," replied Sabrey, "or we should have been sent back at once, to the British camp, as we expected; but, believing he shall meet with no serious opposition, and probably fearing I should find some means to escape, if sent back, my magnanimous persecutor concludes to drag me round with him and his minions, that I may be watched more closely, till, having completed his anticipated triumphs, he is ready to return."

"But where *is* Peters?" asked the other; where *is* that remarkable gentleman *now*, that he don't present himself here, to pay his respects or make his apologies, or assure you of your safety, or frame some story by the way of accounting for his conduct, or at least, of smoothing the matter? One would suppose the fellow would want to say *something* on the occasion.

"Yes," replied the former; "but he wishes to see me as little as I do him, I presume. Should he find it impossible to avoid me, however, he would probably come up boldly, and say my detention was a mistake of his subaltern; or that he only directed it to afford me a safe escort to my friends in the Grants."

"There would be a deal of love in such doings."

"He entertains none; not one particle now, if he ever did, for me, Vine."

"What the deuse, then, does he want with you?"

"Indeed, I hardly know myself."

"Marry you?'

"If he does still aim at that, it is with no honorable motives. I have had some strange suspicions, lately, and I feel but too thankful at this prospect of a battle, for I shall cheerfully meet all dangers I may encounter from the flying bullets of our people for my chance of a release."

"Chance, Sabrey? Why, I know our side will get the victory, when we shall be made prisoners to — well, to about the right sort of fellows, probably," added the girl, with a merry laugh.

The conversation was here interrupted by the scattering reports of musketry somewhere in front, which instantly threw the whole line into commotion. An immediate halt was commanded, and the troops hastily formed in order of battle, as well as the ground

would permit. Glancing over the line in front, from the sma.
elevation on which they chanced to have stopped, the girls perceived that the head of the column had reached the banks of the
stream that here crossed the road, and were rapidly deploying
into the fields, to the right and left, to be prepared to receive
their yet invisible foe. The bridge over the stream had just been
torn up, and its scattered wrecks were seen floating down the
stream below. While Baum was hurrying forward his artillery c
the front, a body of about two hundred Americans emerged fr.
their coverts in the bushes, some distance from the opprsite bar :,
and, with an ominous shout of defiance, discharged their gui
and disappeared over the hill beyond, before the slow Cerman,
who alone were yet near enough to do any execution with muc
kets, were ready to return a single shot. A strong guard cf
pickets, consisting of tories and Indians, were now sent forward
to ford the stream, and keep watch of their retreating assailants,
while the few wounded and dying wretches who had experienced
the effects of American marksmanship were carried back on
hastily-constructed litters to a house in the rear, affording the
shocked maidens, as they were borne by groaning and writhing
in their agony a sad and sickening foretaste of the fearful scene
of blood and carnage they were destined soon to witness. As
soon as the bridge was repaired by the engineers, who were
occupied nearly two hours in rendering it passable, the column
was put in motion, and again moved forward, but much slower
and more cautiously than before ; for there was something in the
manner of this attack, as unimportant as it was, and even in the
shouts of their assailants, that had disturbed the minds, and cast
a visible shade of thoughtfulness over the countenances, of these
hitherto self-confident and boastful invaders of the Green Mountains. For the next three or four miles, however, they moved on
unmolested ; when, coming to a hamlet of log-houses scattered
along the highway on both sides of the stream, that, here again
crossing the road, wound through a smooth meadow of considerable extent, the word *Halt ! halt !* rang loudly, and from company to company, through the line, with an emphasis and significance that instantly apprised all that trouble was at hand.
The next moment all were in commotion, hurry, and alarm.
Amidst the furious beating of the rallying drums, and the mingling clamor of dictating voices, the cannon were detached from
the horses, run forward, and unlimbered ; the fences on each side
of the road were levelled to the ground, and the whole force rapidly thrown into battle array, the tories taking position in the

meadow on the right, and the regulars on the more elevated
grounds to the left of the road, there to await t. e foe, understood to
be approaching in unexpected strength just beyond the thick copse
which terminated the opening on the east.   While this was transpiring, the officer who had before taken charge of Miss Haviland and
her friend came forward, and, summoning them from their carriage, hurried them to a large, strongly-built log-house, around
which a company of tories had been posted, when, bidding them
enter and take care of themselves, he hastened back to his post,
to take part in repelling the menaced onset. Neither that day nor
the next, however, was destined to be the one which was to cover
the untrained freemen of New England with the deathless laurels
of Bennington. Stark, after marching out into the open field,
offering battle, and vainly manœuvring to draw the enemy from
their advantageous ground. retired about a mile, and encamped
for the night, leaving Baum to intrench himself in his choser
position, and despatch expresses to Burgoyne to apprise him of
his unexpectedly perilous situation, and ask for reënforcement.

CHAPTER XII.

"Sad was the year, by proud oppression driven,
When transatlantic liberty arose,
Not in the sunshine and the smile of Heaven,
But wrapped in whirlwinds, and begirt with woes,
Amidst the strife of fratricidal foes." — *Campbell.*

THE house, into which our heroine and her attendant had been ushered for safe keeping during the expected conflict, was divided into two compartments, and separately occupied by a couple of young farmers, and their still more youthful and recently espoused wives, twin sisters, by the names of Mary and Martha. But as happy a social circle as these close and interesting ties should have continued to render the inmates, the fiend of discord, with the approach of the opposing armies, had just entered in among them. One of the young men was a whig, and the other a tory; and the wives had very naturally adopted the predilections of their respective husbands. The young men had, as yet, however, taken no active part in the public quarrel; and, while the war was at a distance, their difference of opinion had not been permitted very essentially to disturb their friendly intercourse. But now, as the war was brought to their door, the sight of the two hostile armies, coming together for deadly conflict on the great issue in which their hitherto repressed sympathies were oppositely enlisted, had aroused the demon of contention in their friendly bosoms. The boastful assumptions of the tory, uttered in his excitement at beholding the imposing display of the British forces around him, were promptly met by the counter predictions of the other. Retort, recrimination, and darkly-hinted menaces followed, till jealousy and rancor seemed completely to have usurped the place of all those fraternal feelings that lately blessed their peaceful abode.

Such was the painful and ill-omened scene which was passing in the apartment of the brother who had espoused the cause of his country, where both families were assembled to witness the anticipated battle, when the unexpected entrance of the girls put an end to the altercation; and it soon after being announced that the Americans had retreated, the tory, followed by his wife, retired

with an exulting sneer, to his own room, leaving the fair strangers, as it happily chanced, to the care and more congenial com
panionship of the young patriot and his warmly sympathizing
Martha, who now kindly supplied their wants, and then conducted
them to their attic chamber, where, it being now nearly dark,
they immediately betook themselves to their homely but grateful
couch. And, overcome by the fatigues and harrowing anxieties
of the day, they soon fell asleep, expecting to be roused in the
morning by the din of the battle, which they felt confident was
yet to take place before the invaders would be permitted to advance farther on their boasted mission of plunder and outrage.

But the next day was to be marked by the battle of the elements, rather than of men. The morning was ushered in by a
storm of unusual violence. And as the day advanced, so seemed
to increase the power of the tempest. The black, flying clouds,
deeply enshrouding the mountain tops, and dragging the summits
of the low, woody hills around, closer and closer begirt the dark-
ened earth. Heavier and heavier dashed the deluging torrents
against the smitten herbage of the field, and the trembling habitations of men ; and louder and louder roared the wind, as it went
howling and raging over the vexed wilderness, as if in mockery
of the intended conflict of the feeble creatures of earth, who now
stood shrinking and shivering in its rain-freighted blasts.

Miss Haviland and her friend, in the mean time, closely kept
their little chamber ; and as little enviable as were their sensations
under the terrors which the tempest, as it roared around the
rocked dwelling, naturally inspired, it was soon with feelings of
thankfulness that they found themselves permitted to remain even
there unmolested ; for their ears were continually shocked, and
their liveliest apprehensions often excited, by the profane vociferations, the noisy ribaldry, and lawless conduct of the tories, who,
driven from their drenched tents, which afforded them but a feeble
protection against the fury of the storm, had crowded into the
lower rooms of the house, where, half stifled, and jostled for
want of space, they filled up the stairway, and repeatedly attempted to force open the fastened door of the trembling inmates
of the apartment above. But the latter were at length permitted
to experience a temporary relief from this source of annoyance
and apprehension. Towards night the tempest lulled, and the
rain abated, when the tories left the house, and joined in the universal rejoicing of the troops of the encampment, that the discomforts and sufferings of the storm were over. It soon became
manifest, however, that they had been relieved of one evil only

to be disturbed by another. In a short time, the Ame can scout
ing parties began to show themselves on the border of the field
in various directions around the encampment. Presently, the
sharp crack of the rifle, followed by the whistling of bullets, and
the fall of one of their number, in the midst of the startled camp,
apprised them of the danger of remaining longer inactive. And
Baum, astonished at the temerity of his foes, and scarcely less so
at their evident ability to do execution with small arms at such a
distance, instantly issued orders to fit out parties of tories and
Indians, to go and dislodge them. At this juncture, the girls
received a visit from their friendly hostess, who, with a troubled
look, entered their room, and, after telling them that she and her
sister had been, like themselves, little else than prisoners in the
other chamber, proceeded to inform them that her husband, impressed with a sense of duty to his country, had secretly stolen
off, during the preceding night, to the American camp ; and that
his tory brother-in-law, from whom she had contrived to conceal
her husband's absence through the morning, had just discovered
the fact, and, with bitter imprecations, seized his gun and rushed
out to join the parties fitting out to fight his countrymen. Scarcely
waiting to finish her hurried communication, the agitated woman
hurried down and joined her no less excited sister in the yard, to
witness the expected encounter of the opposing skirmishers ;
while Sabrey and Vine, sharing with the sisters, though less
keenly, perhaps, in the interest of the event, took post at their
window, which commanded a clear view of the scene of action,
and looked forth for the same purpose.

A company of tories were cautiously stealing along a low,
bushy vale, towards the most westerly of the opposite woody
points, from which the firing had proceeded. On the extreme
right of the field, under a clump of tall evergreens, was seen the
encampment of the Indians, who were in lively commotion, and
evidently preparing to join in the meditated sally. One, whose
stature, accoutrements, and bearing denoted him to be a chief,
and principal leader of the band, appeared to be actively engaged
in giving orders, and pointing out the course to be taken to reach
some designated station in the woods. But just as the whole
party were beginning to file away in their usual fashion, their
steps were suddenly arrested by a rapid discharge of rifle-shots,
that burst upon them from behind an old bush fence on the border of the forest, about a hundred yards to the east ; when the
tall chief, and three or four of his followers, in different parts of
their line, were seen leaping wildly into the air, and then pitching

headlong to the earth, to rise no more. The next instant, every dark form had vanished, and their places of refuge were only dis tinguishable by the occasional reports of their guns, as the pro- tracted skirmish gradually receded within the depths of the forest

Meanwhile, the tories had proceeded on their destination undis. covered, till they reached the termination of their screening ridge on the left, which brought them within fifty yards of the bushy point where the largest party of their opponents lay concealed. unsuspicious of any immediate attack. Here the former made a brief pause, when they rushed forward with a loud shout, and, after a rapid exchange of shots, and a brief hand to hand con. flict, drove the others from their ground, and compelled them to flee across the intervening opening to the opposite jungle, for protection. A cry of exultation now burst from the lips of the wife of the tory, as she witnessed this successful onset of her husband's party, and, crowing over her disappointed sister, she began to treat the insignificant result as the certain precursor of the speedy flight of the whole rebel army. But her triumph was of short duration; for, almost the next moment, the discomfited party, in conjunction with the band of their associates, to whose covert they had retreated, sallied out, and, returning impetuously to the charge, sent a fatal shower of bullets into the huddled ranks of the unprepared tories, and soon routed them entirely from the woods, from which they were seen flying, in wild dis- order, towards the encampment. The rallying wife of the whig now, in turn, broke out in retaliatory exclamations of joy and ex- ultation. But her triumphs, also, were destined to be cut short as speedily as those of her equally thoughtless sister, but in a dif- ferent, and far more sorrowful manner.

A man, bearing the lifeless body of one of the slain on his shoulders, now emerged into view, and came hurriedly stagger- ing along over the field, directly towards the house. The instant the careless eye of the elated Martha fell on the approaching figure, it became fixed as if enchained by a spell. The half- uttered word she was speaking suddenly died on her faltering tongue. An instinctive shudder seemed to run over her; and, for nearly a minute, she stood gazing in motionless silence.

" What is that? O! what is that?" at length burst sharp y from her blanched lips.

But no one answered; and she again relapsed into the same ominous silence, and continued gazing with the same burning intensity, till the man, with a look of conscience-smitten agony, came up, and laying down his burden on the grass, gently turned

12 *

it over, and presented to her the face of her slain husband; when
shriek after shriek broke, in quick and startling succession, from
her convulsed bosom, and she was carried, in a state of wild
and fearful frenzy, into the house. The homicide was the tory
husband, who, having met his victim in the fight, and acting, as
he averred, under an irresistible impulse, had singled out and
slain one, whom, the next moment, he would have given worlds
to have been able to bring to life.*

The scattered forces of the sky now again began to collect,
the rain to descend, and the angry winds to roar through the surrounding forest, compelling both the assailed and assailants to
retire from the fields and woods to their respective places of rendezvous for shelter. And soon night closed over the scene, and
shrouded every object from view with its Egyptian darkness.

Widely different were the feelings and impressions which the
events of that afternoon had imparted to the troops of the two
opposing armies. The advantages gained, though not very important or decisive, had yet been almost wholly on the side of the
Americans. Their different parties of scouts and skirmishers,
who, with the first slackening of the storm, had filled the woods
in every direction around the British encampment, had slain or
disabled, in the various encounters of the day, more than thirty
of their opponents, and, among them, two Indian chiefs, whose
destruction caused a rejoicing proportioned to the exasperation
which their presence here had occasioned. And the effect
of the whole had been to banish the last remaining doubts
of success from their bosoms, and make them long for the hour
when they should be permitted to meet the foe in regular battle.
The losses and defeats of the royal forces, on the other hand, had
proportionally depressed their feelings, and filled them with dark
forebodings of the fate which was in store for them. Nor did
these feelings, in conjunction with the natural effect of the gloom
and physical discomforts of their situation, long fail of a characteristic manifestation among the contrasted bands of that fated
army. And strange and fearful were the sights and sounds which
their encampment exhibited during the night of storm and darkness that followed. The sullen oaths and outlandish grumbling
of the Germans, delving and splashing away at their unfinished

---

* The scene here introduced is drawn from an incident belonging to the
local history of the battle of Bennington, and is but one among the many
sad and touching occurrences which tradition has preserved us connected
with that memorable conflict.

intrenchments, — the noisy execrations of the exasperated tories moving restlessly about from tent to tent, and swearing revenge for the losses, — the sputtering of the Canadians, — the frightful whooping of the discontented savages, as their dark forms were seen darting about in the flickering light of their camp fires, and finally, the groans and blaspheming curses of the poor wretches who had been wounded in the skirmishes of the day, all mingling with the wailing of the wind, and the ceaseless pattering of the rain, combined to form a scene as wild and dismal as language could well paint, or even imagination conceive, and throw over this devoted spot of earth more of the air of the regions of the damned, than of the abodes of human beings.

But what, in the mean while, were the thoughts and sensations of the hapless maiden, whose fate and fortune seemed to have become so strangely involved in the movements and scenes we have been describing? To her the day had been but a varying scene of gloom and wretchedness — of maidenly terror and pain-ful excitement. And night had come only to be made still more hideous by its accumulated horrors. Shuddering at the strange and appalling sounds, that constantly assailed her recoiling senses from without, and pained and distressed at the ceaseless wail-ing of the bereaved and heart-broken wife within — often startled and alarmed at the noisy intrusions of the heartless tories in the room below, and their frequent threats, and even occasional at-tempts to get into her apartment above, and tortured by the anxi-eties, suspense, and apprehension she felt respecting the fate fo which she might be reserved, independent of the more immedi ately-menaced evils around her, she lay, hour after hour, during the first watches of that fearful night, tremblingly clinging to her less-troubled companion, and earnestly praying for death, or the approach of morning, to relieve her from some of the horrors of her situation. But at length her exhausted system yielded to the requirements of nature, and her senses became locked, and her cares lost, in the forgetfulness of slumber.

She and her attendant were awakened, the next morning, by the reveille of the clangorous brass drums of the Hessians, and the mingling hum of the stirring camp around them. Attiring themselves with that haste which, whether required or not, is usu-ally consequent on a state of great anxiety, they ran to the win dow and glanced out over the landscape. But what a contrast with what it yesterday presented! The black storm-cloud, that had so closely brooded over the earth, had been rolled away, and the cerulean vau't above was as calm and cloudless as if storm and

tempest had never disfigured its beautiful expanse. The air was
full of balmy sweetness; and soon the golden sun, slowly mounting over the eastern hills, poured down his floods of light upon
the varigated landscape, transforming the still-weeping forest into
a sea of glittering diamonds, converting the hitherto unnoticed
openings on the surrounding hill-sides into bright spots of smiling
verdure, and adding a brighter tint to the yellow fields of waving
grain, that stood ripening in the valley, soon to be trod and tram-
pled by other than peaceful reapers' feet : —

> " For here, far other harvest here
>   Than that which peasant's scythe demands,
>   Was gathered in by sterner hands,
> With musket, blade, and spear."

Slowly rolled the bright hours of that calm and beautiful morning away, as Miss Haviland, with her attendant, sat by the window, often and axiously glancing along the road to the east,
to catch a glimpse of that army, in whose movements all her
hopes were centred, making its expected advance. But it came
not.   No American — not even a scout or skirmisher — any
where made his appearance ; and no signs of a battle were visible
in any quarter, unless they might be gathered from the busy labors
of the British troops in putting their arms in order, or the unusual
stillness and the air of anxious suspense that seemed to pervade
their whole encampment. Noon came ; and still all remained
quiet as before. That hour, and the next, also, passed away with
the same ominous stillness ; and the desponding girl began seriously to fear, that the Americans had indeed retreated from the
vicinity, and left her and the country alike at the mercy of the
foe. But just as this depressing thought was taking possession
of her mind, a sound reached her ears from afar, that caused her
suddenly to start to her feet with a look of joy and animation that,
for weeks, had been a stranger to her countenance.

CHAPTER XIII.

"Death to him who forges
Fetters, fetters for the free!" — *Eastman.*

" Did you hear that?" exclaimed the maiden, with flushed cheek and kindling eye.

"Hear what?" asked her surprised and wondering companion, who had heard nothing to warrant so sudden a change in the other's demeanor.

"That sound from the forest yonder," answered Sabrey, pointing over to the wood bordering the opening to the south. "But hush! listen! it may be repeated. There—didn't you hear it then?"

"I heard nothing but the hooting of an old owl over there. What do you make out of that?" responded Vine, still surprised and doubtful.

"I make much out of it: but let us listen further," answered the other.

They did so; and presently the same slow, solemn hoot of the bird just named rose more loud and distinct than before. And scarcely had the last sound died away in its peculiar melancholy cadence, when the solitary report of a musket sent its echoing peal over the valley from the forest in the opposite direction.

"There! the story is told," exclaimed Sabrey, exultingly. "Three hoots of the owl is the secret watchword of the Rangers. The admirable imitation we have just heard was doubtless given by him who communicated to me this fact, and gave me a specimen of his faculty of making the sound as we were coming through the woods in our recent flight. It here shows, unless I greatly err, that his regiment is passing round to the rear of the enemy; while the gun we have just heard must proceed, I think, from some other force going round through the woods on the opposite side, — these sounds being a concerted interchange of signals to apprise each other and General Stark of the progress they have made towards the appointed station. In fifteen minutes, this camp may discover itself surrounded and assailed on all

sides by men who know what they are fighting for.   Then,
Vine then comes the struggle we have been praying to witness.
O, may Heaven prosper the defenders of their homes, and enable
them to triumph over their haughty foes."

The conjectures of Miss Haviland respecting the plan of attack
which the Americans had adopted were well founded.   Colonel
Herrick, with his brave and spirited regiment of Rangers, had been
despatched through the woods to the rear of the enemy, where
he was to be joined by nearly an equal force of militia, under the
command of Colonel Nichols, coming through the forest, also, in
an opposite direction; while the remaining and larger portion of
the army was to advance in front, in time to commence with the
former the general attack.   And, in a short time, the long, deep
roll of drums, swelling louder and louder on the breeze, announced that Stark, with the main body, was in motion, and
rapidly approaching along the road from the east.

Quickly every part of the British camp was in lively commotion.   And the hasty mounting of field-officers, the flying of the
scattered troops to their respective standards, the furious beating
of the drums to arms, and the deep, stern words of command,
mingling with the rattling of steel, and other sounds of hostile
preparation, all plainly told that they were at length aroused to
the conviction that their opponents in front were coming down
in full force upon their encampment; and that something more
might now be required to insure their safety, than the empty
vaunting, and the supposed intimidating display, of British uniforms and brass cannon, which had thus far marked the expedition, and constituted its only achievements.   And scarcely had
the different divisions of their motley army become arrayed and
fixed in their line of battle, which consisted of the regulars
within their strong field-works on the elevated plain on the left,
and the Canadians and tories behind their more imperfect defences stretching from the former across the meadow on the right
—scarcely had this been done, before their line of pickets, which
had been placed among the trees at the eastern termination of
the field, suddenly broke from their station, and came disorderly
rushing back to the encampment.   Presently a dark body of men
in motion began to be perceptible through the openings of the
wood along the line of the winding road; and, in a moment
more, Stark's noble little brigade of sturdy and resolute peasant
warriors came pouring into the field.

Wheeling in beautiful order into battle array, they came to a
halt in the open plain near the border of the woods.   Stark, then

advancing, rode slowly along the front of the line, and, at length pausing, ran his practised eye collectedly over the firmly-standing ranks and dauntless faces before him ; when, raising his massive form to its full length, he raised his glittering sword, and pointed to the hostile lines.

" Yonder, my men," he said, in a voice whose clear, deep, and ringing tones, in the stillness which at the moment prevailed, distinctly reached the attent organs of our fair listeners — " yonder, my brave men, stand the red-coats, your own and your country's foe — their army a mongrel crew of Hessian hirelings, fighting for eight-pence a day, or thereabouts; of tories, who come to ravage and enslave the land that gave them birth ; and lastly, of Indians, dreaming of scalps and plunder ! Are you not better men ? Have you not nobler objects ? Call you not yourselves freemen, with hearts to defend your homes and country ? If so, then let your deeds this day prove it to the world ! As for myself, my resolution is taken, — the field and foe is ours by set of sun, or Molly Stark this night will sleep a widow."

Three hearty cheers, bursting spontaneously from the listening ranks before him, told the gratified leader that he had not overrated the spirit and enthusiasm of the men to whom his brief but effective appeal had been addressed.

The British forces, in the mean time, awaited the approach of their opponents in silence. Baum even forebore to open upon them with his cannon, in the delusive hope that they would prove to be one of the large bodies of friendly inhabitants, who, he had been assured, would rise up in arms to join his standard as he advanced into the interior. His suspense, however, was soon ended. A scattering volley of musketry, followed by a distant shout, rose from the woods in rear of the station occupied by the Indians. And suddenly the whole body of the savages, contrary to their usual custom, quitted the woods, and came rushing into the camp of their allies with manifestations of the greatest surprise and dismay. The next moment, Herrick, at the head of his long files of Rangers, emerged into the open field, rapidly formed them into column, and advanced towards the rear of the enemy's intrenchments ; while, at the same time, Nichols and his corps were seen approaching from the forest in an opposite direction, to form the contemplated junction, and move on with the former to the combined assault. The moment the Indians obtained a view of both these forces, and perceived they were converging together so as to form a continuous line of battle along the rear, they began to manifest the greatest uneasiness and alarm. And

heir innate dread of being surrounded soon becoming too strong
for the restraints of discipline, they broke from their position, and,
like a flock of wild horses, commenced a tumultuous flight across
the field towards the woods in open space between the two approaching forces of their opponents, who, quickly changing
fronts, poured in upon them a rapid succession of destructive
volleys. A fierce shout now burst from the ranks of the assailants; and, when the smoke rose, a line of dark, lifeless forms
marked the green field nearly to the woods; others were seer
crawling, like wounded reptiles, to the nearest coverts; while all
the rest of the savage foe had disappeared forever from the
field. Herrick and Nichols having now resumed their march,
and Stark put his corps in motion, the three divisions, with two
small flanking detachments, despatched along the woods to the
right and left of the main body, all moved steadily on to the
different points of attack. They were not permitted, however,
to advance far unmolested; for suddenly every part of the
royal lines became wrapped in clouds of mingling smoke and
flame; while the heavens and earth seemed rent by the deafening crash of exploding muskets, and the jarring concussions
of cannon, which instantly followed. Unmoved, however, by
the tremendous outbreak, the American forces all moved steadily
and rapidly forward till the forms of their opponents could be
discerned beneath the lifting smoke, when they poured in a
storm of fire and lead which told with dreadful effect on the
shrinking lines before them. The general fire thus fatally delivered was speedily returned; and the battle now commencing
in fearful earnest in every part of the field, both armies became
so deeply concealed in the whirling clouds of smoke, which
enveloped them, that the opposing forces could be distin
guished only in the fierce gleams of musketry and the broader
blaze of cannon that burst incessantly along the lines, filling,
with the mingled uproar of a thousand thunders, the rocking
valley and reverberating mountains around.

In the mean while, our heroine and her companion, who, at the
first shock of this terrible onset, had shrunk back in consternation from view of the scene, sat listening on their humble couch
to the fearful din that assailed their recoiling senses in every
direction around them from without, with feelings which can be
far more easily imagined than described. For more than an
hour, while the battle continued to rage with increasing violence,
and showers of bullets were heard every moment striking and
burying themselves in the logs composing the walls of their seem

ingly devoted shelter, the amazed and trembling girls remained in the same position, dreading to look out upon the field, lest their eyes should be greeted with the sight of the death and carnage which they full well knew must there be going on to a fearful extent among both friends and foes. But Sabrey's increasing anxiety for the result, at length, mastering all other considerations, she arose, and, against the remonstrances of her companion, advanced towards the window.

"How awful!" she exclaimed, as she glanced out on the terrific conflict.

"Too awful to witness, unless there were some use in so doing," responded Vine. "If we were permitted to mingle in the fight with our friends, I, for one, would be willing to brave all the horrors of the battle for the good I might do; but, as this cannot be, why should we expose ourselves to danger so uselessly? Now, I do entreat you, Sabrey, to venture no farther, she continued," as the former, reaching the window, leaned forward for a full view of the scene. "Step back from that dangerous spot; don't you hear the bullets rattling, like hail, round the building?"

"Yes, but there is no danger where I stand, I presume, but if there were, I could no longer forbear watching the issue of a contest in which my own fate, as well as that of friends, is so deeply involved," replied Sabrey, with desperate calmness, as she continued to rivet her gaze on the field below.

"If you *will* look, then," said the other, "tell me what you see going on."

"I will," answered the former, "as far as I can distinguish any movements. But, at present, both sides are so completely concealed in the smoke that enshrouds them, that I can only discern dark forms in active motion along the lines, as the blaze of their fire-arms reveals portions of their ranks. The struggle, however, is evidently a dreadful one! In that continued, deafening crash which you hear, flames and smoke seem to be vomited forth from the earth, as if from the mouth of a volcano."

"There seems to be less firing now," observed Vine, after listening in silence a few minutes. "Can you perceive any new movements afoot? Can't you distinguish any of the words of command, or any thing that is said among that uproar of voices, which, between the booming of the cannon, once in a while, plainly reaches my ears?"

"Ay," returned the other, intently bending her ear towards the scene of action — "ay, I think I can, now. Hark! I hear one voice in particular, rising loud over all others; but it is the voice of one in prayer, invoking the God of battles to strike with the free and aid in bringing down quick destruction on their foes. How mightily he cries to Heaven for succor and success!"

"Where is he? among the rest in the fight?"

"No, not directly in the battle, I should think, but a little aloof, in the rear of this end of the American lines. There! I can now distinguish his form coming obliquely out of the smoke in this direction."

"Who is he?"

"I know not; but he seems a venerable old man, and his long, white locks are streaming in the wind, as, with a grasped musket in his hands, and the cry of *The sword of the Lord and Gideon* on his lips, he rushes towards the foe."

"What! to encounter them alone?"

"Yes, alone, and in advance of all others. Now he takes his stand in front of a group of tories partially concealed by the bushes on the bank of the stream. There! he raises his gun, and crying, *God have mercy on your soul*, fires, and his victim pitches headlong to the ground. They return his fire, but harm him not; and he again raises his gun, and, with the same prayer for mercy on the soul of the foeman he has singled out, fires, and another tory falls heavily to the earth. Mercy! they are now rushing forward to slay the old man! But now they are met by a party of the Americans, running forward with shouts, *For the rescue of Father Herriot!* Both sides fire; and again all are enveloped in the cloud of smoke that rolls over them."

"Father Herriot — Father Herriot," said Vine, musingly. "I have heard a great deal said about one they call Father Herriot, lately; but can he be here fighting?"

"Why, who and what is he, that he should not be here?" asked the other.

"A sort of preacher, I believe," answered Vine, "but rich enough to have bought several large tory estates; though where he came from, or how he got so much hard money as he seems to have, nobody can tell."

A fresh and general outbreak between the opposing lines here interrupted the conversation, and turned Sabrey's attention again to the field. And for nearly another fearful hour did she keep her stand at the window, heedless of the danger from the bullets which were whistling round her head, and unable, in the agonizing anxiety she felt for the result, to withdraw her eyes from that dread field, where the continued thunders of the art'llery and musketry, shaking the solid earth along the line of conflict proclaimed the battle to be still raging with unabated fury.

At length, a brisk breeze sprang up in the north-west, and the battle cloud rolled heavily away before it from the field, disclosing, not only the relative positions of the opposing forces, but the awful picture of carnage that every where strewed the blackened earth. Mutually anxious to avail themselves of this opportunity to ascertain each other's situation, both parties at once suspended operations, for the purpose of obtaining observations which should enable them to resume the battle with more deadly effect. The deafening roar of musketry which, for nearly two hours, had shaken the embattled plain like one continued peal of thunder, was now heard rolling away, in dying echoes, among the far-off hills, leaving only the monotonous din of the martial music, kept up to drown the cries of the wounded, and the heavy booming of Baum's artillery, that still maintained its regular fire on the hill, though only to send — as it now became evident it had done from the first — its iron missiles high and harmlessly over the heads of the Americans, into the tops of the crashing forest beyond.

"Is the battle over?" asked Vine, as the noise of fire-arms thus subsided.

"No — that is, I conclude not," hesitatingly answered the other, still more closely rivetting her anxious gaze on the unfolding scene before her. "No, I think not — I trust not; for the British yet remain unconquered."

"Can you see them now?"

"Yes; the wind is driving away the smoke, and both armies are now fast becoming visible."

"Do our men maintain their ground?"

"Ay, and more. They have advanced almost to the hostile intrenchments; and there they stand face to face with their foes; and with ranks less thinned, thank Heaven, than I should think possible after withstanding so long the dreadful fire to which they have been exposed; though I can distinguish the forms of many poor fellows stretched upon the earth."

"And have not the ranks of the enemy suffered also?"

"Severely, it is evident. The ground along their lines as far as I can see, and especially that part opposite to the station occupied by the Rangers, whom I can distinguish by their green uniform, is thickly strown with the bodies of the slain. And if our men could see the destruction they have caused behind those intrenchments to encourage them! But stay! what means that commotion? Can it be? Heaven forbid! But it is so. They fly!"

"Who fly?" eagerly demanded Vine.

"The Americans — Stark's division — and all is lost, when one more effort might have given them the victory! O that they could but know the advantages they have gained! If my feeble voice could but reach them, I would rush out and raise it, though I perished in the attempt!" rapidly exclaimed the heroic girl, agonized at the thought that her countrymen were actually retreating from a field she believed so nearly won. "Ay, and who knows but I might be heard, or, at least, understood?" she added, glancing hurriedly through the window to the grounds round the house, to see what might be there to prevent her from trying to put her half-formed resolution into execution.

In looking out, with this object, her eye fell on the rude portico running along that side of the house, the narrow, flat roof of which rose within a few feet of her window. And, suddenly changing her purpose, she hastily tore out the fastenings of the window, removed the sashes, and leaped down to the roof of the portico, and stood in open view of the greater partion of both armies. But still regardless of her exposure, she advanced to the verge of the roof, and, turning towards the Americans, waved high her kerchief, and essayed to lift her voice over the tumult, in words which, she hoped, would catch their attention and arrest their supposed flight. But the Americans, who had only fallen back a short distance to avoid the now unobstructed aim of the enemy, and prepare for a fresh onset, had already come to a stand, but were at first too busily engaged in loading their guns, and watching the motions of their foes, to observe her. The tories, however, whose forces were posted in the more immediate vicinity, instantly noted her appearance, and pointed her out to their officers, who, at once, appeared to read her intentions. And the next moment Colonel Peters, now for the first time presenting himself to her sight since her recapture, rode up; and, with a countenance flushed with suppressed passion, commanded her to retire within the house. A look of ineffable scorn was the only reply the maiden vouchsafed to give him, while she redoubled her exertions to attract the attention of his opponents. Stung by this public exhibition of her disdain, and defiance of his commands, the tory chief hastily raised a pistol towards her, and, in a fierce and menacing tone, demanded an immediate compliance with his orders.

"God have mercy on your soul!" was at that instant heard issuing from a covert near the American lines, in the well-known voice of Father Herriot. With the exclamation came the report of a musket, and at the same time a bullet struck and shattered in his hand the raised pistol of the dastardly Peters, who, casting away the remnant of the weapon to which he had been indebted only for his life, hastily wheeled and galloped back to his post barely escaping the shower of balls that, as he had rightly anticipated, was sent after him from the nearest of his foes.

But although the maiden had failed at the onset to attract the attention of the Americans by her attempt, as she had designed, yet the incident, to which the bold step she had taken gave rise, more effectually subserved her purpose. The firing had at once drawn all eyes to the spot. Presently the low hum of questioning voices was heard running through the American lines, while many an uplifted hand was seen pointing to her conspicuous form, as, still undeterred from her purpose, she stood waving her signal kerchief towards them. And the next moment the loud and cheering cry, *Forward, to the rescue of the Tory's Daughter!* burst from the Rangers, and was speedily caught up and echoed in lively acclamations, from detachment to detachment, through the whole encircling lines of the assailing army, which, with one impulse, now threw itself forward towards the foe. And, unmoved by the tremendous but hasty and misdirected fire that every where met them on the way, they swept onward like an avalanche to the very foot of the tory intrenchments; when, pausing only to pour in their devouring volleys, they mounted the works, and raising their clubbed muskets, dashed down, with shouts of defiance, upon the recoiling ranks of the amazed and panic-stricken foe, who, unable to withstand the force and fury of the onset, instantly gave way and threw down their arms, or scattered and fled in every direction.

Astonished and alarmed at beholding all his outworks so suddenly and unexpectedly stormed and carried, Baum seemed immediately to have resolved on a desperate effort to retrieve the fortunes of the day. And in a few minutes he was seen at the head of a long column of his grenadiers, issuing from his intrenchments on the hill, and bearing down with hasty step on the assailing forces below. But the next moment, that imposing column, with its luckless leader, disappeared before the enfilading fire of the death-dealing Rangers, like frost-work before the breath of a furnace; while, nearly at the same time, an upleaping cloud of smoke and flame, followed by the shock of an exploding ammunition wagon within the principal works, completed the only signal of encouragement that was wanted by the already flushed assailants to decide them on an immediate attempt for the completion of their triumph. And before the dull roar of the explosion was lost

13 *

among the echoing hills, the deep-toned voice of the intrepid
Stark, ever eagle-eyed to see, and prompt to seize, an advantage,
was heard rising over the tumult, in ordering the final assault,
which, having leaped from his horse, and sprung forward to the
head of a forming column, he was the next moment seen, with
the air of a roused lion, leading on in person.   In one minute
more, all the various forces, not required to guard the prisoners
already taken, were in motion, and, with flashing eyes, and
rapid, determined tread, charging up the ascending grounds
towards the different sides of the doomed redoubt; in another,
they were furiously rushing over the embankments, and pouring their bristling columns in resistless streams down upon the
weakened and dismayed forces of the Germans and British in
the enclosure.   Then succeeded the rapid, scattering reports
of pistols and musketry, the sounds of fiercely-clashing steel,
and the wild cries of those struggling hand to hand in deadly
contest, and the wilder shrieks of the wounded, all rising in
mingled uproar from the spot.   Then all was hushed in a mo
mentary stillness; and then rose the long, loud shout of a
thousand uniting voices, pealing forth to the heavens the
exulting acclamations of victory !

CHAPTER XIV.

"The strife, that for a while did fail,
Now trebly thundering, swelled the gale." — *Scott.*

LIKE the rapidly-flitting scenes of some dioramic exhibition
passed the crowding events of the next half hour before the half-
bewildered senses of our heroine. The sudden appearance of
Woodburn in the now deserted yard of her prison-house, whither,
the moment the battle was won, he had hastened, with the usual
anxiety of the lover made intense by the distracting fear that she
might have been carried off by the escaping tories, — his eager
inquiries for her presence and safety, — her own involuntary
but silent response to his calls, by rushing out to meet him, and
placing herself under his coveted protection, — the hurried con-
gratulations that passed between them, — the complimentary
greetings of the gallant hero of the day, and other distinguished
persons soon gathering around her and her fair companion, as
they stood shrinking from the admiration and applause which the
conduct of one, and the position of both, had called forth from
the lips of all, — their welcome escape from the embarrassing
scene, in a carriage, under the guidance of Bart, to whom they
were given in charge by Woodburn, as he hastily departed, at the
head of a chosen band of followers, in pursuit of Peters, and a
body of tories that were discovered to have escaped, — the passage of the vehicle through the contested field, ploughed up by
artillery, blackened by the fire and smoke of battle, and strewed
with the dying and the dead, among whom the busy groups of the
dismissed soldiery were every where scattered in pursuit of their
different objects — here to collect plunder from their slain enemies, and there to minister to the wounded, or search among the
fallen for missing comrades, — all these followed so rapidly upon
a victory, the sudden announcement of which had nearly over-
powered her with joyful surprise, that it was not till she and her
companion had passed beyond the confines of the battle-field, and
entered upon the comparatively solitary road leading towards the
village of Bennington, to which they were now directing their
course, that she could realize her happy deliverance. Then, for
the first time during that terrible day, the woman in her prevailed.

and she melted into tears. But they were the tears of joy and gratitude, that she and her native land, whose immediate fate had so singularly become interwoven with her own, had alike been permitted to triumph. We must, however, leave her and her friend to indulge their overflowing feelings, and listen to the recitals of the no less happy Bart, who had been in the hottest of the fight, while they pursue their unmolested way to their present destination — we must now leave them, and return once more to the field of battle, where the dismissed troops were still busily engaged in gathering up the trophies of war, preparing refreshments, and exulting over the glorious result of the conflict, little dreaming of any further appearance of the enemy after so signal a defeat.

But hark! What means that heavy firing which suddenly comes echoing over the forest from the west? Does it portend only some skirmish on the line of the retreat, where a portion of the foe have come to a stand to shield the rest, or favor their escape? No; it is the booming of the deep-mouthed cannon, and not those of the defeated forces; for they have left all theirs behind them. While every eye and ear, through the hushed field, were turned in anxious perplexity towards the ominous sounds, a horseman came dashing at full speed along the wood-begirt road from that direction, loudly proclaiming, as he drew near, the startling intelligence, that the broken and flying bands of the enemy had been met and rallied by a reënforcement of five hundred fresh veteran troops, well supplied with artillery; and the whole, making a more formidable army than the first, and evidently resolved to retrieve the lost credit of the day, and revenge themselves on the victors, were rapidly approaching, and within two miles of the place!

The next moment the loud and quickly repeated cry of "To arms! to arms!" rang far and wide over the field. Then followed the rapid roll of the alarm drums, the rattling of hastily-grasped muskets, the trampling of hurrying feet, and the confused clamor of voices; while the scattered and commingling bands of the surprised troops were seen throwing down their plunder, or leaving the half-partaken meal, and flying, in all directions, to their respective rallying points, to be ready to meet the menaced onset, and die, or keep the field they had so gloriously won. But notwithstanding the spirit and alacrity with which the troops responded to the call, so rapid was the advance of the enemy, that, before Stark, with all his energy, could collect much more than half his former forces, refit them with am

munition, and bring them into line, the British, led on by the cool
and experienced Breyman, and driving before them the detachment of Americans sent in pursuit of the fugitives, came pouring
into the field ; and, immediately throwing themselves into battle
array, opened a tremendous fire, with cannon and small arms,
upon the half-formed lines of their opponents, gathering to dispute their passage in front. The Americans returned the fire,
which, though partial and irregular, was yet so well directed as to
put a temporary check upon the advance of the foe. But the
latter, seeing the unprepared condition of the former, and becoming confident of an easy victory, were soon again upon the
advance ; while Stark, destroying the breastworks that had shel-
tered the foe in the first action, as far as the time would permit,
and dragging the captured cannon along with him, slowly fell
back, continuing to make his dispositions, and pour, from time to
time, as he went, his well-aimed volleys upon the thinning ranks
of his pursuers. At length, however, he took his stand, resolved,
in despite of all his disadvantages, to make a final and desperate
effort to regain the lost mastery of the field. But closer and
closer pressed the exulting and determined foe ; and, although
well and bravely did his weakened and exhausted men repel the
fierce charges of their assailants, yet it soon became evident that
they could not long withstand the repeated assaults of those heavy
and disciplined columns upon their unequal lines. Both the men
and their officers began to exchange doubtful and despairing
glances ; and even their bold and unyielding chief was seen to
look uneasily around him. But at that critical juncture, when
the fate of the free seemed trembling doubtfully in the balance,
an inspiring shout rose from the copse-wood bordering the road in
the rear. And the next moment, the far-famed regiment of Green
Mountain Boys, whose earlier arrival had been prevented by the
storm of the preceding day, emerged into view ; and, led on by
the chivalrous Warner on his fiery charger, that would know no
other rider,* advanced with rapid and resolute tread directly to
the scene of action.

"Warm work, warm work here, Colonel Warner," said Stark,
as the other dashed up to his side for his orders.

---

* It may be interesting, to the antiquarian at least, to learn that the
splendid war-horse, which Warner was known to have rode in all his
battles, could neither be mounted nor managed by any except the colonel
and his son, then a lad of sixteen or seventeen, who attended his father
in the service mainly on that account. This fact I have from the lips of
Colonel W.'s second son, now living in Lower Canada.

"Ay, general ; but we will make it still warmer for the Red coats, at leas', if you will give us a chance at them in front of your line," promptly responded the gallant officer.

"That chance you shall have, with the thanks of my exhausted troops, to whom, and myself, your presence, at this time, my brave friend, could scarcely be more welcome," said Stark, with a frankness and cordiality of manner which attested the pleasure he felt at the other's timely arrival.

"Thank you — thank you, general," replied Warner, galloping back to his regiment, and commanding their attention.

"Soldiers," he exclaimed, in his clear, trumpet tones throwing back his tall, superb form, and displaying his noble and beautifully-arched brow — "my brave soldiers, shall this be *our* battle, and *our* victory ?"

A deafening cheer was the affirmative response.

"In God's name, on, then !" he resumed, in a voice of thunder — "on, and avenge yourselves for country's wrongs, and for your hugging at Hubbardton."

In eager obedience to the welcome command of their idolized leader, who now led the way, with flashing eyes and waving sword, they all swept on through the opening ranks of their loudly-cheering companions in arms, rapidly deployed into line, and, the next instant, wrapped themselves in the flame and smoke of their own fire, which burst, with an almost single report, into the very faces of the astonished foe, whose ranks went down by scores before the leaden blast of that terrible volley. And, by the time they had recovered from the shock of the unexpected assault, the relieved and encouraged forces of Stark, now strengthened by the arrival of additional numbers of the scattered militia, and formed into new and more effective combinations, returned with fresh ardor to the contest. And, as the different detachments, moving resolutely on, with flying colors and rattling drums, to the various points of attack assigned them in front and around the hostile squares, reached their allotted stations, they successively poured in their withering volleys till the rebounding plain trembled and shook beneath the tumult and thunders of a conflict, to which, in obstinacy and sanguinary fierceness, few engagements on record afford a parallel. On one side was discipline, with revenge, the hope of reward, and the fear of the disgrace attending defeat, to incite them to action. On the other side, the stake was home and liberty ; and these as the trained officers of Europe soon found to their astonishment often more than compensated for the lack of discipline and military experience ; for, in contending for a stake of such individual moment, every man in the ranks of freedom, though frequently wholly untrained, and in battle for the first time in his life, at once became a warrior, fighting as if the whole responsibility of the issue of the battle rested on his own shoulders. And, in every part of the field, deeds were performed by nameless peasants rivalling the most daring exploits of heroes. Here a company of raw militia might be seen rushing upon a detached column of British veterans, firing in their faces, and, for want of bayonets, knocking them down with clubbed muskets. There old men and boys, with others who, like them, had come unarmed and as spectators of the battle, would spring forward after some retreating band, seize the muskets of the slain, and engage, muzzle to muzzle, with the hated foe. The intrepid Stark, harboring no thought but of victory, and as regardless of exposure as the unconscious charger that bore him through the leaden storm, was every where to be seen ; now heading an onset — now dashing off to rouse or rally a faltering column, and now leaping from his horse to show his inexperienced men how to load and fire the captured cannon ; while Warner and Herrick, fit men to second the efforts of such a chief, were constantly storming, like raging lions, in the smoke and fire of the hottest of the fight ; here breasting, with their brave and unflinching regiments, the desperate assault, and there, in turn, leading on the resistless charge.

Thus, with the tide of war alternately surging to and fro, like the wild waves of the ocean lashed by contending winds, continued to rage this fierce and sanguinary conflict, till the sun went down in the semblant blood with which the smoke of battle had enshrouded him.

But now, soon an unusual commotion, attended with new and rapid movements, was observable among the contending forces of the field. Presently an exulting shout rose from the American lines ; and the enemy were seen at all points to be giving way. Their retreat, however, though rapid, was yet, for a while, conducted with order ; and they repeatedly turned and made desperate efforts to resist the fiery tide that, with gathering impetus, was rolling after them. But vain and fruitless were all their attempts ; for, while their whole rear was wasting with frightful rapidity, under the terrible volleys which were poured upon it, in one incessant blaze, by the hotly pursuing squadrons of Stark and Warner, a strong detachment of the heroic Rangers, under the daring lead of the now half-maddened Woodburn rushed forward and fell upon their flank with a fury that threw their pierced and staggering columns into such disorder and con- fusion as to destroy their last indulged hope of escaping in a body from their infuriated pursuers.   And, the next moment, their whole force broke, and, abandoning their cannon and baggage, fled in a tumultuous rout from the field, some escaping along the road, some yielding themselves prisoners on the way, and others, to avoid their outstripping pursuers, seeking refuge in the surrounding forest.   But neither road, nor field, nor forest, were this time permitted to afford many of them the means of escape, or shield them from the harassing pursuit of the exasperated Americans, who, in furiously-charging columns, overthrew, shot down, or captured, all their broken and flying bands within reach, in the road and open grounds, or in small parties, or singly, closely followed and boldly encountered them in the woods, whose dark recesses soon resounded with the scattering fire, the clashing steel, and the hurrying shout, of the pursued and pur- suing combatants.

But of the scores of promiscuous conflicts and personal en- counters which marked the *finale* of this memorable triumph and made so conspicuous the prowess of the heroic men by whom it was achieved, it were in vain for us, within our limits, to attempt a description.   There was one of these encoun- ters, however, which the approaching development of our story requires to be more particularly noted.   And, for this purpose, we will now change the scene to a wild glen, far within the depths of the forest, where, hedged in by an impassable morass in front, and steep ledges of rocks on either side, a gang of a half dozen of the fugitive tories, headed by an officer in British uniform, had turned round with the desperate ferocity of wild beasts, to give battle to the indefatigable pursuers, who had fol- lowed them from the battle-field with a vigilance and speed from which there was no escape, and with such demonstrations of marksmanship as had already told fatally on nearly half their numbers on the way.   But those pursuers, as wary as they were brave and untiring, with the double object of concealing the in- equality of their numbers, which were but four, and securing the advantages that a choice of positions in all sylvan contests especially affords, had instantly fallen back to a line of hastily- selected coverts, stretching across the gorge, and had now be- come wholly invisible to their advancing foes, who soon paused in turn, and, shielding themselves behind the bodies of trees

stood eagerly peering out to catch sight of the objects of their aim.
Suddenly the sharp report of a rifle burst from a bush-covered
cleft in the rocks nearly abreast of one of the exposed flanks of
the tories; and the tallest of their number, with a wild start, and
half-uttered oath, floundered into the bushes and fell. The next
moment, our old acquaintance, Bart Burt, who, having conveyed
the ladies to their destination, had sped back to the battle-field
in time to participate in the last part of the final action, was seen
stealthily creeping round the point of the ledge, from which the
fatal shot had issued, and approaching the leader of the concealed
assailants, who, as the reader may have already anticipated, was
no other than Captain Woodburn.

"Bart," said the latter, "you have executed my order as no
other man could. But whom have you slain? Not Peters?"

"No—couldn't get him in range; but did as well, though—
may be better—fixed out the only one whose aim I was 'fraid
of—the big, fierce-looking whelp that shot father Herriot, in our
last sally in the field; the same that made that bullet-hole in
your coat on the way here; and the same, too, who would have
finished me, likely, but for the glancing of his bullet on a bush
before me. But I have settled all the grudges at a blow, now."

"You have done bravely; but did you discover who they
are—any of them besides the leader, Peters?"

"Yes, two of 'em, who are, as Dunning and Piper surmised,
Dave Redding and Tiger Fitch, that beauty of a constable, who
bothered us so in old times, at Guilford. He's now some kind
of an officer among 'em, guess; and, dead or alive, I'm bound to
have him; though, if you've any particular plan, captain, I'll
follow it, instead of going round to 'tother ledge for another pick
of the flock."

"I have one; and that is, to draw their fire, or most of it, and
then rush upon them. You may creep on, then, to Dunning and
Piper, and, with them, contrive and execute some plan to effect
that object, and I will stand here ready to order, and lead the
charge, at the favoring moment."

Bart now, with the noiseless tread of a cat, rapidly glided
away into the bushes and disappeared on his errand. In a few
minutes, the cracking of sticks, as if under the pressure of cautiously moving feet, was heard in a thicket of bushes within full
range of the guns of the tories, who, now safely ensconced behind the new coverts, to which, in alarm at Bart's fatal shot, they
had betaken themselves, instantly turned their attention in that
direction, and, levelling their pieces, keenly watched for the

expected exposure of the persons of some of their opponents. Soon, the dim outlines of two or three apparently human forms could be traced in the thicket, rising up one after another, with the quick hesitating motions of men intent on a stealthy *reconnoissance* of the objects before them. And, the next moment, every tory, but one, sent the contents of his gun at these supposed forms of the lurking besiegers. But instead of beholding, as they had anticipated, the riddled bodies of the dreaded foe dropping to the earth, they soon discovered, to their astonishment and dismay, that the empty coats and caps, which the outwitting Rangers had raised on their ramrods over their prostrate persons, were the only sufferers.

"Der — der— der — ditter ready!" shouted Dunning, in a voice which at last went off like the terminating clap of a rattling thunder peal, as he and his two associates leaped, coatless, from the ground, to be prepared for the instant execution of the expected order.

"On, then, and suffer not a wretch of them to escape you alive!" exclaimed their impatient leader in reply, dashing forward himself, and leading in the headlong onset which they all now made on the foe.

Taken by complete surprise by this rapid and unexpected movement of the assailants, now bursting upon them with cocked and levelled rifles, the dismayed tories, at first, made no attempts at escape or resistance ; while part of them threw down their half-loaded guns, and stepped out from their coverts.

"Surrender at discretion, or take the consequence!" sternly cried Woodburn, pausing within twenty yards of the tory leader.

"We are in your power, sir, I suppose," replied Peters evasively, and in a tone of affected submission, as, avoiding the burning gaze of the other, he threw a significant glance to the tory who had reserved his charge at the fruitless fire just made by the rest of his party.

In an instant, the gun of the latter, who still stood behind a tree shielding him, as he supposed, from the other Rangers, was levelled at Woodburn, whose attention was too intently fixed on his chief foe to notice the movement. But before the finger of the assassin was permitted to tighten on the trigger, a bullet from the unerring rifle of the watchful Dunning had pierced his brain, and his gun, as he fell over backwards, exploded harmlessly into the air. Three of the tories, however, taking advantage of the momentary confusion occasioned by the noise and smoke of the

guns, made a desperate spring for the surrounding thickets and
succeeded in breaking through the line of their assailants, three
of whom instantly gave chase, leaving Woodburn to cope alone
with the rival foe, whom he had vainly sought through the day
to confront in battle. Peters threw a quick, furtive glance around
him; and, for an instant, seemed hesitating whether he should
attempt to follow the example of the rest of his band; but another glance at the watchful and menacing eye of his opponent
gleaming at him over the barrel of the deadly rifle, taught the
folly of any such attempt, and, throwing down his weapons, he
said, —

"I yield myself a prisoner of war, sir."

"A prisoner of war!" exclaimed Woodburn, repeating the
words of the other, in a tone of bitter scorn. "After signifying
your submission, and then instigating an attempt to shoot me,
you hope to be received as a prisoner of war, do you? Villain!"
he added, advancing and presenting the muzzle of his piece
within a yard of the other's breast — "villain, your last claim to
mercy is forfeited!"

"You would not slay an unarmed man, and a prisoner, would
you?" said Peters, recoiling, and casting an uneasy glance at his
opponent.

"Yes,' replied the former, with increasing sternness, "if,
like you, in defiance of all the rules of war as well as honor, he
would do the same to me the first moment he had it in his
power. No submission shields the life of an outlaw from any
one disposed to take it. But you shall have one minute for
uttering your last request, if you have any such to make."

Being now thoroughly alarmed by the words, as well as the
demeanor of his incensed captor, the once haughty loyalist
fell on his knees, and humbly besought the other to spare his
life.

"Live, then, wretch!" said Woodburn, at length moved to
both pity and contempt by the entreaties and abject manner of
the former — "live then, if you choose it, to be dealt with as
a traitor and a spy, by men who will award you your deserts with
more coolness, doubtless, than I should have done, but with no less
certainty."

"O, spare me from that," pleaded the abased supplicant, with
redoubled earnestness "Kill me on the spot, if you will; but
spare me from that fate. Allow me to be delivered up as a
prisoner of war, and I will consent to any thing — yield any
thing you wish. I will ensure you, by my influence at the

British camp, any advantage in a future exchange of prisoners you may ask ; and ——— "

" Peace, miserable craven ! " interrupted Woodburn. " I could promise you no exemption, if I would, from a punishment which our exasperated people will justly say you have brought upon your own head."

" And I will also," resumed Peters, encouraged by the somewhat softened tone, and slightly hesitating manner of the other — " I will also relinquish all claims, and forego all inter-ference, in matters that may have stood in the way of your private interests and wishes."

" I will make no pledges, nor grant, nor receive any terms, at your dictation, sir," said the former, haughtily.

" I will trust to your magnanimity to a fallen foe," then, re-joined Peters, rightly appreciating, for once, the character of his conqueror. " Here, take this," he continued, drawing a care-fully-preserved document from his pocket, and extending it to-wards the other — " take it, and deliver it to the one whom it most concerns. Tell her it was voluntarily relinquished, and that I will trouble her no more."

As small as was the measure of credit which Woodburn's judgment told him should be accorded to the motives prompting this unexpected course in his old enemy, it nevertheless quickly banished every vindictive feeling from his generous bosom ; and after a momentary hesitation, he took the proffered document, glanced at its contents, and silently deposited it among his other papers. But soon growing jealous of himself lest he should compromit the policy which his superiors might deem it just and wise, under the sanction of the stern rules of war, to enforce, he restrained himself from making any immediate reply. And, the next moment, he was relieved from what apparent necessity there might be for so doing, by the approach of the first of the returning Rangers.

" Where is your prisoner, Piper ? " he asked, turning to the latter, now coming up.

" He would not be taken alive, sir ; and the order was to let none escape in that condition," replied the broad-chested subaltern with a significant look.

" In order, then, that you go not home empty-handed," re-joined Woodburn, " I will give you charge of *my* prisoner, Colonel Peters here, whom you will conduct to Bennington Meeting-House, whither the prisoners of the day were ordered and where you will deliver him to the officer in command

as a prisoner of war — at least for the present; for any doub
that may arise about his final disposal can be settled her
after."

" Der well, captain," exclaimed Dunning, whose tall, gaunt
form, in the rear of his prisoner, the infamous David Redding.
whom it had been his lot to capture, was now seen emerging
from a thicket near by — " here is one, about whom we shan'
be bothered with der doubts, a great while, if his captor can have
his say."

" Aha! — but what *is* your say about him, sergeant?" said
Woodburn, smiling.

" Der well," replied the other, " I say, if the ditter devil don't
take him from a traitor's gallows, then we may just as well have
no devil."

" I shall not be the one to gainsay you in that, sergeant,'
responded Woodburn. " But hark! what is the uproar yonder?"
he added, pointing out into the woods in a direction from whence
the sound of an occasional stiff *whack!* followed by groans,
curses, and calls for protection, were now heard to issue.

On turning their eyes towards the spot, the company beheld
Bart, with his rifle in one hand, and a long beechen switch in the
other, driving in before him the whilom constable, Fitch, who
was chafing, like a chained bear, under the lash which his
catechizing captor was administering every few yards on the
way.

" Why are you so rough with him, Bart?" expostulated Woodburn, as they came up.

" Well, captain, I have a reasonable wherefore for it — may
be," answered the former, gravely.

" What is it?" asked the other.

" Why," replied the imperturbable Bart, " perhaps I don't remember, and perhaps I do, how a chap of about my size sat
sweating near two cool hours, at the sight of an ugly-looking
bunch of beech rods, that a certain constable had ordered for his
back. And as 'twas no fault of his that the matter wasn't carried
out at the time, and, as I always thought there was a mistake
made as to the one whose back ought to take it, I felt rather
bound to have the order executed now, and in a manner to set al'
to rights between us."

" Well, well, boys," said Woodburn, with a good-humored
smile, " you must all be indulged in your notions, I suppose, at
such a glorious hour as this. But you may now be moving

on with your prisoners to the field, and thence by the road to
Bennington.   Business calls me there by a nearer route, and
at a quicker pace.   You shall find good cheer awaiting your
arrival."

So saying, he struck off rapidly from the rest, and soon disap
peared in the forest

CHAPTER XV.

"Sing it where forests wave, —
From mountain to the sea,
And o'er each hero's grave, —
Sing, sing, the land is free."

IT was evening; and all that met the eye was joy and anima
tion in the little village of Bennington, in which, not only the
great body of the opposing armies, either as conquerors or prisoners, but the best portion of the patriotism, wisdom, and beauty
of young Vermont, were now congregated. There her statesmen
and sages — many of whom had mingled in the strife of the day
— were gathered to rejoice over a result which their own heads,
and hearts, and hands, through the anxious days and nights of the
preceding month, had been unceasingly engaged in securing for
their country and their homes. There, too, the old men and
striplings, drawn from all the neighboring settlements by the
ominous sounds which had reached them from the distant battle-
field, and there the maids and matrons, whose solicitude for the
near and dear ones, supposed to be engaged in the conflict, would
not permit them to stay behind, were all found mingling with the
victors, and participating in their exultations. Bright lights were
streaming from every window, or dancing in every direction in
the streets; while the smiling faces and animated voices, every
where seen and heard among the commingling throng, seemed to
tell only of a scene of universal joy and triumph. But as joyous
and lively as was the scene, in its predominating features, it was
yet not without its painful contrasts. The broken sob, or the low
wail of sorrow, was heard rising sadly on the night air, in every
interval that occurred in the more boisterous but irrepressible
manifestations which characterized the hour. And, even in the
same dwellings, these two contrasted phases in war's exciting but
melancholy picture were not unfrequently presented; for, while
in one room might be heard the notes of joy and exultation, in
another might be distinguished the stifled groan of some wounded
soldier, or the lamentations of the bereaved over the body of a
slain relative.

Among the most noted of the class last mentioned was the late residence of Esquire Haviland, situated in the outskirts of the village, and recently occupied as the quarters of the officers of the Rangers, on the invitation of the patriotic but singular and mysterious man, who, at its sale by the commissioners of confiscation. had purchased the establishment, among several others of a valuable description thus sold in this section of the country. To this residence, the scene of a former portion of our story, we will now once more, and for the last time, repair.

While in one part of the building the officers just named, with other distinguished persons, were engaged in discussing the incidents of the day, in another and more retired apartment, on a pillowed couch, lay the wounded Father Herriot, who, having been stricken down in the last moments of the battle, as before intimated, had been borne hither to complete the willing sacrifice he had made of his life to the cause of his country. On a small table, within his reach, lay several documents, which were fresh from the hand of that ready writer, the accomplished secretary of the Council of Safety, who had just left the apartment. And around his bed stood those in whom all his private interests and sympathies had been for some time secretly concentrated, though to two of them personally unknown till a few hours before, when he had been brought in wounded and committed to their care. Those persons were Henry Woodburn, Bart Burt, Sabrey Haviland, and Vine Howard, who, ignorant of his particular wishes or intentions, and wondering why the presence of all of them should be desired at the same time, had been summoned to his bedside to hear his last communication and receive his blessing.

"My prayer is answered," said Herriot, after looking round affectionately a while upon his expectant auditors, who, at his request, after the room was cleared of other company, had advanced to his bedside. "My last prayer has been to be permitted to see all of you, in whose personal welfare I have been led to take a peculiar interest, assembled before me while life and reason remained, so that I could commune with you; and the prayer has been graciously answered. Still, when, at the close of our first, and, as we all then supposed, final triumph to-day, Miss Haviland, with her friend, at my request, was conveyed here to her former home, of which I had become the purchaser, I then thought to have met you all here this evening under circumstances in which I could have actively shared with you in the rejoicings that our victory so naturally calls forth, as well as in the happiness, which, as far as regards you, I believed I could superadd by my own acts. But He who holds the fate of indi viduals, as well as that of armies, in his hands, has seen fit to deny me such participation ; and *He doeth all things well.*"

" Your wound is not necessarily a mortal one, Father Herriot and I trust you may yet live to enjoy the fruits of a victory you have contributed so much by your bravery to win," observed Woodburn, feelingly.

" That may not be. I feel the destroyer busily at work here, undermining the citadel," responded the other, placing his hand on that part of his chest where the bullet had entered. " But I regret not having made the poor sacrifice of my life for so righteous a cause. And though I shall not live to see the happiness I would be the means of imparting, yet the wish and the duty of doing what I proposed to that end remains to be fulfilled, and for this purpose I have requested your presence."

The speaker here paused, as if at a loss how he should open the subject which seemed to rest on his mind. But at length he resumed : —

" Miss Haviland, what you have done and suffered for the cause, in which you so nobly took your stand, is known to many. The part you have acted in the events of this day is known to still more ; but have not those events had a bearing on your happi‐ ness beyond what would arise from the bare liberation of your person ? "

" They have, sir," replied the maiden, frankly, but with an air of surprise at the unexpected question.

"And have I been correctly informed, by the person who has just left us, and who has long been my confidential friend and adviser, that, by the relinquishment of a certain contract, you are now left free to bestow your hand on one whose character and feelings may be more congenial with your own ? "

" Why am I questioned in so unusual a manner, and by one so much a stranger ? " asked the former, in a half‐remonstrating, half‐beseeching tone.

" I knew," rejoined the other, " that you, as well as the rest of those present, might, at first, wonder why and how I should have kept myself apprised, as I confess I have long done, of all that concerned the individual interests, and even inclinations, as far as could be conjectured, of each of you. And I know, also, that my ways are not like those of other men. But cannot you trust to the motives of a dying man, and let him proceed in his own man‐ ner ? "

" I can — I will, Father Herriot," answered Sabrey, touched by the appeal. "And I will not affect to misunderstand you. I

have been freed from fetters under which I have suffered — per
haps unnecessarily — both persecution and embarrassment of
feeling.   And I am thankful," she continued, throwing a gratefu.
glance to Woodburn — " greatly thankful for that generous for-
bearance by which this was effected without bloodshed.   Yes, I
am free, doubly free ; but whoever takes me," she added, slightly
coloring, " must now receive a penniless bride."

" Perhaps not," said Herriot, musingly — " perhaps not.   But I
did not mean to be understood as imposing any conditions to the
act I was about to perform, after ascertaining your entire deliverance from the power and supposed claims of one whom I deem a
bad man, as well as a foe to his country.   Here, deserving girl,"
he continued, taking up one of the documents from the table and
extending it towards her, " here is a deed of gift, from me to you,
of all this, which was your father's estate.   Take it ; it is freely
given and worthily bestowed."

Surprise at an act as unexpected as it was munificent, kept all
mute for some seconds ; when Sabrey, whose sensibilities were too
deeply moved to permit her to speak, threw upon the donor a look
which her grateful emotions made more eloquent than any language she could have summoned for a reply ; and then, turning,
she silently extended her hand to Woodburn, with the deed still
'ying across the open palm.

" Which ? — the hand or the paper ? " asked the latter, in a low
tone, and with a slightly apprehensive air.

" Either, or both," replied the maiden, as a blush stole over her
conscious cheek.

" The hand, then," exclaimed the delighted lover, grasping the
coveted prize, and bearing it in triumph to his lips.

" It is all right ; but no words," said Herriot, making a motion
for silence to Woodburn, who was about to address him — " no
words.   I have much to say — let me proceed.   Bart," he continued, after a thoughtful pause, as he turned to the young man
who had stood mutely noting the proceedings with a puzzled look
— " Bart, do you remember the old Rose Homestead, which
was confiscated, and also purchased by me ? "

" Well, yes," replied Bart, looking up with an inquiring, doubtful expression — " yes, for as many as two several reasons, or
more," he added, with one glance to Woodburn, and another,
and more significant one, to Vine, who was standing demurely at
his side.

" Would you like it for your own ? " asked the former.

' My own ! " exclaimed Bart, casting an incredulous but

searching look at the other's countenance, in which, however, he read something that at once changed his demeanor; and, in a softened and respectful tone, he replied to the question, " Yes, Father Herriot, as soon as the smell of toryism got fairly out of it, I would like it grandly, that's a fact."

" It is yours, then, as this deed will show," said Herriot, handing to the surprised and hesitating young man the instrument in question ; " it is yours ; but have you no one to share it with you ? "

" Well, don't know exactly, but may be the chap that helped me fix up my spy disguises, and gave me so many good hints for ferreting out the tories, won't object much to that, seeing we have had considerably the start of the captain and his lady here, in the way of finished bargains," replied Bart, turning, with an expression of droll gravity, to the blooming girl at his side, who, thereupon, with an arch and blushful smile, placed her hand in his, which had been extended to receive it.

" Who are you, Father Herriot ? " exclaimed the now completely surprised Woodburn ; " who are you, to take such an interest in us, and bestow on us gifts so valuable, with so little hope, as you can have, of any adequate return ? "

" Listen, and you shall be answered," replied Herriot ; " for the time has now arrived when you all should know the relation in which we stand to each other ; and I know not but I have already delayed the disclosure of this fact too long. Perhaps I should have made it, as I had nearly done, when, at the breaking out of the war, you and Bart visited my hermit cabin in the vicinity of the Connecticut. But when I found you about to embark in the cause of liberty, for which I stood ready to make any sacrifice, I concluded to defer it, lest the discovery, which I had but then just made myself, should turn you from a service that I thought none were at liberty to withhold. I therefore, after communicating to you enough to lead you, in case of my death, to all the knowledge I wished you to obtain, encouraged you on your way. And it has all, doubtless, been for the best ; for who knows but your individual exertions were needed to turn the scale which has been so long trembling at equipoise? But the events of this day," continued the patriot, kindling at the thought —" the events of this day, which will be memorable through all time, have turned that scale in favor of American freedom. I read it with a prophetic eye, which is made for me too clear for error or misconception. Our avenging armies will henceforth go on conquering and to conquer, till the last vestige of British usurpa tion is swept from the land."

Here the speaker paused a while to recover from his exhaus
tion, and indulge his mental vision, apparently, with the enrap-
turing glimpses he was catching of the future destiny of his coun
try.   But soon arousing himself from his reverie, he resumed, —

"Harry Woodburn, you had once a paternal uncle ? "

"I have been told so," was the reply.

"Who, by his folly and wickedness, disgraced himself and
ruined your father," proceeded the former.

"I had such an uncle," responded Woodburn, with an expression of gathering interest and surprise; "or, rather, I had an
uncle, who, though not a bad man, was, I have understood, at one
time, a very indiscreet one ; and, by his indiscretion, lost his own
property, and deeply involved that of my father.   But I do not
feel to condemn him as much as your words imply you expect I
should."

"Or as he has always condemned himself," rejoined Herriot,
with an air of deep self-abasement.   "But I thank God for giving
me the means, and the will, for making ample restitution to such
as remain of my injured brother's family, or of my own.   Harry,
I am that uncle.   I am the erring Charles Woodburn."

"I am surprised, deeply surprised," said the other; "for, attributing the interest you have taken in me to other causes, I
have, till within a few minutes, been totally unprepared for such
a revelation.   And now it seems as if it could not be.   You could
not have much resembled my father, and you bear another name."

"I did not strikingly resemble my more staid brother, in per
son or character," responded the former, meekly ; "and my reasons for assuming another name are explained by the circum
stances under which you first saw me, the accused of a revolting
crime, of which, as I then declared, I was never guilty.   And
this the wicked men, who combined against me, and hunted me
out, even in this new settlement, full well knew.   But they knew,
also, that I had somewhere at command the large amount of
money that had been left me by a wealthy and heirless gentleman, whom I had previously rescued from death.   Are you now
satisfied that I am the man I claim to be, and, as such, willing to
acknowledge me ? "

"Fully, now — not only satisfied of the identity, but willing,
nay, proud to acknowledge the relationship," said Woodburn,
with warmth and rising emotion.   "Nor is this all, my uncle,
my friend !   The acts you have just performed will ever —— "

"Enough, enough ! " interrupted the former ; "but let me go
on.   I have still another and more humiliating duty to perform

Bart," he continued, turning, with an agitated countenance, to the young man, "as forsaken and guideless as you have been, many a parent has had a less deserving offspring. And had you not done more for yourself than he, who should have been your protector and guide, has done for you, you had been less than nothing among men. But listen; for the story of your origin, which, thus far, has been as a sealed book to you, must now be disclosed Your father contracted a private, but legal marriage, with a woman, who, as the world falsely esteemed it, was below him in station; and, in his pride, he refused to acknowledge her, and, having squandered the property that should have been applied to her support, absconded from the country. In after years, however, conscience drove him back, but only to find her dying of destitution and a broken heart, and to learn from her last words that the offspring of their connection, a male infant, had been thrown unacknowledged on the charity of the public. Aroused by a new sense of duty, he diligently sought for the child — followed it from its first lodgment to its next asylum in the city; from that to another in the country; and then, through various shifts and wanderings, till the trace was lost far in the interior; when he gave up the search, and again left the country. In the process of time, he once more returned to New England, in altered circumstances, and located himself in this settlement, where he soon met with a youth, whose countenance so strikingly resembled that of his deceased wife, as to put him instantly on inquiry and research, which, in a few weeks, resulted in supplying the broken chain of evidence, and in identifying the youth as his lost son. Bart, you were, and still are, that son. I was, and still am, that father. Do I die, my much injured son, acknowledged and forgiven?"

The young man was too deeply affected by his surprise and emotion to utter a word in reply; but tears, which all the wrongs and hardships he had endured had failed to wring from him, now stole out on his sunburnt cheeks, testifying, not only his gratification at the discovery, but that the slumbering fountain of a naturally generous nature was now effectually stirred within his bosom. And the speaker, seeming satisfied with the answer which this evidence implied, soon proceeded: —

"Little more now remains to be imparted. You remember, Harry, that at the visit at my cabin, to which I have already alluded, I showed you two small casks, labelled ' *Printer's Type*,' concealed under a stone in the cellar?"

" do; and the impression they caused of the absurdity of

bringing that kind of property into our new settlement," replied the other.

"They were so marked for greater security," resumed the former; "for they contained silver coin, and, at that time, nearly all the property I possessed. Of these, one has been recently appropriated to the purchase of confiscated estates, whenever a lack of money in others was likely to prevent a sale at a fair value. The other remains in the same spot. And this, and the rest of my property, except what I have just conveyed, and except, also, bequests of small farms to Dunning and Piper, for their friendship to you, and faithfulness to the cause, you will find, by my will here on the table, to be equally divided between you, my son and nephew. And now," he added, in a faltering tone, and in accents of touching tenderness, now, my children, having said all I wished to communicate, I will commend you to our common Parent above. Kneel and receive my blessing."

Hand in hand, and side by side, with the fair sharers of their gushing sympathies, the young men now reverently knelt around the dying patriot, and bowed their faces beneath his outspread hands to receive the proffered blessing, which was then pronounced with much fervor, but with the last words he was destined ever to utter; for after waiting a while after he had ceased to speak, the tearful group gently removed his hands from their heads, and arose to be greeted by a face pale in death.

CONCLUSION.

On a summer afternoon, nearly a year after the occurrence of the events last described, there was an unusual gathering in the village of Bennington. As early as one o'clock, multitudes of people were seen pouring in by every road leading into the place from the surrounding country, and filling up the streets with a promiscuous crowd of all ages, sexes, and conditions. And as the hour of two approached, the commotion increased to a degree which plainly showed that some crisis was at hand ; and soon the dense throng, gathered in the vicinity of the Green Mountain Tavern, then the principal place of public resort, broke away into groups and companies, and began to flock towards a newly-erected gallows, standing, at no great distance, on the neighboring common. Here arranging themselves, as they came up, in a circle round the ill-omened structure, they assumed the attitude of spectators awaiting the advent of some promised spectacle.

Presently a clamor rose from the outer part of the crowd, as, with the exclamations, " *There comes the new Overseer of the Tories !* " * " *There comes Dunning and his gang of beauties !* " They pointed to a column of some dozens of variously-clad, dejected-looking men, headed by a well-armed officer in the continental uniform, just coming round a corner into view, and advancing towards the spot.

" Der open there to the right and left ! " cried the commander of this unique company, as he marched them up to the crowd. " Make way for Mother Britain's ditter darlings ! The coming sight is as much for their der benefit as your ditter fun. There, halt ! " he continued, bringing the submissive creatures into their allotted place. " Now, the first one of you that attempts to sneak away from the sight, takes a der pistol bullet. So face the music without flinching. It will ditter do you good."

Scarcely had this transpired before the crowd, whose attention,

---

* The Overseer of the Tories, an officer peculiar to the times, and perhaps to the locality, was one to whom was intrusted the general surveillance and control of that class of persons, to prevent them from communicating with the British, and see that they did not pass over the limits of the farms, or town lines, within which, under various penalties, they were doomed to remain, unless called out by such officer for some public service, such as clearing out the highways, &c., to which they were held subject.

for the moment, was too much engrossed to notice the approac:
of the principal procession, now close at hand, was again thrnwr
into commotion by the sound of a muffled drum, followed by tne
loud cry of, " *Clear the way for the prisoner and his escort !* " ir
a voice whose well-known tones never fell unheeded on the ears
of a Green Mountain assemblage. With magic quickness, a clear
space opened through the ranks of the receding throng, in the
direction of this fresh summons, when the first object that met the
eye was the towering form of Ethan Allen, mounted on a large
black horse ; he having recently returned from his captivity, and
been appointed, in the quaint language of his commission, " *to conduct, in behalf of the state, the trial and execution of that inimical
person, David Redding.*" * Next to Allen came the prisoner,
riding in an ox-cart, and sitting between two armed men, who
were acting as his special guards. Then followed a company of
soldiers, under the command of another of our old acquaintances
Bill Piper, who had been promoted to a captaincy in a voluntnei
service then recently projected ; while the president, secretary,
and members of the Council of Safety, succeeded by a band of
private citizens, brought up the rear of the procession. On reaching its destination, the team was brought to a stand immediately
beneath the gallows, which was a naked cross-tree, set into the
ground like a sign-post, and wholly unprovided with platform, or
other of the usual adjuncts of such structures. The prisoner was
then ordered to stand up in the cart, when the noose at the end
of the rope, dangling from the arm above, was securely adjusted
round his neck, and every thing made ready for the awful mo
ment.

Ira Allen, having mounted some object at hand, then addressed
the people in an eloquent exhortation on the duty and policy of a
faithful and unwavering adherence to the cause of the country,
which he enforced by giving a rapid sketch of the character and
career of the wretched traitor before them, as contrasted with those
who had been true to that cause, and especially those who had
captured him.

" Of the four brave men," he said, in conclusion, " who, at such
odds and risk, pursued and took the prisoner and his party, on that
glorious occasion, two are present, and in positions which amply
testify the high estimation that has been placed on their gallant

---

* David Redding, the only person ever executed in Vermont for political
offences, was, after changing two or three times from the American to th?
British cause, ard two trials, hanged July 1!. 1777. at 2 o'clock, P. M.

conduct. The others, the two Woodburns, who remained in the city, are — as I learn from letters I have recently seen from them or their scarcely less heroic young wives, left to conduct the affairs of their respective homes — now in New Jersey, acting under the eye of their beloved Washington, whose confidence in them in their different spheres of action — one as the honored colonel of a regiment and the other as the most trusty and adroit manager in the secret service — they consider their sufficient reward, and one that was only wanting to crown that which, on the eve of our memorable battle here, they received in their wives, and the wealth obtained through the romantic disclosures of their dying relative, the lamented Father Herriot. And of the party taken alive by those gallant men, the tory leader, Peters, was exchanged for several of our imprisoned officers, and at a bargain which secured us advantages not to be obtained by stretching his worthless neck ; and he has retired into Canada, to sink into insignificance, despised and hated by those whom his misrepresentations respecting the alleged easy conquest of our state so completely deceived. Fitch, after having ransomed himself by the payment of all he could raise, offered through his fear of a fate to which, after all, he probably would not have been condemned, sneaked back to his old haunts in Guilford, where he perished miserably by the hand of one whom former wrongs, committed in acts of official cruelty and extortion, had made desperate. And the other, and last of the infamous trio, now stands before us, to make atonement for his crimes by an ignominious death on the gallows."

When the speaker had concluded, the prisoner, after glancing around him, with that fitful, furtive, and restless expression, which at all times so strongly marked his countenance, turned to Ethan Allen, and meekly begged permission to address the multitude.

" Why — yes," hesitatingly replied the rough old hero, who had been sitting upon his horse, moodily looking at his watch lying in his broad palm, and occasionally exhibiting signs of impatience at the length of his more wordy young brother's remarks — " yes, it may be right enough, that you should have your say unless you want to preach some more of your damnable tory doctrines to the people. But be short, sir. Your hour is nearly up ; and I do not intend that the earth shall be polluted by your living presence one moment beyond the time."

Immediately availing himself of this ungracious permission, the prisoner turned, shrinkingly, towards the crowd, and said, —

" All you who hear me, I hope, will take warning by my miser

15 *

able end — an end to which I have been brought, in my opir:on on'y by my inconstancy.   In the first place, I adhered to my oatl cf allegiance, and supported the king; but, finding myself in danger, I enrolled myself under the new state, and went for the authority of Congress.   Conscience, however, quickly carried me back to the royal cause, which I again supported a while; and then, being over-persuaded by my neighbors, I came out once more openly for the state, and went for it till the approach of Burgoyne emboldened me to risk another change, and go for my old master.   But, being soon taken in arms, I must now untimely perish.   It is, therefore, my advice to you all — never fluctuate as I have done; but you who are for the States, stick by the States; and you who are for the king, stick by the king, and prove ———"

"And so," fiercely interrupted old Ethan — "so you would have an interminable war, would you?   Take your treason along with you to Tophet, ye doubly-damned miscreant!   I will have no more of it here.   Teamster, drive on the cart!"

The teamster did so; and the next moment the traitor Redding was launched into eternity.